Peter Yeldham's extensive writing career began at the age of seventeen, and has included short stories, radio scripts, and a newspaper column. He lived in England for almost twenty years, where he became a leading film and television writer and also wrote six successful plays for the theatre.

Since his return to Australia, he has won numerous awards for his work, which included screen adaptations of *The Timeless Land, 1915, The Far Country* and *The Battlers*, and many original works including *Captain James Cook, The Alien Years*, and *The Heroes*.

He and his wife live on the Central Coast of New South Wales. *Land of Dreams* is his seventh novel.

Also by Peter Yeldham

REPRISAL
WITHOUT WARNING
TWO SIDES OF A TRIANGLE
A BITTER HARVEST
THE CURRENCY LADS
AGAINST THE TIDE

LAND OF DREAMS

PETER YELDHAM

Pan Macmillan Australia

First published 2002 in Pan by Pan Macmillan Australia Pty Limited
St Martins Tower, 31 Market Street, Sydney

Copyright © Peter Yeldham 2002

All rights reserved. No part of this book may be reproduced or
transmitted in any form or by any means, electronic or mechanical, including
photocopying, recording or by any information storage
and retrieval system, without prior permission in writing from
the publisher.

National Library of Australia
cataloguing-in-publication data:

Yeldham, Peter.
Land of dreams.

ISBN 0 330 36331 X.

1. World War, 1939–1945 – Japan – Fiction. 2. Australians –
Japan – Fiction. 3. Man–woman relationships – Fiction.
I. Title.

A823.3

Typeset in 10.5/12 pt Sabon by Post Pre-press Group
Printed in Australia by McPherson's Printing Group

To Alex and Winifred Faure

Ah, love, let us be true
To one another! For the world which seems
To lie before us like a land of dreams,
So various, so beautiful, so new,
Hath really neither joy, nor love, nor light,
Nor certitude, nor peace, nor help for pain;
And we are here as on a darkling plain
Swept with confused alarms of struggle and flight,
Where ignorant armies clash by night.
Matthew Arnold
1822–88

PART 1

CHAPTER 1

He woke, and in the darkness heard the sound of screaming. For a confused moment he thought it was the girl, but that was impossible; it had been twelve years ago and part of another lifetime. He was not on board the ship; he was alone in a dank concrete cell, wrapped in a blanket on the hard stone floor because there was no bed, nothing but a malodorous slop bucket, and the nauseating glimpse of an army of cockroaches scuttling away from it.

The next scream shocked him into full consciousness. It came from the room above, and was unmistakably a man in terror as experts of the military police, the Kempetai, tortured him. This was a part of their technique, allowing others to hear and thus share the consequences of being interrogated; unnerving those awaiting similar treatment, knowing the victim would soon be confessing, spilling his guts, admitting to whatever crime they might decide to level against him. As if in confirmation of this, the screams stopped; the ensuing silence was infinitely more threatening.

Despite the cold, he began to sweat. He wondered who the victim was, what he had done, and whether he in turn would be taken up into that room and questioned? If so, could he stand the pain? The Kempetai were known for their draconian methods; nothing was too extreme. In his seclusion, he faced the prospect that he may not be able to remain silent. Few managed to do so, even the bravest, and he did not consider himself brave. Therefore, he must somehow avoid being tortured. To do that, he had to convince them he had nothing to hide, which would be difficult, for there was a great deal to hide, matters he had vowed to keep secret. Revealing them would not only betray others, but condemn himself.

He knew his future was perilously speculative even if he survived interrogation, because for the past three days – since his arrest – they had been shooting prisoners in the courtyard behind the prison. Constantly he had heard the booted tread of escorts, the snap of command followed by a volley of rifle shots. Executions without ceremony. One of the paradoxes of this arcane land. Opponents considered heroes were beheaded in the *Bushido* tradition. Spies and traitors were hanged after the most rigid formal trials, whereas those arbitrarily classified as enemies of the state were summarily shot. In these demented days, it was not difficult to be an enemy of the state.

Particularly for those with European features, marked out for special attention. Stared at with dislike or suspicion in the street, stopped by random patrols, ordered to produce their papers, sometimes forcibly taken to the nearest police post, their names checked against a register to prove they were neutral foreigners as they claimed. Never before had they known this overt antagonism, where appearance and racial origins made them outsiders, 'despised *gaijin*', instead of accepted residents who had lived here most of their lives, a great many even born here.

The hatred was like a rampant virus, but it was not only directed at foreigners. In a land that once prided itself on decorum and traditional courtesy, Japanese civilians had been pulled off trams in Tokyo and beaten for the crime of not being in uniform. Their attackers were mostly groups of soldiers on leave, sometimes riot police, and once he had seen a large party of women berating two middle-aged men, demanding to know why they were not prepared to die for the honour of the Emperor. One man had listened to the tirade impassively, then politely bowed, reached for a walking stick and limped slowly away.

Bands of officials, recruited as 'economic police', stopped people in the street, accusing them of hoarding black market goods. They made embarrassing public searches, while other people, strangers, gathered to watch the hapless victim's humiliation. Such incidents were now daily occurrences. The mood in the country was one of anger and disenchantment. If this was how they treated their own, what would they do to him if they knew the truth?

Trying not to think of his present plight or uncertain future, he chose instead to remember that other life of his childhood. Knowing what he did now – about the past and about his own family – he felt surprise that it had seemed so safe then, so uncomplicated and secure.

Kobe had been a tranquil place when Sam was ten years old. His family's home, the substantial residence of a prosperous French businessman, looked down on the bay of Osaka. The two-storey house was set in spacious grounds; a pond containing golden carp was the centre of a much-admired sculptured water garden, and on the lawn there were cherry trees and clusters of maples. In spring and summer, the grounds were vivid with colour.

His father had come to the Far East from Paris as a young man, and after meeting and marrying his mother, a twenty-year-old White Russian refugee, had started an export firm specialising in cultured pearls. It had prospered and brought them a comfortable lifestyle. Henri and Tamara Delon were a handsome addition to the French colony in Kobe and became leading figures in the close-knit foreign community. They had remained childless for a considerable time, for so long in fact that their friends assumed there would be no family. Sam was told they had been married nine years before his arrival. The birth of his sister, Angelique, had come less than eighteen months later.

When Sam was ten and Angelique nine, their father came home from the office one evening and surprised them with the news that instead of their usual holiday trip to France, they were taking a vacation in Australia. They would enjoy the sunshine and the beaches of Sydney. It had all been arranged by an exchange of letters with a good friend, Miss Florence Carter. They were to stay in a hotel at a seaside resort, and would meet Miss Carter, who was not only a fine lady but also Sam's godmother. Sam was startled; it was the first time he had heard of her, and until then he was unaware he had a godparent at all. The subject had somehow never been mentioned, and he wondered why.

'What shall I call her,' he asked his mother, and

received no answer. So he raised the question with his father. 'Is she to be Miss Carter or God-mama?'

He hoped it might bring a smile, but his father seemed preoccupied, and muttered that no doubt it would work itself out. His mother appeared upset, as though she disliked the prospect of this journey, or perhaps did not like Miss Carter. He became aware his parents were having rows, and often at night heard raised voices from their bedroom, his mother's accented English in moments of stress replaced by an angry stream of her native Russian. Though he didn't understand the words, the acrimony was unmistakable. The friction puzzled and disturbed him. It increased noticeably as their departure drew near.

They boarded an almost new Dutch passenger liner, the *Batavia Star*, at the end of November. Winter was due in Japan, summer in Australia lay ahead. It was to be a leisurely three-week voyage through the Dutch East Indies to Perth and Sydney. The first week was pleasant, the sea calm, the weather warming with each day as they approached the equator. His mother seemed to relax; both his parents were more amicable than they had been for months. They all went ashore in Saigon and, while the vessel refuelled, spent the day sightseeing.

It was on the second night out from Indochina, en route to Djakarta, that the ship caught fire.

CHAPTER 2

No-one ever knew exactly how it happened: if it was a careless smoker, an electrical fault, or perhaps sabotage. Sam and Angelique, sharing a cabin, were jolted awake by the continual clamour of the ship's horn blaring, then the sound of terrified screaming coming from outside on the boat deck.

'What is it? What's the noise?' Angelique asked sleepily.

Before he could answer, the door burst open. Smoke gushed in and they could feel the fierce heat; it took a moment to realise the two frightened people in the doorway were their parents. Hours earlier, Henri and Tamara Delon had come from their own cabin to say goodnight before attending the gala dinner, their father in his tuxedo, their mother beautiful in a ballgown with her pearl necklace and best jewellery. Now he was dishevelled, clad only in scorched pyjama trousers, and she was in a flimsy nightdress without a negligee. Her hair was hanging loose halfway down her back, and it seemed to be smouldering.

'Quick,' their father said, and picked up Angelique. Sam followed, grabbing his mother's arm, hearing her say she must get to the cabin to dress and collect her jewellery. Henri Delon shouted at her to forget the fucking jewellery – there wasn't time to waste. His children stared at each other, their astonishment at his fury and his language almost as great a shock as the hysteria around them.

Outside the air was hot, the scene chaotic. People were gripped by panic. The wind blew and the night was filled with flying cinders; the ship's horn was even more deafening, and the sound of the wild screaming much closer. The starboard side of the ship was in flames. Passengers as well as some of the crew were trying to reach the lifeboats, some of which were already on fire. Others dangled helplessly, ropes burning before they crashed into the sea. People were drowning. Sam glimpsed one lifeboat overturn in mid-air; before his horrified gaze the occupants were trapped beneath it.

Still the same violent screaming continued. It could only have been moments, so much was happening at once – but this was the worst sound. It felt inhuman and terrible. And then they saw her, and knew why.

It was a girl, and she had no clothes on.

Her whole body seemed to be enveloped in flames. Her face and hair were hardly recognisable, but Sam knew it was the young Filipina called Yvette, the one the passengers had labelled the captain's whore – although his mother had persisted with the fiction that she was his fiancée, while his father said if that were so, the engagement was for the duration of this voyage only.

The Dutch captain was standing there, almost naked, while he shouted helplessly and tried to make a fire extinguisher work. He did not seem to know how to operate it, and one of the sailors snatched it from him and yelled that he was a drunken idiot – then almost walked into the flames while he sprayed Yvette, and managed to drag her out of the fire. Part of her body was black, part red raw as if it were melting.

'Oh Jesus Christ,' Sam heard his father say, although it was meant as a whisper to himself, 'the poor bitch is still alive.'

Down below, the electrical system had failed, and the lower decks were in total darkness. A crush of frightened humanity tried to fight its way out, but the companion-ways were blocked. People unable to breathe were trampled on; the strongest fought clear and reached the top decks. Up there, they saw the ship was tilting, but the port side was not yet burning; the remaining lifeboats, untouched by the fire, were swinging on their davits and still empty. There were angry demands for them to be used; what were empty lifeboats doing at such a time? An officer yelled it was hopeless. There was no way they could be safely lowered, he shouted, with the deck careened at such an angle.

'What's it mean, careened?' Sam asked his father, but the reply was lost amid the fury of the frightened passengers pushing past them, calling the officer a bloody liar, and accusing the crew of saving the boats for themselves. Henri Delon held Angelique and Sam protectively to prevent them being trodden on by the crush.

'They've all gone mad,' he said. 'Come on, stay with me. I know where there are lifeboats.' He lifted his daughter with one arm, extended a hand to clutch Sam and told Tamara to run.

Behind them they heard their mother protest,

reminding him about the jewellery left in the cabin. And that she had no clothes, and could go nowhere without clothes. He took no notice of her complaints. He ran with both children down the main companionway, through the second-class dining room, until they reached the stern of the ship. It was packed with people, but was more orderly than the frenzy on the boat deck. The last three lifeboats were filled and almost ready to be launched.

'Only women and children,' one of the crew ordered.

'Two young children here,' a loud voice bellowed, and Sam realised it was his father's. People gave way. Henri Delon handed Angelique into the boat, pushing Sam in after her. A moment later he saw his mother, as his father assisted her to clamber aboard while some of those in the lifeboat tried to stop her.

'We're full,' one protested. 'Any more, we'll drown.'

'Lower the bloody thing,' an officer ordered.

'It's overcrowded,' another passenger complained.

'Release the ropes,' the officer yelled. 'Let it down!'

Sam could remember his mother trying to find a seat in the swaying craft. His sister was crying. His father waved and blew a kiss. They hit the sea with a splash. It felt as if they could sink with the weight of so many people, but the lifeboat settled. There was only a few inches of freeboard, and it was so crammed that the late arrivals could not sit down. It was now possible to see some veils being removed, and the faces of a few men revealed.

'So much for women and children only,' Tamara Delon said, looking disgustedly at one who was a member of the crew.

'At least you and your kids got aboard, lady,' he said, 'so you shut up. These boats should take thirty, and there's over fifty of us. We're too low in the water, and termorror there'll be sharks looking for a meal. If they get hungry and decide to attack, we'll all be dead meat.'

She swore at him in Russian, saying he was a cowardly pig and not to frighten the children. The lifeboat began to drift from the ship, and Sam could see people on deck lit by the flames. Somewhere among them, though it was now too far away for them to identify him, was his father.

The morning came too soon. First, with the rising dawn was the shock of finding themselves alone. The sea, deadly flat and calm, revealed no sign of the liner, nor were any other lifeboats in sight. The air was sticky and humid. As the sun rose, they began to feel the strength of its heat, and knew it would be a dreadful day.

Later, they saw the fins.

The sharks cruised and encircled the drifting lifeboat like confident predators, aware their quarry was at the mercy of the tides and unlikely to escape. People in the crowded boat tried not to look at the fins, but there was a sense of terror. Some of the children were crying with fear; others were too hungry and fretful to care.

At the far end of the lifeboat, Sam glimpsed the body of the girl, the deflagrating figure he had seen on deck. He wondered how she could have survived the fire, and thought she must be in terrible pain, then someone told him she was unconscious. Another added that hardly a piece of skin on her body was left intact. Space had been made for her by other survivors, and she was wrapped in a sheet. The top of her head protruded; all her hair was burnt off.

The boiling sun began to be a torment, and there was

no shelter from its blistering heat. Their mother was the first to realise the answer. She opened the hatch, which covered the bilge where the lifeboat's water tanks and food supplies were kept, and dragged Sam and Angelique inside the tiny housing before anyone else could guess what she intended. There was room only for the three of them. The air was putrid, and their feet encountered slimy water at the bottom of the bilge, but at least they were sheltered in the hatch from the sun's direct rays. It was a blessed but temporary respite.

Above them, people began shouting for water, and it was soon realised the storage tanks were empty. Not only was there nothing to drink, but the sole emergency food consisted of packets of thick sea biscuits which needed to be soaked in water to make them edible. Some of the survivors demanded the biscuits, and held them over the side, dunking them in the salt water before eating them voraciously. Others realised the danger of this, and tried to fight the twin torments of thirst and hunger. But as the day passed, the conditions became more and more intolerable.

In the heat of noon, desperation overcame reason, and most people by now were drinking salt water and trying to ease their craving with more biscuits. They began to vomit, which drew the sharks closer, and others tried to avoid this by retching into the boat. They relieved themselves where they lay, too torpid to care. Most of this effluent found its way into the bilge. Sam, his sister and mother had to scramble out of their shelter, unkempt and reeking with the smell of urine, faeces and vomit.

Tamara Delon, used to finery, clad only in her elegant nightgown – no longer satiny, but stained and filthy – ripped a piece from it and soaked it in sea water in a vain attempt to clean both children. People were babbling wildly. Some prayed, others raged and sought someone to blame. 'That hopeless bastard of a captain,' one of the men said, 'no water, no provisions, too busy fucking his tart of a girlfriend to run his bloody ship.'

'I blame her,' another said. 'Whoring and drinking with him day 'n' night. Talk about take his mind off the job!'

'Well, you canna blame her any more,' a Scots woman spoke up angrily. 'The lassie's dead. She's been dead for hours.'

They threw her body into the sea, and tried not to look back at what happened as the fins cleaved the water. Later in the day others died, and by then it was accepted routine to feed their corpses to the sharks who trailed them. When the sun touched the western rim of the sea, and began to vanish below the horizon, it was a blessed relief. Even if the fins still pursued them, they could no longer see them, and the twilight was a solace after the searing heat.

Their bodies tortured and blistered by the equatorial sun, they could not imagine how bitterly cold the night would be. Or that, after hours of sleepless shivering on the dark sea, they would soon pine for the morning and the warmth of the sun again.

Florence Carter sat on the verandah of her house, which faced the crescent-shaped beach at Collaroy, and felt despair. She had read the story of the disaster in the *Sydney Morning Herald*, and listened to the news on the radio. She felt deeply responsible, for it had been her letter that had persuaded Henri to waive his customary trip home to France and bring his family – and in particular, Samuel – to spend the summer with her in Australia.

She waited for more information, even a snippet of hope would be a relief, but apart from the first announcement that the *Batavia Star* had burnt and sunk with a massive loss of life – and reassurance that the dead did not include Australians – there was a singular lack of further detail. No additional facts, no lists of survivors. It was absurd – unbelievable – that an ocean liner could be lost in the South China Sea and there was such a paucity of news. She remembered the clamour when a Sydney ferry was rammed by an overseas vessel with the loss of forty lives; it had been tabloid headlines for weeks. But within days the fate of the *Batavia Star* had become a tiny story buried on the inside pages; after that, it was not mentioned at all, no longer considered to be of interest.

She telephoned newspapers. She rang radio stations and criticised, with scant success, their lack of coverage. She was reminded the vessel was a foreign ship with only foreigners aboard, and there were a great many matters more apposite to local listeners. Wasn't she aware, for instance, that the country's most famous racehorse, Phar Lap, was dead, believed poisoned in America? Or that the English cricket team was here for the Ashes Test series, and was introducing unfair tactics called bodyline? If it was world news she wanted, over in Europe, in Germany, a bizarre bloke called Hitler was trying to gain power. But he and his peculiar Nazi party would never succeed.

Florence Carter was twenty-seven years old, by nature a polite but determined young woman. She went to all the newspaper offices in turn, but they had nothing with which to reassure her. One journalist suggested a dinner date, and he would see what he could do. Instead she phoned the Dutch Embassy, but they said Djakarta had sent them only the names of citizens of the Netherlands. They had no knowledge of this French family. So she sent a series of cables to French consuls in places like Manila, Singapore and Saigon. She could do no more, except wait for word, and when that failed to materialise, wonder if her beloved Sam was dead or alive.

The second night in the lifeboat was colder, and by then over a third of the people had perished. The lack of food and water was taking a toll, and it was obvious they could not last much longer. The full moon and clear sky promised another day of the same relentless heat; tropical rain would have been a blessing. In the moonlight, Sam could see his mother and sister huddled together, trying to keep warm, until a man crept towards them, roughly pushing Angelique aside, cuddling his mother and whispering urgently to her.

'You bastard,' she said, elbowing him in the face. The man fell back with a startled cry, complaining she had made his nose bleed. The people in the boat managed a laugh when she said she should've kicked him in the balls and drawn blood where it mattered.

Sam was restless and awake most of the night. He missed his father, afraid he had not been able to escape. Finally he dozed, dreaming about the mysterious and unknown godmother whom he might never meet now. In the pewter-grey light of dawn he did not hear the shouts or see the American freighter until it was almost alongside them.

* * *

Surabaya, the first mate confided to Sam, was the arsehole of the earth, but to the others he merely said it was a seaport with a naval dockyard. They might pick up a ship for Australia, and there was a French Consul in residence there. He wished it was a more agreeable place, but the freighter had already steamed way off course to land them in Java, and now had to resume its passage to the Philippines.

Their family had experienced great kindness on board. An officer had vacated his cabin for them. They had enjoyed the luxury of a hot shower and clean clothes donated by the crew. When they stepped ashore they were barefoot, but only because none of the sailors had shoes to fit them. But at least they were on dry land. It was an industrial town and the military base of the Dutch East Indies army, with barracks and heavy fortifications. But little else.

'We want the best hotel in town,' Sam's mother said, and was told there were no good hotels in Surabaya.

'The best available,' she said, but no hotel was willing to accommodate them because they had no money.

'Come back when you can afford to pay,' a Javanese desk clerk said, indifferent to her predicament.

'If I could pay, I'd hardly come back to such a garbage tip,' she told him, and they set out to find the French Consulate.

It was shut for lunch, but outside waiting impatiently was a figure Sam had almost given up hope of seeing again.

'Papa,' he shouted.

It was indeed his father, but barely recognisable as such. He was barefoot and wearing a native sarong. He saw them and began to run across the road, almost being hit by an army truck that honked furiously. The driver stopped to shout abuse; Henri Delon stopped to swear at him in French, while the rest of the military convoy tooted on their horns, and his children risked the traffic to run and hug him. Finally safe on the footpath, he explained what had happened; he had seen the crew throwing deck chairs and furniture into the water, realised they were floating, and jumped in. He had grabbed a table top and clung to it until just after dawn the next morning, when he had been picked up by a Malay fishing trawler. He had been landed further down the Java coast and had spent the past three days walking to Surabaya.

'Walking, Papa?' Angelique was overcome by joyful laughter. 'Are you sure you didn't persuade some bearers to carry you?'

'If I could've found them, darling, I would have.' He hugged her and Sam again, close to tears of relief.

'I'd truly given up all hope,' he said. 'Here we are, all of us alive, and safely together.'

'Thank God,' Tamara clung to him. 'Now can you take me to a store, and buy me some underclothes and a dress? I'm rather weary of wearing men's clothes – apart from looking ridiculous.'

'My dear girl,' their father said, 'Buy you a dress? I haven't a centime to buy anything. My wallet and bills of credit, like our passports and your jewellery, are all at the bottom of the China Sea.'

The office of the Netherlands Line overlooked the harbour. They were asked to wait, and an hour later were still waiting. They knew they were the object of amusement; the husband in a native sarong, the wife in the trousers and sweater of a deck hand. Both shoeless. It did nothing for Henri Delon's mood. By the time he was finally allowed an interview with the chief shipping clerk, he was livid.

'Where's the manager?' he asked.

The manager, the chief clerk regretted, was unavailable. He was in hospital suffering a nervous collapse after the disaster. The whole company was in a state of shock, and Mr Delon was privileged even to be granted an interview at such a critical time. What did he want, for as he could see, the office was in turmoil?

'I want a number of things,' Henri said. 'I want first-class passages on your next ship leaving for Sydney. I want funds for my family, in order to replace their clothes with something more suitable, and I want a suite at a hotel, paid for by your company . . .'

'But sir . . .'

'I haven't finished,' Henri said. 'I also require a letter of liability to claim for the loss of all our belongings.'

The chief clerk seemed sincerely apologetic. He regretted there would be no Dutch vessel here for another month. Nor did he have the authority to issue funds, or offer impossible luxuries like hotel suites. As for liability, the company would strenuously deny any obligation existed. The sinking of the *Batavia Star* was a tragic disaster, and in the terms of mercantile indemnity, an act of God.

'You can't be serious,' Henri said, reminding him they had lost all their possessions, and that assistance was a matter of contract.

The clerk said he was indeed serious, and the passenger should apply himself and try reading the small print on the back of his ticket.

'My fucking ticket,' Henri shouted, 'is at the bottom of the sea, along with your ship and its captain.'

'I can show you a replica,' the clerk helpfully suggested, 'so you can study the terms and conditions.'

'Bugger your replica. I intend to discuss your company's attitude and this matter with my country's Consul,' Henri said, and slammed the door on his way out.

The Consul was at a long lunch, and kept them waiting until late in the afternoon. He was amiable and unsteady after what had clearly been an enjoyable repast. Sympathising with Monsieur Delon's predicament, he regretted he had no resources to bestow funds. Now if Monsieur were in Singapore or Manila, that would certainly be different, but Surabaya . . .

Such a place! The *derrière* of the world!

However, he would do his best, and offered provisional passports for the family which would get them to Australia – if they could find a ship and raise the money for their fares. The rest was up to Monsieur, the Consul said, and wished him *bon chance*.

The vessel that arrived in harbour was the SS *Hakone Maru*, a freighter of the Japanese NYK line, unloading cargo and leaving for Melbourne and Sydney that same night. It was an opportunity, Sam's father said, that he didn't intend to miss. His wife asked him to keep his temper this time, and try not to shout. She knew it was difficult, but she had a feeling that in Java nothing could be achieved by a man in a sarong getting into a tantrum and making a spectacle of himself with third-rate shipping clerks and drunken consuls. If they were not third-rate, then they wouldn't be in Java.

'Take Sam,' she suggested.

'Why?'

'He speaks Japanese, and it might impress the captain. It might even stop you losing your temper. Angelique and I will wait on the dockside.'

Sam and his father found their way barred by a guard at the top of the gangway, who called an officer.

'No visitors,' the officer said in English.

'We've been shipwrecked,' Sam said in Japanese, and told them about the fire, and being adrift in the lifeboat, and even about the girl who had been burnt and died. He was aware of several of the crew and another officer coming to listen, and his father staying silent and allowing him to tell the story. Finally, after a muttered debate between the officers, they were taken to see the captain.

'I'm in a difficult position,' Henri said, after the usual exchange of bows and greetings, 'I'm a rich man but I have no money.'

This news did not appear to please the captain. He studied his visitors with considerably less enthusiasm. 'A rich man, without money?'

'Temporarily without. What I require is two cabins on your ship, and a loan of some cash to buy clothes.'

'Impossible, Delon-san.'

'Two cabins – and a loan of all the cash you can spare.'

'I would say you are being ridiculous.'

'I would say you should listen, Captain. In Kobe, I own an export business. I use a lot of shipping including your NYK line. You can confirm this by sending a telegraph to Japan, but I doubt if there will be time for a reply. So you must take me on trust.'

'Indeed,' the captain said. 'Why should I?'

'Because if we don't travel on this ship, your company will not do any business with me again. Whereas if you help, you will be repaid when we reach Sydney, with a personal bonus. Plus, all my cargoes will be transferred to NYK, and the president of your company will be advised the credit for this is entirely due to you and your judgment. So, would you like to consider that, and let me know your answer?'

The freighter's captain considered it. He bowed and said two of his officers would vacate their cabins, and asked if a loan of a hundred American dollars would assist. Henri bowed and assured him he had made a wise decision. It would bring him great credit. They sailed that night, hoping never to see the Dutch East Indies again.

CHAPTER 3

The Hotel Manly looked down on a white beach and a large, crowded swimming enclosure. Shrill shouts enlivened the day as children built castles with turrets and moats on the wet sand, while others played in the shallow water. Beyond this, older swimmers ploughed their way out towards the protective shark mesh.

'Are the sharks all waiting on the other side?' Sam asked, and Auntie Florrie laughed and told him sharks were rare on Sydney beaches, no matter what the papers said. There were lots of people killed in road accidents now because of so many motor cars, but that never made the news like a single shark attack did.

'I know you had a dreadful time, Samuel, but you must try to forget it,' she said.

She always called him Samuel.

At first it seemed strange, but after one attempt to say his real name was Sam, he accepted it; even grew to like it, because he liked her so much. He had from the very first, the day after their arrival, when he and his father had taken the tram to Collaroy, and he'd seen the tall, slim woman waiting outside her beach cottage, then waving and running eagerly to meet him. He had been unsure whether to kiss her or shake hands, but while trying to make up his mind she had lifted and hugged him, saying in a voice that sounded strange, almost like she was crying, 'Samuel, my dear boy. How you've grown.' She had laughed then and said it was just as well, wasn't it, since the last time she'd set eyes on him he'd been a baby, just six months old, and Sam had liked her laugh, and felt utterly at home with her.

She and his father had shaken hands, and the conversation had become more formal. She spoke about the trip; how devastating for them, such a tragedy with so many people drowned. How were his wife and his daughter? Was the Hotel Manly satisfactory? It had a good reputation and should be nice for the children, the surf beach on one side of the town and the harbour pool on the other. Then she said something else that puzzled Sam.

'It was good of you, Henri. I know it meant a change of plans, and I daresay Tamara wasn't pleased, but I do appreciate it.'

'I made a promise,' his father said.

'You kept it, and I'm grateful. Tell Tamara he's a credit to her . . . that's if you don't think she'll mind me saying so.'

They both sensed Sam's confusion, and she changed the subject, saying they'd have their lunch on the verandah, so they could enjoy her favourite view of the high headland called Long Reef and the small beach which her house faced. Its real name was 'Fisherman's Beach', she told him, but to the locals it was affectionately known as 'the basin'. After lunch, they had left his father dozing and walked together, his small hand in hers, past the fishing dinghies at the far end of the beach, up the steep path beside the golf course, where they stopped to look out on the ocean. It was low tide, and a shoal of rocks could be seen below with waves lazily washing over them. To their right was a much larger beach, wide and empty with brilliant white sand, stretching all the way to the cluster of pine trees and the next headland.

'It's beautiful,' Sam said.

'Yes, it is. I hope your parents will let you come and stay a little while with me.'

'Yes, please,' he said enthusiastically, on the point of adding 'Miss Carter' for he was still unsure what to call her. She smiled as if she read his mind.

'My name's Florence, but I'm called Florrie. I expect for the sake of convention you'd better make it Auntie Florrie.'

'Or just Aunt?'

'Too English. "Auntie" is Australian.'

So Auntie Florrie it was, and a week later, after a lengthy parental discussion, his mother agreed he could go and spend a few days with her. His father took him there, and he and Auntie Florrie had a quiet and serious talk while Sam went exploring the beach and wondered why there were so many discussions going on. Later they both saw his father to the tram stop.

'If you behave, and Miss Carter doesn't get tired of you, you can stay a week,' he said as the tram approached.

'Whacko,' Sam said loudly, to his father's astonishment and her amusement. They stood waving as he left, then walked back to the cottage.

'Now we're alone,' she said, 'you can skip that Auntie nonsense and just call me Florrie.'

It was a joyous time. They went hunting for shellfish on the reef, and swam in the rock pool where the surf splashed in at high tide. They met the fishermen who took the dinghies out at night, and watched them winch the boats up high on the sand early in the morning when they returned with their catch. Sometimes they collected shells or driftwood on the beach.

After she had convinced him there were no sharks in the placid bay, they began to swim directly in front of the house. Sunbaking turned him a deep brown, though she insisted on a liberal application of coconut oil to prevent burning. Most days they had a picnic lunch on the sand. They took a tram to its terminus in the seaside resort of Narrabeen, hired a boat there and rowed on the lake. Once she took him to a picture palace, where he saw his first movie, an Australian film called *On Our Selection* with Bert Bailey.

It was over too soon. The week had become a fortnight, after a phone call to his parents who had finally agreed. Sam wanted to stay longer, but Florrie thought another request for an extension might not only upset them, but be rejected.

'Why?' he asked.

'Well, because you're their son, and ... well, they want to share the holiday with you. It's only natural.'

'I'd rather share it with you.'

'My dear Samuel ... that's awfully nice ...' She seemed to be stuck for words, and suddenly said, 'Let's buy an ice-cream,' and they walked to the milk bar opposite the surf club and had a malted milkshake as well as an ice-cream.

Sometimes after that she came to Manly for a visit, but it wasn't the same. The town was packed for the school holidays, the hotels and boarding houses filled with visitors from the country. Ferries arrived every half hour with picnicking families from the western suburbs. *Seven miles from Sydney and a thousand miles from care* was the famous slogan, and in the January heat the beach was so crowded that it was difficult to find space on the sand, whereas the basin had felt like their own private kingdom. At Manly, he and Florrie sat amid the throng, mostly with Angelique, and sometimes with his father. On the rare occasions when his mother joined them, she and Florrie were so carefully polite that Sam could tell they didn't like each other.

Once in a while it was just Florrie and him alone because the rest of the family had taken the ferry to the city for shopping. When this happened, she took him to the Corso where they bought fish and chips and went to the ocean beach among the Norfolk Island pines, and those were the best days.

He said he felt sad because they would be going home.

'Of course you mustn't be sad,' she said firmly. 'You have a nice family, and there'll be other times like this.'

'Do you really think so, Florrie?'

'I hope so. We'll try to make sure it happens.'

'How?'

'By keeping in touch, writing to each other. I don't think your mother will mind.'

'Why should she?' He was puzzled.

Florrie hastily corrected herself. 'I don't know why I said that. Of course she won't. And perhaps in a few years time . . . we'll keep our fingers crossed. But by then you'll be quite grown up and I'll hardly recognise you.'

'I'll send photos,' Sam said. 'Each birthday.'

'That'd be nice. Don't forget.'

'I promise. I'll think of you, you lucky thing, swimming and walking on our beach.'

'It won't be as much fun alone,' she said. 'And soon I'll only be able to swim at weekends. I'll be back at work.'

Sam knew she worked as a secretary in a solicitor's office in the city, and had taken special leave for the time they were there. Unpaid leave, it was called. He also knew she was twenty-seven, not as old as he'd thought a godmother would be. He'd worked that out from hearing his mother say Florrie was three years off thirty and still unmarried, and his father's reply that she had once been engaged, but her fiancé had died. Sam knew so much about her, except what he most wanted to find out. He remembered being told that straight questions were the best way to acquire knowledge.

'How did you happen to know me when I was a kid?' he asked. She gave a fleeting smile at his choice of word, then hesitated for so long that he wondered if she was going to answer.

'Was it in Australia?' he tried to prompt her.

She nodded.

'So I was in Australia before?'

'When you were a baby. Just for a short while.'

'With my parents?'

'Yes.'

'How old were you? Seventeen?'

'Nearly eighteen.'

'Did Mama and Papa ask you to be my godmother?'

'Yes,' she said, but looked away.

He finished eating his chips in silence, and she took their greasy newspaper and put it in one of the rubbish bins beneath a pine tree. Then they walked back through the town. Sam wasn't sure whether to take her hand or not. For the first time since the day they had met he felt uncomfortable with her. Somehow he knew she had not told him the real truth.

CHAPTER 4

The letters arrived regularly, along with presents and sometimes there were photographs of places they had seen together. In childhood, doubts dissipate, the congenial well-loved memories remain. Sam looked forward to her letters, and unfailingly replied. They became a link between them in the ensuing years.

Collaroy, July 1937.
My dear Samuel,
　I hope the ship arrives on time, and this reaches you for your birthday. The small cheque enclosed is for you to buy a book, or anything you wish as long as you enjoy it. Don't be persuaded to put it in your savings account at the bank; I know your father believes in such thrift, but there's time enough for that later.
　I hear strange reports of the war in China, but I hope the papers exaggerate. They make rather wild statements about the brutality of the Japanese soldiers, but tell me what people living there think. Is it as bad as our press

makes out? Such a pity the League of Nations seems so ineffective because it was supposed to stop wars, but I suspect all they do is shuffle paper in Geneva. No more serious talk. Enjoy your birthday. I'll put fifteen candles on a cake to feel I'm a part of the occasion. Perhaps by your next one we might even meet again. I'll write and ask your parents. Here's a photo of the basin to show you it still looks the same. Very tranquil and awaiting your return. Like I am.
With fondest love, Florrie.

Kobe, September 1937.
Dear Florrie,
    Thank you for the birthday cheque. I hope you don't mind, but I did put it in the bank, not to be thrifty, but because I'm going to save up to help pay my fare to Australia in a few years time. Soon it will be your summer and our winter. Papa has promised to take me skiing – if he has the time! That's the trouble, he's always busy because he has started a new office overseas in Saigon, Indochina. I'm late with the usual birthday photo, but here it is. I've grown three inches in the past year, and my voice has now completely broken. Angelique says I sound like a frog, but she and I are always fighting these days, ever since I told her I wished she was my brother. In revenge she scribbled on the photograph of the basin pinned on my wall and ruined it, so will you please send me another?

    About the Chinese war, our English language newspaper, the Japan Times, *says its purpose is to impose peaceful change. It says the war is justified, but my friends and I think that's just propaganda. Have you heard this word propaganda? One of our American teachers says it means giving governments permission to distort and deceive.*

I keep thinking of Sydney, and wish we'd been able to come this year. I would have liked that even more than going skiing. Perhaps next summer.
Love, Samuel.

Collaroy, February 1938.
My dear Samuel,
I loved your Christmas card of Mount Fuji, and am pleased your father found time to take you skiing, even if it was only for a weekend! It was a busy January here, with Sydney celebrating its 150th birthday. I'm back at work in the office, secretary to a new solicitor who has joined the firm. He's a refugee from Germany who speaks very good English, but had to spend an extra year qualifying to practise law here, even though he was well qualified and ran his own firm in Munich.

The news is certainly not good. This Herr Hitler seems to make promises, then break them, and his government are specialists in your 'propaganda'. I like the remark of your American teacher, who sounds enlightened. Just think. This year you'll be sixteen. Too young, I suppose to travel alone, but let's plan for when you turn eighteen. Don't forget more photos, or at the rate you're growing I won't recognise you when we meet.

God bless, fondest love, Florrie.

The Bluff, Yokohama April, 1939.
Dear Florrie,
Note the new address. Sorry I haven't written for such

a long time, but something's happened. I'm sure no-one has told you, so I feel I must. My parents are getting divorced. After twenty-six years of marriage it ended in a public shouting match that was like some awful stage farce. It almost made me want to laugh. I can't admit that to anyone except you. Divorce is supposed to be painful and sad, and my sister was very upset. Mama was too angry to be sad, and seems to have recovered, but it has made a big change in our lives.

What happened was this. Papa went on a business trip to Europe. He cabled he was coming back on the Trans-Siberian Railway to Vladivostok, then by ship to Kobe, but could not confirm the dates. Mama found out when the ship was due and decided we would be there to give him a surprise welcome home. But it was her and us who got the surprise.

He left the ship accompanied by a lady – very stylish – and looked startled when Angelique rushed forward and hugged him. Even alarmed, I thought. Then after we'd all exchanged greetings, he introduced the lady, who was Italian and most attractive.

'This is Signorina Maria Valerio,' he said, 'we met on the train. Miss Valerio, may I introduce my wife and children?'

She said how delightful to meet us, and felt she knew us all, as the Signor spoke with such affection of his family. Then a porter brought a trolley with suitcases, some of Papa's and the others belonging to the lady. Mama went and looked closely at the labels on the cases, then turned and slapped his face. She called him a bastard so loudly that everyone heard it. Then she really got started. 'Met on the train, did you, you lecherous old goat? So why does her luggage have the same hotel labels as yours?'

He hardly opened his mouth before she slapped him again. By then, other passengers and people on the dock were watching and listening. My parents didn't seem to care in the slightest who heard.

Papa said, 'Now be sensible, Tamara. Maria and I are just good friends.'

That didn't help. She went off like a firecracker, no longer in English but in a stream of Russian, which happens when she's really angry. From what I've been able to make out, she called her a cheap tart, a two-faced trollop, and a conniving dago cow. (I'm sorry to be so graphic, but it helps to explain what happened.)

My father finally admitted that Maria was his mistress, but he was deeply shocked by Mama's behaviour and her display in front of others, let alone us children. I had no chance to protest that we were hardly 'children' any longer because Mama was shouting at him.

'You just hoped to sneak her into a cheap hotel, as cheap as possible, where you could call in each day and play tootsie, a bit of morning glory in the afternoon, you treacherous rat.'

Truly, Florrie, that's what she said! In front of everyone! I wanted to hide. Or run! Or jump in the harbour!

Papa told her not to be absurd. He said he and Maria had discussed it, and they had a proposal to make.

'I can just imagine,' Mama said.

'No, you can't, Tamara. We'll talk of it later.'

'We'll talk of it now. What proposal?'

'I'd prefer to talk later.' He seemed at last to realise we were wide-eyed and listening. By now there was quite a crowd, and even the immigration and customs officials had stopped work to listen.

'Now,' Mama insisted.

'Very well. It was never my intention to be secretive

about this. If you'd take the trouble to know her, you'd find Maria is a very nice person. So what I propose is, we give it a trial.'

'Give what a trial?'

'I really think we should wait for more privacy . . .'

'Give what a trial?'

'The idea of Maria moving into the house, and the three of us living together as a family. With the children, of course.'

Angelique and I were mesmerised. Mama had run out of words to say. Her mouth opened, but nothing happened. Papa seemed encouraged and went on to explain what he had in mind.

'You see, I have to admit I'm in love with Maria. And I'm very fond of you, Tamara.'

'Fond?'

'No – that's the wrong word. More than fond. I'm still in love with you – I'm besotted by you. That's the word. Besotted by both of you. I'm in a cleft stick, unable to choose between you – so this seems the logical solution. After all, a ménage à trois *is simply a love affair between three people. You and Maria and me.'*

'What?'

'All three of us . . . living happily together in harmony.'

You can imagine what my mother said to that! In half an hour we were packing, while she made travel arrangements and talked to a lawyer. Papa arrived at the door, but she bolted it and said he could have the place when she was gone. The next day we moved to Yokohama, where she found this house to rent, and Papa's been told he has to buy the lease. It's smaller, but in a good neighbourhood, and Mama has lots of friends who live here. I've had to change schools, of course, and I'm now at St Joseph's College run by the Marist Brothers.

I hope you don't mind me being so candid about the way they spoke to each other. It was peculiar – and funny – and awful, and I had to tell someone about it. I miss Papa, and the friends I grew up with in Kobe. It's fine here, but different. Angelique took it very badly, and needed me to lean on – so we no longer fight. In fact, we're quite friendly. So I suppose some good came of the family breakup. But it certainly is broken up, well and truly. It's been a rotten year, but I feel so much better now I've written all this to you. I think it's therapeutic, is that the word?
Love, Samuel.

Collaroy, May 1939.
My dearest Samuel,
 I'm relieved to hear from you after so long, and glad you felt better for writing about it. Therapeutic is exactly the word. You know you can tell me anything. Always remember that. What a bizarre day! Your letter made me laugh, then feel sad, and then worry for you and Angelique. Meanwhile, how is your father and his Italian lady? A ménage à trois? Goodness me! Write soon.
 The rest of the world also seems to have gone slightly mad, but in a different and alarming way. Mr Chamberlain dashing to Munich, and Mr Hitler making him look like an absolute old fool, with his umbrella and his piece of paper. Carl says there will be war for certain. His name is Carl Eisler, and he is the solicitor from Munich I told you about, who is a part of the firm – and has now become a part of my life.
 If you can tell me your secrets, I will gladly tell you mine. We're very much in love, and he has asked me to

marry him. Imagine it, almost thirty-five and in love like a schoolgirl! I will admit it only to you. We are going to have a small private wedding in about six weeks time. I know it is impossible, but I wish you were here to make my day complete.
Yours, very happily, Florrie.

The Bluff, Yokohama, June 1939.
Dearest Florrie,
 How wonderful! I'm thrilled. Congratulations. I hope my present will arrive in time. It is a woodblock carving by an artist friend of Mama's called Paul Jacoulet, who is quite famous here, and I think you'll like it. I hope Carl is wrong about the war, but even here there's talk of it.
 Papa has moved to Saigon with Maria, and shifted much of his business there. He seems happy, but I don't see him often, as he only rarely visits Japan. This is written in haste because I have exams. If I pass I'll get a scholarship to the International School, and from there I can try for Harvard University.
 I spoke to Father about spending next summer in Sydney, since I'll be eighteen and old enough to travel alone, but all he did was complain about the cost of paying for two households. I said that was his choice, so we're not very good friends at present.
Love, Samuel.

Yokohama, 28 November 1939
No news. No wedding picture. Are you all right?
Samuel.

Yokohama, January 1940.
Dear Florrie,
No answer to my cable. Please write and tell me things are fine and there isn't any trouble. I know Australia's in the war with England against Germany, but you're so far away that I'm sure you're safe.
I got the scholarship. Another year here to graduate, and then Harvard next stop, in 1942! Please find time to write and tell me that all's well. Or tell me what's wrong. Love, Sam.

CHAPTER 5

There was a smudge of smoke from the funnel of a navy vessel far out at sea, and along the empty beach towards the Dee Why lagoon a group of soldiers was stringing barbed wire. Ever since the declaration of war on September third, there had been a gradual attempt to fortify the vast coastline of Australia with wire and tank traps. The irony of this, to Florence Carter, was that these defences were erected mainly on remote and rarely used beaches. The popular bathing spots like Bondi and Manly were only patrolled by lifesavers, and people surfed and sunbaked there as if there were no war at all.

Others, young men eager to fight or perhaps just see the world, were on their way to what they imagined was high adventure. Recruitment had been brisk, ever since the night when the measured and rather sepulchral tones of Prime Minister Menzies announced on the radio that – 'it is my melancholy duty to inform you, because of Germany's refusal to withdraw troops from Poland, England is at war, and therefore Australia is also at war.'

Why, she had thought then, and thought it again now. *Why is it our war?*

But she knew she was in the minority. Open opposition to the war was muted. Australian battalions were already embarked on board troopships – one of them the former luxury liner, the *Queen Mary* – en route to places with curious names like Bardia and Tobruk in the Middle East; there, as the local newspapers put it, to fight the Italians and teach them a lesson. Air force volunteers were being sent to Canada to be trained as pilots and navigators, and then dispatched to bolster the Royal Air Force in England. In the meantime, it had become known as the phony war because, apart from a few skirmishes and deployment of troops, little had happened. The much-mocked German bastion, the Siegfried line, had sparked a song that was popular with comedians: '*We're gonna hang out the washing on the Siegfried line – if the Siegfried line's still there!*'

The breeze from the south was freshening, and the radio had predicted a late afternoon storm. Time to leave the Long Reef headland, walk down the path and across the sand to her empty house. *I must write to him*, she thought. She had been trying to urge herself to do so for months, and felt annoyed and ineffectual that she had been unable to pick up a pen. *If you can tell me your secrets, I will gladly tell you mine*, she had confidently said in her last letter, more than eight months ago. It seemed like eight years.

She went into the house, made herself a cup of tea, and sat on the porch looking at the beach. It was humid, a typical February day, but the predicted storm had failed to appear. Protected from the wind by the promontory, the air around her cottage felt heavy and lifeless. Like her thoughts. She wished for the storm;

she had always loved the abrupt ferocity of southerly busters, the first gusts, the grumbling thunder and forked lightning, and finally the turbulent rain on the iron roof. It was a lovely nostalgic sound; for many people, it was a childhood memory they carried with them all their lives. A friend who had lived abroad for years said she still missed the drumbeat of real rain on galvanised roofs.

One night when Samuel had been staying, a southerly had blown up, and she could clearly recall his ten-year-old face, his eyes at first alarmed, and then excited, as the elements unleashed and rain almost drowned the house, a downpour so loud on the roof that they could not hear themselves speak, and they had stood at the window watching the storm lash the panes of glass and felt protected and safe. *I wonder if he remembers that*, she thought, and felt sure he did. All at once she stood, went inside the house and sat at her desk with a pad of writing paper and a fountain pen.

My darling boy, she wrote carefully, then frowned at the wording, ripped up the page and began again.

It was waiting there on the dining table when he came home from school. Her firm and upright handwriting, unmistakable, even to his mother. She had left a note propped beside it, saying that here was a letter from the elusive Miss Carter at long last, and that she would be at the club until late; his sister was staying with the Shroders, and cook-san would give him his dinner. His mother was at the club a great deal lately, ever since meeting the German who worked for Reuters. Richard Sorge was a journalist from Berlin, talented but flamboyant, and inclined to be openly possessive of his women friends, the latest of whom, it was clear to all and sundry, was Tamara Delon. It worried Sam.

Angelique had told him not to be a stick-in-the-mud. Why make such a fuss? Their mother was entitled to have some fun as well as sex in her life. She wasn't so old, not ready for retirement from active service; why should she live like a nun, when Papa was regularly fucking his girl-friend in Saigon? Angelique often used words like fuck lately, since becoming best friends at school with American Kitty Shroder, who doubtless had expressed her views on the liaison. Kitty with her Californian twang and dark inviting eyes, was alluring and disturbingly mature at the tender age of seventeen. Angelique frequently spent nights at the Shroder house, not only for girls' talk, but because of a secret infatuation with Kitty's older brother, Simon.

Sam had patiently tried to explain that their mother having an affair with anyone was not the problem, it was the amount she and Sorge drank that concerned him. They were invariably the last to leave the club bar at night, and people were noticing. His mother had always liked a drink or two, but now was in danger of becoming a drunk.

He took Florrie's letter into his room and sat on the bed. He had a premonition of disquiet even before he started to read it.

Collaroy, April 1940.
My dearest Sam,
I can't apologise for all these months of not having written, of not thanking you for your lovely gift or replying to your letters and cable. I can only tell you we had a wonderful day, married on July the fifth, and although it was winter the sun shone and I was happy. I was

happy for two months, and then on September the third war was declared in Europe, and within hours Australia had loyally joined onto the skirts of what we call 'the mother country' and we were also officially at war with Germany.

Two nights later they came in a police van, some rather burly men in plain clothes with warrants, and asked Carl if he was Carl Eisler, formerly of Munich? When he said that was his name, they arrested him as an enemy alien. He tried to explain that he was a Jewish refugee and if he had stayed in Hitler's Germany would have risked being taken to a concentration camp like so many others. That he had escaped, sought a place of sanctuary, and thought he had found it here in Australia.

They didn't even listen. Just pushed him out the door, marched him to the van and put him inside. I haven't seen him since that night. I've filled in letters of complaint, written declarations, had interviews where I've lost my temper and shouted at people, but it's like beating at the wind. These faceless officials say we're at war with the Germans, he's German, therefore he must be confined. It's called acting in the national interest, though what harm my dear Carl could do this country truly bewilders me.

I wanted to write to you so many times, but felt I should not burden you with this, that it would upset you needlessly, and I could hardly concoct a letter saying I was happily married and all was well. Which is why I didn't write at all, clearly upsetting you in a different way. I'm sorry for that. In the end, I felt I had to talk to someone, even on paper, like you did about your parents, and you're the person I feel closest to. Does that surprise you? After one brief summer when you were ten, all those years ago. Someday, perhaps, we'll talk more about it.

Meanwhile, I'm delighted about the scholarship, and the prospect of Harvard. I only wish you could come via Sydney, but this wretched war makes travel dangerous. Though, of course, if you came on an American ship it should be safe, for America seems determined to stay out of the war and remain neutral.

Don't worry about me. I'm going to keep on fighting my own personal battle – I haven't finished with those wretched bureaucrats yet. I feel better for telling you, even though I've torn up two (censored and sanitised) versions of this letter.
Fondest love, Florrie.

He wrote back immediately, abandoning his homework to spend care and time over it. Knowing it would be weeks before the letter arrived by ship, he went the following day to the overseas telegraph office and sent her a cable. Thinking the less said the better in these awkward times, it merely stated: LETTER RECEIVED. WRITING. LOVE, SAM. That afternoon he told Angelique, then had to relate the details to his mother, who realised something was amiss.

'Barbaric,' she said. 'Uncivilised. They're all so quick to accuse the Germans, but the truth is they're just as bad.'

Not quite, Sam thought, *you've been listening to your friend, Richard Sorge*. But he said nothing.

'Poor woman,' she shrugged. 'When you write, tell her I'm sorry about it. I never disliked her, even if we could hardly be friends. That would've been expecting too much.'

He was on the point of asking what she meant, why was it so impossible they could be friends, when the doorbell rang. A chauffeur from the German Embassy inquired if Madame was ready.

'Madame is changing into her new dress,' she called out, emerging soon after in the new outfit and wearing her best jewellery. They saw her driven off in a gleaming Mercedes.

'What is it tonight?' Sam asked his sister. 'Not the club?'

'Not togged up like that,' Angelique said. 'Richard has invited her to a cocktail party.'

'Trust Richard! He's fond of cocktail parties.'

'This isn't just any old bash. This is the cocktail party of the year. At the Imperial Palace.'

'You're joking! The Emperor?'

'Not quite. Prince Konoye, the Prime Minister, is giving a private party for a few close friends. Among them is dear Richard, who is very influential and moves in select circles. Mama is going up in the world.'

'She sure is,' Sam said, wondering why it bothered him.

'He isn't so bad. You must admit he takes her places she'd never go to otherwise, and gives her a good time.'

'I suppose so. She did enjoy getting into that limousine, with the chauffeur saluting and all the neighbours watching. I just hope to God she doesn't have one too many and fall flat on her arse in front of the Prince.'

Angelique laughed, told him he was horrible, and that she was going to Kitty's place for dinner.

'How's Kitty?' he asked.

'She says she has fantasies about you.'

'Really?'

'Late at night. In bed.'

'Bullshit,' he said as she hid a smile. 'How's Simon?'

'Insufferable.'

'Last week he was gorgeous.'

'That was then! He hasn't even sent me an invitation for his twenty-first birthday party. Everyone else seems to be going, but he's too full of himself to remember I'm alive.'

'It's over then? The romance of the century? The one they said would be bigger than the Duke and Duchess of Windsor.'

'Go fuck yourself,' his sister said.

The man was rigidly polite but implacable. He had a small office in Bathurst Street, with a view that overlooked the entrance to the Museum Station, and in the park beyond she could see figures rugged up against the winter. In her handbag was his sudden request that she attend the department on Friday at eleven o'clock, and in a moment of hope she had applied for and been granted the day off. The man's name was Watson: H.W. Watson it said on his door, and his rather peremptory summons nestled in her bag beside Sam's latest letter, the third he had written since his cable, always solicitous, so anxious for her, always expressing his hope the war would end soon, and her nightmare with it.

But the war was not about to end. If it did, it would end badly. The war had erupted; after the long inactivity, an astonished world had watched Hitler's blitzkrieg conquer Belgium and France, had seen the newsreels of German soldiers strut the streets of Paris, with Britain alone, her army in tatters, her only weapon seemingly the defiant voice of Winston Churchill.

'Mrs Eisler . . .'

'I beg your pardon?' The name was unfamiliar; she had had so little time to be Mrs Eisler. Carl had suggested, perhaps with foresight, that she kept her own name at work. It was only in places like this she heard it.

'I said you must really stop this.'

'Stop what, Mr Watson?'

'The stream of letters, phone calls, abuse.'

'I don't mean to be abusive. I'm trying to point out my husband is being unfairly detained.'

'Legally detained. And now this latest impertinence. How dare you send copies of your letters to the Minister for Immigration, let alone the Prime Minister.'

So that's it, she thought. *Someone has leant on him from higher up*. She felt renewed optimism. Perhaps he was being so curt and dismissive because he had been overruled. Perhaps . . .

'I've been told to order you, for your own good, not to continue doing this.'

'I helped elect them. Is it an offence to write to them?'

He stared at her, and took a deep breath before he spoke. 'You see, that's the kind of thing we'll no longer put up with in this department. That sort of talk doesn't help you, it doesn't help your husband, nor us.'

'I'm not here to help you,' she said, and then regretted it. She was stupid to make an enemy of the man. Yet he was her enemy.

'Perhaps not. But I'm here to help you.' Mr Watson smiled and she felt a chill, for it was not a friendly smile. 'It would be stupid for you to needlessly lose your job. But you certainly will if you continue this. Some of my colleagues are in favour of approaching your employers. Cusack & Noble, I recall. Fine old law firm. Very prestigious. The partners would be upset to hear of this futile campaign you're waging.'

'The partners gave Carl a position there.'

'Before the war, Mrs Eisler. And before we possessed

facts that give us grounds to believe your husband is a security risk.'

'What're you talking about?' She felt confusion and a growing alarm. 'Security risk? He was interned because of being classified as an enemy alien. A decent man trying to begin a new life, imprisoned because he was born in the wrong country.'

'Not quite that simple, Mrs Eisler. We had already been given other information. A number of internees have been cleared of any complicity and released. Your husband won't be.'

'Are you saying he's a spy?' She didn't know whether to laugh or cry at this new insanity.

'I'm unable to discuss it,' Mr Watson replied. 'Except to say he came here in the guise of a Jewish refugee seeking asylum.'

'But he is a Jewish refugee – with the papers to prove it.' She wanted to reach out and slap the bland face on the other side of the desk. 'You can't deny he was forbidden to practise law in his own country by the Nazi Aryan decree.'

'Perhaps he was,' he shrugged. 'I can't say any more about the matter. Except this... we're not vindictive. We do try to help most of these people. It doesn't always work out.'

'These people? Why do you call them *these people*?'

'I don't know why that should upset you.'

'Because it's derogatory. Has it ever occurred to you that it suggests you're speaking of a group you don't really like?'

'I'm afraid we've strayed from the point of this meeting. Our time is up, Mrs Eisler.'

She stood, collecting her overcoat from the rack before he could offer to hand it to her.

'I think you ought to realise that we're obliged to protect the country against these people, or whatever *you* wish to call them.'

'You creature,' she said, overcome with such a feeling of futility that it enraged her. 'You awful racist turd.'

She could hardly believe it was her speaking in this manner. All the way home in the tram she felt ashamed.

CHAPTER 6

The rumours had been circulating all year in Yokohama and Tokyo, but few in the foreign community believed them. The gossip claimed that prominent people, some of them powerful political figures, were being taken in for questioning by the security police – and that an espionage probe was being carried out which included some of the highest persons in the land. Despite the persistence of these stories, nothing appeared in the newspapers. No editor was prepared to risk the consequences, for the names whispered about were celebrated and influential.

Yet the hearsay continued, and seemed to gain veracity. Sam heard it at college and was afraid. He tried to discuss it with his mother who dismissed the whole thing as a vindictive pack of lies. She asked him to please not mention it again, nor waste his time listening to such rubbish: he should instead get on with his studies if he wanted to shine at Harvard next year. But while it was a taboo subject at home, Angelique, now eighteen and attractive enough to rate the attention of Simon Shroder, heard about it on her visits to the Shroder house. As a wealthy ship owner, Simon's father was a frequent guest at the American Embassy, where speculation about the matter was rife.

But when it happened, the foreign colony were astounded. It was the charge that was such a bombshell. The news broke in the Tokyo Press Club; within hours everyone knew that Richard Sorge had been taken into custody – accused of spying for the Soviet Union.

As chief correspondent of the *Frankfurter Zeitung*, with connections in Berlin extending to the high echelons of the Nazi party, all the rumours had implied he was an agent for Germany; reporting on Japan's military strength, while recruiting politicians to sway the government into joining the Axis alliance.

But a Soviet spy!

It left his friends and acquaintances bewildered. It was even rumoured he had been a double agent, paid by Berlin, but with his real loyalty to Moscow, and had warned the Kremlin of Hitler's surprise plan to attack Russia. It made sense to many. The shock invasion had occurred three months earlier, and the Russians had seemed remarkably well prepared for it.

Sam came home, dreading the thought of having to break the news to his mother. There was no need.

'I had telephone calls,' she said. 'Some nice people that I always thought were friends, they just couldn't wait to tell me.'

She refused any dinner and went to bed early. Long past midnight, he heard her weeping in her room.

The cars placed themselves at either end of the street, effectively sealing the area, while one stopped in the laneway behind the house. This was the squad car that Sam happened to see from his window, where he was doing his best to study. It had been a terrible week. Not only the headlines in the newspapers and reports on the radio; far worse were the constant telephone calls, some sympathetic, others abusive, a few of them silent threats without a word until the connection was abruptly terminated.

At least the headmaster of the International School had been understanding. He said the only thing that mattered was Sam's looming exams, and his pursuit of an economics degree in America. That was his future; the current scandal was nothing to do with him, and he must not allow himself to be distracted. Where would he feel most comfortable until the matter died down? Did he prefer to put up with the curiosity at school, or work at home?

Sam had chosen the latter, which was how he saw the two men open the rear gate and enter the yard. He guessed they were police the moment the cook came out of her bungalow room in the garden, bowed in a frightened manner, and retreated hurriedly as they came to the back of the house and waited. A moment later the front doorbell rang, followed by an insistent knocking. As if this was a signal, the back door was kicked open.

The men who poured into the house wore hats which they didn't bother to remove. The officer in charge showed a warrant, and loudly announced they were members of the Special Police, here to conduct a search of the premises. Sam felt a shiver of dismay. It was a division of the Kempetai who investigated major crimes against the State. They were an authoritarian organisation with unlimited powers, akin to the German Gestapo.

If his mother felt any alarm, she gave no sign of it. The leader of the group spoke in Japanese, which she understood, but she deliberately addressed them in English.

'An outrage,' she said. 'How dare you treat us as if we are criminals? It is rude and disgusting not to take off your hats in the presence of ladies.'

Nice try, Ma, Sam thought, knowing it would make no difference. But at least they removed their hats, then in retaliation proceeded slowly and methodically to search each room in the house. While they did, his mother fiercely denigrated them, her strongly accented English growing more erratic with increasing agitation.

'Bluudy bastards,' she muttered, well aware it was loud enough for them to hear. 'What rubbish do they look for?'

Sam knew it was a rhetorical question; the secret police ignored her while they opened drawers and peered into wardrobes. They searched the kitchen cupboards and even the oven. It goaded her into another attempt to provoke them.

'Superintendent,' she said loudly to the man in charge, knowing he was a junior inspector. 'You know what they say in my country, if there is a sudden silence?'

'Madame,' he was brusque, accustomed to people being terrified rather than angry: 'I have no idea, nor do I care. We have a job to do.'

'When such a silence happens, all the Russians, they say, "Somewhere a policeman is being born".'

Sam had heard it before, many times. It was one of his mother's fond tales of old Russia, the real one, she always declared – before the Bolsheviks killed the Tsar and the Tsarina. The inspector's shrug of indifference reinforced her annoyance.

'I am a White Russian who fled from the revolution

and hates Soviet communists. Why in the name of God do you invade my house, and what are you looking for?'

'I am obeying my orders,' he said, 'and you would do well to remember it. Your good friend has been arrested.'

'This is not a secret. But I knew nothing of this work he did, and he has not even been proved guilty.'

'He will be,' the inspector said.

'Of course! The trial will be a farce.'

'No need for a farce . . . when there is so much proof. Now shut up and stop annoying me.'

His anger finally warned her into silence. The search moved to Sam's room. They rifled through his reference books and scattered his work papers. He knew better than to complain. One of the policemen opened a desk drawer and took out a bundle of letters tied with a ribbon. He undid them and they spilled onto the floor in a heap, as he called his superior. They studied the pages while Sam fumed.

'What are these?'

'Personal letters.'

'All in the same handwriting.'

'They're from the same friend.' As they continued to carefully scan each page, Sam found their behaviour absurd, and rashly said in exasperation, 'They're letters from Florence.'

The inspector gazed at him.

'From Italy?'

Sam had an absurd desire to laugh, and knew it would be dangerous. He tried to explain as patiently and politely as possible.

'From someone *named* Florence. Florence Eisler.'

'And what is this word that always begins the letters.

Corr-a-roy.' He had the usual difficulty with pronunciation. 'What does that mean?'

'It's the place where she lives. Collaroy,' he said, careful not to sound as if he was correcting the other's use of consonants. 'It's a beach suburb of Sydney, Australia.'

'Australia?' They moved aside and had a brief murmured conference that excluded Sam, then the policeman gathered all the letters together. Sam put out his hand for them, but the inspector shook his head.

'It is no longer a friendly country, Australia. We will have to keep these.'

'*What*?'

'They should be more thoroughly verified.'

Sam forgot caution in his anger at this blatant stupidity. 'For Christ's sake, they're private letters from my godmother. Years of letters. I keep them because I'm fond of her. There's nothing of any interest in there.'

'If not, then they will be returned. Meanwhile we will take them for our experts to examine,' the inspector said.

The neighbours had seen the raid. Everyone on the exclusive hillside called The Bluff was aware of Tamara Delon's affair with Richard Sorge. That was the trouble, Sam reflected, she had enjoyed flaunting the relationship so openly. He didn't blame her; after the fiasco with their father she had felt a deep sense of betrayal, and for months had stayed home, shunning friends and her regular bridge games at the Country Club. It was during that time that the heavy drinking had started, alone. After meeting the journalist, the fact that he drank as much as she did was one of the bonds that had coalesced their intimacy.

The neighbourhood they lived in was unique; occupied only by foreigners. The government owned the land and had leased it to those who built houses under a treaty signed when Yokohama was still a fishing village. It was an expensive district; Sam knew they could only afford to live there because his father had paid for the house at the time of the divorce, as part of his mother's financial demands. Because of this, they belonged to a close-knit community, its exclusivity resented by wealthy Japanese who envied the prime position denied them. The people on The Bluff knew this; it created a special camaraderie, and while not prepared to be too open in case it attracted the attention of the Kempetai, most tried to act as if there were no scandal attached to Sam's family.

Besides, more disturbing events were taking place. A bitter quarrel between Japan and America over trade. The replacement of Prince Konoye as Prime Minister by the militarist General Tojo. People on The Bluff agreed it was unsettling but there must be no panic, it was really just a thread unravelled in the smooth fabric of their lives. They attended each other's parties, played tennis and golf, and within weeks were unsurprised to see Tamara back at the Country Club, sitting with her friends at the bridge table instead of perched at the bar, even if a gin and tonic was by her side.

Meanwhile, half a world away, Florence Eisler wrote a long letter to Sam. An important letter that he never received, for his name was on a list and his mail was now being intercepted.

It was September and bitterly cold; officially spring, but the weather denied it. The chill winds made the tram trip home unpleasant and interminable. She tried to read an evening paper, but a large man dozing and smelling of beer in their shared seat made it difficult to turn the pages. She thought instead about Carl. Two years since he had been so abruptly imprisoned, and despite her letters and appeals, no word of where he was held. No permission granted to see him. It was unjust, abhorrent, but without help what could she do?

Of the partners, her employers, Mr Cusack had been the most sympathetic. Mr Noble was inclined to caution, and felt if the authorities were taking such draconian action, they must have a good reason. One had to trust the government, he believed. Both lawyers assured Florrie she would not lose her job, although she sensed their anxiety that she should not become too radical. They warned nothing could be achieved by creating trouble, and counselled patience. *When the war ends*, she thought, recalling their advice, but wondered how it would end. In chaos? Hitler was the master of Europe, his army was dominant in Russia, his bombers battering London. Now there was talk about Japan. An uneasy suspicion they might declare war and join the winning side. Thank God Sam would soon finish his exams and leave for Harvard. She had become accustomed to calling him Sam, no longer Samuel, although the longer biblical name had a sentiment he would not understand, and she would never tell him.

As the tram clanged its way through Brookvale, she began to speculate on exactly when Sam would be departing for America. By the time she reached her stop beside the Long Reef golf course, she had already decided she would write to him after supper. But when she reached home the porch lights were on, and a figure was waiting.

'Carl?' She said it disbelievingly, then ran so wildly

towards him she would certainly have fallen had his arms not tightened around her.

Towards dawn Florrie woke and knew the joy of not being alone, feeling the warmth of Carl's body and hearing the soft regular breathing as he slept. Her lips felt bruised with his passion, her body exhausted with the ecstasy of their love-making. Gently she slipped from the bed, pausing as he seemed to miss a beat, then the rhythmic sound of his breathing resumed, and she went softly into the kitchen, closed the door so as not to wake him, and made a cup of tea.

They had hardly known what to say to each other after her first incredulous realisation.

'When did you get here?' she'd asked. 'How? Why didn't they tell me, so I could meet you?'

The questions came tumbling out. The answers took longer to absorb.

'A week ago,' he said, 'I was brought before a panel.'

'What panel?'

'People. Officials, some committee. There are always committees. They said there had been an error.'

'An error?'

'Someone had made a mistake.'

'But Carl . . .'

'Some wrong information. A person made a report I had come here unlawfully, that I was a communist . . .'

'Dear God,' she whispered, 'a mistake. Two years for their mistake.'

'Even worse than that.'

'What could be worse?'

'The strain of those seven days after they told me, before they set me free. I counted every minute of every hour of those dreadful days. I began to wonder if it was false, if they were trying to trick me. Sheer paranoia, of course, but in prison if you know you are innocent, you go a little crazy. They said there were . . . what was the word? . . . formalities . . . papers to be prepared for me to sign.'

'The bastards,' she said, feeling the enormity of what he had been through, 'the awful bloody bastards. We'll sue them for false imprisonment. I'll talk to Mr Cusack.'

'We can't,' he said.

'Of course we can. There must be compensation. Not for the money, but to stop them doing this to someone else.'

'The formalities, the papers forbid it. I had to sign that I would take no action against the Commonwealth.'

'But under duress!'

'I had to state I signed of my own free will.'

'Oh God,' she said, 'we should go to the newspapers, but I suppose we can't . . .'

'Especially not the newspapers.'

'Then what? Just accept it, this injustice?'

'Accept it's over. Try to forget.'

'But it's wrong. There must be something we can do.'

'There is,' he said gently, and took her hands. 'We can have dinner, talk about you, then we can go to bed and make love.'

The kettle for her tea was about to boil, and she turned off the gas before the sound of the whistle woke Carl. Outside it was still dark. There was a north-easterly breeze, and she could hear the comforting sound of the sea washing on the shore.

A mistake.

There was no way they could even establish that. People like Mr Watson would have locked away the file. Two wasted years, and no way to reveal his innocence. It would drive her mad, but Carl was right. They had to try to forget. Yet before she did that, she needed to express her feelings. At least someone must be told. She sipped her tea, collected her pad and pen, and began to write.

Collaroy, September 1941.
Dearest Sam,

A most miraculous and yet infuriating thing has happened. The miracle is that Carl is free. The fury comes because the idiots who ordered his arrest discovered they were acting on false evidence, and it was all a mistake. So while I am filled with joy I am also consumed with rage that they have made us suffer, and have forced him to sign papers which will prevent him from proving their culpability and his innocence. It is most unjust. Carl wants me to forget it, which I must, but the act of letting off steam helps me, so now that you're a tall, broad-shouldered young man of nineteen, I pass the baton to you.

I only hope Carl can get his job back. I think I can sway Mr Cusack, but Mr Noble is a capital C conservative. However, if he refuses he will have to get a new secretary, and I've been there so long and my filing system is so complex, that I pity the poor wretch who takes my place. They might even have to call for help, which will give me a lovely chance to impose my terms – a salary increase and Carl's reinstatement!

Now listen to me, my darling. There are worrying rumours here that Japan might get involved in the war. I have some money saved, and would gladly pay your fare if you felt it prudent to hop on a boat and come south. As for Harvard, it should be easy enough to catch a boat here, and sail to your Ivy League destination. Or you could get into Sydney University, as I once said.

You will know better than me what the feeling is there, but the feeling here is one of deep concern. Please write as soon as you can and tell me what you think. Fondest love, Florrie.

The letter was among overseas mail brought by the freighter *Takana Maru*, and cleared through the Tokyo Central post office. A member of the Kempetai internal security section checked the recipients against a list of names he had, and those letters were kept for scrutiny. They were taken to a highly specialised unit where a staff of code-breakers and experts in foreign languages were employed. The letters were steamed open; if considered harmless, they were resealed and put back in the mail system.

Florence Eisler's letter was studied intently. There were a number of expressions that puzzled the decoders.

'I pass the baton to you,' one said. 'An unusual phrase. It could hide other information.'

'Hop on a boat and come south,' his colleague pointed out clearly meant an escape to Australia.

They pondered if Mr Noble being a capital C conservative had any special meaning. And whether Ivy League destination could be a code word. Meanwhile, the English linguist noted that the letter spoke openly of Japan making war.

They decided it should be withheld and kept for closer scrutiny. After all, the young man's mother was a paramour of the notorious spy, Sorge. One of many, but the latest one. While nothing had yet been proved against her, she would remain listed in their files as being under suspicion. And so, they agreed, would her son.

Seven weeks after this, at the end of October, a letter came which puzzled Florence Eisler. It was in the mailbox when they came home from work: Mr Cusack had prevailed, and Mr Noble had finally and with some reluctance agreed Carl should return to their office. He was soon busy conveyancing and appearing for clients in the magistrate's court, and after a few weeks it seemed as if he had never been away. In fact, he was a welcome addition, even Mr Noble admitted, for the founders of the firm were elderly and the workload had become unmanageable. Carl and Florence found this entailed them arriving at the office early and leaving late. There were times when it felt as if they were beginning to run the practice between them. She was the senior secretary; Carl was always so alert and attentive to the clients that people were starting to ask for him in preference to the partners.

If they worked slavishly in the week, at least the weekends were theirs. Carl swam, declaring the water beautifully warm; she said she'd take his word for it, but felt she would stick to jogging and sunbaking until warmer days in November. The spring meant picnics and barbecues, and Florrie's friends warmed to this goodlooking and affable husband, who had been given such a raw deal, but would not hear a word against his adopted country. Her friends liked that; it was unanimously decided that Carl was a good bloke, which, with the country at war with his homeland, was a peculiarly and rather notable Australian accolade.

'What is it?' he asked, as she frowned over the letter and he brought two glasses of wine to the table.

'Sam.'

'Is Sam in love? Made a girl pregnant? Or what?' Then he saw her concern, stopped teasing and sat beside her. 'Trouble?'

'I'm not sure. It's rather odd.'

'What is?'

'I wrote to him in early September. I remember clearly, because it was the day after you came home.'

'I remember you posting it. And . . .'

'His letter was sent a month ago. He would surely have received mine by then, but there's no mention of it.'

'No?'

'Not a word. Nothing about the news of you being home, or the situation there, not even a reaction to my proposal that he leaves the country before there's any trouble. It's all about that man Sorge – how deeply upset his mother is, and the way the police came and searched their house and questioned them.' She stopped as she saw his expression. 'Carl? What is it, darling?'

'I hate to say this, but if they searched and questioned them, then they would most assuredly monitor their mail.'

'Would they really do that?'

'My darling, in times like these all foreigners are suspect. And yes, of course they would do it. We paranoid ex-prisoners know to what depths secret police like the Kempetai or the Gestapo stoop. I would say it is quite clear; he never received your letter.'

CHAPTER 7

The streets of the summer resort were empty, the air chilly with the onset of winter, the town unnaturally silent. There were no voices, no sound of bicycle bells or the laughter of their riders in the lanes. From the verandah of the house he could see distant mountain peaks, their tips powdered with snow against the skyline. The landscape was uncharacteristically bleak; peach trees bare of blossom, groves of azaleas inert against the frost, the graceful birches stripped of foliage and abandoned by birds who would not nest here again until the northern spring.

Most of his life Sam had known this village of Karuizawa. He and his friends had chased dragonflies and collected their cicadas here. Ever since he was a child, this had been the family's holiday home, the haven where they migrated each July to escape the city heat. Perched high in the hills, a thousand metres above sea level, its cool air and idyllic climate had, years ago, seen it transformed from a rustic community into a fashionable retreat with expensive chalets, palatial residences, and European-style villas.

He wondered why he and his father had come here.

To talk, Henri Delon had explained, after his surprise arrival from Saigon, but he had omitted to specify about what.

It was like a ghost town; the big hotel closed, restaurants vacated, tables and chairs stacked away; the holiday chalets locked up until the summer. The living room of their house contained a rarely used fireplace. Sam helped his father gather wood, and they lit the fire. If it was unusual being here in November, it was even more unexpected to be alone like this with his father. In the two and a half years since the divorce, they had rarely met. The distance, their mother's hostility, their father's devotion to the new woman in his life, had made any encounter difficult. So the news his father was in the country, and his invitation that they take the mountain train together, had come as a surprise to Sam. One not welcomed by his mother.

'Karuizawa? Why?'

'I don't know, Ma, but I'm going.'

'Ridiculous. Who in their right mind would go there in winter? But then your father hasn't been in his right mind ever since he met that tart!' She assured Sam it would be freezing.

In fact the house was soon warm. It was companionable in front of the fire, the afternoon darkening outside, wood flickering in the grate.

'Everything all right now at home?' his father asked.

'Settling down, Father,' Sam said, deciding not to go into further detail. 'How is it at your home?'

Henri Delon reminded himself his son was now nineteen. Perfectly entitled to make such a remark. 'Peaceful,' he said, with a trace of a smile. Recalling the uproar of his parents' separation, Sam smiled in return. 'But things are happening, which make it vital I talk to you. We may not get another chance like this.'

'What things?' Sam asked.

'You know there's going to be a war?'

'We know there are rumours. We hear them all the time. What we don't know is whether to believe them.'

'Take my advice,' his father said, 'believe them.'

'I've been trying not to,' Sam said, weighing the impact this might have on his future. What of Harvard? All year he'd been preparing to go to America and ignoring the signs that might make it impossible. He realised his father had abruptly changed the subject.

'I had a letter from Miss Carter.'

'From Florence?' He turned in surprise.

'Yes. Unexpected. I gather you two write regularly.'

'We have for years.'

'Did you know her husband has been released?'

'Carl has? He's no longer interned? But that's really wonderful news. She's been so unhappy . . .'

'Sam,' his father interrupted, 'she wrote and told you.'

'No. I haven't heard from her for months.'

'She did write, in early September. You never got it?'

'I'd have replied straight away – and sent a cable to wish them joy. It must have gone astray.'

'She thinks your mail is being diverted and checked. I think she's right and her letter is in some police file.'

A dry log in the grate crackled like a pistol shot, and Sam flinched. Why, he was about to ask, then suddenly he knew why. His mother and bloody Richard Sorge. The security police, the house search, his letters which had finally been returned. But not this one – if they had it. It was a disturbing thought.

'She wrote to me,' his father said, 'because she felt it unwise to write again to you. We're both afraid for your safety, which is why I flew from Saigon immediately. We needed to have a serious talk in private, and that's why you and I are here.'

'Afraid... for my safety?' A spark flew onto the hearth, and he put the mesh guard in place. 'Afraid of what?'

'It's difficult for me,' Delon stared into the glowing fire as if he might find assistance there. 'To help you understand, I have to explain something. You were never to be told this, it was part of the arrangement, but now I feel you must know. You're adopted.'

Sam sat looking at him in numbed disbelief.

'You're not my father?' was all he could finally ask.

'Well, yes. But your mother...' he stopped, then tried to continue. 'She... that is, we... came to an agreement.'

'Someone else is my mother?'

'Er... yes...'

'Who?'

'Sam, don't get upset. Listen to me.'

'Who?'

'This is the most difficult conversation I've ever had.'

'If it's difficult for you, think how I feel about it, Father!'

'I don't blame you for being angry.'

'I'll get angrier if you don't answer. Forget trying to make excuses for yourself. It's never been a secret that you were a randy bastard. The stud of Kobe. The French Ram, as some of my friends called you. I know of at least four affairs you had when I was growing up.'

He looked astounded. 'Good God,' he said, 'do you?'

'So you had another, and this time I was the result.

And you thought you'd never have to tell me. Let me live the rest of my life not knowing.' He shook his head in disbelief.

'I'm sorry, Sam.'

'Bugger being sorry. Tell me the truth. Who was she? And where is she now?' It was then he had a moment of perception. The memory of the beach house in Collaroy when he was ten years old, and the spontaneous way they had found such a kinship.

'It was Florence,' he said, gazing at his father.

'Not Florence. She would never have given you up for adoption. Not if you were truly hers.'

'What does that mean? Who in God's name was it?'

'Her sister. Catherine.'

'I didn't know she had a sister.'

'I met her on a business trip to Sydney. A solo trip – I daresay I don't need to add that.'

'No, you don't.' Sam felt dazed. 'What happened to her?'

'She died when you were six months old.'

'How?'

'Pneumonia.'

'Where were you?'

'Back in Kobe. Things were awkward in our marriage.'

'Things were always awkward in your marriage, the way I remember it,' Sam said, not caring if he offended him.

'One thing I never did was hide my frailties.' He seemed to feel this was a virtue. 'I told Tamara about the affair, even told her I'd done my best to persuade Catherine to have an abortion.'

'Jesus Christ, did you have to tell me *that*?'

'I'm sorry. But it wasn't easy for an unmarried woman to have a child out of wedlock in those days.

And her family hardly helped the situation. They were particularly upset.'

'I can imagine.'

'No, you can't,' Henri Delon retorted. 'You can't begin to imagine. Her father was an Orthodox Jew. Both parents were strictly religious, and appalled their elder daughter had got herself pregnant, let alone to a married man who wasn't a Jew and didn't even live in the same country.'

'Shit,' Sam said.

'I think they might've welcomed an abortion. Catherine refused. She insisted she'd cope alone.'

'I'm fortunate my natural mother had such strength of character,' Sam said. 'Otherwise we could hardly be having this conversation.'

His father ignored this: 'When Cathy died, Florence quarrelled with her parents over the way they'd treated her. She left the family home, and took you with her. She went to stay with friends, and wrote to me that she wanted to bring you up. She was not even eighteen, she had no money, it was impossible. Whereas we'd been married nine years without a child. The doctors believed Tamara couldn't have any. We went to Sydney, persuaded Florence. It wasn't easy. In the end we convinced her it would be best . . .'

'Best for whom?'

'For you. Your future. My wife was willing to accept you as her son, on condition that you were never told. Florence had her own conditions. After the adoption we'd have a Christian baptism with her as godmother. Then, when you were older, we must bring you back to Sydney, long enough for her to properly get to know you. I made that promise, and at least I kept it.'

'You did. Thank you for that,' his son said, remembering words spoken outside the beach house years ago.

'After it was all settled we came home to Kobe. By then Tamara was pregnant with Angelique. So the doctors were wrong.'

'Would she have wanted me, if she'd known at the time?'

'She knew. Before the papers were signed, she knew. Sam, she wanted you. I know she hates my guts, but you'd do me a favour if you keep this to yourself. She's been a real mother to you all this time, and she's proud of you.'

'I'd never want to hurt her. I'll do my best, but you explain why you had to tell me. Why, after so long?'

'God knows I didn't want to. But I thought you had to know it all. The whole damned thing.'

'I asked *why*?'

'Because of the danger. Because Florence is afraid. In her letter she said you should get out of Japan.'

'Oh.'

'If the letter was intercepted, it could be used against you. She thinks – and so do I – that the sensible thing is to leave. The sooner the better. When the war comes, Australia and Japan will be enemies.'

'But Papa, I'm French. In any war, we'll be neutral.'

'You're Australian by birth.'

'But you're my father.'

'I wasn't there. I'd left her. Your mother registered your birth in Sydney. You're only French by adoption.'

'But how would anyone find that out?'

'They may not, but only a fool takes chances. There are papers that had to be lodged here. Adoption of an Australian child. There are people still living in Kobe who know. They had to be told. After all, we arrived home with a baby. People guessed.'

'What people?'

'A few good friends sworn to secrecy. But these days can even friends be trusted?'

He rose, stacked more wood on the fire, then said he'd heat up the food they'd brought with them.

'Think it over, Sam. In the end, it's your decision. But you need to make it quickly.'

Sam heard him go into the kitchen, saw the lights flicker in protest as the electric oven was switched on. Power was not one of the most dependable features of the house, which needed rewiring. In the grate the wood flared and the fire warmed him. He stared into the flames, remembering Australia when he was ten years old, trying to come to terms with all that he had been told.

'Sam?'

He turned. His father was looking at him curiously.

'Yes, Papa?'

'The food's nearly ready. I thought you were asleep.'

'No, just watching the firelight. Remembering things. Florence and Ma, how they didn't like each other. Florrie telling me some story about you and Mama choosing her as my godmother, which I felt wasn't true. Things that puzzled me for years.'

'Will you go?'

'Yes,' he said.

'Good.' His father nodded, relieved.

'When and how?'

'There's a cargo ship. Leaving in ten days time.'

'Only ten days!'

'I wish it was less,' Henri Delon said.

Early next morning they locked the house and went down to Karuizawa station, where they boarded the Tokyo train. While they had breakfast, his father outlined the arrangements.

'It's a freighter leaving from Kobe. Safer than taking a

boat from Yokohama. I'll be there, trying to sort out the office for a few weeks, and I'll have my secretary buy you new clothes. When you leave home bring only a weekend bag. You're coming to visit me before I fly back to Indochina. Right?'

'You really believe in taking precautions.'

'I know these security police. Evil bastards. We can never be too careful. I don't know what to suggest about Angelique and Tamara, or what you say to them. But please make sure there's no gossip or tearful public farewells.'

Sam nodded. He would have to think that one out before he reached home. He could hardly tell them the full truth, but he had to say something.

'The ship is the *Honshu Maru*. By the way, I made the booking through Saigon, but your aunt insisted on paying the fare.'

'My aunt?' Sam said with a smile. 'Yes, that's right, of course, she is. And I'm half Jewish.'

'Don't go around announcing it,' his father said.

At Tokyo Central, Sam accompanied him to the Kobe train. They shook hands beside the carriage. The train was hissing steam, the guard's flag poised to signal departure.

'I'll be expecting you. I'll send a cable to tell Florence.'

'Is that safe?'

'Perfectly. I send it to the senior partner in the law firm she works for. It'll merely say the contract is being dispatched and give the date you leave.' He smiled. 'We're learning the cloak-and-dagger business, Florence and her husband and me.'

He climbed aboard as the guard's whistle shrilled.

'She really loves you, your aunt. But you know that.'

'I know. And it's mutual,' Sam said.

CHAPTER 8

Mr Cusack gave Florrie the cable, and saw her smile with delight. It was astonishing, he thought, that he had never previously considered her beautiful. But the smile gladdened his heart. Her eyes were so lively and bright, she moved with a fluid grace, she was, ever since Carl Eisler's release, an extraordinarily attractive and vital woman.

'The contract is being dispatched in nine days time,' she said. 'He'll be here before Christmas.'

'Wonderful news, Miss Carter.' Mr Cusack still called her Miss Carter, for he didn't like change. She had been Miss Carter when she came here as a slip of a girl, and would remain so until her retirement, although by then Mr Cusack assumed he would be long gone from this earth. He had felt some twinges lately; irritation of the old ticker his fool of a doctor had said, trying to reassure him, but Mr Cusack knew better than to listen to such placatory nonsense. He was aware what it was. His father had died of a heart attack in his fifties, and

Charles Cusack was now in his late sixties. Getting old. But not too old to admire the transformation of Miss Carter, he admonished himself, and tried to resume work.

The calendar on their kitchen wall had a big cross in the space for November the twenty-seventh, which was the day the freighter would sail from Kobe. Florrie made yet another list of the many things to be done before Sam's arrival, and Carl sat opposite and watched her frown of concentration.

'Such intensity,' he said fondly.

'It's a list.'

'I know. You like making lists. Especially this one.'

'So much to do in the next few weeks.'

'I can imagine,' Carl said. 'Paint his room. Finish the quilt for his bed. Ring the shipping company for the exact date and time of arrival . . .'

'You peeked,' she laughed.

'No, I read your mind. Then we talk to the university. To see if they have an economics degree that might tempt him to give up Harvard. Plus a welcome party. And a Christmas present.'

'You don't mind me being a bit excited, do you?'

'I love you being a bit excited,' he said. 'You know why? Because you look exquisite when you're excited.'

She felt warmed by his admiration. *Exquisite indeed*! But Carl had a way of saying things and gazing at her that made her feel so wanted, and always invoked a response.

'It's getting late,' she said, 'let's go to bed.'

* * *

Sam decided there was no way to avoid an emotional farewell to his mother, so the prudent thing was not to tell her he was leaving. It would avoid days of drama; she might be upset enough to confide the news to her gossiping bridge friends. The deceit troubled him, but she was not renowned for keeping secrets.

In his own mind she remained his mother, and he had no problem with that. In fact, he returned home with a new affection for her; it was true, as his father said, she had brought him up as her own. There had never been the slightest difference in her behaviour towards Angelique as her natural child, and the one forced on her by her husband's philandering. Which was why, on arrival he had hugged her with unusual tenderness.

'So! Relieved and happy to be back,' she said, pleased by this display of affection. 'Frozen by the mountains, back to nice warm civilisation!'

Typical Mama, he thought, and hugged her again.

'And how was the old *roué*? What did he want?'

'He thinks there's going to be a war soon.'

'Always the pessimist! Except with women, then he was every time an optimist.'

'I think you mean an opportunist.'

'Do I? Well, whatever I mean, you couldn't trust him in or out of bed. Anybody's bed. Why did he drag you to Karuizawa?'

'He wanted to see it again, a sort of nostalgia trip. We walked a lot, talked over old times. He'd like to be friends with us.'

She looked scornful at the idea. 'With me? Fat chance. How's the Italian tart?'

'They seem to be happy.'

'Hmph! What else did you talk about?'

'My hopes for Harvard. Nothing special. It was

strange being up there, the place was so empty.' He added casually, 'Papa's in Kobe sorting out his office there. I'll go and see him off, when he leaves for Saigon.'

'Why?' she asked sharply.

'Because he asked me to.'

All week he felt guilty, agonising over how she would feel when she learned the truth, and if he should tell Angelique first, and beg her to explain after he was at sea. In the end he told them both, but not until the night before he was due to leave. He told them facts, but left out details. Florence Eisler barely received a mention. He said his father had convinced him there would be a war. His best hope of a university degree was to leave while there was time, and if it had to be Australia instead of Harvard, so be it. If that was selfish, he was sorry, but it was the rest of his life he was talking about. He waited for a furious outburst, but as always Tamara surprised him.

'Of course you must go,' she said. 'Why couldn't that silly old bastard have come and discussed it with us, like any normal person? We'll miss you, it's all so sudden, but you'll be back when you graduate.' He saw her eyes were suddenly moist, and held her tightly. Her muffled voice speaking against his chest said it would be best if they said goodbye at the house, because it might not be wise to have any tearful public farewells at the station.

The freighter *Honshu Maru* was two days late leaving Kobe. The departure was delayed by the ship loading extra cargo, intensifying his father's anxiety. In this uneasy time, with the pair using the apartment of a friend, Sam learned some surprising details about Henri Delon. His father had secrets of his own. In Saigon, he personally wrote and circulated a newsletter for members of the Free French in the Far East, actively campaigning against the puppet government which now ran France.

Sam was concerned. Until that moment, he'd had no idea; he thought of his father purely as a businessman, an estranged parent, certainly not a political activist living what might be a dangerous existence. 'Does anyone suspect what you're doing?'

'Not so far. It began with a group of us in Kobe keeping watch on German ships. When France was defeated and De Gaulle fled to London, he asked us to continue. He sent proof of the things happening under the Vichy regime in France. Men and women being arrested and shot, or sent to work in slave labour camps. We do our best to keep people informed so they won't believe the Nazi lies.'

'But the risk, Papa . . .'

'Don't you start, or I'll be sorry I told you. It's hardly a risk at all, but sometimes Maria feels nervous.'

'Jesus Christ.' He felt oddly inarticulate and, for the first time, rather proud of his father. 'What was it you said? Learn about cloak and dagger? Sounds like you're up to your neck in it.'

'Don't worry. The police there are amateurs, not exactly the Kempetai. More like Keystone Kops. And if things ever get tricky, I have some friends in high places – in case they're needed.'

Sam thought about it as the freighter left Osaka Bay, and the land dropped away. He had a feeling his father had minimised the risk, and he spared a thought for Maria who sometimes felt nervous. Strange things happened to people. For so long Henri Delon had been a remote figure to his son, his interests centred mainly on accruing money and acquiring other women, not necessarily in that order. The war far away in Europe seemed to have transformed him into a patriot.

Tomorrow his father would leave for Indochina. He had a seat booked on the plane that refuelled in Formosa then flew to Saigon. From there he would communicate, through the law firm in Sydney that Florrie and Carl worked for, using whatever code they had arranged between them. Sam realised he might even be able to send greetings by this method at Christmas time. It would be good to remain in touch with Papa after so long a period of alienation. He stayed on deck until it became dark, the breeze freshening off the sea, then went into his small cabin. He was the only passenger.

On December first, the ship reached the Philippines and unloaded cargo in Manila. The captain said they had already made up useful time. They would save another twelve hours by his change of schedule; instead of two days in harbour, they were to leave that evening on the tide. He hoped to reach Sydney by the scheduled date, picking up the lost two days by spending less time in port. Besides, their only other major debarkation was Morotai, not a place anyone would wish to remain for long. In that case, Sam said, he'd buy his Christmas presents in the brief stay ashore.

The streets of Manila were full of American troops. In the shops and the hotel coffee shop where he lunched, the likelihood of war seemed to be the sole topic of conversation. People discussed it with animation, many eagerly welcoming the prospect. If the Japs wanted to strut around waving Samurai swords, a man said loudly at an adjoining table, let them stop posturing and get on with it. We'll kick the shit out of them. He begged the pardon of the ladies within hearing, but the ladies all said they absolutely agreed with him.

The mood of self-confidence was tangible. Everyone Sam spoke to asserted the army was better, bigger, and far bolder under the command of General Douglas MacArthur. There was an air of local certitude about MacArthur. He had frequently declared the base impregnable, and was believed implicitly. Japan would never dare attack here, people said, and if they did, the General would sure teach them one hell of a lesson.

After leaving harbour that night, the *Honshu Maru* headed south. They made good progress through the Celebes Sea, unloaded freight at Moratia, and left there at dawn on December fourth. Ahead was the Torres Strait and the coast of Australia. Soon Sam would see the great twin headlands and Sydney Harbour again. He might even – if they arrived in daylight – see Manly's crescent beach and the hotel where they had stayed nine years earlier. And Florrie would be forewarned and expecting him. Sam thought about her a lot. He wondered if she had changed, and hoped he would like Carl. He warmed himself in the tropical sun, read books, studied the daily chart of their headway, and tried to contain his growing excitement.

In another part of the Pacific, far to the north east, a great fleet had been at sea for eight days. An armada of warships, it converged to group north of the Volcano Islands, then carefully headed in the direction of Hawaii with every vessel's transmitter sealed to preserve strict radio silence. Protected by the convoy of cruisers and battleships were all of Japan's aircraft carriers, laden with a combined strike force of three hundred and fifty bombers and their fighter escorts.

At dawn on Sunday, December seventh, the warships stood in their allotted positions to the north of the Hawaiian island of Oahu. The sun was soon to rise over the unsuspecting playgrounds of Waikiki beach and Diamond Head. Before it did, coded orders launched the first wave of aircraft from their carriers in a surprise attack. As the decks were cleared, new planes were called into position. Within the hour, a second and then a third strike were to follow.

Before the morning was gone, the highly fortified United States naval base and the American Pacific fleet at anchor in Pearl Harbour had been almost totally destroyed.

The radio operator of the *Honshu Maru* sat listening to the chatter of the morse message, then began to write. Wide-eyed and trembling with the significance of the news he had to impart, he ran towards the bridge. Sitting peacefully outside his cabin, Sam heard the commotion; he saw the captain read the message and witnessed the crew's excited reaction. Rising to his feet, Sam drew close enough to hear the conversation, followed by a rapid exchange of orders. Within moments he understood what was happening.

Japan was at war with America. Two days earlier, there had been an attack, although the radio operator was not sure which side had been the attacker. But the report he had decoded came from a source in New Guinea, and declared other allied countries had now declared war on Japan, including Australia. If they sailed on, they would soon be in enemy waters; if they were foolish enough to dock in Sydney, the crew would face certain internment.

As their sole passenger, the captain paid Sam the courtesy of explaining their predicament. They had a large load of freight, but sadly it was no longer possible to deliver it. He deeply regretted he was also unable to land his passenger at any destination. All ports posed danger. It was his imperative to save his ship, therefore the flag was being lowered, the vessel turning about, and they were heading back to the safety of their homeland.

CHAPTER 9

On the Sunday evening, Angelique and her mother heard a musical programme on the radio abruptly interrupted by a fanfare. Then came an announcement that there was to be a statement from the Prime Minister, General Tojo.

'I can't stand that man,' her mother said. 'He's like a toad. A toad with buckteeth and shifty eyes.'

'Shhh, Mama. Listen.'

'Why should I listen? I never understand what the nasty little toad is saying. And I wouldn't believe a word of it, even if I could understand.'

'Ma, please, shut up,' Angelique said.

The rather desiccated voice on the radio proceeded to announce that the cowardly Americans had attacked the Japanese fleet without warning, and that the Japanese navy and air force had responded with superb courage to inflict a resounding blow on the enemy. The American fleet had been crippled; a glorious triumph following the treacherous attack. He finished by promising victory; the war would be over within months, and Nippon would assuredly prevail because the enterprise had the divine blessing of Emperor Hirohito.

Angelique switched off the set as the sound of the national anthem began. Despite the constant rumours of war for weeks past, both women were shocked; their immediate thoughts were for Sam.

Was it possible he could reach Australia?

It seemed unlikely; his estimated arrival was still a few days away. Might he have managed to persuade the crew to land him somewhere adjacent, like New Guinea, from where he could get transport? Or perhaps the ship would be stopped by the Australian navy? Angelique found a school atlas and they pored over it, trying to work out where he could be.

In the house on the beach at Collaroy, Florrie and Carl heard a different version of the same news. It was on every radio channel; Japan's relentless and unexpected attack on Pearl Harbour had stunned the world.

'This is a day that will live in infamy,' President Franklin Roosevelt proclaimed in his declaration of war before a joint sitting of the US Senate and Congress. Australia, Britain, Canada and their allies had immediately joined the United States and declared war on Japan as the world divided into two armed camps.

Florrie had carefully worked out the probable progress of the ship, since receiving a cable from Henri Delon after his return to Saigon, advising of the two-day delay. Without any real feeling of hope, she telephoned the local office of the shipping agents the next morning. They had no news as yet, but promised to advise her if and when they had word from the vessel.

It was almost a week later before they confirmed what she dreaded, but inwardly knew was inevitable. The *Honshu Maru* had kept radio silence until the captain had judged the ship's position safe, then radioed the owners in Kobe. A copy of the message had been dispatched to Sydney. The large consignment of cargo bound for Australian wharves would not be delivered there; the freighter was already within a few days sail of the southernmost Japanese island of Kyushu, and on its way home.

When Henri Delon heard the news in Saigon, he slammed down the phone in his office. He could hardly believe they had failed by such a cruel margin. His staff could hear the sound as he raged and swore loudly and furiously.

'Fuck,' he shouted. 'Not even a week. Just a few fucking days.' His senior clerk hurried in to ask if there was something he could do, and Henri yelled at him to fuck off. Later he came out and apologised, and gave the clerk a cable to send to the firm of solicitors, Cusack and Noble, in Sydney.

It read: REGRET CONTRACT RETURNED. WILL TRY TO ADVISE IF ANY FURTHER DETAILS AVAILABLE BUT SITUATION MAY MAKE IT DIFFICULT. DELON.

Then he went to one of the bars in Canal Street and spent the afternoon getting thoroughly drunk.

The *Honshu Maru* was assigned a docking berth in Kobe so that the holds crammed with the undelivered cargo could finally be unloaded back at their home port. Sam was met by Koki Ogawa, his father's contact in the NYK shipping office.

'Deeply regrettable,' Ogawa said, but whether he meant the war, the loss to his firm, or even Sam's failure to reach Australia was uncertain. He told Sam he had sent word to his father. Also that there would be a limousine and chauffeur available to transport him home to Yokohama, supplied with the compliments of the company. He reiterated his regrets for the circumstances, bowed and departed. Sam bowed his thanks with all the equanimity he could muster.

He had been extremely careful, ever since the fateful day when the ship had turned about, not to show his frustration or feeling of despair too openly. When the captain had expressed his apologies at dinner, Sam had merely smiled and shrugged. He said his studies would have to wait until the war was over. In the meantime, he would rejoin his family. Secretly he wondered if the freighter might be captured by one of the many British warships that were based in Singapore. It was his only hope – a faint one – which evaporated as they sailed northward without sighting another vessel. In a week they had passed Okinawa, and were back in Japanese waters.

He made his farewells to the captain and crew, and went ashore. There was a car and chauffeur waiting for him as Ogawa had promised, but when Sam stepped off the ship two men moved to confront him. They identified themselves.

'Kempetai,' one said. They showed him a warrant, and told him to accompany them.

The interrogating officer was polite. Disturbingly so. He occupied a large office in a building that overlooked the port, wore a well-cut business suit, and introduced himself as Major Ito. In fluent English, he told Sam to sit down.

'May I know why I'm here?' Sam asked in Japanese.

The Major replied – once again in English – that he had certain questions to ask him. Sam remained outwardly calm, trying to act unconcerned. He responded – in Japanese – that he would do his best to answer whatever it was they wished to know. It became aberrant; the Kempetai Major speaking perfect English, with Sam answering in his flawless Japanese.

'You were intending to live in Australia?'

'For a few years.'

'Why?'

'To study there.'

'For what purpose?'

'To obtain a degree in economics.'

The Major referred to some papers in front of him.

'According to your school headmaster, you always hoped to attend Harvard University in America?'

'Originally, yes.'

'Why did you choose Australia instead?'

'I sensed there was trouble developing between Japan and America. That Harvard might not be my best option.'

'And now we're at war with Australia. That was hardly a good option.'

'I didn't know that, Major, when I changed my mind. We weren't at war then. I didn't know anything about it until we were almost . . . almost there.'

'Almost safe? Is that what you were going to say?'

'Why would I say that? I was going there to study, not for any other reason. My home, friends and family are all here.'

'Then why not choose to study in this country?'

'Because of the language difficulty.'

'You speak it exceptionally well.'

'But I can't write in Japanese, or read it. So it would've been impossible for me to attend university.'

'Hmm,' the Major said. He made a note about this, then after a pause asked, 'What do you propose to do now?'

'Return home. My mother and sister will be anxious.'

'No doubt. And then?'

'Try to find a job in Japan.'

'You think that possible, in wartime?'

'I hope so. I'm a French citizen, and this country is not at war with France. I hope we'll be treated as neutral, and allowed to work and live our normal lives.'

'Do you have relatives in Australia?'

'Not exactly a relative. A godmother.'

'Ah yes.' The Major referred again to papers in front of him. 'A Miss Florence Carter.'

'Yes, before her marriage. She is now Mrs Eisler.'

'Eisler.' The Major wrote it down, and Sam felt sorry he had mentioned it. 'That would be the man referred to as Carl?'

'Referred to in what?'

'Just answer the question.'

'Yes, his name is Carl.'

'And what is he, this Carl Eisler?'

'A lawyer. A refugee from Germany, who was interned. But I've never met him. How can I answer questions about a man I don't know?'

The Major stared at him thoughtfully. Then, as if having had enough of this charade, he resumed the interrogation in Japanese.

'We have a letter sent to you, signed by someone named Florrie. Obviously the godmother you mentioned.

She suggests that you should leave Japan as soon as possible, because it might be dangerous to remain here.'

Sam frowned as if deeply puzzled. He shook his head in apparent confusion, and this time replied in English.

'I never received such a letter.'

'I assure you it exists.'

'Where?'

'Here, on my desk.' The Major began to lose some of his careful composure.

'But why didn't I get it?' Sam asked, attempting a blend of perplexed ingenuousness and indignation. He was aware of the Major's scrutiny, knew this was becoming dangerous, but he was committed to the strategy. 'Did it go astray? Where was it?'

'It was of interest to another branch of security.'

'You mean it was opened?' Now he could exhibit shock and disbelief. 'I didn't know things like that went on in this country.'

'I'm quite sure you know they go on in every country, when it's required in the national interest.' He pushed the letter across the desk to Sam. 'Here.'

'Thank you, Major.'

'Read it.'

'You mean now, sir?'

'Now.'

Sam looked at the familiar writing. He carefully read the letter, while the Major watched him intently. He began to realise why Florrie had been alarmed enough to contact his father, once she suspected the letter had not reached him. But he tried to conceal this.

'I think she's just worried about me. We're good friends. I only met her once, when I was a child, but we write regularly to each other.'

'You don't seem unduly surprised by her remarks?'

'I would've been, Major – if you hadn't told me the contents. I'm pleased her husband's been released.' He shrugged. 'Mostly I'm just shocked that any letter of mine was opened by the security police. And then it was kept from me.'

The Major looked at him for what seemed like a long time. The man was relatively young, in his late twenties, Sam thought. He had sharp, perceptive eyes.

'Why do I feel this doesn't really come as news to you?'

'I don't understand why you'd say that, Major.'

'You're good, Delon-san.' Major Ito smiled ironically. 'Most people shit themselves when they come in here. Guilty before I even ask a question. A few try to match wits with me, try to be smart. They invariably fail. But you're polite and plausible. I'm not sure if you're secretly shitting yourself, or trying to be smart. We may find out some day.'

He pressed a buzzer, and the door was opened from the outside by a uniformed guard.

'You can take the letter. We have a copy.'

The car and chauffeur was still waiting for him down at the docks. His luggage was in the back seat, the driver clearly looking anxious. Sam guessed the man had spent the past hour wondering if his passenger would return.

He sat in the front beside the chauffeur. They drove away from the docks and through the main part of town. On the outskirts of Kobe, Sam signalled for the car to stop. He got out just in time. He vomited, again and again, until he was weak with exhaustion and his stomach was empty.

PART 2

CHAPTER 10

The changes in Yokohama were startling. On The Bluff, so long the sole enclave of foreigners, many houses already stood empty. There had been swift action within hours of war being declared as people – sometimes entire families – vanished into internment camps. Stories abounded of their arrests. A Melbourne journalist had wired a last report as the door of his press agency was smashed open. A New Zealand artist, noted for his watercolours of local flowers, was arrested; his work impounded as likely evidence of espionage. The Shroders had planned a farewell party before sailing home to San Francisco. Instead of guests, police arrived; Kitty, Simon and their parents had not been seen since. The Country Club was raided and Tamara Delon's bridge group was decimated.

Australians, Britons, Canadians, Americans, no matter how long they had been resident, were enemies now. There was concern; no-one knew where they were being held, or under what conditions. Tamara was outspokenly irate at the stupidity of detaining women who had few interests in life other than shuffling cards and playing bridge. Angelique was inconsolable. Kitty had long been her best friend, and Simon had become an event in her life. The return of Sam was a consolation, but after hearing of the Kempetai interrogation, they were both afraid for his future.

Sam had to go to the police station to register as a neutral alien. The constable there was arrogant with new authority. 'Follow regulations. Carry your identity card at all times. You cannot leave your district without a travel permit, and you must report each month to have it stamped. If you travel without a pass, the penalty is a heavy fine or seven days gaol. Do you understand?'

Sam understood all right. It was payback time. If some Europeans could evade captivity because their countries were not at war, living conditions would be made as onerous as possible. For too long the *gaijin* had enjoyed advantages here, handsomely housed, well paid – with lavish expense accounts that enabled them to live far beyond most people's standards. The esteemed Japanese courtesy was sometimes a veil that shrouded a deep and silent resentment.

Things would be different now.

They became different with astonishing rapidity, in some very personal ways. Sam saw his former headmaster being arrested. A group of students watched in stunned silence as he was roughly bundled into the back of a police truck. On his rostrum he had always appeared an imposing figure. Now he stared through the mesh, looking far smaller; untidy and frightened. Two other teachers, both British, were tossed in beside him.

The next day, Sam and his closest friend, Claude Briand, went for a run with their rugby team at the

Country Club – a select haven situated above the bay. It boasted a fine sports ground, tennis courts, and a luxurious clubhouse with library, dining room and bar. For most of the expatriate community in Yokohama, the club was the popular meeting place and the centre of their social life.

When Sam and Claude arrived, militia were on guard and a notice announced the premises closed. The Irish secretary had just been escorted from his office by two police officers.

'We came for rugby practice,' Claude said. 'Where is everyone? What the hell is going on?'

The secretary was flushed with fury at his humiliation. 'Can't you see? The club's shut.'

'Until when?'

'God knows. Until the end of this bloody war, I expect.'

'But why?' Sam asked.

'We're a fucking security threat.' He could not conceal his anger. He had been Secretary here for almost a decade. For him, it had been a way of life, and he had served the members with enthusiasm and distinction. Now his office had been locked, his keys taken, and he was being removed from the premises like an intruder.

'Security threat?' If they had not realised the other's distress they might have laughed. 'What threat?'

'We're foreigners,' the secretary replied. 'Dangerous people, Sam. As the club has such a good view of the harbour, the authorities believe we might spy on ship movements. Have you ever heard such fucking codswallop?'

'Never.'

'Nor have I. But we're closed down, locked out. Rugby practice is suspended until further notice.'

Also closed was the local racetrack, turned into a prison camp. The headmaster and his teachers were taken there, together with businessmen, missionaries, and other enemies. On the lush turf where horses had galloped, barrack accommodation was erected. Sentries with rifles and bayonets patrolled the perimeters. Most of these were veteran soldiers, recalled to duty but wishing they were with their victorious army cutting a swathe through South-East Asia. The army's meteoric advance made headlines in every paper. At the cinemas, crowds came in droves, not to see the feature but to applaud the newsreels. There, in the motion picture dark, they watched their troops take territory after territory.

Hong Kong fell on Christmas Day, the Philippines a week later. Ironically, Sam recalled the confidence displayed in Manila, as there were reports that General MacArthur had fled his impregnable fortress – taking his family and his furniture – heading for the comparative safety of Brisbane.

The British battleships, *Prince of Wales* and *Repulse*, both claimed unsinkable, were sunk. The Dutch were driven from their East Indies. Burma was invaded. By January, an army was cycling down the Malay Peninsula to Singapore – to make a mockery of the naval bastion's legendary guns. Realising that these faced out to sea, the Japanese approached from behind, by land across the causeway. The guns – pointing the wrong way – had no enemy at whom to fire. Chinese, British and Australian defenders were overwhelmed and captured.

Incredibly, this had taken only two months to accomplish. By the end of February, Japan was the master of Asia.

* * *

Florence read the latest war news in the evening paper on the way home. Carl glanced at the lurid headlines, then stared out of the tram at the dismal scene. The light was fading, and there were no streetlights or illuminations in the shop windows. The 'brownout', as it was called, was now in force. There were times when Carl felt homesick for Munich, but he tried to be impartial. The pre-war Munich he knew was a buoyant city, home of the *Oktoberfest* and lively beer halls, but it had also spawned the first Brown Shirt bullies with their swastika armbands, and the rise of Adolf Hitler.

For a long time, far too long, Carl had believed there was no real danger, not until his young cousin, Rosa, had been arrested and sent to a concentration camp. Her crime had been denial, refusing an SS officer the use of her body and her bed, but this was not placed on her charge sheet. It would hardly be in the best interests of the *Schutz Staffel* for one of their elite to be accused of wanting to copulate with a Jewish girl. He could be demoted for such corrupt conduct; instead his Yiddish quarry had been arrested on a charge of inciting treason, dispatched in a cattle truck to Ravensbruck, and was dead soon afterwards at the age of nineteen. It was when he heard of Rosa's hideous fate that Carl had realised how fragile his existence was, and he'd fled; pre-war France, then Britain, arriving with just enough money to pay for a passage to Australia.

'Look,' Florrie said, and he turned to her, his thoughts of the tragic past forgotten. Just gazing at her, he felt filled with love, sometimes barely able to contemplate his amazing good fortune in coming so far across the world to find someone like this. Even his time in internment had not spoiled that. He wished he could take her to Munich, but the city he had known as a schoolboy and then as a law student was no longer there.

'What is it, liebchen?' he asked, realising she was upset by something in the newspaper.

She pointed to a small paragraph buried at the bottom of an inside page. 'Indochina.'

'What about it?'

'According to this news, the Vichy government in Saigon has invited Japan to occupy the country. Can you believe it?'

'Unfortunately, yes. France and her colonies are under German rule since their surrender, which means they're allied to Japan. I doubt if Saigon had much choice. I'd say it was a matter of invite them in or be invaded.'

'But we'll lose contact with Henri Delon. He was our only way of keeping in touch with Sam.'

Carl knew Florrie was disturbed, but privately he thought the chance of remaining in touch with Sam had always been unlikely. He tried not to reveal this. 'Let's wait and see. There's always a hope something can get through.'

He knew he did not sound optimistic. He took her hand and held it, trying to console her, hating this damned war for its heartbreak, even though it had brought him love and bliss.

Sam recognised Koki Ogawa at once. His father's friend from the NYK shipping company arrived at their house late one afternoon, and said he had brought a letter from Saigon.

'Then you'll stay for dinner, Ogawa-san,' Tamara Delon said, insisting he join her in a drink before she went to tell the cook.

Over a meal, Koki, as he requested they call him, said it was a dangerous business, carrying letters, but he and Henri Delon had been friends for many years, and this was nothing to do with the war or being disloyal; on the contrary, he was a patriot. This was simply to establish communication between Henri and his family. He said the letter was written in French, which he could not read, but Henri had assured him it was not seditious. However, it would relieve him if Sam read the letter aloud – it was addressed to him – and would convince Koki they were not up to any kind of mischief. He meant no offence, he said hastily, but these were strange times.

'Of course,' Sam said, and proceeded to translate for Ogawa as he read. It was a brief letter containing mostly bleak news. His father was relieved to hear he was safe, but disappointed he had not reached Australia. He had sent a cable to the law firm in Sydney, advising them of the situation.

About money, things were going to be difficult. All his capital had been invested in the business, and as the export trade was now impossible, the Kobe office faced ruin and he had been forced to shut it. He felt sad dismissing loyal staff, but there would no longer be money to pay them. All foreign firms like his faced disaster. He would try to survive in Indochina, but had no hope of helping them with finances. Tamara should budget for a long war. For a start, she should try to be less extravagant!

His mother interrupted angrily. 'How dare he,' she said, 'that man never changes. Always lecturing me about money.'

'I think he is wrong about a long war,' Ogawa observed. 'With Japan's great success, it will soon be over. By the summer, America will sue for peace. Admiral Yamamoto predicts it.'

No-one replied to this.

'May I finish reading?' Sam asked, and continued aloud without waiting for an answer: 'You and Angelique must somehow get jobs. I know it will be difficult, but write to Count Louis de Boulanger at the *Bank de l'Indo Chine* in Tokyo. And Mama could speak to her Swiss friend, Sophie Rambert: that rich husband of hers has fingers in lots of pies and may be able to help Angelique find work. God bless, much love to all of you. Papa.'

'No love to me, thanks all the same,' his ex-wife said, draining her glass and immediately pouring herself another, 'but I *will* speak to Sophie. Even your father has an occasional good idea.'

Later, Sam walked with Koki Ogawa to the train.

'It was kind of you to bring it all this way, Koki.'

'I was told personal delivery was safer than by mail. Delon-san's own words in his note to me.'

'Then it was even kinder.'

They stood on the platform waiting for the express, with the station brightly lit. The government had announced blackouts and air-raid shelters – essential for their enemies – were unnecessary here, for American planes were incapable of flying far enough to reach Japan. It was one more illustration of supreme confidence that gave people a sense of impending victory.

'You really think this war will be over soon?'

'It's inevitable,' Ogawa said, 'If we conquer all of Asia, America must sue for peace.'

'What about Australia?'

'They can hardly stand alone. In a few months, we will occupy the cities, and you can go there to begin your studies. I will write to your father and tell him NYK will be honoured to provide your passage, and since we were unable to deliver you last time, this voyage will be at our expense.'

Sam nodded his appreciation. About to voice his thanks, the words suddenly registered. 'You can write to my father?'

'Of course. We communicate on a number of matters, with regard to business.'

'Could I write to him?' Ogawa looked startled, as Sam continued hurriedly: 'After all, you said yourself it's only communication between the family. I'd like to explain that I'll write to Count de Boulanger, but not to expect too much. Tell him how tough it is nowadays to get a job. There are virtually none for foreigners any more. People don't even bother to be pleasant – they just shake their heads, or kick you out. One told me to try a munitions factory. I doubt if the government would agree. You could tell my father these things, but it's not the same – if you see what I mean.'

'You miss him?'

'I do. All I hear is Mama bitching about him. If I could write, it'd make a difference. We wouldn't feel like strangers.'

Ogawa studied him. 'Let me think about it,' he said, then added thoughtfully, 'we would have to be careful.'

It was a wild idea that kept Sam awake and excited later that night. Before the train arrived, the polite and correct Ogawa had agreed.

'I'm patriotic,' he had again repeated, 'but friendship of so many years must be respected. It would only be family matters, after all. We would be doing no harm, betraying no secrets . . .'

'Of course not,' Sam said.

'You would send any letter to me at the office. I would open it, and reseal it in an NYK official envelope. Such mail never attracts the attention of censors – or anyone else.'

'And you could read the letters, before you forward them on to him.'

'You write in Japanese?'

'I can't,' Sam admitted. 'It would be English or French.'

'I speak a little of each, but can't read either.'

Here we go, Sam had thought. *Shit or bust.*

'Give them to one of your colleagues to read,' he had said casually, and smiled as he recalled Ogawa's reaction.

'I don't think that would be a very good idea. Colleagues are sometimes rivals who cannot always be trusted. I prefer to believe you would write nothing of concern.'

'Just family matters.' Sam had used the NYK man's own phrase as the train came in.

Now he lay awake in the dark, making plans. Tomorrow he would try to seek an appointment with the grandiose-sounding Count Louis de Boulanger, though he did not feel optimistic about the outcome. After that, he would write a letter to his father, one that could stand any scrutiny, no matter what Koki Ogawa had said about not showing it to colleagues. Perhaps it should be in French, rather than English; it might seem more natural. Within the letter, carefully oblique, would be a reference to Florrie, and if his father was smart enough he'd work it out. It was simply a request for help.

From Japan, it was impossible to write to her. Whether it was remotely possible from Saigon he had no idea, but one thing he did know. His father had useful contacts there. He always had useful contacts, wherever he lived. If there was any way to contact her, it was through Saigon. Sam fell asleep thinking it might be perilous and irrational, but for ten years he had written to Florrie, using the letters like an intimate diary to express all his feelings; thoughts, dreams, ambitions, and disappointments, there was nothing he could not share with her. Growing up, everyone had a need to confide secret concerns and emotions, and he had entrusted his to Florrie. Isolated from her, he felt a painful sense of loss.

The bombers left Ambon in the Dutch East Indies at first light. Ahead of them lay a journey of eight hundred miles, and they spread out across the sky with full payloads of high explosive – but they were not the main attacking force. That was already positioned in the Arafura Sea, a huge concentration of naval vessels; four of Japan's largest aircraft carriers protected by heavy cruisers and destroyers. Many of these ships – and the fliers waiting by their planes – had taken part in the attack on Pearl Harbour two and a half months previously. Now they had a new target.

After briefing and weather reports, a total of one hundred and eighty aircraft were launched. The course was compass bearing 148 degrees, their destination a mere hour's flight away, the objective the unsuspecting town and port of Darwin.

Off Melville Island, a fishing boat saw the sky crowded with planes, but had no time to consider what to do before a Japanese fighter swept low and raked the deck with machine-gun fire, followed a moment later by a dive-bomber with a direct hit that turned the vessel into a blazing inferno.

As the second force, the bombers from Ambon, passed over East Timor, a coast watcher saw the armada of aircraft moving inexorably south east, and ran to his jungle hut to transmit an urgent message. He knew it was dangerous to use the radio: there were enemy troops in the vicinity, and it had to be a rapid signal.

Hundreds of aircraft sighted was all he had time to send before a hand grenade was flung into the hut, destroying the radio and killing him instantly. The truncated message was received at the telegraph office in Darwin, where the puzzled operator rang defence headquarters, and talked to the duty officer.

'Whose aircraft? American or enemy?' The duty officer was brusque, for there had been a constant series of false alarms since Christmas.

'The message didn't say, sir.'

'Sighted going where, for Christ's sake?'

'I'm sorry, I've no idea, sir.'

'Are you sure it's from an authenticated source?'

The telegraphist was young and new to the job. He had no concept; he thought he should simply pass on the message.

'Keep in touch, if you get more reports, and let's hope they make sense next time,' the irritated duty officer said, wondering if he should alert Port Moresby. It seemed the most likely target, but on the other hand hundreds of planes sounded extreme, a bit alarmist and melodramatic, and why hadn't the wretched coast watcher – if it was a genuine message and not someone playing silly buggers – why hadn't he informed them where the bloody aircraft were heading?

He decided he should leave the matter to his Colonel.

It was the privilege of rank to make decisions, so he sent a hasty note to his office, not knowing the Colonel had met a soubrette from an army entertainments show the previous night, and was still in bed with her. The message lay in the Colonel's in-tray until a clerk read it and wondered if the air raid warning should be sounded.

Meanwhile, there was another warning, this one from Bathurst Island, and a coded alert from Dili, but it was far too late. The attackers were already over Darwin harbour, and no air-raid siren had been sounded. Filled with Allied warships and a great many merchantmen, the vessels were anchored, unprepared, and had no chance of escape as the scream of dive-bombers signalled the beginning of the mass slaughter. An oil tanker caught fire, a hospital ship with its protective Red Cross was strafed with machine-gun fire by fighters, while the heavy bombers bracketed the wharves and killed waterside workers.

Eight ships were sunk, another twenty damaged; crews in their dozens died of burns or drowned. While the authorities tried to control the situation and apportion blame, the second raid from Ambon concentrated its attack on the town and the airfield. Heavy bombs and cannon shells damaged the main buildings, hit the hospital and police barracks, demolished the main post office and killed everyone inside it. Meanwhile, a bomb short-circuited the air-raid warning system. While people died in the streets and homes were reduced to rubble, the sirens blared the all-clear signal. They had never sounded the alert. By midday the planes were gone, leaving at least three hundred dead, ships sunk or burnt, and twenty aircraft incinerated on the ground.

Within an hour the panic began. People fled. They left

unlocked homes and unfinished meals. By early afternoon, the road south was crammed with terror-stricken refugees. Some had trucks or cars, prepared to drive them until the petrol ran out; others rode bicycles, drove road graders, or had horses and carts piled with their belongings, while the unfortunates with no transport trudged on foot, as they left the ruined town.

Despite the February heat and the wet season, fear drove the refugees inland from the coast. They were mostly townspeople, but there were also soldiers and airmen, sworn to defend the realm; their uniforms discarded and wearing civilian clothes, all of them frightened of another attack – or more likely now the air raid had smashed the fragile defences – the chance of a full-scale invasion. The prospect of a sea full of landing barges with troops swarming ashore, troops with bayonets whose brutality towards non-combatants had become a byword, terrified people and drove them to escape from what they believed would be a bloody massacre.

Among those ordered to remain in the town were naval and army personnel. Military police were instructed to patrol the streets and maintain order. Some were conscripted to this duty against their wishes; resentful and afraid of being left in danger, they invaded abandoned and ruined pubs, and seized the opportunity to steal all the liquor they could carry. Later, when they were drunk enough, they began to systematically loot the town.

There were alarming rumours circulating among ferry passengers as Florence and Carl made the journey home after work that day.

'Nothing in the afternoon papers,' a man said. 'But

then that's censorship, ain't it. If you ask me, the Japs are halfway to Alice Springs by now.'

There were even more rumours by the time they boarded the tram from Manly to Collaroy, some asserted with authority amid an air of growing hysteria. The Japanese success had been so complete, so rapid, what was to stop them from invading the huge undefended stretches of Australian coastline? A man sitting opposite them voiced a loud opinion.

'If the buggers can take Singapore with all its guns, who the hell will stop 'em gettin' here?'

'But in Singapore the guns were not intelligently placed,' Carl said, and Florrie wished he hadn't.

The man stared at him belligerently. 'What sorta flamin' accent's that?' It was pointless not to answer; it would only provoke him. As Carl hesitated, the other said accusingly: 'A bloody German, I reckon. Sounds like it to me. German. Y'er a frigging hun.'

'I came from Germany, yes.'

'Stinking bloody hun. Sunk the *Sydney*, the huns did.'

'I know this. I'm sorry.'

'Sorry! My cousin was on that ship, and all you can say is you're bloody sorry! Who let you into the country, yer flamin' German bastard?'

'Just shut up,' Florence said suddenly, and all at once the other passengers near them, until now trying to avoid this confrontation, started to take an interest.

'Who're you tellin' to shut up, missus?'

'I'm telling you, you rude, ignorant fool. My husband was born in Germany, but he escaped from the Nazis.'

'Bullshit. They all say that.'

'He'd hardly be here if it wasn't true.'

'Bribed someone to get in, I'll bet. Sunk the poor old

Sydney, killed me cousin. And fought against our mob at Tobruk. Bloody dirty rotten spy, if you ask me.'

'Who did ask you?' a woman sitting near spoke up. 'As far as I can see, you're a drunken pest. If you're so worried about the defence of this country, go and join up.'

'Hear, hear,' another voice said amid other rather careful murmurs of agreement.

The tram came to a stop and the man swayed to his feet. He stared at Carl, then spat directly in his face.

'Youse can all go and get fucked,' he said, then lurched off into the gathering dark.

She looked out at the moonlit beach. It was disfigured by barbed wire, and up on the Long Reef headland she could see the silhouette of the gun emplacement. It no longer felt like her beach, where she and Sam had built such lavish sandcastles. The thought of Sam was like an enduring pain, for he had been so close, could only have been days away from joining them. He and Carl would have liked each other. Things would have been so different. This bloody awful war kept them apart, as well as all the other hurt it caused.

Carl was pretending to read the evening paper. She sat on the floor beside his chair, and rested her face against his legs.

'He was just a drunk,' she said.

'Sometimes they're not drunk, liebchen.'

'Who aren't?'

'The people who turn and stare when I speak, or call me names, filthy, abusive names. Because there have been others.'

'All right. Ignorant people. Ratbags, larrikins . . .'

'Some look quite respectable. Until they start calling me Adolf, or something equally wounding.'

'It'll change, Carl. A lot of people are scared, and it makes them stupid or vicious. The war seemed such a long way off, and suddenly it's on our doorstep. We're the next place they'll come; they're in Java and Timor and Papua encircling us, and people are terrified that we can't stop them. I'm a bit terrified myself.'

He stroked her cheek, and leaned down to kiss the top of her head. 'That's the irony. So am I,' he said.

In the morning they heard the early news on the radio, before leaving for the office.

'The first attack on the Australian mainland was carried out yesterday, when Japanese planes bombed Darwin.' The measured tones of the newsreader had an English accent, considered obligatory by most radio stations. 'Initial reports indicate some damage to shipping in the harbour and to the town itself. The Minister for Air announced that fifteen people had been killed and twenty-four wounded. The Prime Minister, Mr Curtin, in a brief statement said there was no cause for alarm, and promised the government would keep people fully informed.'

'Not as bad as the rumours made out.' Florrie expressed her relief as they locked the house and headed for the tram.

'I hope not,' Carl said.

'Don't you believe it?'

'I'd like to. But there is such a thing as censorship.'

'Darling, be an optimist.'

'I'd love to be. But truth is the first casualty of war, isn't that the expression?'

That week newspapers, learning of the extensive damage, seeing photographic evidence of the panic and looting in Darwin, began to prepare new front pages. But before they could be printed, an official government directive imposed a notice that this news was counter to the national interest, and therefore could not be published. Almost three hundred people had died, and hundreds more were injured; there had been a mass exodus in which both army and air force personnel had deserted, but it was considered best not to tell the public that the first attack on Australian soil had ended in ignominy and chaos.

CHAPTER 11

Tamara Delon, despite her outburst, had taken careful note of her ex-husband's words of caution. She realised that if the war lasted long they could be in a perilous position. They were on tolerance as foreigners; accepted as neutrals and free from internment, but there would be no financial help. The French Embassy had already stated they would not provide monetary assistance. She had a small amount of savings, but it might soon be necessary to dispense with cook-san, and also abandon the holiday house at Karuizawa. With some of these problems in mind, she consulted a Russian *émigré* friend, a jeweller. Quietly and selectively, she began to sell her few remaining diamonds.

In the following month, food rationing was introduced. Dismayed foreigners learned there would be no coupons for them; they were for issue only to Japanese nationals. Tamara Delon alone in the household was unconcerned. She disliked most Japanese food, and rarely allowed it to be served. She was also vigilant of all home-grown vegetables.

'Filthy stuff,' she said. With her strong Slavic accent she found the word excrement difficult, so she asked how anyone could possibly eat food grown in human shit. 'They call it fertiliser, but it's just shit. How can you enjoy eating food that's smothered in crap from the honey carts?'

Since meat was unobtainable, the family lived on a diet of fish from black marketeers, plus items like bread and jam that were not in demand. They illegally bought vegetables smuggled from farms outside the city, which were taken home and thoroughly scrubbed to remove all trace of offending substance to Tamara's complete satisfaction.

They had to be careful about such purchases. Each household was now required to belong to an association called the *tonarigumi* under police control, where neighbours kept watch on each other and reported infringements. Black market trading was a major crime, but even a lack of patriotic fervour was a reportable offence. It developed into something very insidious: a network of informers spread from each precinct and village across the country; silent accusations, complaints and anonymous allegations made people afraid to talk aloud or speak their minds.

Sam had no reply to his request for an interview at the *Bank de l'Indo Chine* – the French Bank, as it was called. His friend, Claude, was also vainly chasing a job, and time hung heavily for them both. Avid film fans since their teens, they went to a movie but did not enjoy the experience. American and British pictures were now banned. The days when they could see Gary Cooper in *Beau Geste*, or films like *Stagecoach* were over. Instead there was a crude local feature, and endless newsreels showing Japanese victories; the packed cinema rising to the sight, cheering and shouting *Banzai*!

Among these triumphs was the bombing of Darwin; ships burning, planes blown up on the ground, and Sam felt a deep concern that an invasion was almost certain to engulf Australia. He wished for news from Ogawa, in order to write to his father and then to Florrie, but had heard nothing.

When he arrived home, there was a short note from the Count Louis de Boulanger. Sam was to present himself in two days time, at eleven in the morning, and kindly not be late.

The French Bank was in the central business district, only two streets from the Ginza. Sam reached Tokyo Station so early that he walked the rest of the way, in an attempt to pass the time. He found the bank without difficulty, a modest wood and stucco building that faced the canal. It consisted of two main floors, and what appeared to be a tiny top story. Nestled against one side of the massive Bank of Japan building, it looked like a delicate miniature in comparison.

It was a sunny day, and the vibrancy in this part of the city lifted his spirits. He had slept badly, and on the train journey had felt a growing anxiety, realising how much depended upon securing this job, for there might not be another. A year ago, firms like this eagerly sought foreign staff, and anyone who spoke English and French, as well as Japanese, was assured of employment. Now obtaining a job was like winning a lottery. The world had changed. He was here as a supplicant, conscious of how badly the family needed a wage earner.

On the ground floor was an entrance hall that led into the main banking chamber. Behind the tellers' counter was a series of desks and cubicle offices. He was directed to one of them.

'You do realise you're extremely early?'

The Count de Boulanger's private secretary was a petite Frenchwoman with features that gave her a bird-like appearance. Neatly dressed, her nails and hair immaculate, she was like an elegant sparrow. She wore gold-rimmed pince-nez, and the glasses seemed to reflect the light from the window, and made it difficult to read her expression. But after her mild rebuke at his premature arrival she appeared more friendly, inviting him to sit down.

'You might even have done me a favour, Mr Delon.'

A favour? He was about to ask how, but had no chance.

'Please wait,' she said, and entered the adjoining office. Sam sat mystified, unable to hear what transpired. He could see her name displayed on her desk: *Mlle. C. Patou*. He wondered what the C stood for, and later found it was Cecile, but she was never called anything except Mademoiselle Patou.

'You may go in.' She startled him because he had been rehearsing what to say, and had not heard her return. 'Monsieur Le Comte will see you now, and I can rearrange his later appointments. It's a busy day, so your early arrival is welcome. And young man . . .'

'Yes, Mam'zelle?'

'Try not to fidget, and don't look so nervous.'

'No, Mam'zelle.'

'And if you should come to work here, I prefer the more correct term of Mademoiselle.'

'Of course. My apologies, Mademoiselle.'

'You'll have to apologise to the Count if you keep him waiting. Not to mention upsetting my arrangements.'

She sat and resumed work, as if his future was no longer her concern. Sam knocked and heard a distant murmur invite him to enter. He entered the Count's office, which presented a startling contrast to the modest banking chamber, and Mademoiselle's office. This was a luxurious room, beneath a huge crystal chandelier, richly carpeted and decorated with impeccable taste. At the far end was a marble fireplace with an open grate; near it stood carved bookcases and an ornate antique desk.

The Count Louis de Boulanger was an imposing man, very much at home in this lavish setting. Looking rather like photographs of General de Gaulle, he was not as tall, but more handsome, and he had a considerably smaller nose. He wore an immaculate suit, and imparted an aura of privilege and old money. He rose and shook hands, inviting Sam to be seated, switching from a greeting in French to fluent English, hoping the train journey had not been tedious, the weather outside not too humid, and his family in good health. During these minor courtesies a door opened, and a servant appeared bringing a tray with coffee.

While they drank this, the Count asked if there was news of Sam's father, and expressed the hope his business would prosper in Saigon. He then took a document from his desk, and a puzzled Sam saw it was his scholarship exam result.

'This is very impressive. I gather, if it had not been for the war, you were to take a degree at Harvard.'

'Yes, sir. But I didn't send that . . .'

'No. Apparently your mother felt I should see it.'

Sam felt acutely embarrassed. The Count smiled and handed the certificate back to him.

'Mothers do these things to assist us, and they mean well. I was most impressed.'

'Thank you, sir.'

'But exam results, while important in our lives, have no real connection with the world of banking. Of which, you know absolutely nothing. Am I right?'

'Well, sir . . . I'm more than willing to learn.'

'Of course you are, which is why you're here. We need French nationals to handle confidential matters. We train them – so you'd be back at school in a manner of speaking – this time learning the business of the bank. If you make good progress for six months, we'll sit down again, and discuss the matter of a salary.'

'In six months?' Sam began to feel a growing dismay.

'Six months precisely. I'll make a note in my diary.'

'No salary . . . until then?'

'We don't pay students. Tuition in banking is a privilege. You're here to be trained for the future.'

'The future . . .'

'The long view, young man. Anyone who begins work accepting a small wage, invariably ends life still on a small wage. Their attitude denotes the philosophy of a mere employee – with limited ambition. No career vision.'

'Sir – can I just get this clear?'

'By all means. I thought I'd made it clear.' The Count was relaxed, graciousness personified.

'Are you offering me a job – without remuneration?' He wondered if remuneration was overdoing it; he knew he must clarify this, but was trying to be diplomatic. Instead he felt uneasy, flushed and tongue-tied.

'My dear fellow,' Count de Boulanger said cheerfully, 'the first matter we must establish is that you and I are not speaking of anything as crass as a *job*. What we're proposing is to offer you a *position*. By age-old tradition, the custom is that you learn first, then we assess your aptitude. As far as remuneration – as you term it – goes, if you show ability, you'll be well and truly rewarded.'

'In six months time,' Sam mumbled.

'Precisely,' smiled the Count.

'He told me it's the system used in France, and a great many other countries. Apparently it's traditional.'

'Traditional Gallic graft,' his mother said. 'What tripe! He's taken advantage of you, and expects you to be grateful.'

'I must admit I was a bit surprised.'

'You're too soft, Sam. You should've been shocked. I most certainly am. I'm outraged by his impudence!'

'He runs the bank. Those are his rules.'

'You can't possibly accept.'

'I have to. There's no work anywhere else.'

'This isn't work – this is helping his wretched bank make a profit. Let's wait and talk about it.'

'No, Mother.' Sam knew it was time to be firm. He'd made up his mind. 'It's their custom. The only way to a future is to accept – work to the best of my ability, and hope he keeps his word.'

'Trust the French to think of such effrontery. How do I tell my friends you have a job that pays nothing?'

'It's not quite nothing. I get my train fares . . .'

'Brilliant,' she stated.

'And there's a staff dining room that serves a low-priced lunch. I get mine free until I'm on a salary.'

'How very kind,' his mother said acidly. 'How typically condescending! To think I wasted a postage stamp, sending him your scholarship results.'

* * *

The following Monday he began work. It was an uncomfortable hour's journey in the packed commuter train, his first experience of the frantic rush hour. After that, the pleasure of walking through the Tokyo streets, past bars and bookshops, and a variety of exotic shops and eating houses. A brisk ten minutes brought him to the canal and the building. *Bank de l'Indo Chine*: the name shone on a gleaming brass plate above the entrance. His place of employment.

It may be employment without pay, he thought, *but at least I have a job*. It was a matter of some pride in this difficult time. Few of his school friends had found work. Most accepted the view that there would be no trade, and no jobs until the war was over – whenever that might be.

The doors of the bank were already open, and in the entrance hall a number of men and women were busily shaking hands. It seemed a formal and lengthy affair, as every person who arrived met and welcomed each other.

'*Bonjour, Monsieur.*'
'*Bonjour!*'
'*Bonjour, Madame.*'
'*Comment ça va?*'
'*Très bien. Merci.*'

Most of the greetings were in French, some in English. As they included inquiries about each other's wellbeing, questions on the health of their families, as well as comments on the state of the weather, it was a protracted morning ritual.

While the French went through this daily observance, the Japanese staff – men too old for military service and young female secretaries – performed their own ceremony and bowed to each other. After that, they all bowed to the French. The French bowed in reply. Sam was to learn this strange procedure occurred every morning, and not until it was over did the business of the day begin.

Mademoiselle Patou met Sam, and complimented him on being granted the position. She called to one of the young Japanese typists. 'Kimiko, this gentleman is Monsieur Delon, our new trainee clerk. Introduce him to the staff, show him the premises, then see he is on time for a meeting with Monsieur Le Comte at nine forty-five.'

'Yes, Mademoiselle,' Kimiko said. She bowed and spoke to Sam in a strange French accent, that had clearly been acquired at a local language school. 'May I welcome you, Monsieur, and say we are glad to have you join the French Bank.'

Sam wondered if it was always so polite and formal. The muted voices, the sober dark suits of the men; it was more like a funeral parlour than a bank. Six months trial might be as much as he could stand. Which could suit the system – six months work without a salary – but would certainly infuriate his mother.

The Count's secretary left them, high heels clicking on the marble floor, looking even more ornithoid as she hurried away. Kimiko was a cheerful girl in her twenties. When they were alone she spoke in Japanese and asked his first name.

'Sam,' he said.

'Sam is easy to say.' She had an engaging smile. 'But they'll insist you're called M'sieu Delon.'

'No thanks.'

'It is the custom. In here everyone is most conventional.'

'I've noticed. I'm too young to be conventional, and M'sieu Delon is my dad. *Wa kari masuka?*'

'*Hai*! Okay,' Kimiko said with a broad smile.

She took him to meet the assistant manager, where she reverted to her own brand of French.

'M'sieu Ribot, this is Sam. Sam Delon.'

'Ah yes,' Ribot said vaguely, perhaps surprised to hear a Christian name, or trying to remember if this person was important. Ribot was a tall, thin man with a receding hairline, who looked more like a university don than a banker. 'Yes, indeed.' He shook hands. 'I hope to see you later,' he muttered, but appeared to be saying this to Kimiko, before he entered his office and shut the door.

She introduced him to the rest of the senior French staff: the chief accountant, M'sieu Laroche, his assistant M'sieu Sardaigne, then took him on a tour of the building. They went upstairs to the top floor; to his surprise, it was a tiny penthouse which seemed unlike part of a bank at all. He asked her if anyone lived there.

'It's unused now,' Kimiko said, 'but it was once the Count's love nest. His short-time house – for his affairs. Before he met his Vietnamese mistress.'

'He has a Vietnamese mistress?'

'He lives with her. She's exotic and very glamorous.'

'Is there a Countess?'

'They're separated. She lives in Paris. I hear she says Paris is the only civilised city, even with the German occupation.'

My father wouldn't agree, Sam thought. *And if I were in Paris, half Jewish, I'd be a candidate for a concentration camp.*

They went down to the first floor, where she showed him the conference room, and an annexe for reading. Here were magazines and newspapers from France, out of date because of the lack of shipping. He was surprised to see a June 1940 edition of *Le Monde*, with headlines announcing the French surrender, and a huge photo of Hitler in front of the Arc de Triomphe, arm extended in a fascist salute while his army marched down the

Champs Elysées. He wondered why these sombre mementos of defeat had been preserved here? His father had burnt such newspapers long ago.

The rest of the first floor was taken up by an executive dining room.

'This is where you'll have lunch,' she said. 'The French staff eat in here.'

'Where do you eat?'

'The Japanese bring lunch boxes. We sit in the back garden if the weather is fine.'

'What if it's raining?'

She shrugged. 'The cloakroom.'

Kimiko wished him luck and delivered him back to Mademoiselle Patou. Promptly at nine forty-five he was sitting opposite the Count in the same luxurious office.

'Can you use a typewriter?'

'Yes, Monsieur Le Comte.'

'Two fingers?'

'Ten,' Sam said. 'Touch-typing. I had lessons.'

'Splendid. At college?'

'No, a tutorial, to help me prepare for university.'

The Count nodded. 'This war's changed all our lives.'

Sam knew it had changed his. Being a junior clerk was a far cry from his ambition to take a degree. He wondered how it had affected the Count's life, but the banker did not enlighten him.

'We have to hope the end will bring the correct result.'

'Yes, sir.' Sam was noncommittal, but could not help speculating on what the other's idea of a *correct result* might be.

'Your typing will be useful. A bonus.' He saw a lack of enthusiasm and smiled. 'I'm not consigning you to the typing pool. But on occasions there are documents in French too confidential for local staff to handle. I've even had to use a typist from the embassy but in future you can deal with it. I hear you speak fluent Japanese?'

'Yes, Monsieur.'

'Good. None of my senior staff can manage more than a few words. Kimiko handles day-to-day matters, but there are times when I'd prefer a French national. Eventually you may be privy to some confidential matters. I hope I can trust you to be discreet.'

'Of course, sir.' He wondered what secrets he might be called upon to interpret.

'You're going to be an asset to us. I gather you expressed a wish we dispense with protocol, and call you Sam.'

'If that's acceptable, Monsieur Le Comte.'

'It's not been our normal practice here,' he smiled, 'but times change, and I daresay we have to change with them.'

In the late afternoon, the Count de Boulanger was driven home by his chauffeur to his house in Tokyo's fashionable Azabu district, near the Meiji Shrine. When the chauffeur took the Daimler to the garage, the Count enjoyed a moment admiring his garden. It was vivid with peonies, camellias and chrysanthemums. A graceful willow and screens of bamboo sheltered the pool where golden carp swam. In a ceramic pot, set in this landscape, was the garden's jewel, a dwarfed cedar tree. The tree was reputed to be a hundred years old, and was thirty centimetres high. De Boulanger considered it utter perfection.

As he studied the aged bonsai, marvelling at the skill of craftsmen who had maintained its perfect proportions – eloquent almond eyes watched him from within the house. He felt her presence, and went eagerly inside. They bathed together, and afterwards he made love to the slim and elegant Vietnamese woman who shared his life.

The house was quiet, for his servants were trained in the daily routine, and the ritual hour that His Excellency always spent in private with Madame after his day's toil, was well established. They remained in their quarters and only appeared when Moustique-san rang for drinks to be served. But today the Count and his paramour spent more time than usual alone. They had matters apart from physical desire that occupied them. She knew of the decision he had made that day.

'Do you think you can trust him?' she asked.

She lay naked on their large bed, her light brown limbs graphic against the rumpled white sheet. It was a sight he cherished.

'I can train him,' he replied. 'As for trust, we can only hope I made the right choice. Time will tell if he's to be trusted.'

Sam endured the return rush hour. Straphanging, wedged more tightly at each stop as new passengers were forced into carriages by the special pushers, he disembarked with relief when the train at last reached Yokohama. His mother and sister were eager for news.

'An asset he called you? Well, that's a good start,' his mother said. 'Mind you, you are an asset – since it's not costing him a yen – or a centime if they use French currency.'

Despite this complaint, she seemed in a better frame of mind, keen to know more. Was the Count friendly? What about the other staff? Who was this Kimiko he had casually mentioned?

Sam explained that Kimiko was the one cheerful face, and he liked her. The rest of the staff, especially the senior French, were all rather conservative. This comment made her instantly want to know more about Kimiko; what did she look like, where did she live, what kind of family did she come from?

'Give him a chance, Ma,' Angelique said, 'he's only been there one day.' She turned to Sam and asked, 'What *is* she like?'

'Fat,' he said, libelling Kimiko, but achieving its purpose and effectively ending the cross-examination.

A few days later their mother told them she had sold most of her jewellery. It had not brought as much as she hoped, but after all, as her Russian *émigré* friend had explained, this was not a seller's market. Not a good time, but he had done his best.

'You mean that crook, Gregori?' Angelique asked.

'He's not a crook. He's a respectable White Russian, and a reputable dealer in gems.'

Sam sighed at his sister. They knew, having heard from childhood, that all White Russians were respectable. In fact they both agreed that Gregori, the reputable, was a robbing bastard.

'He had a lot of expenses in selling them,' she insisted. 'He had to go to Shanghai to get the best prices.'

'And you had to pay his fare?'

'He went second class.'

While they laughed, she declared herself satisfied with the result. The money would last for six months, until Sam was finally granted an income at the bank. Provided, she said, that the perfidious French kept their word.

CHAPTER 12

Charles Cusack seemed to have shrunk a great deal in the weeks since his last severe attack, becoming so worn and aged that it was difficult for Florence to conceal her disquiet. She kissed his cheek; it felt cold, creased and waxen like old parchment; she smiled into his eyes, once a lively blue, always amused and inquiring, that now seemed faded and unfocussed.

'You're looking so much better,' she lied, and gave him the bunch of flowers she had brought. A nurse came to take them, exclaiming how beautiful they looked, and went to get a vase.

'You're very kind, but you shouldn't waste your money, Miss Carter.' The voice, so firm and emphatic in court, seemed faint and strained; even the few spoken words had clearly tired him. She sat and held his hand. She was very fond of him; he had been her first and only boss since she was eighteen, and had always treated her with the greatest courtesy.

'Let me do the talking,' she said, 'We want you to rest,

so you can get well enough to come back to the office soon.' When he smiled and shook his head, she put her forefinger to his lips to prevent his reply. She had a feeling she knew what that would be, and did not wish to hear it. 'Carl sends his best wishes. He wanted to be here with me, but there's a complicated land settlement at Blackheath to be sorted out for signing tomorrow, so he's spending the night up there in the mountains.'

What she did not say was that Mr Noble had made a mess of the conveyancing closure, and Carl had been asked to step in by both parties. Nor did she say several of the staff had left, finding the atmosphere at Cusack and Noble, now that Mr Cusack was so ill, no longer to their liking. But his eyes were more alert now, watching her intently, so perhaps he had heard some of these things.

It was far better to talk of other matters. He had been in here so long that he might not have heard some of the latest events; the comic and tragic moments of the past few months.

'When you're better, you'll be able to sit by the window, look down at the traffic and see how peculiar the cars have become. Because of the tiny petrol ration, people have fitted gas producers on the backs of their trucks and cars. They burn charcoal. It's cheap fuel, but blows dark smoke and makes an awful mess. There's a story going around that a girl hitchhiker left Sydney as a platinum blonde and arrived in Brisbane as a brunette.' She watched him try to laugh, but he could only manage a nod and a smile.

'I know you've heard there've been more air raids on Darwin, as well as Broome and Port Hedland. But, thank God, no sign of an invasion yet. We all have ration books now, and identity cards. It means the manpower office can draft people into essential industries for the war effort. So far we haven't lost any staff under the regulations, but it could happen. Some of the typists think they'll end up in the land army, or a munitions plant.

'The clothes rationing has gone a bit crazy. The new 'victory suits' for men look awful. And waistcoats are banned. You should see the letters of complaint to the newspapers – from men, of course – declaring it's the end of civilisation! Fancy life without a waistcoat! We women are not allowed new evening frocks, and we've been told to paint our legs, instead of using stockings. And there's a serious shortage of elastic for our undergarments, so some of my friends are keeping theirs up with string.'

He chuckled this time, and squeezed her hand.

'What else? Well, we've got sandbags around the office building; you'd hardly recognise it. Most homes have slit trenches or shelters in the backyards. Schoolkids have air-raid drill. All town and street signs have been taken down: it's to confuse the Japanese invaders, but the only ones confused are the locals. They've even removed the clock tower of the GPO. I suppose that's so the Japs won't know where to post their letters home.'

The nurse came back with the flowers in a large vase. She was a nice-looking girl in a neatly laundered uniform. 'Lovely flowers,' she said. While she straightened the bedclothes, carefully raised Charles Cusack and plumped the pillows, Florrie moved to the window and looked out. His private room in St Vincent's Hospital had a clear view across the roofs of Paddington towards the harbour. Bright stars were overhead, a radiant canopy glistening around the Southern Cross. She remembered Carl saying there were no stars as large and beautiful as those above Australia, and wished he was there with her. Suddenly there were the probing beams of searchlights, sweeping across the dark water.

'Something's happening,' she said, puzzled at this burst of activity.

A moment later they heard the alarming crash of heavy gunfire, the sound of shells exploding, accompanied by the staccato of machine guns. The nurse ran to join her at the window. They could see tracer bullets like a stream of fire, patrol vessels lit like vigilant shadows on the moonlit sea, and the muffled detonations of depth charges.

The nurse started to cry and crossed herself. 'Mary, Mother of God, it's the invasion. They're here.' She ran to inform Matron, although what that would achieve mystified Florence.

There was a massive detonation, that illuminated the shore of the harbour. She saw the fragments of a vessel explode, and perhaps it was her imagination but she thought she heard the screams of terror. She was unaware that behind her Charles Cusack sat up abruptly in his bed, tried to ask what was happening, and died almost in synchronism with nineteen young naval cadets aboard the converted ferry *Kuttabul*, being used as a barracks. They had been killed by a torpedo from a Japanese midget submarine, unsuccessfully aimed at the United States warship, *Chicago*.

It took two days before the news was assessed and released to the newspapers and radio, but by then everyone knew. Three midget submarines, from an underwater mother vessel somewhere off the coast, had slipped through the protective harbour boom with the intention of sinking one of the American ships refuelling at Garden Island. The midgets had carried two men cramped into a tiny space; their only weapons were twin torpedoes. Two of the craft had been destroyed, the third blown up by its own crew to prevent capture.

But the first reports were far from accurate, as events would prove. They failed to say there was a convoy of five mother submarines off the coast, close to Sydney. Or that one had launched a light reconnaissance aircraft the previous day, which flew totally undetected in broad daylight over the harbour, able to plot the position of the submarine boom and reveal details of the battleships and cruisers at anchor.

Some of these disturbing rumours were already beginning to circulate later that week, at the funeral of Charles Cusack. He had been a popular member of the legal profession for many years, and a large crowd packed the church. Florence was gratified to see how many lawyers and his friends used their precious petrol ration, or with smoke-belching gas stacks followed the cortege to the cliff-top cemetery. It was a sunny winter's day, the graveyard a peaceful place, the sea below placid but deceptive – for it was not yet safe.

Three days after he was laid to rest, one of the main submarines surfaced off Bondi and shelled the rich Eastern Suburbs district between Rose Bay and Vaucluse. The bombardment brought terror to the residents, shattered several houses and destroyed a block of flats. Many affluent families packed up and fled to the relative safety of the Blue Mountains. Expensive waterfront homes were suddenly for sale at bargain prices.

Carl sat at breakfast, grinning over an advertisement in the *Herald*. 'Listen to this. Point Piper. Three bedroom modern house close to the water with superb harbour views. Only 800 pounds.'

Florrie laughed. 'No thanks,' she said. 'Tell Mr Noble about it. I heard him say he's looking to snap up a bargain, if the rich are scared enough to sell.'

'You know what? That sounds exactly like him.'

'Doesn't it just! How could those two have been partners for thirty years?' She sighed. 'I do miss Mr Cusack. His lovely old-world courtesy. No-one is ever going to call me Miss Carter again.'

'I'll call you Miss Carter if you're nice to me.'

She blew him a kiss, and they cleared the breakfast dishes and went to catch their tram.

Later that month, three merchant ships were torpedoed off the east coast, and the city of Newcastle was shelled. The war was all at once a great deal closer. On the headlands and hillsides additional anti-aircraft guns and searchlights were installed. Submarine booms were laid across entrances to all harbours. The barbed wire strung along the beaches was reinforced with tank traps and concrete pill boxes. Squads were trained to destroy industrial plants in the event of an invasion.

In the strictest secrecy, the government prepared a plan it called the 'Brisbane Line', in which it would abandon the northern half of Australia and fight to save the southern cities, when it became necessary.

In the *Nippon Times* there was little else but war news, much of it now concerned with the southern continent that would soon become Japan's greatest conquest. The country, according to what Sam read, was on the brink of surrender. Cities had been bombed, unions were on strike, and even General MacArthur, the American commander, had declared the Australians were ready to accept defeat. And now a submarine attack on Sydney Harbour!

Sam tried to imagine where the attack might have taken place. His memory did not encompass naval dockyards or warships, which the *Times* said had been the targets. The newspaper reported many sailors killed, cruisers sunk, and the bottom of the famous harbour littered with drowned vessels. In a matter of weeks supply lines would enable the first troops to land there. Meanwhile, a flood of inhabitants had fled in panic to the mountains, sixty miles inland.

It sounds so logical, Sam thought. *I remember the mountains. It can't all be propaganda.* He felt desperately afraid for Florrie and her German–Jewish husband, and what might happen to them. He put the paper aside; the news was too disturbing and the meeting he had been ordered to attend lay ominously ahead of him.

Late the previous afternoon he had been called into Mademoiselle Patou's office. She said Monsieur Le Comte had been away on business, but would be back tomorrow and wished Sam to attend the bank one hour before the usual time. He was to come to the side door at eight o'clock, and would be admitted.

'A special meeting?' Sam asked her.

'You'll be told in due course, Sam,' she said.

He had no idea what it entailed; not even Kimiko knew, which meant it was a very private meeting, for Kimiko knew most things. She was his source of information. It was Kimiko who had first told him the huge Korean caretaker at the bank was called Frankenstein. Sam thought it cruel, but had to agree he shambled like the monster, and even bore a slight physical resemblance.

'He lives in the basement with his family. His wife's Mrs Frankenstein, and the boys are known as F Major and F Minor.'

Sam had stifled a laugh, for a sound as alien as laughter

in the bank would bring frowns from the senior French staff.

Now he was waiting impatiently for the caretaker. He had knocked on the side door, but no-one seemed to hear. He knocked again. It was almost eight o'clock, and he had slept badly, trying to imagine the reason for this meeting. According to Kimiko, the Count hadn't been away on business at all. He had been skiing at Nagano with Moustique, his mistress. How she knew was a mystery, but if it was true why the subterfuge? Perhaps Sam had not lived up to expectations and was to be fired. He had spent ages lying awake composing a resignation speech, denouncing the French Bank, accusing it of venal, fraudulent behaviour – until he'd run out of invective and, in exhaustion, had fallen asleep.

Breakfast had been tense and moody. Cook-san and his mother were not on speaking terms. There was a milk shortage, and a meat shortage, and the cook protested that as food was rationed she could not be blamed if they didn't like her meals. She did her best, but foreigners got no rations, and she had to buy lousy food on the black market. While this was going on, Angelique had asked if he was in love or had a problem, because he looked like death warmed up. He had abandoned breakfast, told her she talked utter bullshit, declared the place was a madhouse, and ran for the station. Then, on the train, the worrying story of the attack on Sydney in the paper had left him dispirited. He hammered on the side door of the bank again, and it opened so abruptly that he almost fell inside.

'I heard, first time,' Frankenstein glowered at him and mumbled an inaudible complaint. The massive caretaker spent a lot of his time muttering uncomplimentary remarks, but few people in the bank ever knew what he said, or were bold enough to ask.

'I have an appointment,' Sam told him.

Frankenstein gave no response, apart from a jerk of his thumb in the direction of the main offices, and Sam heard the heavy security door clang shut behind him. The Count de Boulanger was at his desk. As always he was impeccably dressed, and his face glowed with a deep tan which could only have come from the ski slopes.

'Sit down, Sam. Here's the *Nippon Times*, to occupy you while I finish with these documents.'

He continued working. It was pointless for Sam to say he had read enough of the paper to ruin his day. He looked at other pages. In the Atlantic, German U-boats were sinking British ships, and England must soon ask for surrender terms from Hitler.

It could not all be lies, he thought. *What happens when Hitler and Tojo and fat old Mussolini win the war? What kind of a world will it be ... or will anyone with a Jewish mother be allowed to live to find out ...*

'Sam, did you hear me?'

'Monsieur ...'

'You obviously didn't hear.'

'I beg your pardon, Monsieur Le Comte. I was worried by the news in the *Times*.'

'Your concern can hardly alter the course of the war.'

'I'm sorry.' He was conscious of how abruptly the Count spoke. It was unlike him, and did not augur well. It began to seem as if everyone was in a bad mood today. In which case, if this was a prelude to dismissal, he would soon be in a similar state himself.

'I asked if you'd had news from your father.'

'Unfortunately, no, Monsieur.'

'I hope he's not in any trouble.'

'Trouble?'

'There were rumours before he left here.'

'About what, sir?'

'There've always been rumours. His political sympathies. Even back in 1939, there was talk he kept watch on German shipping from his house in Kobe. Reported their movements to the British.'

'I could hardly know that. My parents were separated by then. I was in Yokohama.' He hoped he sounded convincing.

'Later, there were suspicions of Free French activities, and talk of a newsletter. Did you know anything of that?'

'No, Monsieur.' He felt no compunction about lying to protect his father.

'He never spoke of security police? The Kempetai?'

'Not to me.'

Sam could not work it out. This blunt interrogation was very strange. The Count seemed aloof, almost hostile. Was this why he had been summoned so early, before anyone else was present?

'What about his business in Kobe?'

'I'm afraid it's in chaos,' he said abruptly. If he was to be examined like this, he'd adopt the same tone as his inquisitor.

'What happened?'

'He decided there were better prospects in Saigon. At the time he had no idea there'd be a war, but now the Kobe office has collapsed. It was in debt; the bank closed the firm down.'

'I'm sorry to hear that,' the Count de Boulanger said after a reflective pause.

'Yes, sir. There were loyal workers there, friends who lost jobs they'd had for years.'

'Can I ask you another question?' The Count's change of tone was conciliatory, surprising Sam.

'Of course, Monsieur.'

'Your mother was a friend of Richard Sorge?'

'She knew him. He sometimes came to tea.'

'I'm told they were closer friends than that.'

'I'm sorry, Monsieur Le Comte. I'm not qualified to comment on my mother's friendships. He took her to parties. People say she's good looking. Sorge liked beautiful women. I was unhappy about the friendship because I didn't like the man, but it was none of my business.'

'You know he's going to be found guilty of espionage?'

'I've heard so. But what's it to do with my mother?'

'Nothing I hope, Sam.'

'Then why all these questions, Monsieur? You ask me about my father, now my mother. What's the purpose of this?'

It was a rash thing to say, but he felt he could no longer endure the probing. It was too persistent, and far too personal.

'Sorge is being tried in court. Is there anything – and I don't meant to offend – but is there anything he could say that might implicate your mother?'

'In what, sir?'

'In his activities. In espionage.'

'You mean is my mother a spy?'

'That's putting it bluntly.'

'Then how should we put it?' Sam asked recklessly, too angered by the implication to care any longer what he was doing to his future prospects. 'Are you seriously asking me if my mother – a White Russian who fled from the revolution – was a spy for Joseph Stalin? How can you or anyone imagine she'd contemplate helping Sorge work for Moscow?'

'I've offended you, Sam.'

'Puzzled me, Monsieur. Yes, you've certainly done that. I'm at a loss to understand some of your questions.'

'I didn't like it any more than you did, but there was a purpose,' the Count said. He pressed a buzzer beside his desk, and his Japanese servant entered with a laden tray. There were cups on it, a coffee pot and a covered silver salver. It was as though he had been poised outside, awaiting the signal. He bowed and left them. The Count waited until the door closed behind him.

'It's a matter of trust, Sam. For the bank's reputation I need someone I can completely rely on.'

'For what, sir?'

The Count ignored this, as he continued: 'I'd be making a very serious mistake choosing a person who might – for any reason at all – come under suspicion.'

'You mean me? Under suspicion because of my parents?'

He felt sweat trickling down his back. Did anyone know about his adoption? About his long-dead mother, who had refused an abortion and registered his birth as an Australian. He should not be sitting here in this office if the truth was known; he'd be far away in an internment camp.

'Anyone can attract the wrong kind of attention. The slightest thing can bring us under scrutiny in these difficult times.'

'Like me, with the wrong parents?'

'Listen to me, Sam. I have to preserve this bank, and in banking trust is everything. Our clients insist; we have to be as credible as priests in the confessional. Even deal with more crucial matters than coveting a neighbour's ass, or committing adultery with his wife.' He smiled at Sam's perplexity. 'There'll be no more questions. They had to be asked, and you answered.

Now we'll have coffee and croissants together, and talk about your future.'

The Count insisted he try the croissants, for they were the equal of any he'd eaten in Paris. He had found a baker who worked in France as a pastrycook, and who supplied them for special occasions. The emphasis placed on 'special' sounded so promising that the croissant tasted delicious. As Sam accepted another, he was told he now had a permanent job and his salary would begin at once. Consequently, the second croissant tasted even better, while he tried to guess what he might be paid. He had hoped for forty yen a month, but as a hedge against disappointment had fixed on a figure of thirty-five. It was then, perhaps due to the excitement, or the second cup of coffee, that he realised he needed to urinate. If the Count did not get on with the details, he might pee himself.

Unfortunately, de Boulanger was now expansive, telling Sam he had come at precisely the right moment, and that his fluency with languages and ability to type secret correspondence all fitted the kind of person he had been looking for. 'We have fewer clients now. So many French nationals are forced to live off capital, with their firms closed because of the war. As a consequence we have to find other avenues in order to keep the bank viable.'

How much a month, Sam silently begged him, and thought if the peroration didn't stop, he would definitely disgrace himself. Which was when the Count finished his coffee and smiled.

'Now about your remuneration, Sam,' he said, 'I intend to pay you a hundred yen a month,' he said.

Shit, Sam thought, *a hundred yen*!

His bladder might be near bursting, but he forgot it as

his mind tried to absorb the figure. *One whole hundred*! Housemaids were paid eight yen a month, cooks ten, senior clerks forty, Japanese managers, if lucky, eighty. It felt like an fortune. *A hundred yen every month*, he thought. *It is a fortune*. He tried not to show his amazement, but doubted if he fooled the Count.

'A good salary,' de Boulanger said.

'Very fair,' Sam managed to reply, and the Count raised an eyebrow and gave a slight smile.

'You'll earn it,' he said.

The regular morning ritual, the handshakes, inquiries about health, families, the weather – all took place as usual that day, when the main doors were unlocked by Frankenstein on the stroke of nine. The Count was waiting in the entrance hall to participate. Sam shook hands with the French, bowed to the Japanese, and tried to behave as if his life was unchanged. It was difficult; he wanted to celebrate, to revel in the news but had been expressly forbidden to do so.

'This meeting won't be mentioned. Your salary is not to be revealed to the rest of the staff. Is that clear?'

'Yes, Monsieur Le Comte.'

'Leave now and return at the normal time. Mademoiselle Patou knows of our meeting, but not the details. Nor will she. I can hardly expect you not to tell your family, but do request your mother to be discreet.'

The insistence on such secrecy came as a surprise. After the relief of a visit to the toilet, the side door was opened by Frankenstein. Sam nodded his thanks, but was ignored. He walked to the Ginza, then back across the Nihon-Bashi Bridge to synchronise his arrival with the moment the bank doors opened. Frankenstein did not even blink. *Perhaps*, Sam thought, *we all look alike to him*. Or else he was chosen for his ability to remain so stolidly phlegmatic.

As a final pretence, Sam and the Count greeted each other and shook hands. He felt foolish taking part in this masquerade before going to their respective work places; the Count to his luxury office, Sam to his desk adjacent to where Kimiko sat at her typewriter.

He had barely begun work before she rose and paused alongside him to ask, 'How was your meeting?'

He stared blankly at her. 'Meeting? What meeting?'

'With His Highness. Our Honourable Emperor.' She made a mock bow in the direction of the Count's office.

'I don't know what you're talking about,' he said.

'A secret meeting, Sam. It must've been important.'

'Kimiko ... haven't you got any work to do?'

'Heaps,' she said.

'Then how about getting on with it?'

'Listen to you, Delon-san. We're more important than yesterday. Giving orders. We have an air of authority today.'

'Shut up,' Sam said.

'You're on the payroll at last.'

'I don't know what you're talking about.'

'By the look of you, it's good news. But forget trying to say there was no meeting. Because there was – at eight this morning, just you and the Count – before the bank opened.'

Sam was speechless. He knew her capacity for finding out what went on, but this was impossible.

'How?' he asked, 'how in hell could you know that?'

She smiled teasingly, but before she could answer, Ribot called her. Would she kindly bring her notebook at once, as he had some letters to dictate.

She murmured to Sam. 'How do I know? Take me to lunch at that new sushi bar in the Ginza, and I'll tell you.'

'You will? Promise?'

'The new place, not that cheap one. Yes or no?'

'Twelve-thirty,' Sam agreed, then after she had gone to Ribot's office wondered if he had enough money for the new sushi bar. Until his salary at the end of the month, he was almost penniless. He could have had his free lunch in the bank's upstairs dining room.

On the other hand, it would mean another dull meal with the same people he ate with each day. They were not a very lively group, the senior French staff. While he liked Mademoiselle, she rarely had much to say, and excused herself as soon as the meal was over. If the Count was present, his executives spent all their time being so obsequious that the end of lunch came as a relief. Sam had never seen adults so sycophantic, although he realised that while the war lasted, none of these men could expect to find another position of such substance in Japan. Nor could they leave the country. For them, it was the French Bank or nowhere, which made the Count's power in this place absolute.

The dining room was not an atmosphere he enjoyed, and he had a feeling that if they knew about this morning's meeting and his salary, they'd resent him. No, the Ginza and the sushi bar with Kimiko was best. Apart from which, he was determined to find out how she knew so much about what happened in this place.

'You don't really want to know,' she said, reaching across with her chopsticks to take a slither of sashimi from his plate. Sam was eating slowly, after a hasty calculation of the prices on the menu against the amount in his pocket. It was going to be a close thing, when it came time to pay the cashier.

'Of course I want to know. That's why we're here.'

She gazed at him and sighed. 'Is that the only reason? You didn't have anything else in mind?'

She leaned across and took a tuna sushi wrapped in nori, topped with red caviar. His meal was disappearing while she flirted with him, and he was sure he'd be ravenous halfway through the afternoon. In fact, he was hungry now. He realised he'd better eat what remained of his lunch, before it vanished entirely.

'I thought you might have had a different reason,' Kimiko said, 'more romantic.' Sam was unable to reply, his mouth filled with delicious prawns and the flavour of vinegar rice. 'Or even sexy,' she said. He mumbled and indicated that his mouth was still full. Kimiko smiled at him.

'After all, most of the staff are old – except us. I'd rather go out with you, than have Laroche rub up against me and feel my bottom.'

'The chief accountant? He doesn't.'

'He does. Every chance he gets.'

'Dirty old bugger,' Sam said.

'Then there's Frankenstein...' she said, and smiled again.

'He doesn't feel your bum,' Sam said, aghast.

'No, but he'd like to. Given half a chance. That's why he tells me everything that goes on.'

'Frankenstein!' *Of course*, Sam thought, realising now how she was so well informed.

'He's always having rows with Mrs Frankenstein, who doesn't like what she calls all that nasty business in bed – so he keeps asking me if I'll go into the stationery cupboard with him.'

'That's dreadful,' Sam said. Unnerved by this revelation, he forgot to eat. Kimiko daintily took a prawn from his plate.

'I won't, of course. But he knows I like to hear gossip, so he tells me because he hopes it'll change my mind.'

'Good God.' He was astounded. The sedate French Bank seemed full of lust; he said as much to Kimiko. It made her laugh.

'You haven't heard it all yet. There's Mr Ribot,' she said. 'Goes to church with Madame Ribot every Sunday. If he confesses all his sins, it must keep the priest busy.'

'What sins?'

'I can only speak of what I know,' she said demurely. 'He exposed himself once.'

'He didn't!'

'He did. Not that there was much to see, and when I took no notice, he pretended he hadn't buttoned his fly. Then he asked if I'd come to work without panties, so he could drop his pencil on the floor and have a look...'

'Jesus Christ,' Sam said, 'it's a hotbed.'

'They'd certainly like it to be.'

'Anyone else?' Sam asked. 'Not the Count...'

'No. Devoted to Moustique. The only nice ones aren't interested – like him and you.' As Sam tried to think of a reply to this, she laughed and said: 'I almost forgot the Sardine.'

'Monsieur Sardaigne?'

'Oily. Hands like tentacles, trying to make a grab. More like an octopus than a sardine.' She leaned across and gathered up the last piece of sashimi on his plate. 'I'll tell you the trouble with that bank,' she said, 'there's not enough customers any more. No real work to keep them busy, so all they can do is think about sex.'

Sam had to borrow two yen to help him pay the bill.

He promised repayment when he received his salary. His confidential salary. At least he felt certain that news wasn't known to her.

'One hundred yen a month,' Kimiko said, as if reading his mind, then laughed at the baffled expression on his face. 'Did you think it was a secret, Sam?'

'I was told it had to be.'

'Let me explain the first rule of office life. The bigger the secret, the sooner everyone knows it.'

As they walked back through the lunchtime crowds, he decided to ask her if she'd heard rumours about Mademoiselle Patou. Kimiko, it was clear, knew all there was to know about everyone.

'Is it true?'

'Is what true?'

'That Mademoiselle has a husband and a mystery life?'

She was silent for a moment. Her raunchy humour gave way to reflective indecision. 'Poor Cecile,' she finally said quietly. 'That's a different story, for another day.'

That afternoon Sam was eager to reach home and impart the news of his salary. But he found his timing astray. His mother was pleased, but absorbed. The household, including the cook, had a new family addition. They had bought a goat.

'Cook-san persuaded me it was the answer to the shortage of milk,' his mother explained. For once in accord, they had gone together to buy it that morning. The man who advertised it for sale had said the goat would eat all their unwanted scraps, give lots of precious milk, and was a pet they would come to love.

But by the time Sam arrived from the commuter train, certain facts had become clear. The goat would certainly eat scraps, but it had also, within a few hours, eaten everything else that grew in their tiny backyard. It had polished off the stems of shrubs already denuded of leaves by the winter. The grass, the contents of the garbage bin, all had been devoured by the goat – who showed no sign of being satisfied by these few tidbits.

They finally went to bed with it tied up and bleating in the cold of the back yard, and his mother telling cook-san that since it was her stupid idea, she would have to keep the creature quiet, or else people would complain and might call the police.

Sometime in the night, Sam was woken by the sound of bleating in the back yard, and he heard the cook plaintively begging the goat to be a good girl and go to sleepies. He tried to do the same, but instead found himself wondering what it would be like tucked up in bed with Kimiko. She wasn't beautiful, but she was sexy. The French all obviously agreed on that. Dirty old Ribot . . . no panties! Sam started to recall her flirting smiles across the sushi table, and felt that making love to her could be really exciting.

CHAPTER 13

'Look at this,' Carl said laughing, and picked up a plaster bookend that not only resembled General MacArthur, but in case of possible mistaken identity had his name cut carefully into the plaster below the eagle face.

'Goodness,' Florrie said, as the owner hurried to greet them, and said the souvenir bookends were in such demand that he had been forced to order more.

'Simply can't get enough,' he told them. 'The Yanks buy 'em and send 'em back stateside. The girls take them home to their mums and dads.'

'And are their mums and dads great readers?' Florrie asked, with such an absence of guile that Carl hid a smile.

'Readers?' The owner of the shop was confused. 'What do yer mean, are they readers? You mean books?'

'Well, these are bookends, aren't they?'

'These are heirlooms,' he told her, recovering from the slight sales setback. 'In years to come, if we don't get invaded, this'll be the bloke who saved Australia. And his plaster portrait will be worth a fortune. An absolute bloody mint, and your kids or your grandkids will be grateful you bought a few.'

'So they'll increase in value?' Carl asked him, looking very serious.

'Increase? Sport, these will be rare. They'll go through the roof. Right through it. I can let you have 'em at the current price, if you want to take a dozen. Ten bob each, and believe me they'll be ten quid before the year's out.'

'So we could make heaps?'

'Believe me...'

'Oh, we do believe you,' Florence said gently. 'But you see, we represent the potter who made the originals, and he's rather upset at all these people making heaps from his clay effigy of the famous general. And as solicitors, he's asked us to represent him and take action against shops like yours that are cheating him.'

'Shit,' the owner said. 'Fuck it.'

'That's exactly the way he feels,' Florrie replied, 'so we'll look forward to seeing you in court.'

It was a strange time. On some days they felt on the brink of invasion, while on others life seemed to settle into a routine of normality. The trams, ferries and trains all ran on schedule; gas and electricity were uninterrupted, except in times of violent storms, and even telephones rang for those fortunate enough to have them.

It was sometimes difficult to realise that the Japanese had progressed four thousand kilometres, that they stood poised in New Guinea, ready to swarm across the thinly defended landscape. While half the population were in fear of defeat, the other half surfed, played

Rugby League, and the papers had sports headlines as large as those on the front page. Racing was popular at Randwick and Flemington; crowds attended the meetings. The English comic, George Formby, was touring in *Turned Out Nice Again*, described as the funniest show in town.

Meanwhile, an increasing flood of American troops were arriving. Greeted at first with relief and enthusiasm, this gradually began to change. The GIs, better dressed in their smart uniforms, and considerably better paid, often ignorant or uncaring of the value of Australian money, were already popular with black marketeers, taxi drivers, and local girls. Australian soldiers, many in battalions returned from fighting Germans and Italians in the western desert, resented their easy success, their swagger, the orchids and nylon stockings with which they won affection. They taunted the Americans on learning that some girls accepted the orchids at night, and sold them back to the florists the next day at half price.

Not all wars were fought against the enemy. Florrie and Carl had been on a rare week's holiday in Brisbane, and witnessed the ferocious battle between Australian soldiers and their American allies. There were serious injuries and fatalities, but the censor, in the interests of comradeship, had decided it should not be reported.

'We're learning more about goats,' Tamara Delon told her friend Paul Jacoulet, 'and the more I discover, the less I like what I'm learning – if you understand what I mean?'

Jacoulet was a noted wood-block artist, who possessed one of the world's most exotic collection of butterflies. Exotic himself, he was an extravagantly overt homosexual who rarely wore men's clothing, and was mostly to be seen in a kimono with his face painted like a geisha. He was rich and notorious, impervious to public opinion, famous enough not to be in danger of harassment by the law, and invariably attended by a cluster of young Korean boys, who now stood watching and giggling some distance away, while Jacoulet and Tamara sat talking together in a teahouse.

'My dear Tamara, you must be utterly insane. A goat?'

'It's for the milk.'

'It's madness. Was it your idea?'

'No, cook-san's.'

'That woman is an idiot. She'll have to go.'

'She will. I've been wanting to get rid of her for years. I keep trying to be brave enough to tell her.'

'The milk must taste revolting.'

'Actually,' she said, 'the taste isn't bad, surprisingly.'

'It surprises me. Don't you dare use it when I visit.'

'Of course not. The trouble is, she eats such a lot . . .'

'Who? Cook-san?'

'No. Gracie.'

'You've given this beast, this creature, a *name*?'

'Well, we had to call her something.'

'Gracie!' Jacoulet roared with laughter. 'Gracie Fields?'

'Just plain Gracie. I'm trying to tell you, she never stops eating. Or shitting. The back yard is full of it.'

'Gracie Crapper!'

'Paul, stop making fun of me. This is serious. She ate a shirt belonging to Sam last night.'

'Sam should take more care where he leaves his shirts.'

'This was hanging on the clothesline. Our shoes, the garbage bin, absolutely nothing is safe. She even tried to eat the fence.'

'My God, if the fence goes,' Jacoulet said, 'she'll be into next door's garden like a scythe. Then the neighbourhood. I can see it now: precinct petitions, protest meetings. They'll form a "Gracie must go committee" and take you to court.'

'Oh, shut up,' Tamara said, becoming cross with him. 'Give her back.'

'The bloody man won't take her back. She provides milk, but her appetite is ridiculous. At this rate the milk will cost more than if we bought it on the black market. I don't know what to do.'

'How about a curry?' Paul Jacoulet suggested.

Angelique said he was an unfeeling murderer, and vowed to become a vegetarian if it happened, quite apart from never speaking to Jacoulet again. In that case, her mother told her, get a shovel and a bucket and clean up all the shit in the backyard, because it looks like a sewage farm. Then she told cook-san to put a rope on the beast, walk her to the park and find some grass where she could graze.

The cook came back soon afterwards in a rage, for the park keeper, after seeing bamboo shoots being scavenged, ordered them to leave, threatening the next time she'd be fined and the goat would be arrested. When asked for his ideas on the problem, Sam said an arrest might be the solution, but it was none of his concern, and he needed his best suit pressed because it was a very important day at the bank.

The clock over the main door seemed to take an eternity to move. Three more minutes. Sam had already made excuses for his absence from the dining room, saying he was meeting a school friend. Just three minutes until Frankenstein shut the doors for lunch hour. Pens would be put down, chairs pushed back, and the rhythmic tap of Kimiko's typewriter would cease. It was almost the only sound apart from the murmur of voices at a meeting in Laroche's office. He knew she was equally conscious of the time, as their glances met.

Today, Kimiko had agreed, she would finally tell him the truth about Mademoiselle Patou. But they should not be seen leaving together. He must exit first. She would wait until the executives had gone upstairs, then make her own way to the Ginza. When Sam asked why the subterfuge was necessary, she told him not to be naive. It would do his future no good if it became known. M'sieu Ribot had noticed them return the last time they had lunch, and had spoken to her. Liaisons between the French staff and employees were not encouraged. They must be careful not to let it become obvious.

'But what are we doing wrong?' Sam wanted to know, after they had found a table in the corner.

'Upsetting old Ribot,' she said, 'not to mention the Sardine and the chief accountant – if they knew about it.'

'What a bunch of hypocrites.' Sam was indignant. 'All trying to get their hands on you. Grabbing your bottom, asking you to come to work without pants. They're disgusting, whereas we're just having a civilised lunch together.'

'Not quite as civilised as last time,' she said, with a glance around the cheaper sushi bar.

He had to grant her that. But it was all he could afford. Yesterday, when she had suggested this, his eagerness had overlooked his lack of money until his first payday.

Embarrassment had been avoided by managing to borrow from his sister. Angelique was an avid saver of pocket money but a reluctant lender, and this sushi bar was the extent of any largesse she was prepared to risk.

'Next time will be somewhere special,' Sam promised. 'But wherever we are, that's all we're doing. Just having a civilised lunch. Hardly doing anything to upset a bunch of sex maniacs.'

Kimiko treated him to one of her lingering looks. Sam thought it surprising he'd never noticed until then she had such luminous eyes. 'They play games that won't get them anywhere. But a civilised lunch is different – who can tell where that might lead?'

'Where?' He wasn't sure if he should ask it, or where she was leading him. Kimiko could be extremely complex.

'People can fall in love over lunch. Change their lives, become engaged, run off together. Lunch can be really dangerous.'

Sam thought this was already becoming dangerous. He didn't want to become engaged or change his life – not yet. He did want to take her to bed if possible, but had no plans beyond some intense and hopefully mutual lust.

'Here's the sushi,' he said thankfully as the waiter arrived, 'now, tell me about Mademoiselle Patou.'

Kimiko reached over and selected a choice squid from his plate. She was always too nimble for Sam. 'Her name's Madame Clermont,' she said. 'Cecile Louise Clermont, nee Patou.'

'Still married?'

'Oh yes, very much so.'

'She prefers to use her maiden name?'

'Her husband insists she use it.'

'Insists?'

'So it won't be known she works to earn their living, while he skis in winter and plays tennis all summer.'

'Good God,' Sam immediately realised, 'that's Jacques Clermont you're talking about.'

'Yes. Do you know him?'

'I've seen him play tennis. He's brilliant. He always wins the summer cup at Karuizawa.'

'Mademoiselle does translations and extra work at night, so he can join all you exclusive people up there in the mountains.'

Sam tried to ignore the gibe.

'I think my father went to dinner at the Clermonts.'

'Then he'd have met Cecile. The quiet one at the table – who was paying for the meal, like she pays for most things.'

'How did you find this out?'

'She was in tears one day. Sobbing her heart out in the ladies lav. I couldn't believe it was our smart Mademoiselle. She wanted to talk, I'm a good listener.' Kimiko shrugged. 'Until now I've told no-one. But you're different. You won't gossip. But some of their friends must realise the truth. Your father probably knows.'

'Perhaps. He's in Saigon, we're not in touch. I always thought that Jacques Clermont was rich.'

'So does everyone. His family in Switzerland were rich, but he had even richer tastes. They gave him money, he spent it all; it seems nothing was too good or too expensive for Jacques. When he got into debt, the family paid. Until finally they'd had enough, and put him on an allowance.'

'In that case, why must she work to pay his bills?'

'Because the allowance doesn't keep him in the style he expects. And since the war, the allowance is no longer dependable. Boats are sunk, banks blown up, cheques lost – it's very distressing. She works, he plays. He's never done a stroke of work in his life, and no matter how short of money they are, he never will.'

Sam was thoughtful, remembering the athletic figure, how he played to win, and the manner in which the ball came back with such a cut and spin on the court that few players could handle it. Jacques Clermont. Often in the newspapers; photographs of him winning tournaments; every winter on the ski slopes, invariably a guest at parties. Women loved him. Men thought him a sterling chap. All of a sudden Sam could recall his father's smile when someone had asked him what good old Jacques did for a living.

'Not a lot,' his father had said, never realising that long afterwards, when he was in Indochina, his son would be working in the same organisation as Jacques Clermont's wife. And until now, unaware of the fact.

They walked part of the way back to the bank together. Sam was still absorbing what he had been told, wondering how he would feel the next time he encountered Mademoiselle Patou. There must be no hint he knew, no change in attitude towards her. He thought of how desperate and lonely she must have been to entrust the details of her life to Kimiko – or anyone else who worked in such proximity.

'You're awfully quiet,' she said.
'I was thinking.'
'About Mademoiselle?'
'Yes. And about us.'
'What about us?'
'In a week I get my first salary. Would you let me take you out to a special dinner that night?'

She hesitated. Sam held his breath, and thought: *She'll say no. Her parents are strict. Or there'd be problems getting home.*

'What a lovely idea,' Kimiko smiled. 'I'll tell my parents I'll be late home.' Then with one of her enigmatic looks, she said, 'I might say I'll stay at a girlfriend's place.'

She went her individual way back to work. Sam waited at a bookshop, then took a different route. He now agreed with her, it was imperative that Ribot, Laroche and the Sardine did not know about them. Or their future intentions. Because her reply was deliciously clear. Neither of them would go home. After dinner, they would go to a discreet hotel. In the morning – he tried to imagine the morning, waking beside her warm body and making love again. No families, no noisy breakfast rush, no trains to catch. They could stay in bed until it was time to bathe, then stroll leisurely to the bank like a pair of innocents looking as if it was just another day.

Only a week. He knew it would seem like forever.

The problem of Gracie remained unsolved. Angelique was fed up with cleaning the yard each morning, only to find it was a mess when she returned from vainly hunting for a job. Their mother had visited Sophie Rambert, whose Swiss husband was a wealthy industrialist and influential in the Far East section of the Red Cross. He had promised to do what he could, but nothing had eventuated. Which did not surprise Sam if the parents were like their son; he and Wilhelm, their only child, had been in the same year at school, and their antipathy was potent and aggressively mutual.

It was Angelique who finally came up with the idea of how to feed the goat. They had a shed full of old newspapers, saved for years, speculating that if there was a war, one of the immediate casualties – apart from the truth – would be toilet paper. Factories making such trifling luxuries would be switched to producing guns. So there was a vast amount of papers stored for such an emergency. Angelique's theory was that the war would never last long enough to use it all, and since the goat ate anything, it should be possible to tempt her into trying a new diet.

It was an immediate success.

Gracie loved the taste of newspaper. There were many editions but it seemed as if she liked the *Nippon Times* the best, although she was quite partial to old copies of *Figaro* and the *Daily Express*. All she craved was a decent-sized paper, a broadsheet for preference, with advertisements and a goodly amount of news.

She munched on the headlines of great events, like Mr Chamberlain returning from Munich in 1938 to make his unfortunate declaration of 'Peace in our time' – then Hitler's army a year later invading Poland, conquering France and marching on Moscow. There were recent local editions with constant references to Japan's rapid victories in Asia, and how it would soon invade Australia.

Gracie ate steadily through the entire night. Silently, with not a bleat to disturb the neighbourhood. It was clearly a triumph for Angelique, and early the next morning they all gathered around while cook-san milked her. The result was interesting. The milk looked like real milk. It smelt like real milk.

Unfortunately, it tasted like newspaper.

CHAPTER 14

The limousine crossed the river and drove along the canal road past the Mitsukoshi department store. Cars were rare now, most powered by charcoal, but this one had no burner; it was either a government vehicle, or it belonged to someone rich enough to afford black market gasoline and a chauffeur at the wheel. It received envious glances from crowds hurrying for the underground in a general scurry from the wet and chilly weather.

Sam was engaged in a bruising struggle to make progress in the opposite direction, buffeted by the wind as he tried to force his way from the store towards the bank where Kimiko was waiting for him. Sleet was falling from leaden skies, and the pavements were treacherous with melted snow. It was almost time for the bank to shut, and he had no wish to be late and find her locked outside in these conditions. It would not be a promising start to the intricate arrangements he had made for the evening.

This at last was his first payday. Finally he was a salaried member of the bank. Tonight he and Kimiko were having their planned dinner together. He had found a cosy restaurant and booked a table for two, then taken time to check a number of discreet hotels in the neighbourhood. Were rooms available for an hour or two, just supposing he was to arrive after dinner with a companion? Indeed, he was told, he would be most welcome! Would he care to pay in advance, and make a reservation?

No, no, he quickly explained; it was only a query at this stage. But what if they should check in for an hour or two, then decide the room was so pleasing they wished to stay until morning? He was assured he would be even more welcome!

It had been a very stressful time. The thought of Kimiko occupied his mind to the exclusion of almost everything else. The prospect of bed together, a passionate few hours – or even better, an erotic few days – was continually in his thoughts. Desire had become intense, frustration acute, for time was unrelentingly slow. If they felt this way about each other, why did they need to wait?

In rational moments, he knew they must. Persuading her to try one of the odious short-time shagging shops, with tiny cubicles that were not soundproof, would be disastrous. There were no other options. Their problem was a familiar one; they had no bed, no nest to nest in, for Kimiko lived with sedate parents, and Sam had no privacy in his own home. He contemplated the penthouse, but there was the lurking possibility of being caught in the act by Frankenstein. He thought of bushes in the park, but it was the depth of winter. There were no friends who could lend them a place.

The strain had begun to tell. He was palpably distracted. Ribot reported his work was slack. Mademoiselle called Sam to a private meeting, and asked if there was a problem that concerned him. Any worries at home? Any little difficulties at work?

Sam had said he could not think of any.

Mademoiselle quietly told him he must settle down. This position at the bank was too important to jeopardise, adding she had decided not to bother the Count with Monsieur Ribot's report. Sam was grateful, promising there'd be no further cause for complaint. Gritting his teeth, avoiding torrid thoughts, he had set about his job with determination. And today at last was payday. Tonight was the night!

He worked through the lunch hour and, in return, asked for a half hour before the shops closed, in which to buy a gift with his first pay packet. Mademoiselle said how it was kind of him to think of a present for his family. How thoughtful. What he bought was a decorative silk scarf for Kimiko. He decided to wait until after dinner before presenting it. He rehearsed the words dozens of times, altered them, came to the conclusion he would not say anything at all, he would just hand it to her and see what happened next. If God was on his side, she would be charmed by the thought, and the scenario that had been constantly in his mind would then follow.

The crowds were even thicker, stampeding from the bleak afternoon and slowing his progress. He moved to the edge of the footpath to avoid them. A limousine splashed past, tyres hitting a pothole filled with melted snow. He had no time to step back; slush sprayed him, and the wrapping paper around the present became wet and discoloured. He caught a glimpse of a figure in the back seat, then saw the car turn the corner and pull up.

That was when he realised it had stopped at the side door of the French Bank.

The sole passenger was rugged in a warm coat and wore a felt hat. Part of his face was obscured by an influenza mask – a familiar enough sight since this cold weather had returned after everyone believed winter was over. Chill winds, sweeping across from South Korea had brought frost and snow – so a facial mask was a sensible protection – for it would be most unwise for the limousine's passenger to be seen visiting here. The man felt it was unsafe to make this visit at all; there were more discreet ways. But an instruction had been given, and he was used to obeying orders. He took an attaché case, reluctantly left the warmth of the car, and rang the bell for the giant caretaker.

From down the street, Sam saw Frankenstein usher in the visitor. Someone had come by special appointment, someone whose car had muddied him. He could only hope the chauffeur's carelessness had not ruined the silk scarf as he hurried to the front entrance. He was just in time; thankfully she was not waiting for him outside in the cold, and the bank had not yet shut its main doors.

In fact, as he entered, Kimiko appeared engrossed in her work. Then she slyly glanced up at him, and his heart accelerated. She had changed into a new dress. A beautiful dress. But it was the intense look she gave him that filled him with joy. The night ahead suddenly had a wonderful feeling of illicit pleasure about it.

He glanced at his watch. Less than two minutes and they would be collecting their coats, all bidding each other goodnight. He and Kimiko would play their parts in the charade, departing in opposite directions, and meeting moments later in the adjoining street. Sam saw Ribot rise and switch off his desk lamp. They all began to tidy their desks and head for the cloakrooms. Kimiko was the first; he thought it prudent if he was one of the last.

It was then that Mademoiselle Patou came and murmured to him that he was required urgently in the Count's office.

Sam had never seen so much money. It filled the attaché case. It was in bundles of twenties, fifties, and hundred yen notes. The Count did not introduce his visitor, who had divested himself of the heavy coat and influenza mask. The room was partly in shadow, and the man sat in a chair away from the light. After a brief glance at him, Sam's attention returned to the contents of the attaché case.

'This is a sum of money which is to be placed on deposit in our strongroom,' the Count said. 'I have a total verified by the depositor, but the bank requires we check the amount. It's a highly confidential matter, so I'll ask you to undertake it, Sam.'

'When, Monsieur Le Comte?' But he already had a deep foreboding about what the answer would be.

'Now, of course,' the Count replied. 'We establish the total while our visitor remains. Then there'll be some paperwork.'

Oh God, Sam thought, *not now, today of all days*. The bank doors would be shutting: soon a puzzled Kimiko would be at their rendezvous. It would be dark as well as bitterly cold, and she would not remain for long. This would take several hours at least.

'Is something wrong, Sam?'

'I had made some arrangements, Monsieur.'

'In view of the importance of this, I'll have to ask you to cancel them. Use my telephone if you wish.'

'Er, no – that won't be necessary.'

'You may be late. Do you want to call your home?'

'There's no need, sir. They're not expecting me.'

Which ironically was true. He had said friends had invited him to stay the night. What a fiasco. All his brilliant plans in turmoil. The table booked in the friendly restaurant, where he could never eat again. And Kimiko in a brand-new dress. A trim, smart dress. The expectant look on her face. He felt it was fair to say the *eager* expectant look! There was no doubt that after an intimate dinner they would have gone to the hotel and made love. Several times! Certainly several times. And perhaps stayed there to wake together in the dawn light.

He remembered a quotation from English class at school. '*When sorrows come, they come not single spies, but in battalions.*' Hamlet. William Shakespeare. This was a battalion of sorrows, all right. It was a bloody great brigade of them.

'I'm sorry if I've disrupted other plans,' he realised the Count was speaking, 'but this must be attended to without delay.'

'Yes, Monsieur.'

'You recall my saying you'd earn your income here?'

'Of course, Monsieur.'

'Then perhaps you should begin counting. We'll send out for supper later.'

It was plain to the staff the next morning that Kimiko was not her cheerful self. At the daily round of greetings she was quite abrupt, and seemed to be in what Andre Ribot later described as a state of acute indignation. Barely civil to anyone. It was most unlike her, he said, to be so irate and in such high dudgeon, but she was furious for some reason and he thought he knew why.

'Why?' asked Emile Laroche, the chief accountant. They were gathered in Roland Sardaigne's office, ostensibly to discuss the day's work, but in reality occupied with this gossip.

Ribot gestured through the glass partition towards where Sam sat at his desk, gazing blankly into space. He looked tired and perplexed, like a young man with a bad hangover.

'Sam,' said the Sardine. 'You mean Sam has been up to filthy tricks with Kimiko? If he has, we'll have him fired.'

'Idiot,' Ribot replied. 'Try to get rid of him and you'll be the one who ends up looking for another job.'

'Me? Don't be ridiculous,' Sardaigne declared. 'I'm the assistant accountant. He's a mere clerk.'

'If you think that,' said Laroche, 'you're an even bigger idiot. Because whatever occurred here last night when the bank shut, only Le Comte and Sam know about it. Which I suggest, despite his youth, makes him hardly a mere clerk any longer.'

'Perhaps he just did some interpreting?'

'Perhaps,' Laroche said, but gave the impression he did not think it quite that rudimentary.

At his desk, Sam could feel the conjecture of the other French staff. Far worse, he could sense Kimiko's bewilderment and simmering resentment. No need to define her expectation of last night; he knew it had been the same as his. The new dress, the look on her face, had told him that. First of all to enjoy flirting over a meal, and then – his mind baulked at the image of them in the hotel, euphoric beneath a quilt.

Eventually Kimiko rose from her desk. She walked

past without sparing him a glance. He saw the note drop, but doubted if anyone else had. To be sure he waited a few moments before picking it up. It was brief and explicit.

WHERE WERE YOU? was all it said.

Where indeed? How could he possibly tell her?

It was after nine-thirty before Sam had finished counting the money. During this time they had paused for supper, when the Japanese servant knocked and the Count de Boulanger, without allowing him inside the room, had brought back a tray of sandwiches and coffee. It was a welcome break, for Sam's fingers were tired from the repetitive tally, and filthy from the used banknotes.

He and the Count had shared the sandwiches. Their visitor declined to eat or drink. Throughout, he had remained in the shadowed section of the room, restless and uneasy. When Sam at last finished, the notes in clusters were packed into a safe-deposit box.

'The exact total?' the Count had asked.

'One million yen,' Sam had told him.

'Good.' The amounts clearly equated. The Count had locked the box, and shaken hands with the man who had brought the money. 'One million is two hundred thousand United States dollars, placed to the credit of your principal's account in Zurich.'

'I beg your pardon, Monsieur Le Comte,' the visitor had said. 'I think there is an error. The official rate is four American dollars to the yen. Which means we are due to receive two hundred and fifty thousand.'

'In normal times, Ozaki-san. But these are not normal times, and this is the best rate I can offer.'

'I think I should discuss this with my superior.'

'I already have,' the Count had said coldly. 'Perhaps he chose not to confide in you. Your job was to make this delivery, and return with a receipt. Which my assistant will now type in French and English.'

Sam could see the man was discomforted, even annoyed by the Count's peremptory dismissal of his protest.

'I think it better, Excellency, before any paperwork is done, if I telephone to confirm this is agreeable to my principal?'

'You will have to accept my word that it is.' The Count's tone was now positively arctic. 'You'll make no call from this office on a matter of such delicacy. I can think of nothing more ill-advised, Ozaki-san. It's dangerous and stupid to believe telephones are safe these days. The only call you'll make is to your driver, asking him to collect you. I suggest you do that now.'

While the man did as ordered, the Count dictated a letter to Sam. He was told to use Mademoiselle Patou's machine in the adjoining office. On *Bank de l'Indo Chine* notepaper he was to type the letter in French, then in English, and make one carbon copy of each. After that he was to destroy the carbon paper, and bring the originals and the copies back to the Count for signature.

Herr Otto Guizot,
Foreign Finance Department,
Banque Commerciale de Zurich

Dear Herr Guizot,
This letter of credit authorises the transfer of two hundred thousand American dollars ($200,000) to be converted into Swiss francs at the current exchange

rate on receipt by you of this authority. All sums, less any bank charges are to be deposited in Account Number 7305.

The Count signed all copies, sealed the duplicates in an envelope, and handed it to Ozaki-san. Already wrapped in his coat and camouflaged by his influenza mask, he had left abruptly without a word. Headlights lit the windows as he was driven away.

'The man's a fool,' Louis de Boulanger had said dismissively, and told Sam to bring the box containing the currency, while he disengaged the alarm and opened the strongroom. When it was placed in the vault the Count reset the alarm and said he felt they had earned a drink.

'Whisky?' he'd suggested.

Sam knew it was far too late to go in search of Kimiko, and also realised this meeting was not yet over. He had been given access to information which no-one else on the staff possessed. Not Mademoiselle, not Laroche nor any of the senior staff. So why him?

'Cheers,' the Count said in English. 'Well done.'

'Thank you, Monsieur.'

The whisky was served in heavy crystal glasses. It was a fine malt, too strong for his taste, but a Scotch that would be spoilt by adding water. He wished now he had asked for a beer.

'I've chosen you as the person I intend to trust in matters of this kind. It's only fair I give you some details, but what I say can never be repeated. You're bound by a banking edict that forbids talk of these transactions, now or in the future. You understand?'

'Yes, sir.'

'What we did tonight, of course, is technically illegal.

You clearly know that. The bank is losing money by remaining open, but our directors in Paris look to the future, and for this reason the Tokyo branch remains. When Japan wins the war, there'll be great opportunity for expansion throughout Asia and the Pacific; those are my instructions, and that's why we remain in business. The man who came here tonight can be forgotten. He was merely acting as a messenger and the money he brought from now on belongs only to a number.'

'7305.'

'Exactly. The number is never to be mentioned outside this room. In time, there'll be other numbers and other transfers, perhaps to other Swiss banks, and your job will be to assist me, and to keep a secret record of them.'

'May I ask a question, sir?'

'I'd expect you to ask several. If I can answer, I will.'

'How is the letter of credit sent?'

'By the diplomatic bag, from our embassy here in Tokyo to Paris. And from Paris to Geneva or Zurich.'

'And the money transfer?'

'We have funds in Switzerland. The client knows Swiss francs will always remain a good currency.' He sipped his whisky with enjoyment. 'So we make money on the exchange rate, in fact on both exchange rates, and also build up a healthy balance of yen.'

'But suppose Japan loses the war...' Sam had stopped, aware of an expression. It seemed a fleeting frown, like a moment of censure, then the Count smiled, and Sam could not be sure he had seen anything.

'Japan lose? That hardly seems likely, does it?'

He had travelled home by a late, almost empty train, after retrieving his overnight case left in a locker at the station. The Count had been surprisingly frank with him; it was obvious he did not trust his senior staff at the bank. *Technically illegal*, he had said, but that was untrue. It was highly illegal and very dangerous; transfer of foreign currency was a crime, and de Boulanger had selected to use him. A lot of trust to place in his newest and youngest employee. Was he the sacrificial lamb, if anything went wrong? That seemed unlikely, for de Boulanger himself would be implicated. Was it because of his special language qualifications, or more importantly that he posed no risk of blackmail or harboured ambitions of promotion?

He had time to think about this while he lay awake much of the night. The goat was bleating softly in the yard. Perhaps pining for her kid, or hungry for newspapers. Some things, the Count had admitted, he could not reveal. One thing Sam had not divulged. He had recognised the name of the visitor – Ozaki. His mother had once gone to a party given by Prince Konoye when he was prime minister, and had met one of his private secretarial staff, Minoru Ozaki.

Konoye was a liberal Anglophile. Might such a man want to guard against the future? Could the Prince, a relative of the Emperor himself, be the Banque of Zurich's account number 7305?

'I waited where you told me,' Kimiko said. 'I waited until I was nearly frozen. Then I went to the restaurant, to ask if you had left a message. They seemed to think that I was a fool, or else perhaps a prostitute let down by a *gaijin*. There'd been no message, and they'd cancelled your reservation. Another couple had been given the table. They were sitting there, happy and smiling at each other, and I felt so angry I wanted to smash the lamp on their table, or anything.'

'Kimiko . . .' he said helplessly.

'Then I went home,' she said. 'And I had to lie to my parents because I'd told them I was going to stay with a friend here in Tokyo, and after that I couldn't sleep and was awake all night.'

'So was I,' Sam said.

'I don't care about you. I care about me. I want to know what happened, and if this was a conspiracy to make me look like a fool. Because that's what it felt like.'

'Of course it wasn't a conspiracy,' Sam said.

'Then what? Where in the name of God were you?'

'Kimiko . . .' he started to say.

'Someone said you were called to a special meeting with the Count. Is that true?'

Sam felt his whole life was in the balance. There was no way he could reveal the events of last night. What was he to tell her?

'No special meeting. He wanted to know if I'd had news of my father in Saigon. They used to be friends. Then he insisted I had drinks.'

He could feel how hollow it was, even as the words issued from his mouth. He could see Kimiko's angry disbelief. But he was sworn to secrecy, and there was simply no alternative.

'I'm sorry,' he said, and wished she had slapped his face. But all she did was shrug and walk away.

It was a dismal afternoon in keeping with his mood as he walked through sleet to the station. He had lingered hopefully at his desk, but Kimiko had returned from the cloakroom rugged up against the weather and left without a glance. Mademoiselle had smiled and wished him good night, but Laroche had stared at him with hostility.

Sam was also aware of resentment from both Ribot and the Sardine. While it was a relief to leave that malice, there was no jollity in the streets. A sense of apathy pervaded the homebound crowds. They trudged to their destinations like robots, trained to accept the dictum that austerity was now part of their lives. They endured the inconveniences with resignation; fewer trains and trams, less coal to heat their homes, food shortages and rationing, as sacrifices for the greater good. Their Emperor had declared the war was just. And Japan, after all, was winning. Amid these imposts it was doubtless a comfort to realise the battles were being fought on islands a long way off.

Yokohama, April 1943.
My dearest Florrie,
I don't know if this letter will ever reach you, and in case it does not I can mention no names, but there is a chance – a faint hope – that we can be in touch again, at least on paper, until these awful years are over. I nearly got there. If only I'd been a few days earlier, or the war a few days later – but 'if only' is the story of all our lives nowadays.

It seems ages ago now, but Father told me the truth. He told me about my mother, your sister, Catherine, and some day when we meet again I hope you will give me a photo of her. I'd like to put flowers on her grave, and perhaps we could do that together. Knowing the truth did explain so much; the way I felt when we came to

Sydney, how in the years since you became far more than a godmother, far more than a friend.

I've been afraid Australia would be invaded – this time last year it seemed certain, and the papers and radio were saying it was a matter of weeks. Now we never hear that, which seems more hopeful. We did hear about the Japanese submarines that sunk shipping in Sydney Harbour, including a ferry, and remembering you writing about how much you enjoy the ferry ride to work, I felt afraid . . .

Sam paused. He thought he heard a sound in the yard, but all was quiet again. Probably cook-san. He wanted to finish and seal the letter before his mother asked questions. In the morning it would start a long journey, first to his father in Saigon. After many months, there had finally come a letter from him, saying the request was difficult – but not impossible. He wrote that his business survived because neutral ships were still able to trade. Sam knew this meant he should send his letter via Ogawa at NYK. Once his father received it, there would eventually be a neutral ship able to trade in Australia. Maybe six months before it finally reached there.

He resumed writing, telling Florence about his work, the bank, his feelings for Kimiko, and with some details omitted, the sad debacle of their planned night together.

So it's over, my first real love affair, really before it ever began. I miss her. She's in the bank each day, sitting close to me, but there's a barrier like a brick wall between us making us both unhappy. I feel as if a part of my life is ended – perhaps the best part – when you're young and new to love, and it seems so exciting and desirable. But at twenty-one I'm sure you felt like that. And it helps me to write this. I could always tell you things that I'd never dream of telling other people – and now I understand why.

I'm so glad about Carl's release, and I hope you're happy. I can see the sand and the beach of the basin clearly in my mind, and wish I was there with you both.

All my love, Sam. (Or Samuel, if that is what my mother wanted me to be called.)

As he sealed the letter, he heard the sound again, and realised it was the murmur of voices. Intruders were trying to break into the house. He hurried to telephone the police, and bumped into a figure in the dark of the living room. It was his mother.

'For God's sake,' she said, 'be quiet.'

'What's happening?'

'We're being robbed.'

'Ma, I was about to call the police!'

'No,' she said. 'Stay still and be quiet.'

'Why?'

'Because they're stealing the goat.'

They stood at the window. As their eyes became used to the darkness they could make out the silhouettes of two men. One had a rope. He tried to throw it like a lasso, but he missed Gracie's head. She bleated, then turned and charged him. He tried to dodge, then landed with a crash as she butted him.

'Jesus Christ,' he said. The accent was Korean.

A light went on in the garden room and they heard

the cook's voice asking who was there? What did they want?

'Shut up, cook-san,' Tamara Delon muttered.

The second man held something, moving to the goat.

'It's a rolled-up newspaper,' Sam whispered.

The man waved it temptingly like a lure, and she blundered after him.

'Gracie!' Cook-san emerged from her quarters, and shouted a warning, but the goat was in eager pursuit.

'Good girl,' they heard the second burglar saying. To their astonishment, he broke into a fractured kind of English. 'Come on, baby. This is real good stuff. It's the *New York Times*.'

The goat went charging after him, as if responsive to this invitation. As they disappeared out the gate, the first man tried to climb to his feet. The cook reached him. She gave a strange karate shout, then kicked him between the legs and he collapsed in a heap.

'Oh God,' he moaned, 'oh fuck.'

Cook-san kicked him again, harder this time, relishing it.

Tamara opened the window. 'Stop it, you stupid woman.'

'But they're trying to steal Gracie,' cook-san replied.

'Good. Go back to bed and stop hurting him.'

In the morning, the goat was gone. The yard was empty.

It was the way Sam was to feel a few days later.

Empty.

The note was on his desk. He began to read it, before he realised Kimiko's desk was cleared and vacant.

Dear Sam, she had written, *I don't know why you*

changed your mind and let me down. I've found another job, and it'll be easier for us both not to have to sit together and pretend. Good luck and goodbye. Kimiko.

CHAPTER 15

It was a warm weekend, and would soon be summer again. The beach was crowded. Flags erected on the sand denoted the safe area patrolled by lifesavers, but out beyond the surf a bunch of swimmers ignored this, disregarding the whistle blown by a beach inspector, until his angry gestures finally induced them to swim away from a dangerous undertow, and join the crowd between the flags.

'Stupid bastards,' he said to no-one in particular, but Florence, passing, heard and smiled agreement. She wore a dirndl skirt, and was barefoot, carrying her sandals and a basket with her shopping. *Nice looking woman*, the inspector thought, and went back to his other task, which was to make sure none of the sun-kissed girls wore swimming costumes which trespassed beyond the bounds of decency. The girls, in the daring new two-piece bathing suits, were spreadeagled on beach towels, gleaming with oil as they tanned their slim young bodies for the coming holiday season.

Brown was beautiful; it was sexy. All the magazines said so.

She walked along the firm, wet sand on her way home. There were children earnestly shaping sandcastles, reminding her of the structures she and Sam had built when he was ten. Young men were throwing footballs, wrestling, turning cartwheels, showing off when not clustered hopefully around the oiled and sunbaking girls. It was sometimes difficult to believe that in other parts of the world a ferocious war was being fought. Quite different now to the fear that had swept the country the previous year, when the Japanese had surged southward and Australia had prepared for invasion.

Florence remembered vividly the night Mr Cusack had died, when the midget subs had shattered the calm of Sydney Harbour. And a week later, the headlines when the submarine surfaced and shelled the rich harbourside suburbs. Not forgetting the amusement as many of the wealthy loaded up their furniture and fled their mansions. *Nothing like a war*, she thought, *to sort out the peculiar Australian egalitarian sense of humour. Or the strange concordat of men who fought each other.* For the recovered bodies of the Japanese submariners had been buried with full military honours.

The fear of twelve months ago had eased, but was not fully dispelled. Darwin was being constantly bombed, a virtual shell after so many raids. There had been air attacks on Townsville and other northern towns. The Japanese occupied much of New Guinea, Borneo and all the strategic islands. They held Asia in an iron grip. The Australian infantry were fighting them on the Kokoda Trail, once turning them back only thirty miles from Port Moresby.

With the passing months, some of the extreme tension

in Australia had begun to ease. The invasion had seemed so inevitable – a logical next step – but the Japanese had paused. Everyone had a theory, but no-one was quite sure why. Carl had suggested the very size, the immensity of the country might have unnerved them. He thought the vastness of the north and the arid centre had been considered unworthy of the effort; the richer prizes of Sydney and Melbourne, and the fertile lands in the southern half of the continent would have risked extending their supply lines too far. They had lost ships in the Battle of the Coral Sea, and were perhaps nervous of becoming exposed and vulnerable.

Whatever the answer, the threat of 1942 was now a distant memory. Even the wealthy, who had so hurriedly evacuated their waterfronts for the safety of the mountains, were contemplating a return. And the beaches, like this one, were crowded as Florence made her way past the rock pool and around the headland to the peaceful crescent where her home faced the sea.

Carl was at the office, working. So often now he spent Saturdays at the office. *He works much too hard*, she thought; in a great many ways he was still European, and had never adapted to the local tenet that the weekend was sacrosanct, reserved for sport, for meetings at the pub or parties. All the offices, banks and postal services shut promptly on Friday afternoons, the shops at noon on Saturdays, and apart from milk bars and a few Greek-owned fruit shops, nothing reopened until Monday mornings. Which reminded her that she had not checked the postbox on their return from town the previous night.

There was only one letter, in a handwriting she did not recognise. She opened it, and inside was another envelope, and inside that a long letter with familiar handwriting that made her gasp with disbelief. She ran into the house, left the groceries in their bag, and sat down to read it, hoping to find out how Sam had managed to achieve this miracle.

Three months later, early in the new year, a letter was brought to the house on The Bluff by a sailor from a Swedish ship. The cargo vessel had been carrying freight to ports in Asia, protected by its neutrality, and the letter was from Saigon. Tamara Delon was the only one at home when the seaman arrived, and she instantly recognised the handwriting as that of her former husband. She invited the sailor to have a drink, thanked him for his time and trouble in bringing it, and waited until he had gone.

The letter was addressed to Sam. Despite this, extremely curious about the strange manner of its arrival, she opened it. Inside there was another envelope addressed to Henri's Saigon office in a hand she did not recognise. She decided to open that as well.

The Count de Boulanger was in a buoyant mood. A cable had come in the diplomatic bag, delivered from the French Embassy by special messenger. It was from Herr Guizot in Zurich, confirming that all transactions since October 1943 were now successfully completed.

The information came as a considerable relief. He would advise all his clients. Sam would write letters of verification quoting only the number of their accounts to ensure privacy. Once this was done, he would hand deliver the letters himself; it was true that Sam knew many of their names, but the illusion of secrecy was paramount and must be preserved for the clients. It was banking protocol.

Among those clients were politicians and industrialists, eminent people who would be relieved the matter had been finalised. Prince Konoye would be pleased. When he thought of the Prince, he wondered – not for the first time – if Sam realised that twice in the past year they had moved money for a close relative of Konoye's to account number 7305 in Zurich. He hoped not; it was vital Konoye and the contacts he provided did not feel threatened.

The Prince was by far his most important patron in the upper echelons of power and the wealthy elite. These were difficult spheres for any foreigner to penetrate; Japanese society had an intricate class system as tribal and clannish as the English, or indeed the French. It was a complex world, and Konoye had proved to be an ally without whom the Count would not be trusted in these circles.

Only recently, the Prince had given two introductions, and two senior politicians had been credited with enough Swiss francs to ensure their future comfort, no matter how the war should end. The two had reservations about the outcome, this was apparent, and being a shrewd banker de Boulanger had seized the advantage and raised the exchange rate. As a result, the French Bank had enjoyed a handsome profit.

Although he never expressed it, the Count was more sanguine than his clients about the future. He believed Japan and her Axis partners would win. While conceding 1943 had not seen the victories of the previous year, it was unrealistic to imagine the initial triumphs could continue at such a spectacular pace.

There had simply been a pause.

The Battle of Midway had not been a success, and the Australians had been surprisingly tenacious in New Guinea. But this was the ebb and flow of combat. More importantly it was being waged far from Japan. Cities remained immune from attack; industrial centres were able to keep up production. This was vital, for the powerhouse of the country, the firms that once made automobiles, toys, or electrical goods, now built the essentials of war: planes, guns and battleships.

There was also the German factor. Hitler still controlled Western Europe. Once he defeated Britain, he would make a pact to neutralise America; then Japan would have a huge and powerful ally. But these were thoughts the Count kept carefully in his own mind. No-one knew of his sentiments, not Moustique, certainly not Sam, who had proved such an asset. De Boulanger was sure – that like his father – Sam would be anti-fascist and hopeful of an Allied victory. So while they were unlikely associates in the matter of keeping the bank alive, sharing the danger, they were in fact on opposite sides. For this reason, the Count was always prudently non-political.

He sent a discreet message for Sam to join him when the bank shut, and arranged for food and coffee. The Minister for War was expected, and they would be working late.

In fact it was almost eleven-thirty when Sam concluded the necessary paperwork. The Minister had a surprisingly large amount of cash he wished to transfer to Switzerland. He had eaten well, refused coffee, asked for whisky, and punctuated the evening with nervous questions about the safety of this small and frail country, surrounded by the

European war. Sam heard the Count placating him, declaring Switzerland would exist as long as people had money to invest.

He means money to hide, Sam thought, but was enmeshed so deeply in these transactions now, he had no choice but to continue. Some occasions were worse than others. The Minister was a greedy and heartless man, encouraging brutality in his troops while busily ensuring he had enough money if the war should end badly for him.

When Sam finally reached Yokohama and pulled up outside his home – the Count had arranged a hire car because of the late hour – he saw there were lights still on inside. His mother was sitting waiting for him. She handed him an opened letter, which he saw at once was from Florrie.

'Tell me how this happened,' she said, and he had never heard her voice so cold or so bitter.

Collaroy, November 1943.
My dearest Sam,
What a surprise, what a joy to receive your letter. How you did it I cannot tell, but you-know-who sent me the name of a neutral ship, and told me to be sure to give my reply to a member of the crew whom he could trust. I'd better not name the man in case this is intercepted, but with luck it will reach our mutual friend, and hopefully soon after that will reach you. Apart from actually meeting again, the next best thing is expressing our thoughts on paper in a meeting of our minds, and how beautifully you do that. It cheered me up so much, I can hardly tell you how thrilled I was.

Catherine would be proud of you. I know I am. I will

treasure the day we can go together and put flowers on her grave. She is buried in a place called the Waverley cemetery that overlooks the ocean, on a peaceful headland, and I go there twice a year to tend the ground and try to say a prayer. I read about your sweet love affair, that never really was one, and felt sad for you and for your now-vanished Kimiko. Yes, I did have such feelings when I was young and new to love, and I'm glad you told me. I'm always here for you to tell me anything you wish. Always, you know that. Carl says he feels he knows you. You'll meet one day, and like each other.

My dear, I may be stupidly optimistic, but I feel the worst of this awful war is over. I know it will take longer, but I think we are safe now from invasion, and you and I will survive, and meet again. I even believe somehow this letter will reach you. It is desperately important to me that it does.
With all my fondest love, Florrie.

Sam finished the letter and looked across the room. His mother's lips were compressed, her eyes angry. He knew she had been drinking, but tried to understand how she felt.

'I shouldn't have opened it,' she said. 'But a sailor brings it. That's strange, I think. Your father's writing on the envelope, and inside is this other letter, so I think to myself what does it all mean? Who is it from? Unfortunately, now I know.'

'Why is it unfortunate, Mama?'

'You still believe you should call me by that name?'

'Why not? As far as I'm concerned you're my mother. Someone else gave birth to me, but you became my mother. I'd like it to stay that way.'

He saw a hint of surprise begin to soften her anger.

'Do you really mean that?'

'Of course.'

'Does Angelique know?'

'Certainly not. And won't, as far as I'm concerned.'

'When I adopted you, we made a pact you'd never know. I won't ever forgive Florence for telling you.'

'She didn't,' Sam said. 'I've known since before the war. Since I went to Karuizawa, with Papa.'

'The bastard,' his mother said, shocked.

'He did it for a special reason,' Sam started to explain, but she gestured for him not to bother with explanations, dismissing her ex-husband as irrelevant.

'Forget him,' she said, 'reason or not, he's still a bastard. Him and all his women – including Catherine. The bastard wanted her to have an abortion. I'll bet he didn't tell you that!'

Sam decided to say nothing. He gave a shake of his head, which could've been a reply, or a repelled reaction to this fact.

'But what I don't understand is you,' she said, puzzled. 'All this time – over two years – and you never spoke about it.'

'And never intended to. That was how you wanted it; I was more than happy for it to stay like that.'

She gave a melancholic Russian sigh. Sam suppressed a smile of relief. It was a sign that the worst was over.

'I'm so foolish. Stupid to open the letter,' she said, then, typically, rebuked him: 'You tell her lots of things you don't tell me. Sweet love affair with this Kimiko, hey? You told me she's fat.'

'Only to shut Angelique up,' he said, trying to be tactful. 'But perhaps I do tell Florrie things in letters, Mama, special things that I sometimes can't talk about.'

'Hmph,' she said, 'I can't see why. You can tell me any troubles or problems – or love affairs. Anything you want.'

And the next day all your friends will know, he thought, but didn't express it. Instead he put his arms around her.

'Look, she's far away, and at times I need to put down on paper what I feel. Besides, she's my real aunt, and I like her.'

'So you'll go on writing more letters?'

'If I can.'

'You never stop to think it might be dangerous?'

'Yes, I often think that,' he said.

There was a strange message on Florence's desk when she returned from taking documents to the court. She went in to see Mr Noble, who was now the sole partner, ever since Mr Cusack's death. The firm was not the same any more, nowhere near as friendly, and Carl had discussed the idea of looking for another job, for it was clear, no matter how hard he worked, that Arthur Noble would never agree to make him a partner.

'This note says you wish to see me, Mr Noble. Something to do with the Swiss Consulate?'

'Yes, what the devil is this, Flo?'

She disliked being called Flo and had tried to tell him, but Mr Noble was not the kind of man to let a detail like that bother him.

'I don't know anything about the Swiss Consulate.'

'Well, they seem to know you. A Mr Joubert phoned, and that stupid new typist put it straight through to me. Before I can say Gruyère cheese, he's telling me there's a letter for you to collect, and you must sign for it. Confounded man talking to me as if *I'm* here to take messages for *you*.'

Florence suppressed a smile. Mr Noble would not have enjoyed that. A *letter*, she thought, wondering if it were possible? Surely not, but . . . who else? Perhaps it was bad news. She began to feel a chill of fear. 'May I phone Mr Joubert, and arrange to collect it this afternoon? I'll naturally make up the time by working later than usual.'

'That would be most inconvenient. I told him you'd go tomorrow in your lunch hour. We don't employ staff to pick up their mail at the whim of a foreigner, and I'm not aware you know anyone in Switzerland so he may have the wrong person.' Mr Noble nodded an abrupt dismissal which was a serious mistake.

'I'm sorry,' Florence said, 'but since the gentleman has been kind enough to advise me of this, the least I can do is collect it. That would only be courteous. But courtesy is not something with which you're closely acquainted, Mr Noble. So I'll go there now, and take this opportunity to give you notice that I'll be leaving at the end of the month.'

'But Flo . . .' Noble said, 'steady on, girl. Don't be stupid. You're a part of this firm.'

'Indeed I am. Like the faded carpet, and the calcimine on the walls. All in need of a change, like I am. So I'm off.'

'You can't leave us,' Mr Noble said. 'At your age you'll have absolutely nowhere to go.'

Neither of them was aware of Carl at the doorway, until he spoke. 'At her age,' he said, 'she's in the very prime of her life. She is not only bright and attractive, but so intelligent that half the law firms in town will bid for her services. If I'm lucky, they might take a journeyman lawyer like me, because they want her so badly.'

'Now look here . . .' Mr Noble began to say, but all he saw was his middle-aged secretary turning to smile at the German chap as if there were no-one else in the room. Then – seeming to remember he was there – they nodded politely and left together. Hand in hand, he noticed, and thought it extraordinary.

It was addressed to her, care of the Swiss Consul, Sydney, Australia. Mr Joubert told her it had come with an explanatory note from the sender; that Mrs Florence Eisler of Cusack & Noble, Solicitors, was handling delicate financial matters for him, and would they be kind enough to contact her and pass on the enclosed letter.

Whether Mr Joubert believed this or not hardly seemed to matter. He was very correct and polite. If there should be any future correspondence from her client, he would advise her.

'He's actually a relative, as well as my client,' she said, for there could be no doubt who had sent it, and his cheek and guile made her want to laugh, but she mustn't. This had reached her under the guise of a business communication, and the Swiss never joked about matters of business. She told Mr Joubert she may be joining a new firm; she would let him know where he might reach her, in case her client had other matters he wished to raise. Mr Joubert bowed over her hand, and said it was a pleasure.

Carl chuckled with delight when she told him.

'Wonderful!' he enthused. 'I can hardly wait to meet this young man. He's realised the most sacred things to the Swiss are privacy and financial trust. The sanctity of secret money transactions is their main contribution to the world. That,' he added thoughtfully, 'and the cuckoo clock.'

Florrie smiled and hugged him.

Yokohama, March 1944.
My dear Florrie,

I've found a new way to send a letter to you, which I prefer as it does not endanger my father, and is hopefully quicker than us waiting on neutral cargo boats. The only problem is, you can't write back, at least until I can fathom a way. So expect a letter from me, I hope, every few months, and save all your replies till we meet. This goes in the diplomatic bag to Geneva, and from there – if I know the Swiss devotion to compliance and convention – it will be sent to the consul in Sydney. We have occasional reason to send letters via Geneva or Zurich, and since I handle this, it is not difficult for me to drop a letter into the sacrosanct bag in which so many secrets are sent.

By the time you get this, it may be June or July. Here at present it is cherry blossom time, and not even a war can spoil the beauty of that. We are going to our summerhouse in Karuizawa this year for the first time since the war began. It's a place I've always loved, high up in the hills, full of people we know. Once we used to go there every summer. Angelique still cannot get work, so she and Mama will stay until late August, but I'll have to go back to work at the bank. I'm glad to say we hear occasional outside news, as some embassies have shortwave radio sets. They are protected by diplomatic immunity, so we can hear the truth, not the propaganda put out by the government to the sound of martial music. We hear the Germans almost got to Moscow, but are now retreating; that there is talk of a second front, which would mean an invasion to free France across the channel. I often think it, but I'll say it to you. Vive la France!

Censorship here is really tight, and it is often difficult for most people to interpret what is happening in the outside world. Because there are no air raids, they are convinced the war is being won. The Japanese have learned from the Nazis to fill the cinema screens and newspapers with phrases that reassure people. 'Military Gods' and 'The Sacred War' have become popular slogans. There are new movies with graphic scenes from planes swooping to attack the American fleet at Pearl Harbour, so vivid the audience feel as if they are in the cockpit with the pilots. Even the newsreels, which were always popular, now try to make everything more exciting by using the music of Wagner. The wretched Doctor Goebbels has well and truly spread his tentacles here!

But it's easy to influence the Japanese people. The war is still remote, still being fought on unknown Pacific islands. They think they will never hear a shot fired or a bomb dropped. It seems unreal, but apart from one fleeting air raid by planes from some aircraft carriers two years ago, which shocked people but did no real damage, no enemy plane has flown over Japan. Most people here believe they never will.

What else? Oh yes – imagine this! A new government edict has banned dancing because it is considered a depraved Western practice!

My only other news is that I think I'm finally in love. Her name is Justine Fournier, and her father is head of Chancellery at the French Embassy. The only problem is, he and his wife don't think I'm good enough. Fortunately Justine is not of the same opinion – so far. Mind you, she's very beautiful and most of the males – including the happily marrieds! – have lecherous ambitions. But I remain hopeful!

My best wishes to Carl, and as always my fondest love to you.
Sam.

CHAPTER 16

Karuizawa seemed an illusion, as if the war did not exist. The town was packed with visitors, the winding lanes lively with the ring of bicycle bells. It had always displayed the visage of a European resort, more like an alpine village than a town two hours train travel from Tokyo. Sixty years earlier, a British scholar had come on a walking tour to study the ancient Nagano road used by feudal lords, and stayed to build the first cottage. Over the years, other foreigners living and working in the East had erected holiday homes and made it their haven. In the summer of 1944, with the world being torn apart, it felt tranquil and unreal.

There were changes, Sam realised. Some of the houses he'd known since childhood had different owners, but not by choice. After the outbreak of war, homes belonging to families now interned were confiscated then leased or sold to wealthy Japanese or Germans. Many of the latter were Nazis working for their government in Hong Kong, Manila and Singapore, who had been liberated on

Japan's march south. Unable to return home, Berlin ordered their embassy to pay them an allowance which permitted them to live in comfort, with the added status of being allies. Sam had heard some of the Germans express the hope the war would continue indefinitely; they had rarely enjoyed such luxury.

It was early June when he and his family came to their cottage in Karuizawa. They had sent word to a local farmer who acted as caretaker, and he ensured one of his daughters aired and cleaned the rooms so the house was ready for their arrival. It was the same all over town as the visitors came by train, unpacked and oiled their bikes, pumped their tyres; some to cycle through the lanes and call on friends, others to visit the stables and book horses, or reserve courts at the tennis club.

Sam rode into the town and past the English bookshop with its sign: CLOSED FOR THE DURATION. He put his name down for the tennis tournament, noting that among the entries was Jacques Clermont. He wondered if Mademoiselle might be coming to Karuizawa, but she had given no hint of it. Besides, much as he liked her, he wanted to entirely forget the bank. He had requested and been granted three weeks leave. He wished he could spend all summer here, but even a brief vacation from the tension at work was a relief. For it was becoming very tense indeed.

From town, he rode towards the *Hanare Yama* golf club. A picturesque course, it was rarely used since the government had decreed golf a corrupt foreign sport. But the French Ambassador, his neighbour Pierre Fournier, and other keen players had prevailed on the greenkeeper to remain, and paid his wages. It was Fournier's house near the links that Sam was cycling past

– not to encounter the head of Chancellery – but in the hope of seeing his daughter, Justine.

They had shared a birthday party when they were nine years old, being the same age and born only a week apart. Justine had been small and tubby with a squeaky voice and unruly hair. Sam hated their sharing a birthday, and suffered from his friends calling them twins and making fun of her. But since then, astonishing things had happened to Justine Fournier. She had grown tall and slim; the squeaky voice had been replaced by modulation, the unruly hair was a soft wavy blonde. Quite simply, Justine had been transformed into gorgeous, and the friends who had mocked then were now envious of Sam, who seemed to have been accepted as her current boyfriend. It was a status he hoped to consolidate, aware of the intense competition and the speculative eyes that admired her.

Their villa was closed and shuttered. Sam circled it, but nothing happened apart from the rotund figure of the Ambassador emerging from his adjacent house. He stared at the bicycle with suspicion, then recognising Sam called, 'She'll be here next week.'

God, am I that obvious, Sam thought. He waved, then rode home. While he did, his thoughts returned to the problem that troubled him in the French Bank; the jealousy, which had been simmering for the past months, was daily becoming more visible.

The Count de Boulanger seemed sublimely unaware, or else indifferent to the resentment of his senior staff at the way a junior appeared to have displaced them. They were unused to this. In their opinion, young men of Sam's age were there to wait until their elders assigned them suitable tasks; attending to the filing, or running messages. No decent bank would tolerate their being excluded in favour of this twenty-two year old!

Sam knew of their envy. It was difficult not to be aware of it. What upset them was the realisation he alone worked with the Count on matters euphemistically known as 'overseas transactions'. What these were, they might surmise – and frequently did – but dared not speculate aloud. Having to accept that a junior had the Count's confidence was a recurring humiliation. Even the ritual morning greetings were now distant and constrained.

Andre Ribot was the most resentful. Since the abrupt departure of Kimiko, he had become increasingly malicious. It was well over a year since her leaving, but the antipathy had intensified. Ribot and Roland Sardaigne – the Sardine – were constantly trying to find fault with their junior clerk's work. Sam realised the situation was coming to a head. He had no idea where it might end, but it would be a welcome respite to have a holiday from the rapidly poisoning atmosphere.

Jacques Clermont easily won the tennis final. Prominent among the spectators was an attractive blonde, who applauded his every winning shot. She was the object of speculation, for local gossip had established he had arrived with her for the tournament, and they occupied connecting rooms in the deluxe wing of the hotel.

Poor Cecile, Sam thought, and wondered how, in their small community, no-one knew he had a working wife to keep him in a style like this. He reflected they must have private means, for her wages would hardly pay for the blonde, let alone the rooms. Then he recalled Kimiko saying the family had made Clermont an allowance.

'I might as well get up and tiptoe away. You wouldn't even notice.' He turned guiltily at the sound of Justine's voice beside him.

'Sorry,' Sam said, 'I was thinking...'

'I could tell. You were miles away. Thinking of what?'

'That even if I hadn't ricked my ankle, I couldn't have beaten Jacques. Not the way he played today.'

'Nobody can beat him,' Justine said, 'which proves you were miles away, because that's what I just said.'

'Oh, did you?'

'He'd qualify for Wimbledon, if it hadn't been cancelled.'

'He's not that good,' Sam retorted.

'Some of us think he is,' she smiled. 'Jealous?'

'Of course not.'

'Who's the blonde? Do you think it's his wife?'

'I doubt it,' Sam said carefully.

'He has a wife.'

'Who told you?'

'I forget,' she shrugged. 'She's supposed to be mousy, not a bit like Jackie-boy. A few years older. So it's not the blonde.'

'Listen,' he said, anxious to end this, 'I've booked a table at the Mampei for a farewell dinner tonight. I leave tomorrow.'

'But don't you think it's strange?' Justine persisted.

'What's strange?'

'A wife none of us knows. Does he keep her hidden?'

'I've had enough of Jacques. Let's talk about us.'

'You don't like him, do you? Honestly, I can't think why. He's good fun – and quite good-looking.'

'You'll have to elbow that blonde out of the way, if you have ambitions there. I doubt if she'll go quietly.'

'Me and Jackie? Sam, you say the oddest things. They must be overworking you. You've become quite peculiar.'

'Too peculiar for dinner tonight?'

'No, not that peculiar.' They exchanged smiles, and

she took his arm. 'Even Daddy will approve of the Mampei restaurant.'

'Provided I bring you straight home.'

'He's only protecting me.'

'From me?'

'From anyone.'

'Especially me. He's a bloodhound. As for us ever getting alone together ... properly alone, and properly together ...'

'We'll get a chance.'

'Not this year. We'll soon be too old to care.'

Justine laughed, then said softly: 'We'd have found a way, if you'd stayed longer. I wish you weren't leaving so soon.'

'So do I.'

'Can't you stay, even a few more days?'

'I'd lose my job.'

'That damn bank. Don't you hate it?'

'Only sometimes,' Sam said. 'Particularly now.'

He particularly hated the bogus charade of morning greetings on his first day back, and the senior staff so artificially polite. Andre Ribot, with a fleeting smile that seemed to cause him pain, it was so acidic; the Sardine saying stiffly how quickly time passed, as if by implication wishing Sam had remained away longer; Claude Laroche, giving a brusque *Bonjour*, accompanied by a forceful handshake. Laroche shook hands as though the gesture were a personal test of strength, and enjoyed making his adversary wince. Sam hardly noticed. In his mind was the grubby image of the chief accountant in pursuit of Kimiko, his hands taking every opportunity to fondle her.

He exchanged bows with the Japanese staff, the oldest of whom expressed a hope that the mountain air had been beneficial. He had never had the pleasure of journeying to Karuizawa, but had heard it was a fine place, much enjoyed by the foreign community. Sam felt grateful for his old-fashioned sincerity, then saw Mademoiselle Patou emerge from her office to meet him.

'Sam,' she said, 'welcome back. How's your ankle?'

He didn't ask how she knew. Her husband doubtless kept in touch by phone, to make sure she was safely in her place.

'Better thanks, Mademoiselle.' He thought it prudent to elaborate. 'I ricked it playing tennis. Had to concede the match.'

'Yes, I heard. Someone told me, I forget who.'

He dismissed it with a change of subject. 'It was a good holiday. I envy my sister and mother. They're staying on.'

'Lucky them. I believe the weather was perfect.'

'Wonderful. Warm sunny days, cool nights.'

'Sounds heavenly,' she said. 'The Count's due at ten. He wants to see you, as soon as he arrives.'

She turned and moved away, a small trim figure, her high heels clicking on the marble floor. *An elegant sparrow*, Sam had thought when they first met. *A wounded sparrow*, he now realised.

'Mademoiselle,' he said impulsively, and she stopped and turned, inquiringly. For a precarious moment he wanted to blurt out the truth about Jacques and the blonde, but sanity returned. 'I'd like to tell you how well you look.' She was gazing in astonishment, and he improvised rapidly. 'I mean, you always made me feel welcome here. Right from the start. The day I was so early, remember?'

'Indeed I do. You were keen. It's no fault to be keen.'

'Anyway, you really do look well, so I just wanted to say so. I hope you don't mind.'

'Thank you, Sam,' she said, so softly he could barely hear. 'I don't mind. Thank you very much.'

He wondered if he was imagining it, or if she was walking more briskly towards her office. Imagination, he decided, because his first thought had been that she was upset and about to cry.

The Count appeared to be in an expansive mood. After he ordered coffee, he said there were urgent matters that had arisen during the past few weeks, requiring instant attention. Sam knew this meant currency transactions to Switzerland, and there would be some late nights ahead for them both. What he was not expecting was the Count's next words.

'Things are changing. Normal daily business across the counter is decreasing every month, and will do so until the war ends. I've been forced to contemplate staff changes. Redundancies, I'm afraid.' He looked at Sam. 'Not you. They'll be announced in due course, but rest assured you won't be one of them.'

Sam wanted to ask about Mademoiselle, but the servant brought in their coffee. By then he had decided it would be unwise to say anything. The Count studied him carefully, and after the servant left, asked what was troubling him.

'Nothing,' Sam said.

'Come on,' the Count said. 'We know each other better than that. What's the problem?'

'Mademoiselle Patou? She won't be made redundant, will she? It's none of my business, Monsieur Le Comte, but . . .'

'You're quite right, it isn't your business,' the other said, 'although I have to wonder why you asked?'

'No particular reason,' Sam replied.

'That won't do, Sam.'

'I worry about her.'

'I see.'

The Count was very thoughtful. Sam took refuge in a gulp of coffee, and wished he hadn't. His mouth felt scalded.

'Do you know something you're not telling me?'

'I just like her, and hope she won't lose her job.'

'She won't lose her job. Now I think you'd better be honest. How much do you know about her domestic situation?'

'Quite a lot,' said Sam, after a pause.

'Who else realises it, here in the bank?'

'No-one, as far as I know,' he was able to truthfully say.

'Is Mademoiselle aware that you know?'

'No, sir.'

'Well,' he took a careful sip of his coffee, 'that seems to dispose of the matter. She's had a rotten life – she's a most capable secretary, and we both like her. Can we leave it at that?' Sam nodded and the Count said, 'Now, if I may continue with what I intended to say . . .'

'I apologise for interrupting, Monsieur.'

'What I was going to say,' a steely gaze warned him not to interrupt again, 'is that it sometimes takes an absence to establish a person's worth. I've been conscious during the past three weeks of how much I depend on your assistance. The work you and I do is keeping this bank viable. So, as I'm proposing to cut our costs, I've been considering the matter of your remuneration. That's the word you like to use, isn't it? Remuneration?'

Oh God, Sam thought, *this is what it's all about. Stay on at a reduced salary. Just when I know Mama is starting to run out of money, and Angelique still can't get a job.*

'I'm planning to give you an increase.'

'I beg your pardon?'

'Anything wrong with your hearing? I said an increase. I think, for all the additional work you do – a hundred and fifty yen a month seems more reasonable.'

Sam blinked. He opened his mouth to express gratitude, but the Count forestalled this. He gestured to the door, and said he now had less agreeable matters that required his attention.

Redundancies among the staff included two of the older Japanese clerks, a typist and a teller. Sam's relief at his survival and salary rise was tempered by regret at these dismissals, but he had no regret at the main casualty among the senior staff. Roland Sardaigne was told the bank no longer required his services. He was given a final payment and a reference, but departed a bitter man, declaring the payment was contemptible and the reference useless, for how could he get another job in Japan? He couldn't speak the bloody language, and the only place he was qualified to work was in the French Bank. The Count had destroyed his life, he angrily announced to anyone who cared to listen. His wife would feel humiliated.

Some of the typists said loudly that the Sardine had not mentioned a wife, when he had pestered, pleaded and even offered to pay them to sleep with him.

Carl went out early on Sundays to buy the papers at the corner shop in Pittwater Road. Florence was making breakfast, trying to pretend that the pale tea in her cup was preferable to the bilious liquid coffee that her husband so disliked, and which the increasing thousands of American troops had called the Aussie revenge for winning so many of their girls. The Americans meanwhile bought up all genuine coffee on the black market as well as importing coffee beans from the United States and announced they were all right, Jack!

It did not endear them to all the local populace.

Meat rationing had been introduced, and furious letters to the newspapers castigated the government, asserting that with such vast quantities of sheep and cattle, this was simply an unnecessary assault on the Australian working man – who could not perform a proper day's labour without a decent breakfast of chops or steak.

Florrie enjoyed the letters to the papers, reduced in number because of the newsprint shortage, and felt they were required reading. Many of them were so determinedly eccentric. With the introduction of tea rationing, there had been a proliferation of ideas for substitutes, everything from the branches of ti-trees – apparently tried by the early settlers – to the use of maidenhair fern. It was, she decided, a mind-boggling idea, which she had decided not to adopt.

'I'm afraid the tea is like dishwater,' she said, as Carl returned from the shop. 'Where's the paper?'

'Banned,' he said.

'What?'

'According to the newsagent. The *Telegraph* has been seized at gunpoint by the Commonwealth police.'

'You're joking.'

'Darling, I never joke about the Commonwealth police. It seems a story about a miners' strike was censored, so the paper was printed with half the front page blank to demonstrate this, and in the middle of the blank space, there was a quote from Thomas Jefferson beneath a photo of Mr Caldwell, the information minister.'

They both knew Caldwell had infuriated the press by a series of suppression orders issued almost daily. Any story he considered against the national interest was instantly censored.

'What did it say, this quote from Jefferson?'

'It said: *Where the press is free and every man able to read, all is safe.*'

She smiled approval. 'I wonder what Caldwell will say?'

They soon found out. The following day, all newspapers were seized by armed Commonwealth police in Sydney, Melbourne and Adelaide; they were forbidden to be sold because they had printed a reproduction of the *Telegraph*'s rebellion. In Sydney, crowds scrambled for copies of the *Sun* and *Mirror*, thrown from windows by journalists, as police with drawn revolvers were photographed preventing truck drivers from removing papers from the loading dock.

Thousands of university students led a protest march; the miners renewed their strike. The press proprietors rushed an appeal to the High Court, where they won a marginal victory. What the army fighting in New Guinea said was not quoted.

The uproar was swiftly overtaken, when Japanese in the Cowra prisoner-of-war camp, armed with homemade weapons – baseball bats, kitchen knives and staves – set fire to their huts and ran through a hail of machine-gun fire in a violent attempt to escape. A number of guards were killed, and almost three hundred Japanese died in the mass breakout. Four hundred found brief freedom but were caught within weeks.

The news of the event made headlines, but readers

were informed that under international agreement, an official report to the enemy country must be made before the full details of the escape could be published.

Carl shook his head when he read it. He thought one side was fighting with words, the other with swords. Would the Japanese security police behave like this?

Major Ito was becoming impatient. He did not like his informant, and having to spend all this time sitting in a car with him was not his choice of a way to spend an evening. It was late and growing cold. His report that the target was back from the mountain village and at work in the bank, could hardly be incorrect. Unless this reptile who wanted payment for his information was lying, but that was unlikely. He and everyone else knew the penalty for misleading the Kempetai. His driver in the front seat was fidgeting; Ito snapped at him.

'What's the matter?'

'It's getting cold, Major.'

'I'll be the one who decides if it's cold or not. How can it be cold if it's still summer time?'

'Yes, sir. Sorry, sir,' the driver said hastily, wondering why it was his misfortune to be on roster tonight with this bastard.

Ito thought he would wait another five minutes, and then abandon the foray. It was almost midnight, and ridiculous to still be optimistic. Either his quarry was tucked up in bed with a bar girl, or else in Karuizawa. He would have the intelligence officer's balls, if the latter were true.

Perhaps he should remain longer, even another half hour. No point in allowing the driver to think he'd had any influence on aborting the surveillance. He would post a man at the house to make the arrest, but he had dearly wanted to be there himself. To relish the moment of recognition. So many arrests brought the same panicked query from the victim: what charge? Ito always enjoyed giving them his favourite answer: that the Kempetai did not need a charge when it was a matter of state security. It never failed to put a sense of dread into all those who heard it.

Major Ito vividly remembered the last meeting with the suspect, although it was two and a half years ago. The war had just begun. Ever since then, he had been convinced the boy had made a fool of him; had lied, politely, deftly, had mocked him and taken the initiative when Ito had asked a question in English and the young smart-arse had replied in fluent and perfect Japanese. It would not happen like that this time.

But it was a bitterly cold night; despite his assertion that it was summer, the days had been cool, the nights unseasonably cold. It was pointless to stay longer, and he was about to say so when they saw the lights of a limousine turn into the street and stop outside the house.

Sam had rarely been home at a normal hour since his return to work. Each afternoon when the bank shut, he and the Count had either met to prepare for the arrival of a client, or worked on private ledgers which no-one else, even the chief accountant, was allowed to view. On varying nights they had met with industrialists, or a secretary to the Cabinet; each time large currency transfers had been arranged.

Sam had taken the majority of envelopes with these details to the French Embassy to be forwarded to Zurich, but one transaction went via the Swiss legation. Aware he would be going there with a delivery for the diplomatic bag, he had prepared for it by writing another letter to Florence. It would be the third he had sent this way. The previous one had been brief, telling her about the night his mother had found out, and how they had reached an accord. She may not have received it yet. This one was more effusive, full of his time in the mountain, excursions with Justine, and news of the war . . .

We were thrilled to hear, via an illicit radio, of D-day. An event as momentous as that could not be hidden entirely, but the Ministry of Information did its best. 'A futile effort to invade France was made by the Americans and British, and repulsed by the German army,' was one local radio report, and newspapers predicted huge losses would lead to retreat and disaster. They called them ill-trained, unwilling soldiers – forced to board invasion barges by their brutal commanders.

If anyone is brutal, it's the Japanese military. Especially the officers. My best friend, Claude Briand, who has a job as interpreter for a French film crew, says the officers are trained to hate – they're like savage dogs – and even looking at them and making eye contact can be dangerous. Claude speaks from bitter experience, as he bumped into a high-ranking officer by accident. It was a colonel who swore at him, then drew his sword. Claude tried to apologise – changed his mind and decided to run for it. The colonel gave chase, but had no chance. Claude was a track star at school. But they're vicious, and beat their own troops mercilessly. It's considered to be training. What it trains the ordinary soldiers to do is be aggressive and shout and order civilians about, keen to try to impress by imitating their brutish officers.

I know you can't write back and warn me to be careful, but don't worry. I promise not to bump into any officers. It's only August here, but as this will take ages via Switzerland, and I never know exactly how long, I might as well say Merry Christmas and a Happy New Year. I think I said so in the last letter as well, just in case that took forever. Still, however long they take, isn't it amazing that despite this bloody awful war, you and I are still in touch. Still able to communicate. No-one else could believe how important that is. And soon, I hope, I'll find a way for you to write and give me your news. For instance, is it true what I read in a newspaper here, that some minister in your government tried to prohibit mention of Santa Claus and Christmas because it would distract from the war effort? It seems bizarre and unlikely, but some day you can tell me if the politicians there are as crazy as those here. Perhaps war makes them all go insane!

Fondest love to you both, Sam.

He had delivered it, sealed and addressed to her care of the consul in Sydney, secure inside a main envelope with its protective insignia of the *Bank de l'Indo Chine*. Fortunately the petite and friendly receptionist was on duty when he arrived, not the surly Vaudois clerk. It was one more letter safely on its way.

Sitting in the back of the hire car, provided to take him home because late trains were so rare these days, he passed the time trying to work out how long before this and his other letters reached Sydney. So much depended upon the availability of neutral cargo vessels. The act of writing them was like an exchange of affectionate dialogue with a very close friend. He missed her cheerful, understanding replies, but was determined he'd find a way to solve that problem.

Sam dozed and woke when the car stopped outside his home. Angelique and his mother were still in Karuizawa, and the house was dark and locked. He thanked the driver and fumbled for his keys. As the hire car began to leave, he was dazzled by the lights of another vehicle parked further down the street. It drove directly at him, pulled up alongside, and an ominously familiar voice spoke from an open window. It was two and a half years ago, but Sam still remembered their meeting.

'Is this him?' The question was in French, directed at a figure in the back seat. A shadowy figure, but one who seemed threateningly familiar.

'That's him,' a voice replied, and the Swiss accent was all the confirmation Sam needed.

'Get in, Delon,' Major Ito said. 'You're under arrest.'

PART 3

CHAPTER 17

He woke, and in the darkness heard a girl screaming. For a moment he was back there on the blazing ship, and they were trying to escape being trampled by the swarm of terrified passengers fighting for places in the lifeboats. But that was another life; he was no longer ten years old with close-knit parents who had seemed in those days so devoted to each other. Instead he was in a concrete cell, no bed, just a stinking blanket on the stone floor; feeling chilled, then sickened by the slop bucket as he saw the scuttling cockroaches. His body was bruised and painful from lying on the solid surface, and his wrists ached from the handcuffs.

Since the night of his arrest he had been left alone, no interrogation, nothing but a surly guard placing food once a day in the tiny cell, then unlocking the manacles but chaining his legs as he made him stagger to the end of the block and empty his bucket, cursing him as a fucking traitor, and when Sam asked why, the guard said everyone in this place was a fucking traitor, and hadn't he heard the bastards being shot behind the prison for their treachery?

Dozens of times, Sam thought, but felt it wiser not to say this. Constantly there seemed to be people marched by his window; it was tiny and too high to see out through the bars, but the sound of rifle bolts and the volley of shots that followed was all too audible. In the three days, he had not seen a sign of Major Ito. He imagined it was deliberate, to build on his fear so that when the questions came he would be too frightened not to answer.

After he had been forced into the car, the limousine that brought him home had paused on the corner of the street, the driver obviously concerned by what he had seen in his mirror. Ito gave a sharp order, and the Kempetai driver took a rifle he was handed and opened his door. He sighted on the vehicle ahead, and fired several rapid shots. The rear window glass exploded, but the car accelerated and sped away.

'That's why you're a driver, not a marksman,' Major Ito said as the man cursed angrily, slid behind the wheel and slammed the car door. Sam was in the front beside him. 'Turn around.' Ito hit Sam's shoulder to emphasise the order.

When he turned, it confirmed his presage of trouble. The figure who sat uneasily beside the Major was the Vaudois clerk from the Swiss Embassy, who worked in the front office. He had seen Sam leave after delivering his letter to the receptionist. They stared at each other, while Ito smiled confidently.

'You're quite sure he's the one?'
'Yes, Major.'
'When was he at the embassy?'
'Three days ago.'
'Doing what?'

'Delivering a letter.'

'To whom?'

'I'm not sure. The girl took it. I had no chance to look at the envelope before it went to dispatch.'

'But he's been there before?'

'Yes.'

'Another letter?'

'Yes.'

'And you were on duty that time?'

'Yes. That time the letter was to a bank in Zurich.'

'Illegal transfer of money?'

'I would imagine so.'

To Sam it was clearly a rehearsed charade, but one which was dangerously prescient.

'He could imagine nothing,' he said, 'since any letter I sent was sealed and confidential bank business. It was certainly none of his business, and this is just pure guesswork.'

The Major leant forward and hit Sam across the face. He must have signalled the driver, who jolted him with an elbow deep into his solar plexus. Sam retched with pain, involuntarily vomiting on the driver, who became enraged and started to punch him fiercely.

'That'll do,' Ito said. 'I want him in good enough shape to answer questions. Delon-san and I have lots to talk about. We need to discover if he's still polite and plausible, or is he now shitting himself? I promised I'd find that out some day.'

They drove back towards Tokyo. On the outskirts, where the car stopped, the Swiss clerk was told to get out and take a taxi.

'But I haven't been paid,' he complained.

The Major handed him a note. The clerk stared at it with bewilderment and disbelief.

'This is only five yen.'

'Your cab fare. You can keep the change.'

'But you promised . . .' His eyes widened with fear as the driver took a pistol from the glove box.

'Never trust a policeman's promise,' the Major said, with a smile that lacked any trace of humour. 'Now find a taxi. Even the world's worst shooter couldn't miss killing you from there.'

The Swiss informer looked as if he were about to cry. He gazed at Sam as if seeking help there. Or perhaps forgiveness.

'He told me you were a spy,' he said. 'And that the State would reward me for your conviction.'

'If you lie down with mangy dogs,' Sam said, 'all you can expect is fleas.'

He saw Ito's flash of anger. Too late he sensed the driver raise the pistol. There was a sickening blow that exploded inside his head, and he knew nothing until the next morning in the cell, when the guards drenched him with cold water and finally managed to revive him.

The Count de Boulanger was puzzled the first day, when Sam failed to arrive for work. At noon, he asked Mademoiselle to find out if there were any rail accidents or extensive delays. After lunch he rang the Delon home number, but the phone was unanswered. The exchange pronounced it in working order. By now, wondering if Sam could be ill, he sent his chauffeur to Yokohama to find out. The lack of a phone call disturbed him. He was far more disturbed when the chauffeur returned to report the house was locked, and a neighbour claimed he had been woken by the sound of shots fired sometime after midnight.

He called the local police to ask if they knew of a traffic accident in the area. Or any unusual incident? The evasiveness of the duty officer began to alert him to the possibility of disaster.

On the fourth day, Sam heard the measured tread of approaching footsteps, and the barred door was pushed open. There were two guards and behind them he saw Major Ito. He was as immaculate as ever, wearing a tailored uniform this time.

'He stinks,' the Major looked disgusted, as if to smell after four unwashed days in a filthy prison was an offence in itself. 'Get him clean, give him something to wear, and have him in my office in ten minutes.'

The moment he left, the guards began to kick Sam. They aimed carefully, at his ribs, testicles, anywhere except his face. Then they fetched cold water and a bar of soap, undid the handcuffs and told him to get washed. And make it quick. He had one minute to satisfy them he was clean enough, because if the Major's nose even twitched in disapproval, they'd bring him back here afterwards and kick him till he wished he was dead.

One guard watched Sam trying to wash his bruised and painfully tender body, the other fetched rough calico prison fatigues. Then they marched him upstairs, across the road to another building where there were suites of offices, and where Major Ito waited.

The Count found it difficult to contain his anger as he faced the quiet, courteous man in his sixties: Mitsuo Toyoshima, Chief Commissioner of Police with jurisdiction over the city and suburbs of Yokohama. It had taken him several days in which he had used all his influence to obtain this appointment, but it was becoming apparent the meeting was a complete waste of time.

'The car was shot at, Commissioner. I can produce the evidence. I can show your detectives the car itself. I've given you a bullet, found inside the vehicle, which almost killed the driver. We also have residents of The Bluff, reputable citizens who all heard the shooting. And a young man in my bank, a key employee, has been missing for four days.'

'Most regrettable.'

'What's even more regrettable is your statement that you can do nothing to assist.'

'Nothing, Your Excellency.' The Chief was scrupulously polite, and his exactitude caused de Boulanger added irritation.

'Do you mind telling me why not?'

'I'm unable to comment on matters that are beyond my sphere of authority.'

'But your sphere of authority is this entire city.'

'In daily police affairs. Matters like petty crime, crowd control, traffic procedures. But not in any concern that relates to the domain of military matters or the national security.'

The Count stared at him, feeling sudden alarm, and trying to prevent it showing.

'The Kempetai? Are we talking of them?'

'I cannot discuss this any further, Excellency. It is out of the question. I hope you understand?'

The Count understood perfectly. He was being given a discreet message that could not be voiced, and while the implications were alarming, at least the journey had not been wasted after all. He rose and bowed, thanking the Commissioner for the generous gift of his time in consenting to the meeting, and went out to his waiting car.

Already he was wondering if Sam had been tortured, and if so, then his own arrest was almost certain.

'This time we'll conduct our interview in Japanese,' Major Ito said. He sat behind a desk in a rather spartan office. In front of him was a bulky folder, nothing else. He made no attempt to hide the name on the front, and seemed amused as Sam realised it was his own dossier.

'Let's begin, shall we? So, you posted bank documents to go to Switzerland in the diplomatic bag?'

'Yes, Major. That's not illegal.'

'It depends entirely on what the documents were. Are you going to tell me?'

'I'm forbidden to, under the banking code of practice.'

'The banking code? Perhaps our interrogators may have to crack your code. But let's hope it doesn't come to that. They are hard to control, our virtuoso examiners, and carefully recruited for their expertise in cruelty. But I expect you know this.'

Sam knew it was scare tactics, and refused to respond.

'Have you written to your godmother lately?' Ito asked so smoothly and casually that Sam wondered if they had forced the Swiss to hand over the mail, despite violating diplomatic immunity.

'How could I?' he answered. He felt he was walking on quicksand; each step, every reply a danger of entrapment.

'Oh, I think you'd find a way, a smart young chap like you. What was her name again?' He made a pretence of consulting the file. 'Florrie. Mrs Florence Eisler, formerly Carter. But is she a godmother, or an aunt?'

'I don't understand the question.'

'Of course you do. A blood relative, that's the question. She was Miss Carter. Her sister, Miss Catherine Carter, gave birth to a child she called Samuel. On the thirtieth of July, 1922, the birth was registered in Sydney. Which is also your birthday, isn't it, Sam? Because that's what it says in your file. You're aged twenty-two, the same age as Samuel Carter.'

He felt as if he was deep in the quicksand, and unable to struggle free. It was impossible for this man to know these things, yet he recalled his father's warning.

Your mother registered your birth in Sydney. You're only French by adoption. There are still people in Kobe who...

Major Ito smiled at the confusion on Sam's face. 'Before you try to deny this and make a fool of yourself, I think you should be told we have agents in many countries. So we'd certainly have them in Australia. The Australians are not adept at distinguishing orientals. So many of us apparently look alike to them. Years ago we recruited Chinese, Koreans, even our own people, who pose as businessmen, restaurateurs, fishermen, market gardeners...' He paused to let this sink in. 'How do you think we knew that coastline and harbour so well, when the midget submarines attacked? How do you imagine we are able to bomb Darwin into scrap and rubble?'

'Why are you telling me this?' Sam asked, but Major Ito ignored the question.

'She's your aunt, isn't she?'

'Yes. You seem to know perfectly well she is.'

'And you write to her.'

'I used to. I can't until the war is over.'

'It upsets me, Sam, when you take me for a fool. If you upset me enough, I'll turn you over to interrogation.

When they've made you bleat everything you know, then they usually kill you. By then, of course, you're glad to die. To escape the pain.'

'How could I write to her?'

'Through the bank, of course. Through Switzerland.'

Jesus Christ, Sam thought, *he really does know*. He felt as if his face was betraying him, but made one last attempt to shrug and look perplexed. Major Ito laughed aloud.

'You fucking idiot,' he said, and the obscenity came as a shock from this meticulous man, 'I've tried to tell you, and you don't listen. Florence Carter became Mrs Eisler. You revealed that yourself when you failed by a few days to escape to Australia. We had her letter, and her address. It was hardly difficult for an agent to find out where she worked, or to learn she and Carl Eisler had left the firm of Cusack & Noble. Or perhaps you haven't heard that?'

Left there, Sam thought, startled. *But how does he know?*

'One of our agents went there,' the Major seemed to be mind-reading. 'He posed as a seaman off a neutral ship, with a message from you. He talked to the partner, Mr Noble ... who was still annoyed his secretary had left. All over a difference about the Swiss Consulate. Apparently they'd phoned to say there was a letter for her from Switzerland; he'd told her to wait, but she gave notice and rushed off to collect it.

'Odd behaviour, unless it was unexpected and very special from someone she cared about, like her sister's child. Now please don't aggravate me by denying it, Sam. You write to your aunt via the Swiss diplomatic bag. I personally can't see any great harm in it, provided you don't send war plans, or anything that could be used against us – and I hardly think you have access to such material.'

'You seem to have it all worked out.' Sam realised it was pointless to deny this.

'That's far more sensible,' the Major said. 'Of course I could report this. You'd go to prison or be shot. Or else I could be less harsh and simply have you interned.'

'But I'm a French citizen,' Sam insisted.

'Australian born,' Ito said. 'So I doubt if you'll win that one. Most internment camps are on Sakhalin, in the north. Freezing winds all year, coming off Siberia. A brute of a place.' He paused to allow Sam time to think about the Siberian winds. 'On the other hand, you could continue life exactly as it is. Your job, your family, nothing will change.'

'I don't believe you.'

'I assure you, it can happen. There need be nothing to fear. Provided you give me the names of those who have sent money out of the country. A complete list of the people and the amounts.'

'I can't do that,' Sam said.

'My dear fellow,' Ito was at his most alarming when he was being friendly, 'you have to do it, if you want to remain alive.'

Sleep was impossible. As though the Major had staged it, there were distant screams from the interrogation room above him throughout the night. The floor was hard and cold, and his body hurt where the guards had kicked him. He felt sick and defeated. He had thought himself clever, rejecting Saigon, using the Swiss to keep contact with Florrie; all the time, Major Ito had tracked him like a hunting dog.

Of course he wanted to remain alive. He had hardly begun to live. He wanted to spend time with Justine Fournier, whose smile promised so much. And return to Australia where he felt he belonged. Perhaps take Justine with him, to walk on the sand, and swim at the crescent-shaped beach he still remembered with such nostalgia. Yet it was not possible to give the Kempetai Major a list. Sam had no liking for the rich industrialists and politicians using their vast sums of cash to buy safe currency against the future. But to betray them, and with them the Count and Mademoiselle, was alien to all his sentiments.

He knew there was no answer.

The night seemed endless, and to pass the time, he tried to imagine what Justine was doing, hoping no-one in Karuizawa would try to take advantage of his absence. Loath to pursue that thought, he let his mind range instead on all he loved about Japan. The great forests of magnolias, the landscapes of hydrangeas and camellias. The traditions, ceremonies, the delicate arts and wood sculpture; the worship of animals like the fox, hunted in some countries, but here called the messenger of the harvest god – the stately cranes and graceful herons, and the *uguisu* nightingale, its fluted night song an exquisite rhapsody in the hills on midsummer evenings.

Whereas in Australia . . . he started to make a list but it was quite different: the wonderful brightness of the light and waking to the sound of a kookaburra's laughter, or the gulls that swooped and cried as they foraged for kelp on the shore. But mostly what counted was a memory of Florrie; the kinship that bound them, her fond smile, her firm stride when they walked, remembering how safe he had felt when her hand held his ten-year-old hand. He wondered if she had changed, and would he recognise her after all this time?

Sometime towards dawn, he fell asleep.

The Count Louis de Boulanger did not sleep. His lover, Moustique, found him at dawn, sitting by the pool where the golden carp swam. He was clad only in pyjama trousers. She wore a silk kimono and brought him a gown. They sat together in silence, and watched the fish glide contentedly by.

'You know what you have to do, chérie.'

'I'm not sure it's possible,' he said.

'You must. He may never be your friend again, but if you sit here and do nothing, you'll all end up crucified. By the press, by the public, and finally there'll be the hangman. Or a samurai sword; they may give you a choice.'

'Don't, my love.'

'I'll probably be conscripted to an officer's brothel. The highest-ranking officers, of course.'

'Stop it,' he said.

'It's not impossible in these terrible times. Face the truth, Louis.' He stared into her anxious eyes.

'I'll try,' he said. 'If it fails, we're all dead.'

Major Ito was in his office early, but decided the interview would take place later in the day. The longer he left Sam Delon to sweat in his cell, the more certain the outcome would be. And if he could produce such a result, there must surely be a promotion at last. It would unquestionably be time; he was ambitious, but the way his career had stalled was a nettle of insecurity behind his outwardly confident demeanour.

He had had an early, meteoric rise. A captain in the army at twenty-four, recruited into the military police and promoted to major, everyone had predicted within a few years he would be one of the group of brigadier deputy-commanders of the Kempetai. This opinion was augmented by the outbreak of war; but the war, strangely, was his undoing. So many senior officers, due for retirement, had remained on active service that there was no opportunity for promotion. He had stayed a major, and began to feel he always would. But if he could provide this bombshell, a list of the leading citizens siphoning their wealth to Swiss banks against the orders of the Emperor . . . he smiled at the thought of the sensation it would cause, which was when the phone rang, and a stuttering sergeant said there was a most secret and important telephone call for him.

The guard kicked Sam awake, and asked if he thought this was a fucking rest camp for traitors? He was to wash, so he didn't offend the Major's nostrils, and then get dressed and wait to be summoned for questions.

'When?' Sam asked, and for his impertinence was kicked again, and told when was none of his business. When it suited Major Ito to call him, that's when, and in the meanwhile he had better pray to whatever pagan god he believed in, because executions had been scheduled for noon today, and perhaps one of them would be his. *When the Major had finished with him.*

The question of what to do with Sam occupied the Major's mind, if only to allay his confusion at his surprise summons. The telephone call had been brisk, but courteous. Would Ito-san be kind enough to present himself for a private meeting in one hour's time? A car would be dispatched to collect him; there would be no need to wear his uniform. A plain business suit would be preferred.

The car passed Hibiya Park, the gardens there bright with peonies and weeping red maples, and turned in the direction of the Diet building and the government offices. *The seat of power*, Ito thought. Someday, if events conspired to help, he might belong here, but his thoughts shied from such grand illusions, and returned to the problem of Sam Delon.

Once he had the list, what was the best thing to do? He could have him shot, or sent to an internment camp. These seemed the only options.

He could hardly set him free.

The two men in the room were both known to him, although he had never met them. The Count de Boulanger had been surreptitiously photographed during the pursuit of Sam, along with most of the bank staff. The older man, tall and distinguished, he knew only from newsreels or photos in the papers. Konoye Fumimaro was an aristocrat and hereditary peer, related to the Emperor himself. He had been in politics for twenty years, president of the Imperial Diet, and three times prime minister until replaced by General Tojo in a coup three months before the outbreak of war.

Both men took chairs, leaving Ito to remain standing stiffly at attention. He had a strong impression they were not friendly towards each other. Adept at detecting ambience, he sensed disapproval and even acrimony here.

'Major Ito,' the Prince said, 'it has been brought to my attention that you are about to do immense harm to the national war effort, and bring dishonour and contempt on your family name.'

Ito was stunned. In all his speculation he had not expected this. Dishonour? Contempt? 'Your Highness,' he ventured, 'may I know what I've done to deserve this rebuke?'

'Good God, man, are you a total fool? How the devil did you reach the rank of Major, if you haven't the brains of a *karei*?'

'A fish?'

'A flounder,' the Prince said icily, 'and I choose the type of fish advisedly. For your floundering could cost us the war.'

'But Your Highness . . .'

'Don't interrupt when I'm speaking. The moment I heard of this I sent for Count de Boulanger, but he's been of little help. So I must clearly take matters into my own hands.'

He paused, but Ito dared not speak unless permitted.

'It was brought to my notice by residents in Yokohama. Neutrals, Westerners, but good friends of Japan. Shots were fired. A young man was arrested. Is that correct?'

'A suspicious character, Your Highness . . .'

'I asked, is that correct?' Konoye snapped.

'Yes, sir. A young man, a bank clerk. He is involved in an intricate matter, sending money to Switzerland . . .'

'Of course he is, you fool,' the Prince said, 'he works for this gentleman at the *Bank de l'Indo Chine*. And they both work for the government.'

'But Your Highness . . .'

'Will you stop interrupting, or do you want to be stripped of your rank and court-martialled for disrespect?'

'I imagine the Major is trying to tell us the transfer of money abroad is illegal.' The Count spoke for the first time.

'I imagine he is.' The Emperor's cousin did not appear to welcome this interjection, either. His tone was as chilly as a north wind. 'And if I'm not rudely interrupted again, I'll explain to him. Where exactly,' he asked the confused and anxious Major, 'do you think we get our guns, our planes, tanks, landing craft – all our weapons of war?'

'We make them, Your Highness.' Ito seemed unsure whether he was meant to speak, and looked relieved when the Prince nodded.

'Exactly. We make them. And where do we get the raw materials to make them? The metal and scrap iron, the fuel for our tanks, gasoline for our aircraft? We buy these commodities, Major. But the world has a habit of wanting payment before they send their goods. So money has to be provided.' He hesitated and studied the Kempetai officer. His manner had changed slightly; it had become more conciliatory. 'What you hear now, you can never repeat. If you did, you'd find yourself reduced to the ranks and fighting in New Guinea, or in an army penitentiary. A high-level decision was taken to send funds abroad, to Switzerland. The matter could not be handled by the Bank of Japan or any government agency, and was entrusted to the foreign bank of l'Indo Chine. You understand?'

'Yes, Your Highness,' Ito said, trying to salvage his situation, 'but Delon-san . . . the one we arrested . . .'

'I may have been harsh earlier. You thought you were doing your duty, after all. But the young man is a key figure in these transactions, and must be released.'

'Has he been interrogated?' the Count asked.

'Not yet. Just questioned by me.' The Major had an odd feeling they were both relieved to hear this.

Prince Konoye said, 'Then destroy his file, close the case and I'll see the right people are told of your cooperation.'

'Will he be allowed to continue sending letters to his relatives in Australia?'

Later, Major Ito would remember the frozen shock on both their faces. He saw the Prince turn and stare at the Frenchman, and the Count's change from bewilderment to a Gallic bluster.

'He'll be disciplined. If it's really true he's doing that.'

'He sends them via Switzerland, in the diplomatic bag.'

For the first time the Major felt on equal terms with them, despite their impressive titles and their riches. He relished the moment as he added: 'He is Australian, but I'm sure you both know that.'

There were three guards this time, all Korean, and Sam knew what it meant. Major Ito stood at the door of the cell and spoke to him in English, because the Koreans did not understand it.

'You have some surprising friends, Sam,' he said. 'I'm to let you go. Which makes me very angry. It seems you've won, but I'm a bad loser. So keep looking over your shoulder, because I'll be there. You can depend on it – I'll always be there.'

He walked away. One of the Koreans pushed the cell door shut. Another grinned with anticipation. The third began to throw punches at him, then suddenly lashed out in a kick-boxing movement so fast and unexpected that his boot sent Sam crashing back against the wall. They came in with bare fists, systematically beating him, making him sick with blows to the stomach, then to the face, breaking his nose and blackening his eyes.

His body was beyond pain; he thought he was going to die. Each time he passed out, he was doused with buckets of icy water to revive him. When they could no longer wake him, they left him there in the cell, bloodied and unconscious.

'I thought you were brilliant,' the Count said, but he knew it was a lost cause. His long friendship with Konoye Fumimaro, which had been so fruitful for many years, was over.

'I told the necessary lies, to save one of my relatives and a number of close friends,' the Prince said, 'but I shall make sure no friends of mine are involved in any future transactions with you or your bank. Certainly not with my approval.'

'I had no choice but to approach you. There was no-one else who could save the situation.' Konoye made no reply. 'Please, I was genuinely concerned that if the Kempetai found out names, it might mean the arrest of all those you'd recommended, and even rebound on you.'

'You were trying to save your own hide.'

'That, too,' the Count admitted.

Konoye poured himself a drink, but did not offer one to his visitor. It was a rare discourtesy that indicated de Boulanger was no longer welcome there.

'You may not wish to hear me say this, but I'm grateful,' the Count said as he turned towards the door, accepting the directive to leave.

'I expect you are. But don't assume the Major believed all he was told. He's no fool.'

'There's very little he can do about his doubts. He wouldn't dare express open mistrust of you.' He paused with his hand on the door. 'I'm sorry we won't meet again.'

'Oh, I daresay we'll meet,' Prince Konoye said, 'but if we do, it won't be by choice. What are you going to do about your Australian?'

'I had no idea of that, I assure you.'

'Then you were extremely careless. I asked what you intend to do about him?'

'I have no idea of that, either.'

The Count had returned to the bank, and the staff were leaving when a car drove slowly along the canal road towards the premises. One of the Japanese typists screamed as a limp, bloodstained figure was thrown out. Sam landed heavily at the bottom of the steps, unaware of hitting the pavement, his face almost unrecognisable from the battering as the car drove away.

Some of the staff thought he was dead, but Mademoiselle Patou told them to stop being hysterical, ran to her desk and sent an urgent request for an ambulance.

CHAPTER 18

It was late August when Florence had a call from Mr Joubert at the Swiss Consulate, and she went there in her lunch hour to collect another letter. He greeted her like an old friend.

'I'm glad you advised me of your change of firms, Mrs Eisler,' he said. 'A larger establishment, I gather, your new post?'

'Much larger, Mr Joubert,' she said, and indeed it was. Houghton, White and Lindsay was one of Sydney's finest old law firms, occupying the entire floor of a building in fashionable Bligh Street. Mr Lindsay, the sole survivor of the founding partners, had arrived on their doorstep one surprising Sunday, introduced himself, stayed to lunch and asked Florrie to come and work for him.

Over prawns and a bottle of white wine that Carl had been saving for a special occasion, she had explained there was a problem. She and her husband wished to work together. When Mr Lindsay declared that need not be a difficulty, she said there was another problem. She was of an age when she would not find it easy to work under another person's direction. Mr Lindsay said he had not devoted a precious Sunday to recruiting a typist: what he wanted was her expertise. She would run his office. A week later, she joined the firm as supervising secretary. Carl had been invited to become an associate, with the possibility of a partnership next year.

She had rarely been happier.

Mr Lindsay gave her responsibility and respect; her staff, fond of her, the typing pool in particular, confided details of their love affairs with American troops, now such a familiar sight in all Australian cities. Thousands were stationed here, over half a million had passed through on leave. Short-term romance was the objective, even if bishops thundered about moral laxity, claiming self-control not contraception, was the answer.

She left the Swiss Consulate with Sam's letter, and walked to the park. It was warm, an early spring. Wattles and grevilleas were in flower. Lunchtime groups fed sandwich crusts to pigeons. A newspaper left on a bench reported Franklin Roosevelt had been re-elected President of the United States. Shock front-page headlines said a Japanese *kamikaze* pilot had attacked the flagship HMAS *Australia* – the plane, packed with high explosive, crashing on the deck and killing the captain and fifty of the crew.

Florence repressed a shudder. The war was far from over, no matter what optimists said. German rockets were raining on British cities; young fliers wrapped in dynamite were suiciding to sink ships. And as armies advanced across Poland, death camps were being discovered that had begun to send tremors of horror through the world.

She read the letter; it had taken only four months to reach her, which was fairly rapid. They were due to go on holiday to this mountain village he liked so much called Karuizawa – but that was in June, and thus it was well and truly over by now. She smiled at his hopes of some progress with the beautiful Justine, and wondered if his next letter might inform her. Or had the summer holiday proved a romantic disappointment? How she wished she could write to him in return.

She frowned as she read of the clash with Tamara, who had opened her letter. Hardly a nice thing to do, but Sam said it was understandable, her curiosity at the way it had been delivered, and he actually felt better now the truth was out in the open.

In his letters, he often wished them Happy Christmas, in case of delay, and he had done so again in this one. *Wouldn't it be wonderful*, she thought, *if we could spend the next Christmas together.*

The private clinic was in Azabu, not far from the Count de Boulanger's residence. He came to hear the result of the examination the day after Sam had been admitted. The Japanese doctor was an elderly man, shocked by the severity of the attack. The Count had explained Sam had been beaten by a street gang. As there were several recent cases of violence towards Europeans, this avoided awkward questions.

'Appalling injuries,' the doctor said. 'We should report it to the police, and if the louts can be identified, press charges.'

Sam had recovered consciousness earlier, but was sedated and hazy with morphine. Despite this, he saw the Count look at him for an answer, and knew what was expected. He shook his head; the slight movement, despite the palliatives, was painful.

'It's an outrage, a disgrace,' the doctor said.

'How long will he be in hospital?'

'Difficult to say just yet. At least a month.'

'So long?'

'My dear Count, it may be longer. He has broken ribs; probably two, but the X-ray will tell us if there's more. His broken nose will mend in time, the facial injuries will hopefully leave him unscarred, but there may be kidney damage. I want to do a scan of his spine, and when we stop sedating him, I must test his reflexes. There could be brain damage, although I hope it's only concussion.'

The conversation, Sam thought, seemed to be taking place a long way off, about someone else. He closed his eyes, feeling he would rather sleep than look at the Count, whose words appeared to express sympathy, but whose eyes contained anger. It was goodbye to the French Bank, he felt certain, before drifting back into the calm of unconsciousness.

It was Saturday afternoon, and Carl was working at the office again. *It's ridiculous*, she thought, *this obsessive working every Saturday. He must relax more.* She decided to take the tram to town, surprise him, and insist they go to a five o'clock session at the pictures and then a restaurant. She was eager to see the new film of *Henry V* with Laurence Olivier and, because it was popular, she rang the Embassy Theatre and booked two seats. She thought of ringing Carl, but the switchboard would be turned off and, since it was only mid-afternoon, there was little chance of missing him, for he rarely left until late.

But when she reached the office, it was locked. She used her key, and found the place completely empty. Not only that, but it was clear Carl had not been in the office that day at all. Crystal clear, especially to her. For everything on his desk was exactly the way it had been when they left there the previous afternoon.

He did not reach home until after dark, and she had long since been to the cinema and cancelled her booking, suffering the irritation of a bad-tempered woman in the ticket booth who said loudly that people who changed their minds were a pest and there should be a fee for cancellation. She had walked to the Quay, taken a ferry, and after that endured a tram trip home in perplexed misery.

Where was he? Why had he lied? And lied with such skill, it seemed to her, as perplexity became anger.

Every Saturday, for months, he had pleaded pressure of work and gone to the office. When she had asked him why, he'd said he needed the extra time as English was not his first language, and legal terms were difficult. If he were to gain a partnership, so important for their future, the loss of Saturday was not such a sacrifice. He promised it would soon end, once he'd mastered all the linguistics of jurisprudence.

Sunday was inviolate, their one day always spent together. If they entertained friends, it was then. Carl often walked to buy the papers at the corner store, bringing them to her with breakfast in bed on a tray then, after the papers were discarded and the tray removed, sliding in beside her and making love. The love-making, she tried to tell herself, was surely real. He couldn't fake that, could he?

When he arrived home, she asked if he'd had a busy day.

'Very complicated, liebling,' he said. 'The Carruthers contract. It took most of the afternoon, and kept me so late.'

She served their dinner without comment, while listening to his lies. The Carruthers contract was an agreement between their client and the government to build new dry docks at Cockatoo Island. She had seen the documents on his desk that afternoon, untouched.

The nurse propped Sam up on his pillows, smiled at them both and went out. She left the door ajar, but the Count rose and closed it.

'Are you fit to talk?' It was really a rhetorical question, for he had been very patient. Ten days since Sam had been taken off morphine, and cleared of kidney and brain damage. He had two broken ribs, and bruises over most of his body. The swelling from his broken nose had subsided, and he could now see out of both eyes.

'Fit enough,' he said.

'Then do you realise the trouble you've caused?'

'If you're going to fire me, M'sieu Le Comte, then you can dispense with the lecture and just tell me I no longer have a job.'

'You're an imbecile,' the Count said. 'An Australian.'

'My mother was. An Australian, but not an imbecile.'

'Don't try to be smart with me.'

'I'm grateful to her. She refused my father's request to have an abortion, for which I have to be grateful. And if she was anything like her sister she must have been wonderful.'

'Be quiet, and listen to me. I've employed and treated you as a confidante for over two years. Treated you damned well. Now I find this out. You could be interned. I could be in serious bother.'

'He told you, did he? The Major?'

'He told us you write to a relative – I presume it's the sister – using the Swiss diplomatic bag. Which is a betrayal of trust, and quite unforgivable.'

'I'm sorry about that, sir.'

'Sorry is nowhere near good enough. You've not only ruined a long and important friendship I had with Prince Konoye, but we've lost credibility. Major Ito has been temporarily stalled, but the man's no fool, and I can't guarantee he'll remain quiet.'

'I think I can,' Sam said.

'Don't talk rot. You know nothing.'

'I know that whatever you or the Prince said dismantled his whole case. What else would make him furious enough to turn three Korean thugs loose, and let them half kill me?'

'I thought the Kempetai did this?'

'No. Korean guards. He said that I had some surprising friends and he was a bad loser. Then he walked off and left them to bash me.'

'You mean this happened *after* he'd talked to us?'

'I'd say directly afterwards. He was livid enough to even let them dump me in front of the bank. Why? Because he knew he couldn't charge me. Someone had made certain of that.'

'Konoye,' the Count said. 'He was very persuasive.'

'Then perhaps I owe him my life.'

'I doubt if he'd wish to know it.'

Sam began to feel the strain; a sudden wave of weariness made his eyelids heavy. The Count's face seemed distant, in a mist.

'Sir,' he murmured, 'if you do intend to sack me, I can

hardly blame you. But I don't think I can stay awake any longer.'

The Count sat waiting until Sam was breathing regularly, then he left. He advised the nurse to keep an eye on her patient, who was still weak and needed care. His car stood outside, but he told the chauffeur he'd walk home. It was only three blocks, and he had a lot to think about.

He had arrived with the intention of dismissing Sam. He still felt that was the sensible option, but it had one serious drawback. It would alert Ito that Sam was no longer protected. A dismissal would clearly signal he was fair game for further investigation. It would not be questions this time, but the full Kempetai interrogation. No-one prevailed against that treatment and the kind of pain he'd suffer. It would be continuous torture until they had milked him of every scrap of information he possessed. Which might well lead to the arraignment of the Count himself on criminal charges, and the ruin of the bank.

It was what you might call a delicate situation, and he was unsure how to deal with it.

All that week Carl knew his wife was upset. There was nothing overt, no hint of it in anything she said, or in the tone of her voice. They travelled to work as usual, they made conversation, and when it was necessary she smiled. But the smile was forced, the conversation polite. There was no laughter, no trace of love; this from someone who cherished laughter and was full of love. Without any word of accusation being expressed, he knew she was angry.

He wondered if he had been careless, if in fact she had somehow guessed or suspected. But how? He was always exactly careful. For instance, because he had mentioned the Carruthers contract to Florence, he'd spent a hurried hour checking the document as soon as he arrived at the office on Monday morning. Then he'd taken it to James Lindsay, casually saying he had been through this on Saturday, and had just double-checked it. There was a clause he felt should be removed, and old Mr Carruthers would want his payments in upfront stages, knowing how slowly the government paid its bills.

'He'd blow a gasket if we let that through,' Carl said, using local slang he'd acquired. 'He reckons getting paid by Canberra is about as easy as catching an eel with a spoon.'

James Lindsay laughed. He thought Carl was becoming more Aussie every day, although his vernacular was a bit weird with the German accent. But he was a good bloke; he and Florence were a fine couple, and it was the best day's work he'd done, engaging them. The office ran like clockwork.

'You deal with Carruthers, Carl. He's an important client, but a difficult old bugger. You handle him pretty well, and he seems to like you.'

'At our first meeting,' Carl said, 'we'd only just been introduced when he asked me: 'How did you get into this country, if you're a bloody Hun?"'

'I said he was difficult.'

'Not a scrap,' Carl said. 'I said I had to skip Germany quick-bloody-smart, because another Hun, a real shitty housepainter called Hitler didn't like me. We've got on famously ever since.'

'Beauty,' Lindsay chuckled. 'Hold out for those advance payments by the government. Take him to lunch on expenses. None of your cheap eateries. Book a table in the Emerald Room at the Hotel Australia. And why not take Florence along as well?'

Carl nodded, then after a moment said, 'Perhaps if it's a client lunch, it should be just me and Mr Carruthers?'

'If you think so,' Lindsay said. He had meant it as a gesture to Florrie in particular, but decided not to say this.

'I think it's best,' Carl said.

When he had gone, Lindsay was thoughtful. He had assumed Carl would welcome the idea. After all, it was just lunch on the firm, a fringe benefit at one of the most expensive restaurants in town. The company could afford it, James Lindsay would have been more than happy to sign the bill for it, but Florence's husband – for some reason that escaped him – preferred that she wasn't invited.

He hoped there was nothing wrong with their marriage. If there was, that might create difficulties regarding certain plans he had for the future. Lindsay, who had been a bachelor for all his fifty-seven years, thought that was the trouble with married life. It often seemed to be so complicated.

'Welcome back, Sam,' Mademoiselle Patou said, and the local staff extended greetings, while the French executives stayed stonily in the background, barely polite. *Nothing much has changed*, Sam thought, thanking her for the flowers she had sent him in hospital, and wondering if Jacques Clermont was still a part of her life.

The Count was waiting, she told him, and had requested he go straight in. It was a day full of appointments; if Sam delayed, it would ruin her schedule. He smiled and said it reminded him of his first time here, when he had been far too early and so eager. *But not so eager now*, he thought wryly, and went into the Count's office.

There appeared no outward change in their relationship. Coffee was served, with croissants, which did suggest a friendly overture. The Count wondered if his family was back home from the mountains, and asked what Sam had told them.

'That it was an unprovoked street attack,' Sam said, 'I thought that was simplest, because it's in the medical records.'

De Boulanger agreed. He said the doctor considered him fit, but how did Sam feel? There was a backlog of work, but it would be foolish to overtax him after such a long stay in hospital. 'Unfortunately,' he continued, 'there is no-one else on the staff who can do this work. I know we've had our differences, but I could hardly train someone new. Even if I could find anyone with your qualifications.'

'Are you sure you can trust me?,' Sam asked.

'What an extraordinary question.'

'No, sir. Please, no pretence. I think you came to the hospital to dismiss me, but changed your mind.' The Count began to shake his head; Sam ignored it. 'I've had all this time to work it out. I think you realised if you did sack me, I wouldn't be protected from further action by Major Ito? Isn't that correct?'

It was so obvious, there was little point in denial. 'It would certainly give him the freedom to make further inquiries.'

'Does that mean we're stuck with each other?'

'Not the most appropriate of phrases, but I suppose that's exactly what it does mean.'

'Would you rather I resigned?'

'Whatever our personal situation, I've said I need you.'

'And I need to work here to keep Major Ito at bay. But are you sure we can work together?'

'We must,' the Count said, frowning at this persistence, 'we have no choice. We're reliant on each other, whether we like it or not.'

Florence wondered how long she could keep up this facade. If Carl would only tell her the truth – whatever the truth was – she felt sure she could handle it. But the pretence, the evasions and lies were a real burden, and beginning to undermine her feelings for him.

She loved him, and that made the deception more hurtful. She wanted to confront him, to say that nothing was worth this artificial way they were behaving, being polite to each other but so remote; surely, she wanted to tell him, no secret was too difficult to talk about. Unless there was someone else, and he wanted to leave her. Or worse, if he had married her for the advantages it would bring; security as a citizen, and a job with prospects.

She tried not to think in this way. She was not proud of herself for letting it invade her thoughts, creeping like a poison into her mind. The trouble was, she really had no-one to confide in. She liked James Lindsay, and enjoyed his confidence at work, but had no intention of burdening him with private troubles. She had friends, who were all good fun, great company, lots of laughs at dinner or a barbecue, but was there one to whom she could pour out her heart?

Well, there was one, because they had always been able to divulge secrets to each other, but he was out of touch. And half her age. The age did not matter. There was nobody else – except Carl, she had to admit – who occupied such a special place in her life. She could talk to Sam, even in a letter, but a letter was impossible.

Was it? What about Mr Joubert at the Swiss Consulate?

When she went there the next day, explaining her need to contact her client, Mr Joubert was most cooperative. He would be glad to assist; any letter would go to Geneva in the diplomatic pouch, then to the embassy in Tokyo. This war would soon be over, Mr Joubert hoped, meanwhile commerce must continue, not be allowed to disintegrate by nations fighting each other. The Swiss, whose neutrality was secure, were there to assist in any way they could.

The following Saturday, after Carl again said he must go to work, she sat on the verandah with a pad and pen. *Dearest Sam*, she wrote, *I don't know what to do, and you are the only one I can entrust with this confusion and misery*.

No, she decided, and tore it up. She would take advantage of Mr Joubert's kind offer; being able to write to Sam after so long would be a delight. But she was not going to upset him with a litany of distress. There was nothing he could do about it, no way he could help, and it would be shameful to put this burden on him. If there was to be a letter, and by some miracle it reached him, let it be the sort they used to write, something that might bring him cheer.

My darling Sam, she began again, *how Carl and I wish you were here to share our happiness. I think of you so often, and with summer coming again, I walk on the beach and remember the lovely sandcastles we built. Now that you are twenty-two, I'm sure you have left sandcastles far behind, and would much rather lie amid the sirens on the main beach, in their two-piece bathing suits. The suits have decreased in size since last summer, and church pulpits are thundering with outrage, but the young girls themselves seem deeply unconcerned. I'm sure they would make a great fuss of you, but perhaps by now you are committed to Justine. What news of that? Do her parents yet approve? I hope Angelique and your mother are well, and your father and his lady safe in Saigon. Trust me when I say the news is getting better, no matter what the propaganda machine tells you, and I believe it will soon be over, and we'll meet again. Take care, my dear. I had hoped we would spend Christmas 1944 together, but that now seems unlikely. Perhaps, as everyone keeps optimistically saying, by this time next year . . . I would truly look forward to that.*

She went on to tell him about her new job – no longer new – but the first he would have heard of it, and how well she and James Lindsay worked together. She signed it with her love, and read it carefully. It would do, she thought. Some day I will tell him the way things seem to have gone wrong, but not like this, not in a letter that would only give him pain.

It was an afternoon in October when the bombing began. The planes came from the south east, from the island of Saipan in the Marianas. A base of no importance, nothing but atolls and jungle was how the news dismissed it when announcing a tactical withdrawal, with troops pulling back to prepared positions. No admission that this was a defeat; no mention of airstrips it contained which had been the reason for the battle to secure it. Not a hint of the B29 Superfortresses, or that these new aircraft were now within range of the *shinkoku*, the 'divine homeland'. Such a possibility would have been ridiculed.

Therefore the shock was greater. Sirens were wailing, and people ran out to see a sight that invoked fear; they saw massed silhouettes of huge bombers, the kind of sky the Germans had seen in places like Hamburg and the Ruhr, but unprecedented here.

The aerial armada broke formation near Hiroshima and proceeded to batter the industrial port of Kure, while the remaining squadrons flew high above the Inland Sea to bomb Kobe. Ground control tracked them turning south, reporting the raid was over, and predicting only minor damage had been inflicted.

No-one was yet aware another flight of Superfortresses was crossing the remote island of Mikura-jima, on a direct approach to the heartlands of Yokohama and Tokyo.

When the sirens went off, no-one in the bank showed the least sign of panic. They thought it was another practice drill, for there had been several in the past two weeks. They obediently put aside their work and filed out to the shelters behind the building. These were no more than slit trenches; two for the Japanese staff, one for the French. It was then they saw the formation of planes like ungainly giants etched against the sky.

From each bomber there appeared to be a trail of smoke. Some Japanese stood beside the trenches, clapping, pointing to the smoke, excitement eclipsing any fear of the attack. The American craft were on fire.

'Hit by fighter planes,' one shouted.

'Or by shells from our guns on the ground.'

The Count was impassive, the French staff uncertain if it was true. Sam caught Mademoiselle's anxious glance. She was afraid for the fliers, wondering if the planes would burst into flames. But they continued, untroubled, unstoppable.

Then the bombs began to fall, and everyone knew it was not smoke they had seen. They dived into the trenches, even though the bombs were on the far side of the city, near the harbour. Later they would come to learn these trails that spilled behind the aircraft were slipstreams, exhaust fumes vaporised by the height that the B29s were flying. An altitude too high for the fighter defence, way beyond the reach of the guns, the Fortresses were like mighty birds of prey throwing their shadows across the city, while they rained incendiary bombs in a cascade of terror and death.

After that, the bombers often came by night. It was worse to be woken by the wail of sirens, to hesitate between fear in a warm bed or safety in the cold, wet backyard trench. At least three times a week Sam huddled there with Angelique and his mother, as well as the cook who shouted at the Americans, calling them barbarians and murderers. As her niece had been killed in a recent raid, there was little anyone could say, except to agree barbarians and murderers were on both sides, and that war was an insane and evil business.

With the incessant bombing, the Japanese began to show signs of tension and a growing rage. A flag with stars and stripes was painted on the pavement for people to spit on. Stores sold small rag effigies – named Roosevelt and Churchill dolls – and women's defence groups taught schoolgirl recruits how to skewer them with bamboo spears. People were changing, hostility was rife, but still optimism remained. They were certain they would eventually dictate the peace terms as victors. No shower of bombs or sleepless nights could prevent that.

Although he doubted if he could ever send it, Sam spent much of his time in their damp trench, wearing out torch batteries and writing of the raids to Florence.

November 10th, 1944.
Dear Florrie
  I may tear up this letter, or else hide it for when we meet again. But I want to tell you the way things are. It's been getting a bit worse for some weeks, but yesterday was hell day. Officially there were three raids. It's not always the danger that matters; sometimes it is the aggravation, the sheer bloody awful stress it causes.
  The first raid came as we were packed in the commuter train halfway to Tokyo, when a flashing red signal light brought it to a grinding halt, and the doors slid open. Alarms were blaring, guards yelling to get out and take cover, and we struggled out of the train and lay on the embankment, to watch the formation as it flew high overheard. I doubt if they even looked down. Not interested! We were never their target.
  We could have stayed on board the train. It took ages to get all the passengers back inside the carriages, and without any official pushers to help jam everyone in, it became a very bad-tempered business. Everyone arrived at Tokyo main station in a filthy mood.
  The second alarm came at lunchtime. Just as we were in the bank's dining room, ready to dip into something really special. The Count had managed to buy some black-market cheese, and Mademoiselle had taken over the cooking to make a fondue. It smelt delicious – then the siren went. We wanted to stay, but the Count said the wardens might be around and they'd report us and cause a fuss.
  Trouble was, it wasn't a proper raid at all. It was just

two reconnaissance planes there to photograph the previous damage, but the sirens went off all the same. By the time this was established the fondue had gone cold and congealed into a gooey mess.

The third raid was later; that same night, at home, just after I'd gone to sleep. This was a real one. Bombs fell in Yokohama, and we had to spend the entire night in the trench. It also started to rain, just to top off a truly wonderful day. I think all the neutrals, as they call us, might be ordered to go to Karuizawa. It's the current rumour. At least it's sixty miles inland, where no bombs will drop, but what worries me is how we'll survive there. I'll have no job. My mother's jewellery is long gone.

I shouldn't write. It's dangerous, but I must, just in case something happens and we never meet again. This time I think perhaps I'll try to send it through our mutual friend in Saigon.

CHAPTER 19

The guard's whistle shrilled, carriage doors slammed as people broke from farewell embraces, the mountain train blew steam, and amid shouted *au revoirs*, *wiedersehens* and *sayonaras*, it began to shuffle out of Tokyo station. It was crowded with foreign families bound for Karuizawa, with as many possessions as they could carry. Sam had found seats for his mother and Angelique, stowing their cases, assuring them he'd tipped the guard to see there was a porter to help them at the main station. It would be late at night when they arrived, and they had to transfer their luggage to the tiny train that took them the last stage of the journey to the summerhouse.

Summerhouse indeed! He clearly remembered the night spent there with his father three years ago, and how cold it had been then. But this was not a brief visit or a single night; this was until the war ended or the bombing stopped, both unlikely in the near future, so there were five bleak months ahead before the spring. Not that he'd said this to his mother, having had enough difficulty making her agree to this unwelcome change in her life.

'You have to go,' he argued. 'It's compulsory for any foreigner not working to leave Yokohama, Ma. There's no choice.'

'Up there in Karuizawa in winter? I'll die of cold.'

'We'll install a fire.'

'Who'll cut the wood?'

'I will, on weekends.'

'If you ever turn up.'

'I'll turn up. Come on, you like Karuizawa.'

'In the summer. Nobody goes in wintertime.'

'Everyone will be there.'

'Who's everyone?'

'Well, the French Ambassador. The neutral embassies. His mother had shrugged, unimpressed by diplomats. 'The Countess...' She'd yawned. He'd kept trying. 'Doctor Wittenberg...'

'Useful, if I get sick. Probably with pneumonia.'

'And Doctor Plessner.'

'I don't need two doctors. Tell me someone interesting.'

'Justine.'

'She's your interest, not mine. Who else?'

'The Bonnards, Paul Jacoulet...'

'Jacoulet!'

'He'll definitely be there.'

'With the young boyfriends?'

'I expect so.'

'Korean boys. Always Korean, why?'

'I don't know, Ma. Ask him.'

'Disgusting, the boys. You know his mother was the only Frenchwoman – the only *Western* woman – who was ever a geisha?'

Yes, Sam had replied, he knew. But she still insisted on

repeating the story; how, as a child, Paul Jacoulet had been brought up in the geisha house, a pet of the women who had dressed him like a tiny replica of themselves, in their traditional make-up and distinctive kimonos. Now in his fifties, a world-renowned wood-block artist, he invariably wore – like a badge of recognition – the same heavy white powder, garish lipstick, and an elaborately brocaded kimono.

'I like Jacoulet!' His mother was cheered by the news. 'He makes me laugh, and I can beat him at poker. We'll play lots of poker in Karuizawa. And I can teach him mahjong.'

While they spent the next few days packing, arguing over what clothes to take, explaining to the cook they could not take her, Sam had fulfilled his promise and arranged for a potbellied stove to be installed in the cottage. He gave his mother the money to pay for it, plus all he could spare to buy food. He promised faithfully to come for a weekend as soon as he was settled, stood watching until the train was out of sight, then took his own suitcases and caught the underground to Nihonbashi. It was late, the bank was closed, but a light glowed inside. He knocked, heard bolts drawn, and the huge figure of Frankenstein filled the doorway.

'*Arigato*,' Sam said, thanking him.

Frankenstein grunted, stepped aside and Sam went into the bank. He carried his suitcases up the two flights of stairs to the small and elegant penthouse on the third floor which was now – and for the foreseeable future – his home.

It had happened so unexpectedly, just days ago. That morning, Sam did not reach the bank until noon. The cause of this was another air raid while he was on the train – a very different delay this time – with bombs dropping, hundreds of terrified passengers, and the track ahead destroyed by high explosive.

It had created chaos, until buses and trucks were found to shift commuters. Forced to queue in drizzling rain, hours had passed while police and civil authorities tried to handle the situation. Those with no urgent need to reach Tokyo were told to return home. Sam was among those who remained to take what transport was available. Uncertain if he still had a job – the bank had been full of rumours about closure – it was vital to reach there to find out. Being half a day late would hardly help his cause. He was eventually loaded into the back of an open truck. It took a further two hours, and he arrived tired, wet and dispirited.

The Count wished to see him. Laroche had conveyed the message, with a smugness that suggested storms ahead. But there were none. Surprisingly – for it was not the custom – Mademoiselle Patou was with him. But that was not the only surprise.

'Monsieur Ribot has left us,' he said. 'I'm not unduly distressed. Nor, I think I can say, is Mademoiselle.'

'He's gone to join his wife and family in Shimoda,' she said, not looking at all distressed.

'Which leaves us one problem. You.'

'You want me to leave?'

'Don't start that again,' the Count said testily. 'The problem is where you're to live.'

'I'll find somewhere.'

'That's not so easy. With the raids and transport delays, you need somewhere convenient. Mademoiselle has made a suggestion. She thinks you should use the empty apartment upstairs.'

Sam was disbelieving. It was too tremendous to be true.
'The penthouse?'
'The penthouse,' Cecile Patou had said.

The Penthouse.
Bank l'Indo Chine.
November 30th, 1944.

Dear Florrie,
My new address, my new home. One bedroom, containing a double bed with a futon. One small but perfect living room. A bathroom, a kitchen, also small but perfect. Everything is small but perfect. Except the view. The view is huge, spectacular. Windows that look across the canal towards the Sumida River. By day I can see barges, trees, the pale November sky. People below like ants, hurrying through the chill late autumn winds. At night if I turn off all the lights, I can sit beside a window and watch the blacked-out city, the dark shapes of buildings, clouds against the moon, sometimes a canopy of stars.

The sheer luxury of it: my own apartment, freedom to come and go, freedom from the tyranny of two hours daily travel – the joy of not being squashed into the commuter train. And I have choices. I can chose to cook a meal, or eat in one of the restaurants that crowd this district. I can sleep alone or invite a girlfriend. Make it my own domain, the Count said. Enjoy it. Kimiko-san, where are you now? If only I knew.

All Mademoiselle's idea. I tried to express my gratitude. I hope she realises – I think she does – how she has changed my life . . .

Sam had not yet sent his letter of three weeks ago, and he decided to try sending them together. The Swiss Embassy was unsafe; it was a year since he had used the Saigon route to his father via the shipping office. He made a discreet phone call after the bank shut.

'Ogawa-san?'

'Sam? Is that you?'

They exchanged formal courtesies, then Sam said: 'I've been wondering if you've heard from my father?'

'Quite recently, yes.'

'I haven't written for ages. I feel guilty about neglecting him. Would it be possible . . .'

'Of course,' Koki Ogawa said immediately. 'Address it to me, with your sealed letter in the main envelope, like last time.'

'Thank you,' Sam said.

That night, adding a second page to Florrie, he realised he had not told her about his frightening experience with the Kempetai, or the weeks in hospital afterwards. He decided he never would.

I had a first anniversary party. One week in residence! Just a few friends including Claude Briand, who still works with the French film unit. He said whenever they film, the secret police come to the set and change the script. Some are no older than us, and strut about wearing military swords, and shout orders to the director. So the films end up looking ludicrous because of all these changes, and people laugh and boo when they are shown. He says he's fed up, and might join his family soon. Along with so many people we know, they're also at Karuizawa.

Claude gave me other news. Richard Sorge has lost his

appeal and will be executed soon. There is an order banning this being published, but it is sure to become known. I'll have to tell Mama. She never mentions his name, but is bound to hear. With so many people in Karuizawa, gossip is the main pastime. It's best I tell her before anyone else can.
Love, Sam.

It was cold outside the house, but private. They walked in the empty garden. Damp leaves lay matted on the ground, the bare branches were moist with thawing frost.

'When? Do you know how many more days?'

'No, Ma.'

'Or what prison he's in?'

'Sugamo, Claude thinks. But you can't go there.'

'Of course not.' She digested the news in silence for a time. 'Thank you for telling me, Sam.'

'Better me than anyone else.'

'When . . . when it happens, will it . . . will there be any report in the newspapers?'

'I doubt it, the way censorship is these days.'

'Yes. Especially as Ozaki, arrested with him, was high in politics. An adviser to Prince Konoye, when he was prime minister.'

'I'd forgotten that,' Sam said, startled. Ozaki in the influenza mask, bringing a million yen for dispatch to Switzerland.

'There was even talk they suspected Konoye,' his mother said. 'Rumours he'd be arrested. You didn't know that?'

'No.'

'Well, it's no matter now. All water under the bridge – or whatever peculiar expression the English say.'

It was becoming colder in the garden. He took her arm and they began to walk back in the direction of the house.

'I'm sorry, Ma.'

'He was stupid,' she said, 'to believe in Stalin. Mad to be recruited as a spy. He could be charming, but he drank too much and in the end he became a traitor and a fool.'

They saw the bizarre sight of Paul Jacoulet in a bright kimono, hair swept in high, lacquered geisha style. He was followed by his adoring cluster of young Korean boys.

'There's another of my fools,' Tamara Delon said, 'but at least he's talented and makes me laugh.'

'And lets you win at poker.'

'He does not let me win – I play my cards far better than he does. I bluff beautifully.'

'Dear girl,' Jacoulet greeted her, 'you bluff outrageously. But today I call the bluff. Today my tea leaves say I shall win.' He kissed her on both cheeks. 'And Sam. *Bello ben proporzionato*! I take Italian lessons from the vice-consul; he says it means handsome. So I say it to all the men!'

'Hello Paul.' Sam smiled, and they shook hands.

'You now live in a penthouse, I hear?'

'For the moment.'

'Very grand. Spare a thought for the poor unfortunates like us, who have to suffer here in deprivation.'

Jacoulet accompanied his mother into the house. Sam doubted if they would see a day when the artist was deprived. He was a rich man. He had a villa adjacent to the French Ambassador's, beside one owned by Justine's parents. It was highly amusing that both neighbours were appalled by his behaviour, but tolerated it as artistic temperament because of his prestige. They even – through gritted teeth – sometimes invited him to diplomatic functions.

Walking past the verandah to fetch his bicycle, Sam could see him inside the house. He stood in front of a large wall mirror, powdering his face and applying more lipstick. He saw Sam's reflection gazing at him, waggled his fingers in a mocking farewell, and laughed at his own grotesque image in the glass.

Sam smiled. It was impossible not to like the scandalous Jacoulet. He mounted his bike, and rode into town. Karuizawa was changing. It was not only that the village was crowded at a time of year when it was normally deserted. There were more Germans, far more than in the summer, he thought. Or perhaps they were so clearly intent on drawing attention to themselves by wearing swastika arm bands; it was now a common sight to see them meet and raise their arms in a militant Nazi salute.

These were not Germans he knew, some of whom had been school friends, whose families had lived in Kobe and Yokohama for years, if not all their lives. These were staff from the Reich's Asian embassies, as well as bureaucrats from Berlin, and party members. There were also security officials drawn from the ranks of the SS. They were loud, aggressive and disturbing. Two of them stood in the street, making Sam swerve his bike to avoid them.

'*Heil Hitler*,' they shouted. '*Sieg Heil*.'

That weekend, Sam bought a whetstone for their rusty old axe, and worked on it until the blade was razor sharp. He took it with him into the woods behind the house. He tramped to a safe distance, for all forests in Japan were the property of the Emperor, and cutting timber in them without a permit was a serious offence.

The ground was soft, wet with rotting autumn leaves. In spring, the soil would be enriched by the mulch, and the forest would be a blaze of wisteria and blossom. The dormant birch trees, red maples and willows would take on their plumage, enlivening the Imperial Estate with a tapestry of variegated florescence. Larks, finches and golden-crested wrens would return, and the exquisite fluted notes of the *uguisu*'s night song might be heard.

He loved this forest; it had been his private playground in far-off summers, when the idea of war – or even family divorce – was inconceivable. This was where he had his imaginary adventures; fashioning scraps of wood into rifles to hunt wild bears and snakes, or setting out on journeys to track eagles. Later, less combative, it was here he sketched butterflies, trying only to capture their tropical beauty. It was Sam's own realm; friends were sometimes invited; sisters never. He had kept this domain Angelique-free by telling her there were dragons in the forest. It was what, in childish awe when any incantation was possible, he had once believed himself.

An animal scurried from hiding, startling him from his reverie. No dragon, he perceived, just an alarmed squirrel. It fled, clawing its way into the safety of an evergreen conifer. He smiled and decided it was time to get on with some work.

He found a dead laurel tree crushed by a fallen oak, and started to cut steadily, until he had a pile of two-metre lengths of thick timber. There was a quiet satisfaction in the wealthy Royal Household providing warmth for his family's winter. Taking as many lengths as he could carry at a time, he shifted the firewood to the cleared ground behind their house. Later he cut them into short sizes, split them, filled the box beside the pot-bellied stove, then stacked the rest below the back verandah to remain dry.

'What if someone steals it?' Angelique asked. At twenty-one she was a pretty girl with a wide circle of friends, mostly male. Several had watched his efforts without offering assistance.

'If they do, you freeze or cut some more. Better still, get a few of those randy boyfriends to help.'

'Who said they're randy?'

'They hang round you and Octavia all the time. Like bees around a couple of honey carts.'

'Charming! Octavia will love to know you called us shit carts. Anyway, what else is there to do? No dances – because it's decadent! Nowhere to go at night, and in the daytime, those Nazis try to start trouble. Fine for you up in your penthouse, able to do what you like, but it's hell being here.'

He nodded. There was no point trying to be evasive about it. There was a difficult time ahead, in an overcrowded town never meant for winter. Nor for such a volatile mix of people.

'Do the Germans really try to make trouble?'

'Mostly the young ones. They look at us and make filthy remarks, even try to grab us by the tits or anywhere they can.'

'You be careful, Angie,' he said, concerned. 'Someone should tell these bastards they're losing the war.'

'But that's the problem. They don't think they are.'

'They must know they've lost Paris, and most of France.'

'They said it was propaganda. One claimed they got sick of Paris and gave it back. And that we should be very careful.'

'Us? Why should we be careful?'

'Because we could be enemy aliens.'

The thought had occurred to Sam before. *They could even be interned, if Japan should decide they were enemies. But surely not. They had all been born here.*

He said as casually as he could: 'I suppose it could come to that. But it's so unlikely, I don't think we should worry.'

'This same German – he wears an SS tunic and a cap – said it'd be worse for those with Jewish blood. He said that in Germany they know what to do with Jews. Mama told me one night, after a few drinks, about your real mother. She shouldn't have, but she did.'

Sam felt a sudden chill. He put his arms around his sister, and could feel her trembling.

'I don't mind you knowing, Angie, but please take no notice of such Nazi garbage.' After a moment he added, 'I thought Ma had cut down on her drinking.'

'Not when she can get it,' Angelique said, and changed the subject, reminding him Claude was arriving, and she and Justine were to play a mixed doubles with them the following day.

Sam rode to town to reserve a court for the four of them.

Sorry, he was told. All tennis courts are reserved.

Sam pointed to the board in the secretary's office. Five of the ten courts had pencilled bookings; the other five were blank.

'They can't all be reserved,' he said. 'Those on the west side are available. How about I take number four court, nine o'clock tomorrow, for a couple of hours?'

'It's not free,' the secretary said. 'Haven't you heard?'

'Heard what?' Sam asked.

'The courts have been divided. New rule of the local

authority. Five can be used by the neutral foreigners, but the five western courts are all reserved for our German and Italian allies.'

Sam stared at him with incredulity. The secretary gave an amused smile and shrugged. They had known each other since the man had been a coach, and Sam first held a racquet. For years, Sam had thought they were friends.

'What happens if they don't want to play?'

'Then nobody does. Those courts are theirs, and not to be used by anyone else.'

'Jesus Christ,' Sam said.

'Don't blame me,' the secretary told him sharply.

'Then who do I blame? Hitler?'

'Watch yourself,' the secretary said. 'Don't say anything stupid. They have a right to this place, the same as anyone else.'

'I see. A right not to use the courts, and not allow anyone else to do so. That's some special right, that is.'

'It's now the rules, so don't be a fucking idiot, Sam.'

He decided there was no reply to that, and left the office. Across the street, he saw a loitering group with swastika arm bands. Some wore *Wehrmacht* uniforms and one had an SS tunic and cap. He realised this must be the one who had threatened Angie.

All of a sudden there was an incident. One strutting figure jostled a middle-aged man hurrying past. The man stopped, shocked by the deliberate contact, clearly confused. The Nazi with SS emblems walked up to him and spat in his face. There was the sound of shouted voices abusing him.

'*Juden*! Filthy Jewish vermin!'

Sam saw with a shock that the man was their family doctor, Klaus Wittenberg. He and his partner, Doctor Plessner who was also Jewish, had lived in Japan with their respective families for most of their lives. As far as he knew, no-one had ever betrayed any kind of anti-Semitism towards either of them before.

'*Juden schmutz*,' they were chorusing. '*Juden schmutz*.' Jewish filth, Sam assumed it meant. Doctor Wittenberg appeared dizzy, as if he might fall. They started to chant louder, enjoying his bewilderment, feeding on his fear.

Sam began to move towards them. He was not keen to be a hero, but this was obscene. He stopped halfway across the street as Doctor Plessner came from the house where they both practised. Plessner moved through the Germans, silently took Wittenberg by the arm, and escorted him away from the chanting men into the house.

It was the one with the SS emblems who noticed Sam still standing in the middle of the street. He nudged the others, and they all turned. It seemed as if – cheated of their sport by the sudden rescue – they were determined on a replacement. Anyone would do, and here was a prospect. Like robots they flung out their arms in a fascist salute. Then in unison so precise that it seemed macabre, they goose-stepped to where he stood. Sam had a moment's choice of turning away from their intimidation, or remaining. He felt it was too late to turn away.

'*Sieg Heil*!' they shouted, and came so close that their combined breath was sour in his face.

'Jew-loving shit,' they said.

'We know you,' they said. 'You're on our list.'

'Dirty yids,' they said. 'We make Jews into soap.'

'Put in a complaint about us. Report us,' they said.

'*Sieg Heil*! *Sieg Heil*!'

They shouted it again and again, trying to incite him with their chants. Hoping he would be provoked to lash out, so they could retaliate. He knew the intention. They wanted to create trouble, and make it appear he had started it. But then they became aware of an audience. The tennis players on the courts set aside for neutrals had stopped their games to watch this. Other people were gathering in the street. Their disapproval was palpable.

'We'll remember you, you dirty French bastard,' they said, and strolled away as if they already owned the town.

CHAPTER 20

Two unexpected things happened in December of 1944, and Florence Eisler would remember them for the rest of her life. The first of these was a summons to a meeting with James Lindsay, who ordered coffee for them both, asked her to shut the door, and told the switchboard he did not wish to be disturbed.

Florence, however, within a brief space of time was quite profoundly disturbed. Most of all when Lindsay rather forthrightly asked if there was any problem in her marriage, any minor or major upset he should know about?

The former Florrie, the one who had given Mr Noble short shrift and a month's notice, would have told him to mind his own bloody business. But the Florrie who had wed in love, lost her husband to an internment camp and fought ferociously for his release, who had shouted abuse at Mr H.W. Watson like a fishwife, had had Carl restored to her three years ago – only to spend the past few months in suspicion and misery – that Florrie just shrugged and shook her head as though she could not find an answer.

'Are there misunderstandings?' Mr Lindsay asked.

'I think it's called the ebb and flow of marriage,' she said, trying not to sound acerbic, for she was fond of James Lindsay.

'Ebb and flow? You mean the tide's out?' His question actually made her smile, and for some strange reason she felt better.

'At the present moment, Mr Lindsay, I'd say that's a pretty fair assessment.'

'Are you still able to work together?'

'Oh yes. We're two consenting adults, perfectly civilised and polite. At least I hope so.'

'But if you were to have far more responsibility, how would he feel? As a lawyer working here, perhaps a partner?'

'If I was to . . .' She was puzzled by his words, and said so. 'Whatever you mean by that, ask him. I can't answer for him.'

'It's your reply I want. Is your marriage going to last?'

She took a deep breath, and kept her temper.

'That really is an impossible question. I can hardly be expected to discuss it with anyone.' *But I nearly did*, she thought. *I wanted to discuss it with Sam, but couldn't bring myself to do it*. 'To be honest, Mr Lindsay, I don't know.'

'Can I help in any way?'

'No,' Florence said.

'I thought you were so happy?'

'I was. But recently, things seemed to have changed.'

'Dammit,' Lindsay said. 'You see, this is important. I want you to take over this firm.'

She felt she hadn't heard him correctly.

'Take over? But I already run the office.'

'I mean run the entire firm. Be the head of it.'

'How? I'm not a solicitor?'

'You're an administrator. My intention is to retire soon and appoint you general manager. The solicitors, including Carl, would be partners. You'd be the senior partner.'

'Good God Almighty,' Florence said, trying to absorb it.

'But I don't want any messy divorce between partners.'

'General manager? Am I capable?'

'Do you imagine I'd suggest it, if you weren't?'

'What would the Law Society say?'

'Probably Good God Almighty, like you did.'

'And the solicitors and partners?'

'Will accept you or move on.'

'Mr Lindsay, I don't know what to say.'

'Well, start by assuring me you're interested in the job.'

'I'm interested. Of course.'

'Secondly, that you feel able to cope.'

'I feel incredulous. But I'll learn to cope.'

'And finally, what about Carl?'

She was thoughtful for quite a long time. He watched her, thinking that many other women – men, too, most certainly – would have glibly asserted it would be no problem. If Florence had a liability it was her honesty, which was an irony, as that was why he wanted her to run the firm he had established.

'Carl and I,' she finally said, 'have spent far too many months being carefully polite and talking like strangers. It's time we stopped doing that.'

'What if you can't sort it out?'

'I don't even want to contemplate that. But neither can we go on the way we are.'

She asked for time to work it out, and James Lindsay suggested there was still a fortnight to the Christmas and New Year holidays. When the office reopened in January, by then he needed to know the situation and how things stood between them. Would that be fair?

Quite fair, she agreed. She went home in a dizzy state of wonder at the prospect of heading one of the city's most prestigious law firms. It would certainly attract newspaper attention, and cause comment in legal circles. The probability of that made her nervous. It might be greeted with derision; lawyers could be lethal with their gossip. She could imagine the shoptalk; J. Lindsay had gone off his trolley, handed the firm to an ex-typist. Or sneaky innuendoes that the crusty bachelor had been a sly dog all these years; why else would he do such a thing? They'd probably christen her Portia. Or Lucrezia Borgia. She almost laughed aloud thinking of Mr Noble's reaction, but felt the late Charles Cusack would have been pleased.

Realising that there might be a flow of vitriolic comment strengthened her resolve. It exceeded any of her dreams, it was the chance of a lifetime, and she was going to make it a success. That would shut them all up, she hoped, and for the rest of the trip home she planned the future. Perhaps she could change the firm's dated name; make it more direct and modern, call it Lindsays. For James Lindsay had always been the driving spirit.

He had begun practice in North Sydney, finding ideal premises directly opposite the police station. He hoped that traffic offenders, drunks and various other miscreants leaving with a court summons, would find themselves face to face with the helpful word SOLICITOR beckoning from his window. A popular and gregarious man, his business had succeeded to such an extent that he structured an amalgamation with Houghton and White, and they had moved into the fashionable comfort of Bligh Street, beside the Savoy Theatre.

They had flourished, progressing from misdemeanours in Magistrate's Courts to company law and higher echelons. The other partners had died, their children were uninterested in the law, and only James remained. It was up to her, Florence reflected, to perpetuate his name. She had not known Mr Houghton or Mr White. So it should be Lindsays; she liked the sound of it.

All she had to do was brace herself for an encounter to sort out her life with Carl. Somehow that had to be resolved, though she felt nervous at the prospect of confrontation. But she was right in what she had said to James. They could not go on like this.

Actual head of a law firm! Her sister Catherine would have been so proud. If there was any mention in the press or the Law Society journal, she'd cut it out and save it for Sam.

There was a bombing raid far to the west of the city, somewhere out near Mitaka-Shi. Sitting at his window in the dark, he could see the incendiaries burst into flames, and knew they must be targeting wooden houses. Sure enough, the sky was lit as an entire neighbourhood began to blaze. The flimsy homes were easy casualties, readily combustible when the B29s came on their carpet-bombing raids, with magnesium bombs primed with oil and iron oxide, or a lethal cocktail of petrol and explosive. There were never enough brigades to extinguish the widely scattered fires caused by carpet-bombing.

In the worst raids, whole areas were engulfed by flame and destroyed. By morning, streets where there had been rows of houses were nothing but ash. If the wind suddenly changed direction, people were often trapped before they could realise the danger and were roasted alive. Others sat helplessly amid the devastation, watching homes and belongings reduced to cinders, impervious to the heat. They were numbed by loss, and beyond pain.

The neutral foreigners were deeply divided over the bombing. Some people, safe in Karuizawa, declared it should be intensified; it was the only way to force Japan's leaders to surrender. Others said it was inhuman, driven by vengeance, compassionless. It was sending young crews into the skies to become murderers.

There was a third group who were convinced it would have a contrary effect, the Count de Boulanger among them. He had voiced it at lunch in the bank, where only four French staff now remained. Mademoiselle Patou declared her distress over the raids, and her concern the civilians were targets. Claude Laroche took the opposing attitude; the Japanese deserved it; they'd asked for it, and now the bastards were getting it back – in spades.

That was when the Count spoke. 'I wonder if the United States realises what they're doing? Don't they know this kind of mass bombing only binds the people, and makes them stronger?'

Sam decided it was a rhetorical question, and did not need a response. His own feelings were mixed. It was terrible to see what happened to people on the ground. What it was like up in the sky, unleashing the incendiaries, he had no idea. But on the ground, he kept encountering people who were damaged, people wounded or burnt. Not soldiers; they were not normally the casualties; the victims he saw were children, women and old people. Civilians who believed their leaders, their militarist government, who had told them that one day soon they would own the world. Now they were bewildered, for they were starting to realise the world hated them.

For a competent woman, Florrie found herself dreading what lay ahead. She felt sure she would be tongue-tied and incapable. When she reached home Carl was in the spare room they used as a study. He had requested the day off to prepare a brief for a Kings Counsel in a case before the High Court in January. The eminent silk was already enjoying holidays in his house at Palm Beach, and the documents were to be sent to him by a special courier.

Florence thought it a waste of time; the barrister would be unlikely even to glance at the brief until he returned to his city chambers; he would be far too busy socialising with the elite who could afford luxury houses on the peninsula.

'Hello,' she called, as she entered the house, and glimpsed Carl in the study, startled at her entry, and seeming to hide some papers. *Stop it*, she told herself, *don't be a silly paranoid bitch*, but already she knew it was going to be difficult. She put down her handbag, took plenty of time, and when she came into the study and kissed him on the cheek, he was engrossed in a familiar folder containing legal documents. 'Hard day, darling?'

'Rather slow progress,' he said. 'It was so hot that I had to sneak a swim. Then I felt sleepy, and the next thing I'd dozed off for an hour. I doubt if this will be ready for the courier to collect in the morning.'

'I'll ring them,' she said, her voice as casual as she

could make it, and went into the kitchen to make a cup of tea.

I'm not paranoid, she thought. *It wasn't that brief he was working on when I came through the door, and I doubt if he went for a swim or slept.*

She brought him tea and biscuits, left them beside him and then said casually: 'Saturday, Carl. I've invited Alfie, Joan and Ron, Cathy and Vince and some others for lunch. A pre-Christmas party. I thought we'd make it a barbecue.'

'Saturday,' he began to say, but she was already back in the kitchen. She sipped her tea, sitting and waiting. In the evening paper, Glenn Miller was missing. Tributes were flowing in for the man who had given the world *Moonlight Serenade*. Believed shot down over the English Channel, on his way to play for troops in France.

'How awfully sad,' she said, 'Glenn Miller.'

'Yes, I heard it on the radio,' Carl said. He stood in the doorway, hesitant. 'Liebchen, about Saturday . . .'

'I thought we'd go to the fish shop and get oysters.'

'I have to work,' he said.

'On what?'

'So many things I'm behind on . . .'

'No, you're not,' she said. 'I do run the administration in the office, or had you forgotten? Why do you treat me like a fool?'

'But liebchen . . .'

'Don't, please.'

'Don't what?'

'Call me liebchen when you're lying to me. It's a term of affection, and it shouldn't be used when you lie. You haven't been in the office on Saturdays for months.'

'Why do you say that, Florence?'

'Because I've checked on you.'

'Checked?'

'Spied, if you prefer, Carl. Ever since a day when I came to surprise you, to suggest we see a film, and you weren't there. So, since then the switchboard hasn't been shut down. Each Saturday I telephone, and each Saturday there's no answer. So now I think it's time to stop lying.'

'You came to the office,' he said.

'On an impulse. Sometimes I wish I hadn't.'

'Why didn't you say so?'

'How could I, when you came home and explained how busy you'd been? It was the Carruthers contract.'

'Dear Gott,' he said, 'all this time?'

'Yes. I should've spoken. Perhaps I couldn't, because I didn't want to know there was someone else.'

'Someone else?' He sounded incredulous. 'Florrie, for God's sake, you don't think that!'

'I don't know what to think. I propose a party for our friends – a party, by the way, which I haven't yet arranged. But you could hardly wait to tell me you work at the office on Saturdays.'

'So it was a trap?'

'If you like. Call it what you wish; I can't live like this.'

'Please listen to me. I love you.'

'Prove it. Tell me the truth.'

'I only wish I could,' Carl said.

They went into town the following day. She had rung the office and made an excuse that she and Carl would be late. Carl had made a telephone call, but to whom she had no idea. On the tram and ferry they could find little to say. She bought a paper; there were already fulsome eulogies to Glenn Miller.

'Isn't it strange,' he broke the silence, 'we feel so sad because we've heard his music. But all those slaughtered Jews in the Warsaw ghetto, perhaps they would've made music, too. Are people sad for them, or are there too many deaths to comprehend?'

'I'm sad about the Jews in Warsaw and everywhere else,' she said abruptly, but that was the end of their conversation. It was such a strange day. He had promised to explain to her, yet could not tell her until they arrived. But where was that? He had not told her where, nor did she feel able to ask.

They left the ferry at Circular Quay, and took a tram through the city. At Bathurst Street, Carl helped her out, and they walked in the direction of the park and the Museum underground station. They stopped outside a small and anonymous building.

'I remember this . . .' she started to say, but all he did was press the buzzer for the antique elevator. Minutes later, they were in the office with the name H.W. Watson on the door, and she was face to face with the same public servant who had been so uncaring and inflexible over three years ago.

'Please sit down, Mrs Eisler.'

She stared at him, then turned in bewilderment to Carl.

'Tell me why we're here.'

'He can't,' Mr Watson said.

'Of course he can.'

'No, Madam, he's not allowed to. Kindly just sit down.'

God, you haven't changed, she thought, hating him, and because there seemed no alternative she sat down.

'I gather you're still making trouble, Mrs Eisler.'

'Mr Watson, you have all the real charm of a funnel-web spider.'

He gave her a bleak look and said, 'I seem to remember you were rather abusive the last time.'

'I never am with decent people. But the kind of man who imprisons my husband for two years, finds out it was all a mistake but never bothers to apologise, is not my idea of decent. Nor the sort of person I want to see again.'

'Florence, please,' Carl said. 'Let him explain.'

'I'd rather you did.'

'No,' Watson interrupted. 'I said he's not allowed to.'

'Why not?'

'Because of the Official Secrets Act,' Watson told her, and she gazed incredulously at him, then turned to look at Carl.

'Am I going crazy? Are you working for him?'

'He is not to answer, Mrs Eisler! Don't make trouble.'

'Have we come here for you to say Carl can't confide in me, and you can't tell me anything?'

'You've come because he telephoned me and said there are difficulties in your marriage.' His expression indicated that he was not at all surprised with such a feisty and awkward woman. 'I agreed I would simply explain he is bound by the Official Secrets Act, but I'm not prepared to say anything else.'

'Am I to gather from this, that you recruited him for some sort of official work – that after the way you treated him, he was persuaded, blackmailed, or cajoled into working for you?'

'No comment, Madam.'

'And this is why he has to lie to me about his whereabouts on Saturdays, and put our marriage at risk? You and your Official Secrets Act! What on earth can be so secret that he can't tell me?'

'Almost everything.'

I'm disgracing myself again, she thought, *but there's something about this man that makes me lose control. I'm hardly fit to run a law firm, if I can't manage to handle a creature like this*. She rose to her feet. There was no point in remaining here, but it was important to regain her dignity and stay calm.

'I won't thank you,' she said, 'because that would be hypocritical. We'd better leave, Carl. We have work waiting for us at the office.'

'To hell with this,' Carl said, in a voice so filled with rage that it startled them both. 'To hell with you and your bloody intelligence mob, and your stupid official secrets.'

'Mr Eisler, that's enough,' Watson said warningly, but Carl took no notice.

'I resent the way you treat my wife. I'm sick of playing your silly espionage games, which is nothing more important than reading pages of German messages and translating them for you . . .'

'Mr Eisler, stop!'

'That's exactly what I'm going to do. Stop. One of my friends said, the best thing about this country – you can always tell someone to go to buggery. Well, you go to buggery, Mr Watson. I quit. Stick your official secrets right up your arse.'

Watson picked up the phone. 'Switchboard? I want a guard here at once. Mr Eisler is not to leave the building.'

'I don't think you can do that,' Florence said. 'No secrets have been disclosed. A man has simply told you he no longer wishes to work for you, even if it was in colourful vernacular.' She smiled. 'I think it was splendidly put, darling.'

'Thank you, liebchen.'

'It was insulting,' Watson fumed.

'Absolutely,' Florence agreed. 'Quite rude. But that's not a crime, not unless he shouts it in the street and frightens dear old ladies. And in this country, even in wartime, a civilian cannot be conscripted for this sort of work against his will. If you try to keep him here, I'll remain with him. You may attempt to remove me physically, but in that case you'll have to answer an allegation of assault. If you do throw me out and keep Carl despite his wish to leave, I'll have a writ of habeus corpus from the Supreme Court by lunchtime. And I think you'll be answering some very uncomfortable questions from our barrister and probably from your superiors. We both know you've well and truly exceeded your authority.'

There was a knock on the door, and a man in uniform entered. He looked at Watson, who seemed momentarily speechless.

'Any trouble, sir?'

'These people,' Watson said venomously. 'Get rid of them. See them off the premises. Get out of my office, Mrs Eisler, and take him with you. The work he was doing was trifling, of no real importance whatever.'

'Interesting you should say that, after forbidding him to speak for fear of the Official Secrets Act. You and your clandestine little empire of deceit. I think you're spurious, Mr Watson, a very small-minded person with large delusions. Ready, Carl?'

'Absolutely,' Carl said, smiling, and took her hand. They walked past the security guard. Florrie had an impression the man was trying to suppress a grin.

In Karuizawa, there were more signs of Nazi swastikas, noisy street encounters with out-flung arms and shouts of *Heil Hitler*. Sam sat with Justine and Claude in the cafe near the tennis courts.

'The bastards act like they're winning the war.'

'It scares me they still could,' Claude said. 'They're hurting England with those rockets. There's a rumour Hitler's got a secret bomb. They're far from beaten yet.'

'If you want to talk about the war,' Justine said, 'I think I'll go home.'

'Instant change of subject,' Sam said promptly, and slid his hand into hers as they exchanged messages with busy fingers. 'What's the local gossip since last week?'

'There's a new German doctor arrived,' she said.

'Who needs him? We've got two doctors.'

'Jewish. The Nazis fear being contaminated by Jews.'

'Personally, I'd let the buggers die,' Sam said. 'Plessner and Wittenberg always treated the German families who live here.'

Claude said, 'Berlin has sent an Aryan party member.'

Justine added, 'Herr Doktor Wirtz is tall, suitably blond, and clicks his heels beautifully.'

'Sounds as if you think he's sexy?'

She hesitated, and shrugged. Claude said: 'Ask me. He's about as sexy as fat Hermann Goering doing a goose step in *lederhosen*.' They all laughed, and Justine and Sam rose. Claude signalled for another coffee. 'What are you two doing the rest of the day?'

Neither replied for a moment. Then Justine smiled. 'Oh, we'll think of something,' she said.

The sleeping bag was Sam's idea. They had debated the options of where to go. Justine was envious of the penthouse.

'It would be perfect,' she said.

'Marvellous,' he agreed.

'Exciting just to think about it,' she sighed, but they both knew it was geographically and parentally impossible.

If she spent a night in Tokyo, her parents would want to know who she was spending it with. All the details. So where could they make love? Not his house. Not hers. That left the woods or the golf course, but it was December, and bitterly cold. Not weather for lovers.

So when Sam said there was a double sleeping bag in the junk room of their cottage, it seemed the answer. It was now packed in a muslin bag on the back of his bicycle. Justine's bike was parked beside his. A casual glance confirmed nobody was paying attention. They climbed on their saddles and pedalled away. Half an hour later the bikes were hidden, they were naked, passionately entwined in the sleeping bag, concealed among pines and shrubbery that provided a hazard not far from the eighth green of the Hanare Yama golf club.

'Oh, God,' Justine said. 'I think I'm coming.'

'Not yet, darling.'

'Please,' she said, 'soon.'

'Soon,' he promised.

It was delightfully warm in the sleeping bag. Somewhere outside their selected hide was the December chill, but their limbs were heated, and being enclosed like this brought about an erotic and sensuous feeling, as if no-one else in the world existed.

'Oh, Jesus Christ,' Justine said.

Sam was about to excite her to a fervent climax with all the carnal phrases he could think of, when he heard a sudden thud followed by what seemed like a rustle of leaves. On the brink of ecstasy they turned to look, fearing an animal. Instead a golf ball rolled through the bushes and came to a halt inches away from them.

Everything in their lives stopped. All senses froze. Sam extricated himself, and leapt from the sleeping bag. Stark-naked and ignoring the cold, he peered through the bushes towards a distant pair of golfers approaching along the fairway. The ball lay on the edge of the sleeping bag like a reproach.

'Who is it?' Justine asked.

'God knows,' Sam said. 'I think it's the Ambassador –'

'Which Ambassador? There's dozens of them here.'

'The French Ambassador,' he said, 'but I don't know who he's playing with.'

'It doesn't matter,' she said. 'Quick, toss the ball out of the bushes. Nobody's going to complain about a lucky rebound.'

'I suppose not,' Sam said, 'but I – Jesus Christ, he's with your father.'

In frantic haste and a tangle of underclothes they managed to gather the sleeping bag and dive for shelter among a screen of jasmine and sacred bamboo. From there, frozen more by panic than the chill temperature, they watched as Justine's father parted the bushes and stalked towards the golf ball. He glared at it, then checked to see where the Ambassador was standing. Clearly he was out on the fairway, out of sight as Pierre Fournier tapped the ball into a more advantageous position, and called to his opponent.

'Armand?'

'I'm here. I suppose you're surrounded by bush and trees. Do you have to take a penalty?'

'No. Piece of luck. It hit one of the branches and is sitting up quite nicely.'

'Oh, really?' The Ambassador sounded disappointed.

'I might even be able to get this on the green, old boy,' he called, proceeding to nudge the ball and improve it to a better lie, as his naked daughter and her beau watched fascinated.

'Your daddy is a dirty old cheat,' Sam whispered in her ear. Justine clamped a hand over her mouth to stifle a giggle, while her parent, oblivious to this, continued to furtively move his ball.

'What's happening in there?' the Ambassador shouted.

'Just taking my time, old chap. Difficult shot.' By this time the ball was on a mound, in as prime a position as possible. 'Ready now. Keep your eye on the green, I'll go for it,' he called, and swung. The golf ball went high in the air and sailed out of sight.

'Fuck.' The Ambassador's annoyance confirmed it had landed successfully.

Pierre Fournier picked up his clubs, and emerged from the bushes. 'It's near the flag. That was a bit of luck!'

'Luck,' the Ambassador was caustic. 'If your bloody ball landed in the duck pond, it would float to the other side – then improve its position.'

'Just one of those days, Armand. We all have our special moments of fortune.'

Amid the bushes, Sam and Justine scrambled into their clothes. They carefully peered out at the fairway, in time to see the Ambassador shank his next shot, and hurl his club angrily in the air. It lodged in the bare branches of a nearby oak tree, and stayed there.

'Shit,' he shouted, 'shit, shit, shit!'

Fortunately his rage drowned a laugh that Justine could not suppress. Sam hushed her, wanting to laugh himself at the club stuck beyond either man's reach.

'Come on,' he whispered, bundling up the sleeping bag.

They left the thicket and ran across the adjoining fairway. Their bikes were hidden in a clump of bamboo. Minutes later they were pedalling hard in the direction of town, completely frustrated, but unable to stop laughing.

Florrie and Carl had dinner on the verandah and drank several glasses of wine, mainly because he kept toasting her in glowing terms, refilling their glasses as he insisted they drink to her vivacity and her vocabulary.

'Stop it,' she said, flushed with pleasure and reaching out to hold his hand, 'you'll get me drunk with your words and the wine, then take advantage of me.'

'What a wonderful idea of yours,' he said, and by mutual accord they went straight to bed and made love. Later, lying awake in each other's arms, there was a cool north-easter through the open bedroom window, and they could hear the gentle lap of waves on the sand. The moon was rising over the sea, and Carl reminded her how long it was since they had walked on the beach at night.

'Let's,' she said, putting on a shift. There was no need for underclothes or shoes.

'I love the feel of Australian sand between my toes,' Carl said as they strolled to the reef in the moonlight. 'When I was a boy in Munich, I never dreamed I'd come to a magical place like this, or meet someone like you. I can't bear to think how close we came to losing each other.'

'Forget it,' she said.

'No, we mustn't forget. Or ever have any secrets or lies between us. I apologise for the lies, but I was rather in awe of their Official Secrets Act, and its penalties. And also,' he observed wryly, 'we Germans are renowned for obeying orders.'

'Why did you work for that awful man?'

'I wanted to do something. For this country, I mean.'

'This country that put you in prison for two years.'

'It also gave me refuge, and gave me you.' They walked to where the sea rippled over the rock formation of the reef. 'I was angry in prison. But I couldn't stay angry for two years.'

'I did,' she said promptly. He laughed and agreed, then kissed her before they retraced their footsteps along the sand.

'I thought about it a lot in there. Doing something, when they let me out. *If* they let me out. I wouldn't be allowed to join the army. But I could interview Germans, or translate any captured document. I wanted to help defeat Hitler, Watson didn't blackmail or cajole me. I volunteered.'

'I can understand that. But why him?'

'There was nobody else. After my release, I asked to be put in touch with the right people. He said he was the right person. I never liked him, but I thought I was helping.'

'I'm sure you were,' she insisted, but the memory of Watson's sneering dismissal of his value lay between them.

'What was the name of the film?' he suddenly asked.

'Which film?'

'The one you wanted me to see?'

'*Henry V*, with Laurence Olivier.'

'It's supposed to be good, isn't it?'

'Wonderful.'

'Let's see it next Saturday,' he said.

CHAPTER 21

There was a strange atmosphere in the bank. Sam came downstairs from the penthouse and felt something was different. There was no sign of the Count or Emile Laroche. The ritual morning greetings had been dispensed with since the departure of most of the French staff, but people still welcomed each other in a less formal manner. Today hardly anything was said. The Japanese knew something was amiss, he felt certain, but they merely bowed to him and each other, and began their work. When Sam went to his desk, one of the clerks came hurrying to murmur that Monsieur Le Comte was in his office, and wished to see him at once.

Not only the Count was there. The chief accountant was also present. Neither replied when Sam wished them good morning.

'I'm afraid we have some bad news,' the Count said. 'I'll let Monsieur Laroche inform you of what's happened.' Abruptly he rose and walked to the window, turning his back on them as he stood looking out at the grey morning. Sam felt a foreboding.

'What bad news?' The premonition was stronger as he gazed at a hint of triumph in Laroche's appraisal.

'You may be surprised, perhaps not,' the accountant said, 'we have a thief in the bank.'

'Who?'

'Mademoiselle Patou. She's been stealing money, regular amounts of it over a considerable time.'

'No!' He spoke emphatically. 'That's impossible.'

'I've gathered evidence. It's on His Excellency's desk.' Laroche's voice could not conceal his satisfaction. 'What we must establish, before calling the police, is if she acted alone or had help.'

'Help? Whose help?' Bewilderment blunted his wits.

'It could only be yours,' the chief accountant said.

In the silence that followed, Sam was aware the figure at the window had turned to watch him. He delayed his reply, trying to control his emotions. The pause lengthened, became uncomfortable.

'Do *you* think Cecile's a thief?' He excluded Laroche, directing his question to the Count.

'I'm sorry. I wish it wasn't so, but the proof's there. M'sieu Laroche has been his usual thorough self.' The venom in his voice, the dislike was unmistakable.

'I merely did my duty,' Laroche said.

Again Sam disregarded him. 'Do you believe I helped her?' he asked the Count.

'It seems unlikely. I would prefer to hear you deny it.'

'If the police are called, I'll wait and tell them.'

'Tell them what?'

'That I find it hard to believe she did it, let alone respond to accusations I might have helped her.'

'There are reasonable grounds to ask the question,' the chief accountant said heatedly.

'The question's been asked and answered,' the Count replied. He turned to Sam. 'I didn't say we'd called the police. There's been no decision on what action the bank will take.'

'She must be charged,' Laroche insisted.

'I'll decide what's to be done. You may go,' he told the chief accountant, and then gestured to Sam. 'You stay.'

Emile Laroche turned brick-red, and it appeared he might refuse to be dismissed in such a peremptory manner. 'I'll take the documents,' he said.

'Leave them,' the Count instructed.

'But they're my evidence, Monsieur.'

'The bank's evidence. Now go back to work, and if a word of this spreads to the staff, you'll be out of a job tomorrow.'

They watched as he went slowly to the door, turned to stare at them both, then went out slamming it shut behind him.

'Dear God,' the Count said, and sat at his desk. 'He's been doing nothing else for days. Like a bloodhound. He enjoyed telling me how she took a little from here, a little from there. Over the past twelve months, she's stolen a total of fifty thousand yen.'

Sam stood there, wondering what to say. In terms of the money they had sent to Swiss accounts, this was small change.

'Sit down, for heaven's sake,' the Count said irritably.

'Where is she?' Sam asked, sitting as directed.

'She's at home. I told her not to come in today.'

'At home? I don't even know where that is.'

'An apartment near Hibiya Park. Very select. The only

kind Jacques Clermont would tolerate living in. I'm sure you know Clermont?'

'Distantly.'

'It's the best way to know him. The man's a complete cad.' The very English expression, in the Count's Gallic accent, made Sam smile, and the other noticed. 'Well, you know what I mean.'

'I know exactly what you mean, sir. But I heard that while he never worked in his life, he had an allowance. And Cecile – Mademoiselle – augmented it with her wages and doing translations.'

'She did. That's how they managed for a long time. But it seems that a year ago his allowance stopped. Whether it was the war, or his family got sick of him, I don't know. Cecile doesn't know. But it stopped. So she had a choice. Let him walk out, find himself a woman with money to support him, or else keep paying his bills.'

Poor Mademoiselle, Sam thought. *Poor bloody Cecile*.

'She told him not to worry,' the Count continued, 'that she'd manage – which was when she started to steal.'

'He must've guessed,' Sam said.

'People like Clermont never bother to guess. They don't care where it comes from. As long as it's there when they want it.'

Sam thought of the blonde applauding him at the tennis, and had a longing to kick Jacques Clermont in the balls. It might curtail his winning ways. He realised the Count was still speaking.

'The bloody man has led her a hell of a life. And now I've got to report this, and send her to gaol.'

Sam hesitated. Then he said, 'Do you have to, sir?'

'Of course I have to. What the devil do you mean?'

'Fifty thousand yen. It's modest, when I suppose she could've stolen a million.' The Count sat up in his chair and stared at him. 'It's twelve thousand, five hundred dollars,' Sam said.

'Of the bank's money...'

'Yes sir, absolutely. I'm only trying to point out how little she took, when she could have taken a lot. I suppose I'm trying to say that unfortunately the penalty is going to be the same.'

'Not necessarily.'

'Well, it's a prison sentence either way. And for a woman like her that would be terrible. I doubt if they separate killers from thieves, or prostitutes and lesbians from other women.'

'Sam, will you shut up!' The Count's usual assurance had deserted him. He was agitated.

'I will, Monsieur. Can I just say something else?'

'You've already said far too much.'

'This wouldn't occur to the chief accountant, but I'm sure it will to you. She only took enough for them to live on. And at times, it must have been an awful temptation when we had huge sums of cash there, before it was put on deposit...'

'Sam, I warned you...' he said ominously.

'That's all I want to say. I felt I could mention it, since it'd be obvious to you. She was desperate, so she took these small amounts. If she'd been a real thief, she'd have taken so much more.'

The farmer had a tiny house; every inch of ground was fertilised in the spring and autumn, when the new crops went in. His land comprised three terraced fields; the lowest of them, which held the water draining off the hillside, was an abundant rice paddy.

Sam and Angelique rode there early Sunday to buy food, before he returned to Tokyo. They had persuaded their mother not to accompany them because she always swore she could smell the human fertiliser, even months after it had been dug into the soil. She conveyed this by sniffing loudly, and commenting that produce grown in shit should be cheaper. It was a lot easier without her.

They parked their bikes at the gate. Cabbages, carrots, onions and turnips grew in profusion. On the terrace below were trees heavily laden with mandarin oranges. The farmer came out of his house to meet them. He was a small man in his fifties, and for years had been caretaker of their house after summer vacations. One of his daughters had cleaned for them. Now both daughters worked in a munitions factory, while the farmer did a lively business selling food to those in the community who did not have ration coupons.

'Nogi-san,' Sam said, after exchanging greetings, 'we need vegetables, eggs, a bag of rice, and a chicken to be plucked and collected next week for Christmas.'

'Very difficult, Sam-san,' the farmer replied, which was a surprise for he was usually keen to do business.

'Why is it difficult?' Angelique asked, equally puzzled,

'How do you pay me?'

'Cash, as usual.' He took out his wallet. It was filled with notes, after being paid his salary increase. Nogi showed no particular enthusiasm at the sight of this. He sighed and shook his head.

'What's the matter?' Sam was perplexed. This was not normal. By now, the old farmer would be smiling, selecting prime vegetables and often tempting them to buy more than they intended.

'Cash no good. Not any more.'

'What do you mean, it's no good? It was good last time.'

'Not now. People don't want it. They want food, clothes, coal. Not cash. Cash is just little pieces of paper that don't keep you warm, or stop you being hungry.'

'But we all need it, to live,' Sam said.

'Why?'

'Because it buys things . . .'

'What things? If I give tangerine to the butcher, he gives me meat in exchange. Or rice to Tanaka-san, he gives me charcoal. Cash don't buy meat or charcoal now – tangerines and rice buy them. Why sell my produce for money, if I can trade it for things I need?'

Sam stared at him in dismay. It was a shock, but it made an ominous sense. In Tokyo he could use his salary to enjoy life; buy meals, drinks, or spend a night at the Kabuki. There were shops that charged black-market prices, but would sell food or clothing. Here, where only basic necessities mattered, it appeared the currency in his wallet was about to become worthless.

'Then you won't sell us vegetables or eggs? Or rice? Even the chicken for Christmas Day? Not at any price?'

The farmer shrugged. 'One yen, five yen – all the same size piece of paper, that don't burn long enough to light the fire.'

'But we need food,' Angelique said, 'how do we live if we can't buy it?' She felt disbelief. They had bought their food from him since forced to move here, and she had known him from childhood. 'Nogi-san,' she asked, 'will any farmer sell us food?'

'Not for money. Nobody believe in money now.'

'Then what can we trade for food?'

The farmer remained silent for a moment. He shuffled his feet, then reluctantly looked at Angelique.

'Clothes,' he said. 'You give me warm coat, Angie-san, I give you food, plenty of food.'

'Bugger that,' Sam protested, speaking to her in French. 'Not your coat, Angie.'

'What else will buy us anything to eat?'

She took off the fleecy coat and gave it to the farmer.

He dozed in the train, and woke to see moonlit reflections on the window as they descended through a pine forest. Further down the mountain, once they reached the villages, the blackout would come into force with blinds drawn in the carriages. It had been disturbing at the farm. Angelique had felt so cold after giving up her coat she had ridden straight home, while he waited to collect the produce. The farmer had been ill-at-ease, bringing him a basket of eggs, a bag of rice, and after that more vegetables than Sam expected, or could carry. They agreed it would be best if he made two trips, and Nogi-san had said next week he would prepare his best prime chicken, and he would also have more fruit and vegetables for them. He was sorry about the barter, but he was only doing what others did now. Sam tried to ease the embarrassment by saying he understood. These were difficult times. When he returned for the remaining supplies, the farmer's wife was outside the house, already wearing Angelique's coat.

It was after ten o'clock when he let himself in the back door of the bank, expecting Frankenstein would emerge to check on his arrival. But there was no sign of the caretaker. Instead he saw a light burning in the corridor that led to the Count's office, and went tentatively in that direction. The office was open, and the Count was at his desk. He had clearly heard the door, for he looked up without surprise.

'Sam.'

He seemed like a different man in casual clothes, a plaid shirt and pullover replacing his usual formal attire.

'Monsieur, I didn't expect you here at this hour.'

'I had a meeting. I assumed you'd take the late train, so I waited for you,' he said, and Sam felt a moment of alarm. Waiting for him on a Sunday night was unusual. 'I caught up on some work, and now it's time for a drink. Beer, or something stronger?'

'May I have a Scotch?'

The Count poured two large malt whiskies, and indicated for him to sit. He resumed his own chair behind the desk.

'I saw Cecile tonight. We met here. I had to tell her my instincts led to the belief you can't steal money and expect to be forgiven. Not if you work in a trusted position in a bank.' Sam was glad he'd asked for whisky. He gazed at the amber liquid in the crystal glass, and took a gulp. It didn't make him feel better. 'I then told her your views on the matter, and how you very nearly talked yourself out of a job as well. Not that it's relevant now, but she said to thank you.' Sam nodded and took another nervous sip. He wished he'd asked for a beer. In a moment this would be finished, and he'd be left toying with an empty glass. 'I'd actually come to a decision on Friday, but I saw no reason to convey it to you. I thought it might do you good to spend the weekend concerned about it.'

Thanks a lot, Sam thought. *I had a great time.* He took a large swallow of his whisky and finished it.

'I'll replenish that, shall I?' The Count rose and refilled the glass. 'I also decided Cecile could wait and worry. I felt some days of anxiety might make more impact, when we talked.'

'Sir . . . could you just tell me if . . . I mean what . . . is she going to be sent to gaol or not?'

'There's your drink,' he became caustic. 'As I've waited two hours for you, at least give me the courtesy of five minutes.'

'Yes, Monsieur, I'm sorry.'

'I doubt if you are.' He raised his own glass and took a long deliberate sip. 'No,' he finally said, 'she won't go to gaol.'

'Thank God.'

'Never mind God. You can thank me. I'm not having her charged, but neither will I have her back here. So she's out of a job, and I daresay that means Clermont will leave her. I said it's the best thing that could happen to her, because he will certainly leave her in the end, but by that time she'll be older, less attractive, and may not find anyone else.'

Shit, Sam thought, *you can be a hard bastard*.

'I daresay you think that was unsympathetic. I assure you, I'm very sympathetic. She's been my secretary for ten years, the best I ever had. She was efficient, pleasant, a nice human being. With a thoroughly reprehensible husband.'

'Yes, Monsieur.'

'I'm flattered you agree with me,' the Count rose to pour himself another drink. 'How did you know about Clermont?' he asked. 'I thought your father might know them socially, but as a couple they rarely mixed in local circles. Was it your father?'

'No, Monsieur.'

'Cecile thought it could've been a girl who used to work here. What was her name again?'

'Kimiko.'

'Ah, yes. The exotic femme fatale who seemed to arouse the passions of our executives. Was it her?'

'Yes, Monsieur. But it wasn't gossip. She cared for Mademoiselle – for Cecile. She only told me, no-one else.'

'So you were fairly close?'

'Yes.' The Count studied him quizzically, but before he could ask a question, Sam answered it. 'No, we didn't, sir, if you're wondering. I mean, we wanted to – even planned it. But our plans coincided with the first night you asked me to help you with the transfer to a certain account in Zurich.'

'Really? So you were busily engaged here, when you might've been – let's say – more intimately engaged with Kimiko?'

'Yes, sir.'

'That's what I'd have to call devotion to duty.'

'I don't think I had a choice. She was very upset about it, asking why I didn't arrive. But it was impossible for me to explain.'

'I see.' The Count considered this self-sacrifice. 'I had no idea I was ruining your private life. Next time you infuriate me with some dangerous and impulsive act, I'll try to remember it. Did she forgive you?'

'No.'

'A pity.'

'Monsieur, may I ask you something?'

'You can always try.'

'What'll happen to Cecile, if she can't get another job?'

'I'm afraid that's not my problem. Or yours. My first meeting tomorrow will be with Laroche, to advise him there'll be no prosecution. He's not going to be pleased. Not at all pleased.'

'Do you mean he might be a threat?'

'He wouldn't be stupid enough to break banking rules. If he was so disposed, he'd never get another post, not in this country or in France. On the other hand, one should always consider the worst-case possibilities. So what are they?'

Sam watched him as he paced the room, realising he was meant to listen, not try to answer.

'He's unpredictable,' the Count said, 'but in this instance fortunately, uninformed. He knows about the Swiss transactions, of course. With his position here, it could hardly be otherwise. But he doesn't know the details. Names, account numbers, the banks in Zurich and Geneva. He has no real information at all. It would be vague and unsubstantiated hearsay, which we could deny. Quite convincingly, I imagine.' He paused, and this time he clearly was expecting an answer. 'Couldn't we?'

'Yes, Monsieur.'

'Thank you, Sam. Goodnight.'

He slept fitfully, with confused dreams. He was in a courtroom taking the oath to swear he was the owner of account number 7305 at the Banque Commerciale de Zurich, and the entire contents were to be distributed to Mademoiselle Cecile Patou, on the condition she divorced Jacques Clermont without giving him even one Swiss franc. Moments later, he seemed to be on a tennis court, hitting wonderful angled winners, while Clermont lost his temper, queried line calls, smashed a racquet, and was booed by the crowd. It was a splendid dream. Unfortunately, just when he was thoroughly enjoying this sequence, a girl in a fur coat who was enthusiastically barracking for Clermont turned around, and he saw it was Justine.

Before he could talk to her, he woke to the wail of an air-raid siren. He went sleepily to the window. The city was dark, the moon almost full, and he could see the bombers, silver and oddly graceful against the night sky. They were well to the south, heading for the docks, and Sam contemplated the prospect of scrambling into his clothes to go down to the freezing air-raid trench to shelter with the Frankenstein family – and crawled back into bed instead. He was sound asleep within moments.

Finally, towards morning he dreamt that he and the Count were at Nogi-san's farm, where they carried a heavy deposit box full of money to his verandah. After a long argument, the farmer at last reluctantly agreed to accept the box containing two million yen, in fair exchange for one cabbage.

He woke and saw a pewter sky. Smoke was rising from the direction of the harbour. It was still early, and the warm bed tempted him to remain there. But instead he headed resolutely for the shower, choosing not to doze and risk any further fantasies.

There was a Christmas party for the staff, and the afternoon before the holidays began they crowded into the boardroom. James Lindsay had asked Florence to arrange caterers; he wanted decent booze, or as good as could be expected in these times of shortages, and good food. It would be his last office party, and he wanted it to be memorable.

He did not ask if she and Carl had come to any resolution, and she felt it best to leave her answer until after New Year, when he expected it. She forgot James had spent over thirty years studying people, assessing if they were honest, trying to discriminate between the innocent and guilty; he was a very good judge of character and aware that for the past two weeks she had been animated and brimming with happiness. Aware also that Carl had a smile on his face that had been missing lately.

When the party was under way, before some of his young lawyers tried to get the typists under the influence with evil intent, he rapped a glass for quiet.

'I'm going to make a speech,' he said. 'I've never made one at the Christmas party before, but it's your bad luck that this year is speech day.' It got a titter but a few senior solicitors rolled their eyes. 'Don't be like that, Victor,' he said to the ringleader, who was in the process of miming a yawn, 'it's going to be a short speech, but I think you'll find it keeps you fairly wide awake. As of today, I'm retiring from this office.'

The shock was immediate, and gratifying. There would be no boredom now, least of all from Victor Barnett and the other contenders for seniority. He allowed the hush to remain as he looked around the crowded room. It was a big firm by the standards of the day. Eight solicitors, four of them partners, articled clerks, typists, secretaries; over twenty employees. All of it beginning from a room in North Sydney. He had worked unceasingly to succeed there, worked so hard he was now exhausted. He wanted his cottage at Whale Beach, the chance to read books, play golf and take up fishing.

'I'm retiring,' he repeated, 'but not abdicating entirely. I'll retain a modest financial interest in the firm, and keep a fond eye on you all from a distance. The current lawyers will all become partners, some of them junior, but those details will be worked out in the New

Year between me and my successor in this chair.' He saw Victor's expectant look, and said clearly: 'Florence Eisler will run the firm. She's to be the general manager and administrator, and I have already advised the Law Society of this.'

There was utter silence. Astonishment on many faces, confusion and bewilderment on some, anger on a select few.

A blonde typist said, 'Florrie, you little beauty!'

She started to clap, and all the typing pool joined in, with the clerks, Carl, and young lawyers following. It became such approbative applause that Victor Barnett and other senior partners felt it expedient to put their hands together in a token gesture.

The signs outside the railway station were in Japanese, which Sam had never learned to read, but the broadcast message was explicit. Due to a bombing raid, the railway bridge at Kawaguchi and sections of the track were damaged. All trains had been cancelled. Crowds were milling angrily on the concourse and inside the station, in a state of disbelief that this could ruin their holidays. It became difficult to hear the voice on the public address system.

'How long did they say?' It was an Argentinian businessman, whose wife sometimes played cards with Sam's mother. He was burdened with luggage and brightly wrapped presents.

'I couldn't hear with all this racket.'

'Goddamn Americans, ruining Christmas,' the man said, 'my kids are expecting Santa Claus. How the fuck is Santa going to get there?'

Sam was in a mood to suggest that he harness up the

reindeer, but sensed it might not be well received. 'I'll see what I can find out,' he promised, and went to queue at the information counter.

'We can't tell you how long,' a harassed girl said. 'They keep shouting at me, but I can't give them an answer.'

'It's not your fault,' Sam said, which seemed to be the first kind word she'd received, for she looked at him gratefully.

'They're determined to wait, expecting a train to leave by morning,' she said quietly, 'but if I were you, I wouldn't bother.'

'No train?'

'Not a chance.' She hesitated, then said so softly only he could hear, 'If the bridge is down, it'll be a week or more.'

Sam found the Argentinian and suggested it was pointless spending the night on the station, waiting for a train, but the man refused to believe there would be no alternative transport. There had to be; this was goddamn Christmas for Christ's sake, and he had a goddam sackful of presents for his kids.

The bank was gloomy and deserted. Even the Frankenstein family seemed absent from their basement. Sam wondered what to do. There was no telephone in their holiday house; he tried Justine at her parents, then the French Ambassador's house, but the operator said all phone lines to Karuizawa were out of order. None of his friends were left in Tokyo, and, expecting to be away, he had no food. He went out to find a restaurant, knowing there would be no Christmas for him this year. There was a drizzle of sleet, and the wind made him shiver.

* * *

Christmas Day in Sydney was cloudless and hot. Florence and Carl had drinks with their neighbours, then went to lunch with Susan and John Dalby, close friends who had three noisy and excited children.

'They're exhausting,' Susan said, as one went hurtling by on a new pair of roller skates that Santa had brought. 'It's been like this since dawn. Santa's had a triumph this year.'

'It's what Christmas is all about.' Carl was smiling as he watched a seven year old ride his new bike around the lawn.

'Mate,' John Dalby said, 'I can't wait for them to find out the truth, so that old bugger in red doesn't get all the credit. You do realise that we give the kids all the cheap presents, while the expensive items come from Santa.'

'He's jealous of Mr Claus,' Susan explained. 'Gets upset the way they insist the beer left out for him is not cold enough.'

'If he drank all the beer left for him, he'd be too full to find his way back to the north pole,' John retorted.

After the meal there was the plum pudding, the sixpences carefully arranged by Florrie and Susan so the children would get the coins. Then they went racing off to play, and the adults were left alone. Carl produced a bottle of French champagne.

'Holy shit,' John said, 'begging everyone's pardon. But where the hell did you get that?'

'Florrie's secretary has influence – with our American allies. She has access to the PX store, where everything seems available. I told her I needed something special. First I wish to drink to good friends. And then I want to drink to my wife, of whom I'm so proud. I think she's a great lady.'

'So do I,' Susan said.

'Me, too,' her husband confirmed. He raised his glass. 'To Florence, who we knew when she was a sexy young secretary. Even before she became a great lady.'

'Stop it, the lot of you,' Florence said, smiling. 'As it's Christmas, I propose a toast to a special person. To Santa Claus.'

'Florrie,' John Dalby said laughing, 'you may be the new boss of a big law firm, but you haven't changed a bit – I'm glad to say.'

In the evening, they walked home. The Dalbys lived only a few streets away, in a rambling weatherboard house that looked down on Collaroy township and the main beach. It had been a lovely day. Carl had played with the kids, and she saw how much he liked children. They were a bit late for that, she reflected ruefully, but realised how she missed a certain ten year old, who next birthday would be twenty-three, and was well and truly grown up. When they reached the house, Carl produced another bottle of the same expensive champagne.

'God,' she said, 'you'll get me tight.'

'So?' He opened it and poured them each a glass.

'Happy Christmas, liebchen.'

'And to you, my darling. And also to Sam.'

'To Sam,' he said. 'Let's hope he's having a happy and a safe Christmas.'

The night had been filled with wailing sirens, and the crunch of bombs. From his window he could see the fires raging across the city. In the morning he had a slice of old bread for breakfast, which he scraped before toasting it, because it had a trace of mould. Later he went for a walk.

Downtown Tokyo was deserted. He had always heard

it was a time of excitement, for December the twenty-fifth was also the Emperor's birthday, and a national holiday. But there was no festivity. It felt eerie in the streets. No people, no trucks unloading, no bicycles or traffic, all the buildings shuttered. He'd never seen it like this. As though the inhabitants had nothing to celebrate, exhausted by the raids and lack of sleep, despondent at the lies they had been told. Activity rarely ceased in this part of Tokyo, but on the birthday of the Emperor this was a strange and empty place.

It was an awful, endless day. He knew there would be lots of parties in Karuizawa, and wondered what they were doing in Sydney. He even considered the Count's liquor cabinet, and a private toast to Florrie, but rejected the notion of drinking alone. There was no-one he could call, until he thought of an address. Near Hibiya Park, the Count had said. He went back to the bank, to see if he could find Frankenstein.

The trees were stripped bare. In the far distance were the walled gardens of the Imperial Palace. Cecile was already waiting there, wrapped in a thick warm coat, fur boots and a hat. Sam thought she looked years younger.

'Mademoiselle . . .'

'Cecile,' she said.

'Cecile,' he smiled.

'Fancy you thinking of sending Frankenstein to bring me a Christmas card.'

'I hoped he'd know your address. He was a surprise. Actually seemed glad to help me.'

'A much misunderstood man, our caretaker. Thank you for the card. Thank you for a great many things, Sam.'

'I didn't do anything.'

'Oh, but you did. I'm well aware you did. And I'm very glad of this chance to tell you so. I'd like to ask you home, but the removalists are there.'

'Removalists?'

'Frankenstein caught me only just in time. I've packed my own belongings. The men arrived to pack for Jacques, since he's not accustomed to that kind of thing, and tomorrow we each go our separate ways.'

'Where?'

'Did Monsieur le Comte not tell you anything?'

'Not a lot. Except he'd said some cruel things to you.'

'Quite cruel,' Cecile said, and to his surprise she smiled, 'but they needed to be said. Things I'd been trying not to face for a long time. Hearing him say them, saying what a fool I was, that I'd become a thief to buy this worthless man who didn't love me, it does make rather an impression – which was what he intended.'

'I didn't know it was that cruel,' Sam said, feeling out of his depth. He was astounded that Cecile seemed able to talk about it with apparent equanimity.

'He only said what I really knew,' she said gently, sensing his bewilderment.

'So now what? Divorce?'

'Whatever he wants. Because I no longer want him.'

'But what will you do?'

'I'm moving into a tiny place. No more absurd rents, or prestige addresses. I've got a good job with a friend of Louis de Boulanger's.' She noticed his expression. 'What is it, Sam?'

'I asked him what you'd do about a job. He told me it was not my problem, nor his. He as good as ordered me to shut up.'

She smiled. 'He arranged it. And a generous allowance

from his own bank account, to help me sort myself out. I'm not supposed to mention this to anyone, but I trust you. Whatever he did to help, of course, was dependent upon my leaving Jacques. The Count said he had no intention of subsiding tennis players or skiers, not to mention a series of complaisant blonde girlfriends.'

'My God,' Sam said.

'Don't feel sorry for me, dear Sam,' she said.

'Not if you're content.'

'I'm content,' she assured him. 'Please believe that.'

He hesitated, then said, 'Actually, I wanted to say when I first saw you that you look so much younger. Years younger. But I thought it might be insulting.'

'If you want to insult me like that, you may do it any time you wish,' Cecile laughed. 'If I look younger – and I hope I do – it's because I feel free. The rest of my life belongs entirely to me.'

When Sam left, he walked to the edge of the park and looked back. She was still standing there. She waved, then touched her hand to her mouth and blew him a kiss. He felt moved, and strangely happy that the rest of her life did indeed belong to her.

PART 4

CHAPTER 22

It was New Year's Eve before the railway bridge was repaired, and Sam was able to take a train to Karuizawa. Because of so many stoppages where the line had been damaged, they didn't arrive at the mountain station until the afternoon of January the first. Thus he not only failed to celebrate Christmas, but also the New Year festivities.

'If you'd come a day earlier,' Angelique said, 'the line would've been open. Why didn't you?'

'Because I was buying you a present.' Sam handed her a fleecy-lined coat, like the one she had traded with the farmer, which was met with exclamations of delight and a fond hug.

'My dear, sweet boy,' Paul Jacoulet greeted him, 'your mother has been teaching me mahjong, and I've become an addict. Do you know how to play?'

'Not really, Paul. I know you have lots of tiles, and the four winds, and you make walls, don't you?'

'Walls to keep demons out. Very oriental! We'll soon teach you. We need a fourth.'

Sam demurred, saying he was only there for a few days, which was when Jacoulet told him his mother was worried. Someone had been there looking for him.

'Who?'

'She didn't tell me his name. Tamara tells me everything, but she wouldn't tell me that. Said it was none of my business. Just as well I'm used to insults, or I might've been upset.'

Sam felt a moment of unease. 'Where is she?'

'Up at the hotel, playing bridge. Boring game.'

'I thought you liked it?'

'Not any more. Too many like that Argentinian bitch. I was unfortunate enough to be her partner. When I went to the toilet, she said, "It'll be the first time tonight I know what he's got in his hand." Bloody bitch,' he repeated as Sam grinned.

'I think I met her husband on Christmas Eve.'

'He was a military man, not in uniform.'

'Her husband?'

'No, this person who came to see you. I didn't care for his looks at all,' Paul Jacoulet said, and went off, a bizarre geisha in full costume with his Korean entourage.

Sam went straight to the Mampei Hotel to find Tamara.

There were two figures out on the beach; one of them Carl in his swimming trunks, and the other a visitor in slacks and shirt. They seemed to be in deep conversation, Florence noticed, giving it little thought, for even their placid beach was crowded in this part of summer. She was on the verandah of their house, sitting with a notepad and writing down the main problems to be faced when they went back to work after the holiday.

Problem one was undeniably Victor Barnett. Which was to be expected, for he had been with the firm almost ten years, and in most people's minds – certainly his own – was the heir apparent when James Lindsay retired. Not that anyone had expected that to come so abruptly. Victor's limp handshake and lukewarm congratulations after the announcement was the reaction of a man stunned; it would be interesting to see his frame of mind when he returned from holiday. She would do her best to make him feel at ease; their future relationship in the office would then be his to choose.

'Darling,' Carl said, 'I'd like you to meet Mr Forbes.'

She looked up and saw the man, in his early forties she estimated, emptying the sand from his shoes at her front gate.

'Mrs Eisler,' he said, 'forgive me for disturbing your peace and quiet here, but I was rather anxious to talk to Carl.'

Not just a summer visitor, she thought, and when he reached the verandah she rose and they shook hands.

'He's from the same department as Watson,' Carl said, and her smile of welcome froze.

'Same band, different tune,' Forbes said. 'Before you throw me out, can I explain?'

'I can't imagine what there is to explain.'

'Well, for a start Watson's gone. We're rid of him.'

'I expect that's an improvement.'

'A distinct one.'

'Mr Forbes got rid of him,' Carl said.

'And came all this way to tell us? How kind of you,' she said, and both men knew she was on the verge of asking him to go.

'Florrie, liebchen, will you listen?'

'To what?'

'To a request,' Forbes interjected, 'before you decide to chuck me out.'

'You were doing a great deal of talking on the beach, Mr Forbes. Does any of this concern my husband? If so, then what can it possibly have to do with me?'

'Carl wants us to discuss it. All three of us.'

'But Mr Watson made it plain I was not to know or be told anything. So how could we discuss it?'

'Mr Watson, begging your pardon, was a bloody fool.'

'Don't beg my pardon. I once called him a turd.'

He laughed and she began to like him. 'I wish I had. He was a bigot – an absolute disaster. The idiot who appointed him has been tranferred.'

'You've brightened my day,' Florrie said. 'Why don't you sit down, Mr Forbes?'

'Thank you, Mrs Eisler. Why don't you call me Frank?'

'Would you like a beer, Frank?'

'That'd go down really well. May I call you Florence?'

'If we're going to have a beer, I think you should.'

The main reception rooms at the Mampei Hotel were monopolised by Germans; the card players were relegated to an anteroom off the bar. In there, amid a haze of smoking and overflowing ashtrays, Tamara and a group of men and women were engrossed in rubber bridge.

'Sam, don't speak until a game finishes, or they'll chew your head off.' The barman, Joe Ishi, was a Japanese born in Hawaii, and thus ineligible for military service. He was the town's main source of black-market cigarettes, which seemed to be extraordinarily plentiful.

'Want any Lucky Strikes or Chesterfields?' Joe asked.

'Maybe later,' Sam said, wondering not for the first time why American cigarettes, illegal and impossible to buy in the rest of the country, were so abundant here.

He went into the bridge room. She was intent on her cards so he had a moment to study her. His mother: he had promised to always think of her as that, and still had no problem with it. She was a handsome woman, fifty this year, and as far as he knew had no man in her life since Sorge. Which was a long time ago, but perhaps the shock of his arrest and execution, the trauma of their house search and gossip afterwards had repressed any desire for intimacy. Or perhaps one of the men here at the tables was a secret suitor.

She looked over her fan of cards, saw him and nodded. He waited until the game ended.

'Partner,' said an irate Argentinian voice, 'did you have to draw my last trump? We should've made that.'

Jacoulet's bitch of the Pampas, Sam thought, and kissed Tamara as she left her table to greet him.

'Hello, Ma. Sorry about Christmas.'

'We were, too. We missed you.' She drew him aside, so no-one could hear. 'Something's happened,' she said.

'I met Jacoulet. He said someone was looking for me.'

'An officer in the Kempetai. I don't know what he wants, and he wouldn't say. But he's staying in town until you arrive. He said you must go to the police station and ask for Major Ito.'

They finished a second bottle of Resch's, while Frank Forbes made small talk, admiring the house and its unique position on the edge of the beach. Then he started to explain to her why he was here.

'I've been in military intelligence since the war started.

I can't go into details, but recently I was transferred to the foreign section where you had some unpleasant experiences. It took about two weeks to find out what sort of a dill Watson was, and give him the boot. And a few people above him. Then I went through their files. About the only thing of any value was the work Carl had done. It was so bloody obvious he was the only competent person they'd recruited, that I want to make him an offer.'

Oh no, Florrie thought. *Oh God*. Despite his friendly manner and obvious decency, she wished Frank Forbes to hell. She could see the pride on Carl's face, with his knowledge that Watson had lied, and his work had not been insignificant. She knew how badly he wanted to work for his adopted country, against the country that had defiled his race and made him flee.

'What I've asked Carl to do is to join me full-time – until the war's over.'

'You want him to give up his career?'

'Briefly. I've given up mine. When it's over I'm a civil engineer again, back in Adelaide. I don't think we're talking of more than six months, but Carl said nothing was possible if he had to keep it secret. I assured him there are no official secrets like that, not in my show. There may be some information I'd ask him not to discuss, but there won't be any deceit. No cloak and dagger. If he goes to interview German prisoners in this country, you'll know. If he was flown to the Philippines, now they're recaptured, or even to Europe, we mightn't say precisely where, but you'd be told he's overseas. I really need him, I've made that very clear. But he says it's entirely up to you.'

'Of course it's not up to me.' She turned to Carl. 'You have to do this, don't you?'

'I want to, very much. But not as much as I want to stay married to you.'

'Well, that's no problem. I want to stay married to you. So work for Frank; you'll be home most nights. And if you have to go away anywhere, you'll be back.' She felt her eyes moisten, and dabbed at them. 'I can't imagine why I'm crying,' she said to Forbes. 'I think it's the beer.'

'No doubt of that,' he agreed. 'Beer is a very emotional drink. I'd like to fill my glass and drink a toast to the pair of you.'

'I have a better idea,' Florrie said. 'Let's all get pissed.'

The police station was a stone building in the centre of town. Sam gave his name and a uniformed sergeant said to follow him. They went through corridors and down some steps to a lower floor, which seemed to be a facility on its own. There were signs the area was private: entry forbidden. In one of the rooms, Major Ito was waiting.

'Well, Sam,' he said, 'no ill effects, I see.'

'Just a few broken ribs, busted nose, weeks on morphine, and a month and a half in hospital. If you call that no ill effects,' Sam said, and took a seat without being invited.

'They're real bastards, those Koreans,' Major Ito replied.

'Bastards are everywhere, Major.' Sam had decided, as he had no idea why Ito was here, the only way to approach this was to attack. Try to show he had no reason to show fear, and nothing to hide. Being timid with a man like this was just a recipe for disaster.

'So where have you been?' Ito asked.

'Stuck in Tokyo. I'm sure my mother explained.'

'The American bombers ruined your Christmas?'

'You could say that, Major. Are you going to tell me why you're here, and why you asked to see me?'

'You've been trying to contact Australia again.'

He took an envelope from his pocket. Sam was suddenly afraid. It was the envelope sent via Ogawa to his father in Saigon, which held both of his November letters to Florrie. It was open. Despite his alarm, he could tell it was empty. He had no idea how to handle this, and blurted out the first thing that came into his mind.

'What's this? Postman's knock?'

'Don't try to be smart with me, you young shit.' The Major's voice was like a whip. 'You may have important friends, but I'm doing my duty. And you'll answer my questions.'

It was vital to remain calm.

'I apologise, Ito-san,' Sam said. 'I was confused. It seems to be an empty envelope. Can I see it?'

'No. It's evidence.'

'Of what? I sent a note to my father, wishing him the compliments of the season. Read it for yourself.'

'Perhaps you did. But you might as well admit this also contained letters to be sent to your aunt, Florence Eisler.'

My God, Sam began to think coherently, *you don't have the contents. All you've got is that envelope.* He feigned a look of confusion.

'Why do you think that?'

Major Ito studied him for what seemed a long time.

'You're fond of her,' he said, 'and you enjoy the risk.'

'That's crazy – begging your pardon, Major.'

'I think she's important to you. Perhaps as close, or

even closer, than a mother. I could help you communicate with her.'

'What?'

'There are ways.'

'Why would you do a thing like that?'

'You could send her a recorded message, and she could send one back. Perhaps we could even arrange a telephone link.'

'It's impossible.'

'Nothing is impossible, if you cooperate.'

'Cooperate? How?'

'Tell me the truth about the bank.'

'But you know the truth,' Sam was already on guard, knowing where this was leading. 'Money is sent to Switzerland for the government. To buy essential materials. I was told by the Count de Boulanger it had been explained.'

'You don't wish to talk to her? To be in contact?'

'Not if it means telling you a pack of lies.'

'You're a fool, boy.' His trace of a smile was calculated to incite fear. 'Or perhaps you're just crafty enough to guess your father burnt the contents of this envelope, before he was arrested.'

'Arrested? When? Why?' Sam began to sweat. 'What harm was done? It was just a note to say Happy New Year.'

'The arrest had nothing to do with you, or your so-called note. He's been doing harm for years. His pitiful news bulletin to the Free French. His activities here in Japan and Saigon.'

'Where is he?'

'He was in prison,' Major Ito replied. 'He died there.'

It was said with such indifference, was so lacking in concern, that for a moment Sam thought it was a bluff.

Dimly he heard the other continuing. 'His office is closed. The business no longer exists.'

He felt sick and numb.

'He died?'

'A month ago.'

'From torture?'

'From illness, or so I heard from my colleagues there,' Ito said with a shrug, and Sam knew he was lying. 'Why did he burn the contents of this envelope?'

'I've no idea, Major.'

'Be sensible. I offered you a choice. I repeat, you can contact Mrs Eisler. I'll arrange it, if you agree to assist me.'

'Why do you keep assuming I can assist you? You were told what the bank does, by people far more important than me.'

The Major's polished veneer exploded into frustration.

'You young bastard,' he said, and ripped the envelope to shreds. 'You could've saved yourself a great deal of trouble. Get out – but don't be stupid enough to think I'll leave it like this.'

'I missed you,' Justine said. 'Christmas was dull without you. My parents gave a New Year's Eve party, and I hoped you'd be there.' She tucked her arm in his. 'Guess who turned up?'

'No idea.' Sam was still in shock from the encounter with Ito, and the news of his father. 'Who turned up?'

'Jackie-boy,' she said. When he looked blank, she repeated: 'Jackie. Jacques Clermont.'

'I'm thrilled,' he told her.

'What's wrong, Sam?'

'Nothing.' He tried not to show his grief. He wanted to forget the bitter times, and instead remember all the things he had loved about his father. The happy childhood in Kobe; his bravery on the burning ship; the joy when they had seen him appear across the street in Surabaya like an apparition. There was the night they spent alone in Karuizawa; the confession and his concern to see Sam safe in Australia. The letters he had helped send to Florrie. After their rift, after the unhappy teenage years, had come a degree of affection and trust. He felt an ineffable sadness his father had died in a police cell under God knew what cruelty, and his circle of influential friends had been unable or unwilling to help him.

'Something is wrong.'

'We'll talk about it later. How did Clermont get here for the party? There were no trains.'

'He drove most of the way, then skied across country. Trust him. Everyone thought it was very romantic.'

Sam returned to work unsure exactly what to tell the Count. Their relationship had once been close to friendship; now self-preservation was the link that bound them. De Boulanger could not let him leave the bank, or Sam would be vulnerable to interrogation. It was why Major Ito had bluffed, and then had to reluctantly dismiss him.

But the Count must be informed of this development, although mention of correspondence with Florrie would be unwise. In the end, Sam gave him the essential details; his father was dead, after being arrested in Indochina. The Major had been in the mountains trying to coerce him, and was angry at his failure. And in view of what seemed to have become an obsession, they should be very careful of him in the future.

'My condolences on the loss of your father,' the Count

said. 'We knew each other well at one time, but disagreed on almost everything. How does your mother feel?'

'Vaguely sorry. As if a distant relative had died.'

'Russians don't forgive easily.' He frowned. 'Damn that Major. You're not still writing letters, are you?'

'Not any more.' He felt it was near enough to the truth and would avoid affecting the other's blood pressure. Then he had his own question to ask.

'M'sieu, if the Kempetai keep us under surveillance, is it wise to go on with the currency transactions to Zurich and Geneva?'

'Perhaps not wise, Sam, but essential. It's all that keeps the bank solvent now. We must remain in business, or we're at risk from your friend Ito.' Sam was about to protest, but the Count said: 'Well, your rash behaviour did bring the bloody man into our lives.'

A week later there was a telephone call from the Swiss Embassy. The Ambassador had moved to Karuizawa, leaving only his nephew and a small staff in Tokyo. The nephew, Bernhardt, who had been at school with Sam, was made Vice-Consul by his uncle. In this capacity, he rang with news a letter had arrived in the latest diplomatic bag. Not for the bank, but addressed to Sam personally. It was from a legal firm, and had the imprint of their consul in Sydney, Australia. Should he send it with a messenger?

'No, I'll collect it, Bernhardt,' Sam had said, and after hanging up crossed to the window. Occupying Ribot's former office, he had a view of the street, and could see two men in the doorway opposite. The men changed, but the surveillance remained there, and had since his return. It was overt, clearly intended to intimidate him, and there was no doubt someone else was watching the main door. It would be that unseen man who would follow him, if he was unwise enough to go straight to the Swiss Embassy.

Florence allowed herself a moment to suspend the problem of Victor Barnett from her mind. She needed time to consider her situation, for the last thing she wished to do in these early weeks was seek help from James. He was busy painting his house at Whale Beach, taking lessons from the golf professional at Mona Vale, and searching boat yards for a clinker with an outboard motor.

To forget her office difficulties she relaxed and allowed her mind to dwell on Sam. In Tokyo, it would be midwinter. In six months he would have his twenty-third birthday, and she had not seen a photograph of him for almost four years. She worried every time she heard news of another bombing raid on Tokyo, unsure where he was living. She assumed he was still in Yokohama – for she had had no letter since last August – and dreaded hearing of the Allied attacks that targeted the rail lines. Surely he could not still be commuting every day.

She wondered if her letter had ever reached him, and how out of date it was, for since then her life had totally changed. Any real communication was impossible. If only she could pick up the telephone, ask for an overseas operator and tell Sam the letter had all been a lie at the time, but things had turned wonderfully upside down. They were deliriously happy, Carl was busy working with Frank Forbes, and she was running one of the largest city law firms. And intending to pay Sam's university fees if he would agree, as soon as the war was over.

That'd startle him, she thought with a grin, and Victor

Barnett, entering abruptly, wondered what she had to smile about. In a moment or two, he'd wipe the contented look from her face.

'I've just spoken to James Lindsay,' he said. 'The phone rang forever, but it seems he was up a ladder with a paintbrush. God knows why, but he's apparently too mean to hire a painter.'

'No, he enjoys painting his house. Was there a special reason, Victor, that you barged in without knocking?'

'Several reasons. I said I disapproved of your changing the name to Lindsays. I disagreed with a former typist being made head of the firm, and unless he was prepared to come and discuss my grievances, I was resigning. And so were Elliot and Humphries.'

'And what did James say?' Florrie asked.

'He listened. Then asked me to pass on a message. You're to call him right away.'

Sam parked the push-bike outside the embassy, and carefully chained it so it could not be stolen. He had faithfully promised Frankenstein it would be returned in good order, after the giant had muttered it was his wife's bicycle, and if it was damaged he would be in big trouble. The idea of Frankenstein in fear of his tiny wife made him laugh. He had also enjoyed seeing the third Kempetai watcher, eyes focussed on the main door as he rode down the lane behind him.

'Vice-Consul,' Sam smiled, as Bernhardt gave him the letter. 'Should I bow?'

'Can't beat a bit of nepotism,' Bernhardt said laughing. 'Looks an important letter. I'll organise coffee while you read it.'

The letter felt long out of date. It must have been

written soon after his summer holiday, and so much had happened since. But at least it was news; she had a new job, she was happy, she said, and bathing suits were more daring now in Australia. It was an odd sort of letter, not quite like Florrie at all, and gave him the strange impression she had intended to write something else.

That's ridiculous, he thought. *My imagination.*

Bernhardt and he had coffee, after which he disposed of the letter, flushing pieces down the lavatory until nothing remained. It was safer to do so. Then he cycled around the perimeter of the Royal Park, through the streets of the Ginza, returning the bike to Frankenstein and asking him to thank his wife.

Florence hung up the phone, and turned to Victor Barnett. He had been joined by the other senior partners, Tim Elliot and George Humphries. There was an expectancy about them; they realised she had listened a great deal and said little. They felt confident this whole absurd aberration was about to end.

'Well?' Victor's air of triumph was manifest.

'Well,' she said. 'James confirms all three of you wish to resign, unless I step down and retire from the firm.'

'That's approximately the position. No hard feelings.'

'Not in the slightest,' she said. 'Let me have your letters of resignation, and clear your desks by the end of the day.'

'What?' George Humphries almost squeaked.

'Us?' Tim Elliot was unprepared for this.

'James said I'm to decide what's best. Clearly it's best to dispense with you three who dislike me, and get some new blood. Some young, enthusiastic lawyers.'

'Don't be rash,' Victor warned. 'This will cause gossip, and harm the firm.'

'I think we'll survive, Victor. Don't slam the door on your way out.'

CHAPTER 23

The B29s were lined up in neat formation, almost wing to wing as far as the eye could see. The first attack group was in position at the edge of the tarmac, awaiting the meteorological report and takeoff. Crews were on edge; there was a long night ahead, and nobody knew what kind of reception they'd meet at the end of it. All they knew from the briefing was this raid would be different. When they were airborne, they would be given further details.

Attempting to relax until confirmation came, the pilots went through pre-flight procedures again, checking gauges and instruments. Others in the crew tested navigation aids, while the gunners made sure their weapons were especially effective. Guns were the conundrum causing the crew's disquiet. The Superfortress normally bristled with defensive armour. It was a well-guarded aircraft. But not on this mission. Most of the turrets were empty; guns removed to allow extra clusters of bombs to be carried. So the gunners wanted to be certain what weapons they had were reliable. They hated the prospect of being buzzed by fighters, unable to return fire. Ground crew, equally on edge, tried to quell their nerves with cigarettes despite the sign: STRICTLY NO SMOKING IN THIS AREA.

Beyond where these planes stood, the jungle had been cut away. The ground had been levelled by bulldozers and laid with concrete. What had been a primitive airstrip was now extended to a huge field, with more squadrons ready to move to assigned positions when the first groups took off. They were all B29s, no other aircraft had the necessary range. This four-engined citadel of the air could fly almost seven thousand kilometres. Saipan, Guam and other conquered islands were a third of that distance from Japan and its main cities. At a speed of five hundred kilometres an hour, it took the bombers just four hours to reach their targets – with ample fuel for a safe return.

On March ninth, 1945, the weather report was good. The sun was setting on a peaceful sea. From airfields across the islands, the B29s took off during the next two hours. The noise was unceasing. Flimsy buildings trembled as squadron after squadron headed north. There were three hundred and twenty Superfortresses. Each carried a payload of five thousand kilograms of jellied-gasoline incendiary bombs. The operation was the largest yet mounted against domestic Japan, and was code-named SLASH AND BURN.

The target was Tokyo.

A cold northerly wind had freshened, and the temperature felt close to zero. Sam was hunched into a thick woollen coat, but could feel the biting wind. He hurried down the narrow street, where open invitations emerged from dark doorways. The district was notorious for erotica; crowds of prostitutes and transvestites jostled for clients in the streets; brothels, sex shows and striptease bars competed in a fusion of alleyways behind Shinjuku railway station.

Nearby was a small building that housed the radio news and information bureau. Across the street from it loomed the garish red windmill of the Moulin Rouge music hall, a replica of the Paris original. Sam went into the broadcasting studio, and found his friend Paul Kranz had just finished reading the early evening news bulletin.

'So who's winning the war?'

'Japan, of course. God, you should hear some of the crap I have to say.'

'I've heard it.'

'Not tonight. I've just been telling our faithful listeners that America is on the brink of defeat.'

'And do the faithful believe it?'

'Implicitly. Every word.'

They ran the gauntlet of hopeful girls working the street outside the Moulin Rouge, and headed for a favourite bar in a less lubricious part of town.

Two hours to the south the night was cloudless, with a sprinkling of stars. There was no moon, and the sea was a black void below. The Superfortresses were flying low, at altitudes between four and six thousand feet. Apart from tiny atolls they bypassed, there was no land mass for another thousand kilometres, hence no danger. Once there might have been the hazard of patrol ships, but the Japanese navy had been decimated in this past six months. On previous raids, approaching the coast they would climb to avoid intercept fighters and anti-aircraft fire, but tonight their orders were to remain at this altitude even over the target.

In the leading B29, the Group Commander handed over controls to his co-pilot. He thought about the mission ahead of them. Flying at this height over the city was going to be hairy. It was also a ruthless, cold-blooded assignment. For tonight, the objectives were not the docks or the great factory complexes; their target zones were the residential areas. The justification given for this was the amount of small industry in backyard plants and workshops in these districts, but it was not an explanation that convinced him. The real purpose was to incinerate as much of the city as possible.

He tried to calculate the number of incendiary bombs they were carrying. Each plane had forty clusters, which meant sixteen hundred per aircraft. He gave up after a few attempts; it was too difficult to work out in his head. Instead he tried to doze, but the co-pilot was talkative.

'Wonder what they're doing?'

'Who?'

'People on the ground.'

'Back home?'

'No, the ones ahead, who don't even know we're on our way to pay a visit. It's eight o'clock there. Dinner's over. I guess the kids are in bed.'

'Shut up,' the Commander said.

'Makes you wonder, though. What all the people in a city that size are doing? Must be a few million of 'em. Some at home listening to the radio. Others out on a date, maybe at the movies, or some guy getting lucky with a broad in the back of a car.'

'Shut the fuck up,' his Commander said.

'Just trying to picture it,' the co-pilot shrugged.

The Group Commander hated to picture it, or talk about it. His job was to take the aircraft there, and bring it and his crew back safely. What happened over the target was the responsibility of the bomb aimers. He knew some of the squadron considered him taciturn, but he had a wife and children of his own in Dayton, Ohio. He had no wish to think about young kids being put to bed in the city they would reach within the next two hours.

'Don't picture it,' he said. 'Just fly the ship, and shut up.' He closed his eyes. Counting might help him sleep. He was going to need it, for they would not be back until dawn. *Three hundred and twenty-five craft, each with sixteen hundred incendiaries, added up to five hundred and twenty something thousand. Plus many high explosive and special phosphorus bombs as well. Holy shit,* he thought. *What in God's name are we doing? That's over half a million fire bombs, in one night, on one city.*

Paul Kranz and Sam had been friends since school days. Paul was Eurasian; his Austrian father and Japanese mother having divorced when he was a child. After an early life being shared between divided homes, Paul shocked both parents as soon as he was old enough to choose, by choosing neither of them, and living with his grandfather instead. Hugo Kranz was a widower, tall, a regal seventy-five. In 1904, he had come from Vienna, among to first travel the new Trans-Siberian Railway, and had started a factory in China making gunpowder.

Stories about him were legion. Grandfather Kranz knew little about the manufacture of gunpowder. But he did know the key ingredient his warlord clients required; that their explosives should make the loudest possible sound in order to frighten the other side. He employed a chemist who found that the traditional mix of sulphur and saltpetre could be enhanced by nitroglycerin. It was dangerously unstable, liable to cause as many casualties among the attackers as the attacked – but noise was what the warlords wanted, and noise had made Hugo Kranz a modest fortune.

'How is the old boy?' Sam asked, after they had settled into a popular restaurant and ordered their meal.

'Independent as ever. Won't renew his passport. Says he'd rather not have one, than deal with Nazi thugs.'

Sam smiled. They were both fond of Hugo Kranz.

'I said we'd be home for a drink later. He sent regrets, but he'll miss you. He's met a widow. An Italian lady in her sixties.'

'A new one. Good for him.'

'She teaches languages, and tonight's a private lesson.'

'The old bugger. Is she a nice widow?'

'Very nice,' Paul said. 'She hates Mussolini as much as he hates Hitler, so they have plenty to talk about.'

Over dinner Sam told him how much the German conduct in Karuizawa had deteriorated. The arrogance seemed more aggressive, the parades and fascist salutes ruining what had been a charming village atmosphere. The Jewish doctors were harassed, and the new doctor from Berlin strutted like an SS officer.

'Hugo wouldn't know the place. They're more militant than when they were winning the war.'

In the distance came the familiar sound of an air-raid siren. Inured to the sound, most customers in the restaurant paused to listen, then continued with their meal. A few stood to leave for the shelters, as mindful waiters rushed to collect their bills in time. It was a well-known ploy, in these days of air raids, to run for safety and leave the tab unpaid behind them.

'How's the job?' Sam asked as they ignored the alert.

'Insane,' Paul said. He was not a newsreader by choice. He had been drafted to the service, run by the propaganda ministry. 'Like I told you, tonight I had to say Americans are ready to surrender. That the country is racked by strikes, there are food shortages, and their warmongering President Roosevelt is dying.'

'Is he?' Sam asked, startled.

'That may even be true,' Paul said. 'He looks old and exhausted. But it was just the start. The script detailed how people hate the President, and blame him for the war. That – quote – the Americans will never take Okinawa, and being beaten there will do them great damage. It will teach them the futility of thinking Japan will ever surrender. End quote. That's the kind of garbage I have to read, and God help anyone who varies from the text.'

'But surely you don't really think anyone believes it.'

'Of course they believe it! Not those with access to a free press. But how few are they? And how does anyone find out that most of what they hear is a lie? I'd love one chance – just one – to broadcast the truth. To say people are exhausted. They're cold and hungry; told they must shed blood for the Emperor, but unsure why. Dissent, real rebellion is just below the surface. People can't understand – if we're winning – why there's so little food and not enough rice; why the public baths are open only twice a week, why hot water's rationed, and why a race that likes to be clean feels dirty.

'Most of all, they must wonder why the bombers can't be turned back. They might even recall the promises of two years ago, that no foreign foot, no bullet or bomb would ever touch Japanese soil . . .' He stopped, with a rueful shrug. 'But before I said half of it, I'd be off the air and in gaol. The bloody studio is full of censors and nobody goes on air without a security man present.'

The owner of the restaurant had been talking anxiously on the phone, and was moving hurriedly around the room. They watched him exchanging a brief word with customers at each table; whatever was said people were taking notice, paying for their meals, collecting hats and coats, and leaving. He reached Sam and Paul.

'It's a big raid,' was all he said. 'Better find shelter.'

He already had their bill made out. They paid him and left the restaurant. Outside, there seemed nothing untoward, except the continuous wail of the siren. The wind had increased. It gusted in their faces as they contemplated whether to see if they could find an open bar or head for an air-raid shelter.

The aircraft remained at an altitude of five thousand feet as the coastline approached. Above the sprawling city, the lead squadron dropped their incendiary cylinders to imprint the first target areas. It had already been decided the focus of the raid was to create fire damage and shatter morale in populated districts, and these markers that the Japanese called 'Molotov flower baskets' lit up and outlined the area where the primary attacks would take place.

Fukawaga, by day a picturesque river anchorage crowded with jetties, wharves and timber warehouses, with a dense residential area, had been selected as the first locality to be incinerated.

Sam and Paul were running for their lives. A half hour earlier they would have chosen to remain in the warmth of the restaurant, but the owner's agitation and his insistence he must shut his doors left them no option. They ignored the crowded public refuges, where they could see people pushing and fighting to get inside, and had instead elected to make for the Kranz house, which had a deep underground shelter in the garden.

But the area was ringed by smoke and choked with fire engines, ambulances and civil defence emergency vehicles, and they could not get through. They turned back, attempting to look for somewhere safer, which was when they saw the western part of the city in the direction of Fukawaga was bright red with flame. As the wind increased in velocity fanning the blaze, the sky itself appeared to be burning.

Everything began to happen at once. The thunder of the Superfortresses flying so low overhead became a monstrous roar that rattled buildings and seemed to shake the ground. A water main burst. An office building crumpled like a house of cards. Around them – in whichever direction they looked – incendiary bombs were falling like rain. But this lethal rain contained a new type of bomb, each making a shrill terrifying sound, spewing flames, as thousands of them plunged earthward.

It was impossible to tell which direction was safe. There had been raids, but never one like this. Never with so many aircraft so low, unleashing such devastation. The phosphorus bombs were having a deadly effect; the heat was so intense it was hard to breathe, and there was a toxic smell of fuming sulphuric acid. People ran, because to remain still was to die. Sam and Paul ran with them; it was a stampede, and there was no alternative except to be trampled on by those behind.

Most of the houses in each street they ran through

were blazing. Cascades of sparks were flung into the air, swept by the wind, igniting other buildings. As they found an open space by a park, and fought their way out of the rampaging crowd, managing to pause for a moment to recover their breath, everything within sight was burning. Wooden telegraph poles flamed like kindling; electrical wires crackled and melted. A man with a pushcart of his possessions tried to run through the park pursued by a firestorm – and just when it seemed he was safe, a cluster of high-tension wires were swept off their poles, liquefying as they fell around the cart, electrocuting him.

Hideous images were encapsuled in fleeting moments of horror. A child engulfed in a ball of fire, her screams turned to whimpers of despair before she died. A mother with a baby on her back, both coated in flames as she desperately flung herself into a canal. A fire truck, with four firemen sitting upright and dead in it, asphyxiated and charred. There were other grisly sights. Hundreds of dead in the streets, shrivelled so utterly by flames their blackened bodies had shrunk to the size of children. It was no longer possible to tell if they had been men or women.

Sometime after midnight, Sam and Paul lost all sense of location. They thought they knew this city, but the only illumination was from the flames, and the smoke and cinders became so dense that familiar landmarks were gradually obliterated. The panicking crowds were the greatest hazard: berserk with terror and hysterical as they tried vainly to find shelter. Some headed for parks, believing that open space was safest, but in the parks the piles of the dead lay burnt beyond recognition. Many made for underground railway stations, which became so crowded it was difficult to breathe, and people were choking there, dying on their feet, unable to fall because of the crush. Others fled for the river, believing that water must be safe. But the water was boiling; the Sumida and the canals were choked with corpses. Even public swimming pools were filled with scorched bodies.

Time became a blur. On at least a dozen occasions, with the wind and flames forcing them in one direction and then another, Sam and Paul thought they must die. Their skin felt raw from the heat, their eyes inflamed from sparks and ash. There was nothing to do but run, and nowhere they ran was safe. At some period during the night – it seemed hours later – they stumbled across a roadside ditch. At first sight in the glare of the firelight it was full of people, but with a shudder they realised all of them were dead.

'What the hell do we do?' Paul asked.

Sam took a deep breath, wrapped his scarf around his face and pointed. They burrowed their way into the ditch among the charred corpses, trying not to be sickened by the smell of burnt and decomposing flesh, while overhead the waves of bombers kept on coming. Just when it seemed they could no longer bear the putrid stench, they began to realise the intensity of the raid was easing.

In fact, it was moving to other areas of the city, ones carefully designated for similar destruction. The lead planes dropped their markers to outline the parameters of each target, before thousands more bombs were unleashed to demolish Nihon-bashi and the Ginza.

Dawn rose on an exhausted and wounded city. There was little visibility because of swirling smoke, and a thick acrid haze stung the eyes. Shocked and bewildered people tried but failed to cope with the horror as daylight began to reveal the extent of it. Streets had disappeared, whole city squares were nothing but soft ash, and small flurries of wind blew it into people's faces like a snowstorm.

What few fishing boats remained set about the grisly task of collecting bodies from the river. Men waded into the canals to retrieve corpses. Pathetic groups gazed at the embers of what had been their homes. A few even found pails and tried to splash water on the smouldering wreckage; inwardly knowing that it was hopeless, but needing to do something other than give in to total despair.

The streets were thronged with dazed survivors searching for parents, other relatives, friends; worst of all, some seeking their missing children. Doctors and nurses were trying to treat the most serious burn cases, with no more in the way of medical supplies than Mercurochrome and bandages. In Sumida Park, pits were dug, thousands of bodies piled into them, and kerosene poured and lit to cremate them before disease began to spread. There was no time for identification or ceremony.

Sam and Paul found themselves in the vicinity of Shiba, once the private domain of the shoguns. In the grim light of day, the ornamental gardens were blackened by fire, statues lay in ruins, and the ground was littered with more bodies. Paul was desperately concerned about his grandfather. He decided he must return to their house, and arrange to get him away from Tokyo. Hugo Kranz was stubborn and would take some convincing. Sam's priority was to first reach the bank – if it was still there. Later, if communication were possible, they would combine forces and do their best to persuade Hugo to leave. Provided, of course, although neither said it, that Hugo was still alive.

When they parted, Sam attempted to make his way across town. It was slow progress, because streets were still smouldering, and emergency crews were trying to cordon off areas they might be able to save. He passed a telephone exchange; once there had been a row of public phone boxes standing there, he knew that because he remembered using them – now their coin containers were fused into a lump of solid metal. In the street was a pair of what looked like black work gloves; as he drew closer, he realised they were charred human hands that had been torn off by an explosion.

He continually met exhausted, frightened people, calling to those they passed for news of other parts of the city. Did anyone know about Sumida-Ka? Or Shinjuku? Was Tokyo station hit? Were trains running? Had the Royal Palace or the Imperial Gardens been bombed?

Amazingly, when he reached it, the French Bank was untouched. It stood tiny but intact beside the massive Bank of Japan building, as if protected by it. Sam let himself in the back door with his key and headed for the penthouse. He met the Count coming down the stairs, each relieved to see the other.

'Thank God you're safe,' the Count greeted him. 'I was worried when I heard you hadn't come home last night.' Sam asked about the Count's house, and was told it was still standing. 'We were lucky. There were dozens of incendiaries, but one of the brigades managed to put the fires out. Mercifully Madame's safe and so are the servants.'

'How did you get here?' Sam asked, 'surely not by car?'

'Part of the way. I walked the rest. There's very little

left of the Ginza. I was sure the bank would be destroyed.'

'Me too. It's a relief.'

'Perhaps a temporary one. There'll be more raids soon, possibly tonight. We have to make some quick decisions, Sam.'

They arranged to meet in the Count's office after Sam cleaned himself. There was no electricity, but at least there was still a cistern on the roof which provided running water for the shower. He threw off his clothes, stained and polluted with the stench of the bodies in the ditch. His face and hair were grimy with soot. He withstood the shock of the freezing cold water, and scrubbed until his flesh tingled, then dried himself and felt the luxury of changing into clean clothes.

He looked around his small penthouse. It had been such a haven for the past five months. He had become accustomed to living in the heart of downtown Tokyo, with the Ginza on his doorstep, free to enjoy its lively allure. But the Ginza was gone, and the charm of the district would be lost with it. He wondered how much longer he would remain here. Not long, he feared, and went to join the Count in his office on the ground floor.

'No croissants,' the Count said, pouring coffee from a Thermos. 'The baker's dead. His shop was bombed and he was in it.' He appeared badly shaken by this news. 'I didn't know until just now. Thousands killed, but the death of one makes it personal.'

And of course it did, Sam thought. Like his glimpse of the burning child, or the mother with her baby in the *obue himo* on her back – these things made it highly personal. The others were just heaps of corpses. Shocking and gruesome to witness, but there was a limit to anyone's capacity to mourn. You could feel angry or repelled by the piles of bodies in Sumida Park, but not sorrow or grief for so many anonymous people.

'It was a dreadful night,' the Count said.

'It was barbaric,' Sam replied. He was aware he and the Count de Boulanger – while they had never expressed it openly – had different aspirations for the outcome of this war, but after a night of such incessant terror, there no longer seemed to be opposing sides. They were all victims of humanity's ability to be inhuman.

They discussed what had to be done. Few staff could be expected to arrive, even if they had survived the raids. No-one would expect the bank to open. In the meantime, urgent arrangements should be made to transfer the contents of the strongroom to safer storage. A direct hit could demolish the building and everything it contained.

'We have to find somewhere to deposit all the currency. It's the only asset that will keep the bank solvent, when this war is over. Though God knows when that might be.'

'Surely it can't be long,' Sam said, feeling it was no longer possible even for the Count to believe in Japan's victory.

'You think not, Sam? If you're saying this country can't win, last night made me agree. I daresay that was the purpose of such a raid, not only to burn and kill, but to crush morale. If so, it was an efficient exhibition of destruction, but the war won't be ended by bombs or fires. It can only end if Hirohito decides it should. That's where America fails to understand the Japanese. They'll go on sacrificing and fighting until there's no-one left, if their Emperor tells them that surrender is dishonourable.'

Sam had his own forthright views about the divine right of an Emperor to let his people be slaughtered while he sat aloof in the sanctuary of his palace. But this was no time to express them, and the Count was in no mood to listen.

'I'm not staying in Tokyo a day longer,' he said. 'This building's being shut, and I'm paying off the staff.'

'Everyone?' It was hardly unexpected, but the suddenness dismayed him.

'Except you. We know why that's necessary. Also, there may be Swiss transactions. We can't simply terminate accounts.'

'So where is the bank going?'

'Karuizawa. Where else? Most of our clients live there now. The Ambassador's summer residence will become the de facto French Embassy. And I've acquired a house. Bought it last month.'

'I thought they were impossible to buy?'

'Very nearly. Enter it on the books as a major asset; our place of business, and my rent-free living quarters.'

'Yes M'sieu.' Running a bank clearly had advantages.

'We'll be accountable to the directors in Paris, so we keep accurate records. Your first job is to stay and tell the staff they're no longer needed. That, by the way, includes Laroche. Give him this letter. It's a reference and six months salary. Can you deal with it?'

'I'll do my best.' Sam doubted if it would be simple. The chief accountant could hardly relish being given his marching orders by a junior clerk, which was how Laroche still regarded him.

'Don't take any nonsense. The rest get two months pay. Sort it out, then get to Karuizawa the best way you can.'

The Count went next door to consult with the manager of the Bank of Japan. He arranged to rent space in their security vault for a number of deposit boxes, explaining they held taxation files and mortgage documents.

Bankers, accustomed to dealing with each other, regarded such fabrics of deceit as accepted practice. The boxes were locked and conveyed to the huge vault in the adjacent building. The paperwork was concluded, the coded password sealed in an envelope, and the Count took possession of the only keys.

Sam was told to place on record that each box contained two million yen, and there were twenty boxes. Arrangements were also made with the French Ambassador that a further three boxes, containing six million yen, would be held in the strongroom of the embassy.

Finally, there were two attaché cases, one packed full of local currency, the other with precious United States dollars. These, the Count said he would take to Karuizawa; there was no need to record it, for they were to be regarded as 'cash expenses' for any emergency that arose. During these measures, Sam began to realise that Louis de Boulanger, despite his outward show of optimism, had long foreseen this day and planned accordingly.

Carl was late home, which was not infrequent now. The European war was in a vital stage, focussed on the attempt to cross the Rhine and begin the march towards Berlin. The start of the working day in London brought a flood of cables and material that reached Sydney in late afternoon, many requiring instant translation. But he was also privy to other material, much of it from the Pacific war, and he was unusually quiet as they ate their dinner.

'Bad day?' Florence asked.

'Not the best.'

'Can you talk about it?'

'I shouldn't. But you'll hear it on the news, once the censor agrees to pass it. I think you should be prepared, so it isn't a shock. Better if I tell you than hearing it on the radio.'

She felt disquiet, for he rarely spoke this way.

'There was a massive bombing raid on Tokyo last night. The Americans kept it to themselves, at times you'd think we weren't their allies at all. Our intelligence says there'll be another. Probably tonight. They're going to burn the city. And I mean burn, because of the matchwood houses. The Superfortresses are packed with incendiaries. The plan is to bomb the place to pieces, smash morale.'

'You mean like Dresden?'

'At least as bad as Dresden.'

Perhaps he's not in Tokyo, she thought, trying to shut out any vision of Dresden, the dreadful photographs and newsreels of a once-cultured city reduced to ash and rubble. It had been mass slaughter and destruction on Valentine's Day the previous month. Eight hundred Lancaster bombers had pounded the city for twenty-four hours, then more appeared the next day to raze the ruins. The death toll was still being counted after all these weeks. If it was that kind of bombing, who could survive? She shivered, and felt Carl's hand take hers, trying to comfort her.

Somewhere in a maelstrom like that was the child she had so desperately wanted to bring up, but lacking the money and family support, dissuaded in the face of reactions ranging from indifference to tight-lipped disapproval, she had made the one big mistake of her life and let him go. She loved him like a son, but because he could never be that, the bonds had always seemed closer.

He should have been safely here in Australia, but for the element of mischance. A few wretched days too late; it could hardly have been closer or more heartbreaking. Now they were bombing and burning Tokyo, and she knew, despite her vain hopes, that he was there.

Please God, she silently prayed, hoping if there was a God her neglect of Him would be forgiven, *don't do this to me*.

CHAPTER 24

It was bitterly cold in the trench and, as the night crept on and the city blazed around them, the only things they could see were flames and crimson skies through shifting shrouds of smoke. The cold in the damp clay trench, despite the profusion of fires, became more intense. These holes in the earth behind the bank had never been intended as real shelters; they had been hastily excavated to conform to regulations, at a time when air raids like these were regarded as inconceivable.

He heard a child crying, and his mother trying to console him. He was in one trench; Frankenstein and his family in the other. Bombers flew low overhead, the huge wings blocking out the colour of the sky like giant predators, using the same pattern of attack, and unleashing their incendiaries indiscriminately. Sam felt certain the raid dwarfed even the ferocity of the previous night. Huddled in the freezing trench, he endured the discomfort, knowing it would be suicidal to go back to the penthouse. He began to believe the Count's assertion was correct; this kind of bombing was intended more to create terror and crush morale than to destroy installations.

Earlier in the night, before the alert sounded, electricity had been restored for a brief period and he had heard the national news on the radio. It was no longer possible to conceal the extent of the air raids. Yet a communiqué put out by the Office of War Information said Tokyo was the only city attacked the previous night, and the death toll had not been unduly high.

Clearly, Sam thought, that was meant to reassure the rest of the country. The dead in the canals and subway stations, the vast piles of cremated bodies in Sumida Park could not refute the bulletin, which typically then became a call to arms.

'The enemy has tried to destroy the city as the earthquake of 1923 once did. What they fail to realise is the nation survived and rebuilt from the earthquake. And if they attempt to destroy our land, we shall survive and rebuild again. We will not only endure, but return their fire a hundred-fold, until they surrender. His Imperial Highness has said, *American aggression must be resisted. Japan is committed to uniting all the corners of the world under one roof.*'

'Bullshit,' Sam said loudly to the radio as the statement concluded with a fanfare, which was abruptly terminated when the lights went out and the electricity failed once again. It was still pitch dark an hour later when the generator-powered sirens had begun to wail their warning. And ever since then, what remained of the city had endured a relentless and pandemoniac inferno.

* * *

With the help of his chauffeur, Count de Boulanger had cleared all personal items from his office by early afternoon. Taking the two attaché cases filled with cash, they had set out in the Daimler for his home. He feared there could be another raid soon and it would be a slow journey with road blocks and damaged streets. He was anxious to collect his mistress and be on the road before more bombs fell.

'You're in charge,' he had told Sam. 'Get out any way you can, tomorrow or the next day. 'Now is there anything else?'

'Frankenstein. Does he stay on here as caretaker?'

'You decide.' The Count was impatient to be gone; details like the giant caretaker were unimportant. 'Leave as soon as you've paid the staff, if any are alive to collect their wages.'

He was driven off in his Daimler. Sam, alone in the bank, tried to work out how to trace the staff and pay them when, to his surprise, the phone rang. The line had been out of order all day.

'*Bank de l'Indo Chine*,' he had said, answering it.

'Thank Christ. I've been trying to get through for bloody ages.' Paul's voice was stressed; something was wrong.

'How's Grandfather Hugo?'

'In hospital.'

'What happened?'

'Burns. Not good at seventy-five, when some bastard drops phosphorus on you. Sophia, his Italian girlfriend, got him into hospital. She yelled at the doctors until they treated him. They weren't keen because he wasn't Japanese.'

'Where is he, Paul? I'll come and visit.'

'No, we're taking him to Shimoda. She has a house

there. I'm driving them down in his car, if we can get through. Besides, the hospital's full and nobody has time to spare for an old man.'

'What can I do to help?'

'A favour for me. Are you going to Karuizawa?'

'Eventually, if I can get away.'

'You know my Datsun?' Sam knew it, a small and noisy old sedan that Paul treasured. 'I wanted to move it, but I have to drive Grandfather. Can you take it with you?'

'Me?'

'Find a garage for it. Up there, it'll be safe from bombs. It's parked in the shed, behind our house.'

'But Paul . . .'

'The keys are under the back steps. There's a full tank of petrol, plus a gallon tin I bought on the black market. It's enough to get you there, I hope.'

'Paul, I haven't got a driving licence.'

'Oh shit.'

'I'm sorry.'

'You mean you can't drive?'

'Well, sort of.'

'What do you mean, sort of?'

'I had lessons, before the war. But not since. I'd never qualify for a licence.' There was a pause. 'Are you there, Paul?'

'I'm here.'

'I thought we'd been cut off. What do we do?'

'I'm thinking.'

'Well, don't think too long. This line may not last.'

'Listen, if a bomb hits, the bloody car's finished, anyway. I'll take the chance, if you will.'

'Right,' he agreed, although it hardly sounded like a vote of confidence. 'Just remind me – how do you find reverse gear?'

That was the moment the line had failed. He was unsure if Paul heard the question; there was no hope of hearing the answer. When the time came, he'd have to try finding reverse on his own.

Towards morning, the planes were still overhead in waves, and the smell of sulphurous fumes was heavy in the air. The cold became so intense that Sam's legs began to cramp. At the other end of the trench he could hear one of the Frankenstein children whimpering. He wasn't sure if it was F Major or F Minor, and felt ashamed he had never taken the trouble to learn their names. But the family lived strictly apart from others, and aside from the father's appearances at work, avoided all contact with the staff. He heard their mother trying to comfort the boy, using the name Yoshi. He hoisted himself painfully out of the trench, and crawled to where the caretaker, his wife and two young boys crouched in equal misery.

'Yoshi, are you all right?' he asked.

There was a startled silence.

'I'm cold and I've got the cramp,' Sam said, and could faintly make out four faces staring up at him.

'I'm cold, too,' Yoshi said. 'What's the cramp?'

'I can hardly walk. All my muscles feel as hard as wood.'

'Will they get better?' the boy asked.

'I hope so,' Sam said.

'You should walk, Delon-san,' Frankenstein said. 'I think the planes are going. You should exercise slowly.'

'Thank you, I'll try,' Sam said, thinking how rarely they had ever had a proper conversation until recently. The huge man had been very quiet, just a nod and a grunt when told he could keep his job, and remain in their basement quarters. Sam wondered if he knew that decision had been his, not the Count's.

'I'll walk with him.' Before either parent could object, Yoshi climbed out of the trench. He was the smallest of the boys, about eight years old as far as Sam could tell in the reflected glow of burning buildings.

'I'll lean on you, Yoshi. You can be my walking stick.'

The boy giggled. They walked slowly up and down the tiny yard. Once another squadron flew low overhead; Sam grabbed him and they lay on the freezing ground, but the planes kept going towards the south and no more bombs dropped.

An hour later, it started to become light. Chilled and hungry people had already anticipated the all clear, and were leaving their shelters. Sam went out into the streets. It seemed, if such was possible, that the aftermath was more terrible than the previous day. The dead were scattered everywhere. There were charred corpses and mangled bodies that could never be identified; the ruins of streets and buildings still smouldering, like a wild scene from a Stygian hell.

He felt sick. It seemed the world was insane. How could there be a God? And if there was, how could He allow such things? Children burnt to tiny scraps in the streets. Many dead dismembered by explosives, unrecognisable. How could He condone this turmoil? Men in machines flying overhead – perhaps some of them kind and educated men – unleashing this havoc, then returning to the comfort of their base? Would they even pause to think about the devastation they had left behind? Or was it just another day, another mission; a course to be flown, killing to be done on command?

The Mitsukoshi department store had taken a direct

hit, but remained standing. Its windows had exploded with the heat and shards of glass littered the pavement. The canal across the street, from where Sam had first seen the bank, was clogged with bodies. He stood and looked back at the quaint bijou building, so frail against the huge Bank of Japan, and wondered how many more raids it could survive, how many more times it could remain there against such odds?

He walked through the ruins of the Ginza, past the corner where a bar had stood. It had been his favourite place: Sumiko, the owner, had always made him welcome. Not only the bar but the entire street had vanished, as if it never existed. Nothing remained except ash and twisted struts that might have been window frames. A girl sat in the dirt, crying. There was something familiar about her.

'Aiko?' She reminded him of Aiko, one of the prettier of the bar girls who had worked there. She looked up, but he couldn't tell if it was Aiko, for her face was burnt and blistered beyond recognition.

'Where's Sumiko?' he asked.

'Dead,' she said between sobs, 'they're all dead.'

'Are you Aiko?' She turned away, as if she couldn't bear to look at him. Or allow herself to be looked at. Sam went to an ambulance crew working down the street, and asked if they could help her. They didn't bother to reply. He was a Caucasian; he could see the hatred in their faces.

Emile Laroche completely lost his temper. He was like a madman, his rage echoing through the empty bank chamber.

'I refuse to be dismissed by you,' he shouted, and was

about to rip up the cheque until Sam pointed out if anything happened to the Count on his journey, there wouldn't be another.

'I know what's been going on here,' Laroche snapped. 'And if the authorities were told, it would put an end to your career, you young bastard. And to his High and Mighty Excellence.'

'And what about you, you fucking idiot?' Sam knew he had to be convincing. There was danger in Laroche's anger. 'Do you really think the police will believe events took place in this bank and the chief accountant had no part in it? Don't be thick! They'll have you in a cell, torturing you to find out how much else you know. And I'll swear you knew every detail. That it was your idea. And since you don't know the real names, you'll shit yourself when you hear them. Because you're going to make deadly enemies out of some important people. If you happen to survive gaol, you'll be as popular as a whore with the clap.'

'How dare you talk to me like that,' Laroche said.

'I mean it. I won't be blackmailed by a prick like you. Take your cheque before I ask the Count to stop payment. Before I tell any firm where you apply for a job that you're a slimy toad who likes to spend his time getting a grip on the typists' arses.'

'I never liked the look of you,' the accountant's voice was shrill, 'from the day you came here, you were trouble. I tried to tell the Count he was a fool to trust you, but de Boulanger is a weak man himself. A slave to that Vietnamese woman.'

'I'll let him know how grateful you are. Now go to hell before I rip up your bloody cheque myself.'

Laroche looked capable of an assault. He spun around as they heard a cough. Frankenstein was standing in the background, his massive figure watching. He pointed a finger at Laroche, then opened the front door of the bank. He stood waiting. Laroche reluctantly went out.

'Sayonara,' the caretaker grunted, then shut the door.

Sam thanked him. It was their second friendly encounter lately, both of them in the space of a few hours.

The news was on the radio, and in the evening papers. Florrie bought the *Sun* and *Mirror* on the way home, but both contained only sketchy details. Even so, it was clear the biggest air raid ever launched had devastated Tokyo. While she cooked dinner, waiting for Carl, she listened to the news. All the scheduled programmes made way for a series of interviews with experts, giving opinions and discussing figures. There was much to discuss, for the Americans, in their biggest triumph to date, had determined to give facts and figures, and spare no detail.

The earthquake of 1923, the city's biggest disaster, had seen a total of 150,000 people perish. In the raids of these two nights in March, 1945, even enemy estimates placed the death toll at seven hundred thousand. The Americans believed it was closer to a million. As for the city, observers in reconnaissance aircraft reported fourteen square miles of it was now little more than a pile of ash.

The Swiss Embassy was intact. It was built of concrete and steel, and appeared to be deserted. Sam hammered on the door, and was about to give up, when he heard bolts on the main door being drawn, and his friend the Ambassador's nephew appeared.

'Sam? What the hell are you doing here?'

'Bernhardt. I need a favour. No, I need two favours.'

'This is not a very good time, Sam.'

'Have you got a driving licence?'

'Of course.'

'Do you have a car?'

'I don't need one. There's an official embassy car, and we have a chauffeur.'

'Wonderful. Would you lend me your licence? I'll see you get it back.' When Bernhardt hesitated, Sam reminded him of their school days. 'Do you remember Wilhelm Rambert?'

'How could I forget him?'

'He used to beat the shit out of you at school, right? Bullied you until I beat the shit out of him? Remember?'

'Why do you want my licence?'

'I've lost mine, and I have to drive to Karuizawa.'

'Can you drive a car?'

'Would I borrow a licence if I couldn't?' As Bernhardt gave it to him, Sam said: 'But the other favour is a bit more complicated. Do you have a communications link with Australia?'

'I can't answer a question like that,' Bernhardt protested.

'Why not?'

'It's top secret. Highly classified information.'

'Which means the answer's yes.'

'No comment. As the duly appointed Vice-Consul . . .'

'Bernhardt, cut the crap. I know there's still a radio telephone to Java. And a submarine cable from Java to Darwin. If you sent a message, it could be there in a few hours.'

'I can't send any messages.'

'I think there's an overland telegraph to Sydney. I need

this, Berny. I'll never ask for another favour, but I need this.'

'Secret messages? I'd be dismissed. My uncle would be disgraced, and I'd never get another job in the diplomatic service.'

'It's not a secret message.' He gave Bernhardt a piece of paper. 'Read it.'

Bernhardt looked at the printed words, then he smiled.

'I'll get it there somehow,' he said.

Kranz's house was still standing. Sam found the keys to the shed where the car stood. It was a four-cylinder Datsun, small and square in shape, the first successful local car before the factory had turned to war production. He tried the ignition key; to his relief the engine started. He experimented with the gears until he felt sure he had reverse, then let out the clutch. The Datsun shot forward and hit a stack of empty oil cans.

'Shit,' he said, stamping on the brake in time to prevent damage. He studied the gear lever, wiggled it into what seemed the correct position, eased on the clutch and felt relief as the tiny car went backwards out of the shed. He parked it on the road, hurried back to lock the building, checked the map to find his best route, and pressed the accelerator. The car stopped.

'Bugger,' he said, realising he was in the wrong gear. Ten minutes later, after a few hops and some anxious moments, he was driving slowly but more confidently. It was not yet noon, and he'd been lucky. After leaving the Swiss Embassy, expecting a long walk with trains or taxis out of the question, he had found an abandoned bicycle. While there were bodies in the vicinity there was no sign of a live owner. Sam had to straighten a buckled front wheel; the bike wobbled slightly, but instead of spending the day trudging across the city to collect the Datsun, he had arrived in less than two hours.

Now he would be able to avoid the main roads and cut across west Tokyo to pick up the start of the mountain road. With any sort of luck, he might even reach Karuizawa before dark.

Four hours later he was not so optimistic. He had travelled less than ten kilometres. Every few minutes there had been diversions, streets blocked by debris; in some cases, emergency crews were clearing corpses for disposal. He had been ordered to detour so many times, he felt he was in a maze.

The police were causing the major chaos as they stopped cars to interrogate the drivers. Each checkpoint brought a barrage of questions. Destination? Your car papers? Driving licence? Paul had left the registration in the Datsun; it was in Japanese, while fortunately Bernhardt's licence was in French and received only scant scrutiny. In this time of panic, any documents were enough.

The crowds were the real reason for his lack of progress. All roads from the city were packed with fleeing refugees. Some pulled handcarts with their belongings, or pushed wheelbarrows; the rest, the majority, carried bundles of food, or whatever had survived the raids and was important to them. Those who had bicycles walked beside them, for the pace was too slow and the road too full of people to be able to ride.

There was no possibility a car could get through this mass exodus. He had tried once to use the horn, but those ahead had refused to give way, turning and shouting at him, and, realising he was a *gaijin*, one of them had kicked the car. Others spat at the window. Someone yelled that he was a fucking spy. It was an ugly and frightening moment, then lassitude prevailed and they trudged on.

Sam felt trapped. All he could do was inch his way forward, aware that proceeding like this would use up the precious tank of petrol more rapidly than driving at a normal speed. The fuel gauge had already dropped to almost half. There was the extra tin in the back, but it contained only a gallon, and there was no easy or safe way to find a black-market source to buy more. In the countryside, it could be dangerous.

If I ever reach the countryside, he thought exhaustedly. The houses were more widely spaced, but this was still outer Tokyo. He estimated he had the best part of ninety kilometres ahead of him. A straight, flat road would be bad enough, but once he reached Okegawa the road would climb, and driving would be difficult. He wished he knew the route better, but few people ever came to the mountains except by train. He realised now there was no chance of reaching his destination until tomorrow, and was unsure if he could continue much longer. Once dark fell, he decided to pull off and try to sleep. By morning, perhaps the road would be less crowded.

In fact, as it became twilight, the people themselves began to find places beside the road to settle for the night. By the time it was dark, so many had left the road that Sam was able to switch on his headlights and increase speed. There were still those pulling carts and riding bicycles, but soon he left them behind. Despite the steep gradient and serpentine road, he felt confident and estimated that he should arrive by midnight.

But midnight was long past when the petrol ran out. He had just reached the crest of a hill, and the headlights revealed a long, level road and scattered farms. He could see occasional tiny houses, but no lights within them. The engine did not splutter or cough the way engines were supposed to do; it simply stopped turning. The car ran under its own velocity for a short distance, then gradually lost speed and finally came to a halt.

Sam tried the ignition again; it was hopeless. He checked his watch. It was after two o'clock. Dawn was at least three and a half hours away, and without the heat generated by the engine, it was already freezing cold.

'Petrol?' the farmer said. 'I ride a bike and push a hand plough. I haven't seen a drop of petrol in two years.'

'Would there be anyone else who could help?'

'Not here. Used to be a black marketeer in Fujioka, about five miles away, but they caught him. Shot him, someone said, but I heard they put him in the army, and the enemy shot him.' He was a wiry man with a creased face and acquisitive eyes.

It was barely light. Sam had been huddled in the car trying to sleep and, when this proved impossible, had walked up and down, attempting to keep warm. He had decided the chance of a welcome was better if he waited until people were awake. No-one would respond kindly to a knock on the door in the dark. Finally, a glimpse of a lantern had alerted him, and he'd seen the farmer emerge from his house to milk a tethered goat. Acquainted with the temperament of goats, Sam had waited until milking was done before approaching.

'That yours, is it?' The farmer indicated the Datsun,

standing forlornly on the roadside about three hundred metres away.

'Belongs to a friend. I'm taking it to Karuizawa for him.'

'Karuizawa?' His gaze was openly speculative. 'I hear rich people live up there. Mostly foreigners. You're foreign.'

'French,' Sam said.

'What'll you do with the little car?'

'I'll have to see if I can find someone to tow it.'

'Nobody has a tractor to do that sort of thing.'

'Or find a farmer with a barn, who could keep it safe.'

'I've got a barn.'

'Yes, I noticed. It looks big enough.'

'Biggest barn in these parts,' the farmer said smugly. 'How long would it be for? A few days? A week? A month?'

'A few months, I'd say. Until he can buy petrol.'

'Black-market petrol?' The other man's eyes were sharp.

'Not worth the risk,' Sam replied hastily.

'He can't buy legally,' the farmer said. 'But when we win the war, the government's promised there'll be all we want.'

'That's right.' Sam was anxious to have it resolved. 'The car might have to stay until then. Luckily our victory will be soon.'

If he thought a pretence of patriotism would help, he was wrong. The farmer struck a hard bargain. He and his neighbours would push the Datsun along the road to his barn. The cost would be fifty yen shared between them. Sam tried to haggle.

'Fifty? I could get it towed by a machine for that.'

'But there's no machines. You want it left where it is?'

'Definitely not,' Sam said. 'How about we settle for ten yen each neighbour,' he proposed. 'That sounds fair to me.'

'Right,' the other said. 'Six neighbours, that's sixty yen.'

'Hang on a minute . . .' Sam started to protest.

'Your idea,' the farmer said. 'Now, the storage charges. Ten yen a week, until he collects it. Minimum of fifty yen. After all, I've got to make room in my barn. And nobody does nothing for nothing, not these days.'

Sam sighed. Of all the locals, he had to choose the most avaricious one. But if he left the car where it was, the wheels and battery would be sold before nightfall. And he was exhausted, badly in need of food and sleep.

'It's a deal,' he said.

'In advance,' the farmer put out his hand. 'I was always told, if you deal with *gaijin*, it's best to get money in advance.'

Sam was allowed a few hours sleep in the barn, after the farmer and his neighbours had put their combined weight behind the Datsun and pushed it along the road to safety. They thought it a huge joke to be so generously paid for so little. But no-one had a horse and cart to take Sam to the nearest railway station when he woke. It took him three hours of uphill trudging to reach Takasaki. There he bought some food, ate it ravenously, and fell asleep in the train, while contemplating the prospect of spending the next day with Justine – and if miracles were on the agenda – perhaps the night as well.

The cable arrived three days after the news of the raids. Three days of torment, during which she could barely concentrate on work. Mr Joubert telephoned and said an extraordinary thing had happened. A personal message had arrived for her at the consulate, and could he save her the walk and read it to her over the phone?

'Please,' she said, her heartbeat accelerating with fear.

'It's brief, but it's astonishing it reached here at all. Quite astounding, these days. But you can't predict such things, can you?'

'Please, Mr Joubert,' she said. 'The message?'

'Of course.' He cleared his throat and read: '*Dearest Florrie, I ducked and they missed. Bound for Karuizawa. Safer to stop writing until the final bugle blows. Love Sam.*' He heard a sound and was unsure if it was a laugh or a sob. 'Mrs Eisler?'

'Yes, Mr Joubert?'

'Are you all right?'

'Oh yes,' she said. 'Absolutely. Thank you so much.'

She hung up, and let the tears of relief run down her face.

CHAPTER 25

Herr Doktor Wirtz was distinctly Aryan, blond and tall, and made no secret of the fact he was a party member. All his aristocratic family were party members. As Claude Briand said, the doctor only required a black uniform and swastika to be a model SS officer. When Hans Wirtz met Justine Fournier it was not by accident. He had seen her in the town, admired her trim figure on the tennis courts, and discovered her name. Then he set about pursuing her.

He had called on the French Ambassador, and over coffee and brandy managed to bring up the subject of golf. He'd heard the Ambassador was a keen golfer, and personally he loved the game. Perhaps a friendly match could be arranged? He and young Wilhelm Rambert: he felt sure the Ambassador knew the Ramberts, a most respected Swiss family? Rambert senior was a director of the Red Cross, and his son ran the local branch for him. If the idea appealed, Dr Wirtz hoped His Excellency would bring his regular golf partner, Monsieur Fournier.

The Ambassador had been pleased to arrange it. Wirtz, who was a very good golfer, managed to lose the match with skilful grace on the last green, and their older opponents were delighted. After Wilhelm Rambert had driven off in his father's Packard, Wirtz suggested he might be allowed to buy the winners a drink. Later, he found himself invited to the Fournier house for tea. He proved an ideal guest, commending Madame Fournier on her tasteful home, wondering, since her daughter enjoyed tennis, if they might perhaps enter as a pair in the mixed doubles?

They had played golf several times since, and the doctor was invited again for tea. He begged to be allowed to return their kind hospitality, asking the Fourniers to dinner, and insisting the invitation should include their daughter.

Things seemed different in Karuizawa. The cold weather lingered and spring was late. Sam already felt time hung heavily, particularly after learning Justine and the doctor were to be tennis partners in the mixed doubles.

'Why?' he asked, meeting her for the first time after he had been back a week. He had tried to see her on several occasions, but she had been curiously elusive.

'Why not?' she countered. 'He's polite. My father and the Ambassador like him, and feel we should be civil to him.'

'Your father's never been civil to me,' Sam said.

'That's different.'

'What's different about it?'

'He's being protective. He knows you're after my body.'

'So what's the Nazi after?'

'Now don't be like that, Sam.'

'I bet he kisses your mother's hand. I'm sure he kisses your father's arse.'

They saw the immaculate figure of Hans Wirtz waiting by the courts. 'It's only a game of tennis,' she said.

Sam sat and watched as she joined the German doctor. Things were certainly different.

He went in search of Claude.

'It's this damn place,' Claude said. 'Like a luxury penal colony. Nobody can leave, and they're bored shitless. Your sister's so depressed she's taken to going out with Swiss Willy Rambert.'

'You're joking!'

'Ask her. He's teasing her with promises of a job with the Red Cross. In my opinion, that's just bait; he's after one thing.'

'If I see the rotten bastard trying it on . . .'

'Sam, she's an adult. Not your kid sister any more.'

'But bloody Swiss Willy . . .'

Claude shrugged. 'It's this charming bugger of a town. Drives people crazy. Fine for a few weeks holiday in summer, but not for this. I wish to Christ I was back with the film unit. You'll soon wish you were back in Tokyo.'

'I already do,' Sam said. 'The trouble is, the Tokyo we knew no longer exists.'

He began to realise what they had put up with living there full time, while he had been able to visit and leave again each week. His mother seemed to have shut out the rest of the world. Her days were spent playing mahjong with Paul Jacoulet, or bridge at the hotel.

'She's still in mourning for that spy,' Jacoulet told Sam. He was adorned as ever like a geisha. 'I can't imagine why. I didn't fancy him in the slightest.'

Sam smiled. 'I doubt if he fancied you.'

'There's no accounting for some people's preferences. So your nice girlfriend plays tennis with the handsome blond doctor. Do they play any other little games together?'

'I don't know, Paul.' It was pointless remonstrating with Jacoulet. He enjoyed being offensive and outrageous.

'Quite a lot of it going on,' he said. 'When people are cooped up together like prisoners for so long, fucking is one way to pass the time.'

'Paul, do you hate it here?'

'Not only here,' Jacoulet said. 'The truth is, I've fallen out of love with this whole country. I remember other times, better times, when it was a joy to live here. It was a place of beauty, a land of dreams. People then were devoted to lyricism; we admired fine *kakemonos*, we prized treasures like *netsuke*, wood carvings, ceramics and origami. We cherished the heron and the nightingale: we loved the lotus. The tea ceremony was an elegant ritual. Even the art of the geisha ... delicate things were revered. But now the colours of our life have been taken away. Lyric art is scorned and forbidden. The delicate and fragile have become objects to be crushed. We are not allowed to be sensitive. We must be warlike, be what they call heroic and courageous. I call it hideous insanity.'

Sam realised Jacoulet was weeping. Tears ran down his powdered cheeks, like rain making splashes in a patch of snow.

Wilhelm Rambert relished the idea of bedding Sam's sister. He had spent time carefully flattering her, even dangled before her the prospect of a job with the Red

Cross, although he had no intention of ever allowing this to happen.

But he fully intended to seduce her. She had a soft, sweet face, and a full curvaceous figure. In his thoughts, he savoured the prospect; he dwelt on the vision of undressing her slowly, arousing them both and bringing her to an excited orgasm; enjoying her while he remembered with hatred her brother, who had knocked him down in the schoolyard one day eight years ago, while the rest of their class had stood around laughing and cheering.

He was determined to have Sam Delon's sister for the humiliation of that day. Even if he had to risk everything to do so. Which was why he telephoned and asked her to come to his office in the village – the small building that was the headquarters of the Red Cross – saying he had used all his influence in Geneva to arrange a job for her. Angelique, he knew, was gullible enough to believe it.

Sam was riding home as she waved and rode by. She seemed in such a hurry; turning to wonder why, he almost ran into the azalea bushes.

'Where's she going?' he asked his mother, who was setting up the table for mahjong. She had a glass of vodka beside her.

'Willy has a job for her,' Tamara said.

'Willy? You mean that Swiss creep, Rambert?'

'Darling, that's unfair. Willy has been trying to get her work. Now it seems he's got agreement from his office in Geneva.'

'Mama,' Sam said, 'don't you know crap when you hear it? That's utter and complete rubbish.'

'Why do you have this dislike for Wilhelm?' she said, carefully arranging the mahjong tiles into a formal three-sided wall

'Shouldn't you wait for the others before you do that?'

'If they don't trust me, they don't need to play. Tell me why do you hate Willy?'

'Because he was a bully at school. And cheated in exams. Apart from being a spoiled brat whose father is so rich that he used to lord it over all of us.'

'You'd better get used to things here, Sam,' his mother said. 'Your friend, Justine, for instance, might be able to say why her family seems to like the Nazi doctor. I find it peculiar. Did you know he said he felt honoured to care for his countrymen, because it meant they wouldn't be polluted by the touch of two Jews.'

'Incredible.'

'He's never spoken to them. One day Doctor Plessner said good morning to him and Wirtz just stared at him then walked straight past. Now neither of our doctors try to talk to him because they know they'll be ignored or insulted.'

'He sounds a real bastard,' Sam said. 'Whereabouts does this medical storm trooper live?'

It was traditional that houses in Karuizawa had a wooden nameplate in front to identify the occupant. Herr Doktor Wirtz's sign was new, conspicuously embellished with the initials of his degrees. He seemed to have a great many for such a young man.

Sam had brought a screwdriver, and a tiny flashlight. He carefully removed the freshly painted sign as Claude handed him Dr Plessner's shabby old board. It was after midnight; nobody was in the street. Sam fixed Plessner's name to Wirtz's gate. They moved off with Wirtz's plate, and strolled through the town.

Early the next morning there was a larger than usual crowd at the tennis club. Nobody was playing; instead they seemed to be busily chatting together while watching the street.

'Here he is,' Claude murmured, and everyone turned to watch. Dr Wirtz strode from the direction of his house. He held a battered sign in his hand, as if it was something offensive.

'And here's Doc Plessner,' Sam said, and from the other direction they saw the Jewish doctor approach. He carried Wirtz's large and ostentatious new sign.

The two men met. They stared at each other, then without speaking Wirtz tossed Plessner's nameplate on the ground. For a moment the older doctor seemed prepared to do likewise; instead he simply held out the board for the other man to take. The watching group broke into spontaneous applause. Until then, neither had been aware of an audience. Now Wirtz turned, realising too late he had made himself look churlish. Then, snatching his sign, he strode off.

Plessner picked up his own tattered name, smiled at the crowd who applauded him again, and walked back toward his house.

'I don't know if you did it. I've no idea who did. I'm saying it's the kind of thing you might do, and in my opinion and that of the Ambassador, it was provocative, stupid and unwise.'

Pierre Fournier was in a rage. Sam had come to visit Justine, but had been intercepted at the front door by her irate father. 'Well,' he demanded, 'what do you have to say about it?'

'I have nothing to say,' Sam replied, 'except that I saw the Nazi behave oddly this morning. He threw Doc Plessner's house sign on the ground. Someone said he's a golfing friend of yours, but I found it hard to believe. Who'd want to associate with him?'

Fournier stared at him, and Sam knew that once again with Justine's parent, he had gone too far. 'I deeply resent that.'

'I apologise, Monsieur.'

'Your apology is not accepted. I *associate* with him, as you call it, because the Ambassador feels it's politically sensible to do so. There is nothing to be gained by antagonising Germans. You should remind your radical friends we're in a precarious situation. The Germans are allies of the Japanese, and in a position to influence them. So far we've survived this war in comfort, compared to those who are interned. Tell those idiots who applauded the Jewish doctor this morning, they did us no favours when word of this leaks out.'

Sam knew he should keep silent. It was the sensible thing to do. Equally, he knew it was impossible. 'The Jewish doctor, sir, has been our doctor and yours for years. He's been a friend. Must we curry favour by being anti-Semitic?'

'I am not anti-Semitic,' Fournier said through clenched teeth. 'I'm also certain you were responsible for this absurdity – this childish charade. Now – was there anything else?'

'I came to see Justine.'

'Go to hell. Just keep away from my daughter.'

Fournier went inside, closing the door. Sam mounted

his bike as an upstairs window opened. Justine looked out and smiled.

'Crazy fool.'

'It was in a good cause.'

'Daddy sounded upset.'

'Never mind Daddy. How does it feel, being locked away like a princess in a tower?'

'You say the nicest things. Sam, I'm bored with Teutonic tennis. He almost clicks his heels every time he hits a winner.'

'Really?'

'And he does kiss mother's hand, and father's arse. Well, as good as . . . he lets him win at golf.'

'Daddy would enjoy that. When can we meet and discuss these important matters further?'

'Tomorrow,' she said, and blew him a kiss.

In Australia, a long hot summer had ended. It was Easter time and rumours abounded. Radio reports said Hitler had called on his youth brigade, ages ten to fourteen, to defend him from the Russians. An equally reliable source knew for sure he had fled to Berchtesgaden, to make a final stand there with thousands of his fanatical SS troops. Yet another declared he was insane, hiding in the *Fuhrerbunker* beneath the rubble of Berlin.

'Your warmest clothes,' Florence said, packing his case. It had happened so suddenly.

Easter Monday, after a late party and looking forward to a lazy holiday, the morning spent in bed, perhaps more love-making, until a phone call had startled them sometime before dawn. She answered sleepily

'Sorry about this, old darling,' the cheerful voice of Frank Forbes had boomed. 'Did I wake you?'

'No, Frank dear,' she said. 'I'm having this dream that you're talking to me without even bothering to dial our number. With such a powerful voice, who needs a telephone?' She heard him laughing as she called Carl, watching her husband try to adjust to the interrupted sleep, then his gathering excitement as he listened to what was being said. When he hung up, he held her tightly.

'Let's go for a swim.'

'It's still dark,' she said.

'One of my last swims. It'll be winter before I get back. We'll have coffee first, and I'll tell you about it.'

'Tell me now. Where?'

'Germany,' he said. 'Tomorrow.'

They went for a swim, then a long walk past the rock pool and along the deserted main beach, hand in hand.

'I'm going to miss all this.'

'It'll still be here when you come home. And so will I.'

They stopped and kissed. An early fisherman, on his way to the water's edge with a rod and his basket of bait, whistled. They waved to him, and walked on with their arms tightly linked as if they could not get close enough.

'You take care,' she said.

He promised to take care.

She felt a strange tremor of anxiety.

All through Easter Monday it persisted. She tried to conceal it from Carl, who made love to her tenderly that night, then asked her to please stop being afraid because there was no danger in what he was doing. If she was going to worry like this, they could find someone else. But she knew there was no-one else, and that he wanted to go.

In the morning she rang the office, dictated two letters

and said Carl was going interstate, so she'd spend the day with him, but if anyone had a problem they could phone her. Her secretary, Dulcie – the blonde typist who had voiced her delight after James Lindsay's announcement, and who regularly detailed all her amorous adventures with American fliers – said any problems could wait. Her boss worked so hard; a day off without any calls would do her and Carl a heap of good. They might try a rest in bed, Dulcie slyly suggested, and Florrie laughed, told her to behave herself, and hung up.

Now the day had ended. A car was due. The plane was leaving late that night. It would take a week via the Pacific Islands, through the United States and Canada. There were frequent fuelling stops before they crossed the Atlantic to London. From there, an RAF plane would take Carl and a group of intelligence officers to Munich. They would process the release of Australian prisoners of war; airmen and soldiers who had been captured four years earlier in the Greece and Crete campaigns. Then they would go to Dachau, Belsen, and the other concentration camps, to see for themselves if what was being whispered was true.

In Karuizawa, the weather turned. Peach trees and cherry blossom enlivened the April hillsides. The sun shone as if in celebration, and the landscape was transformed. Maples were blooming, magnolias and hydrangeas awakening, laurel and birch trees filling with nesting larks and finches. The whole countryside became a bright vista that revitalised people's spirits after the long winter, and in the depths of the forest he knew so well, Sam found the discarded haven of a chamois, which he and Justine called their own.

'Our private suite at the Hirohito Hotel,' she said, naked and snuggled tightly against him, 'since the Emperor seems to own all the forests in this country.'

'I've got news for him,' Sam said, responding to the heat of her body and its delicious invitation, 'this has always been my place. Now it's ours.' In less fevered moments he made her laugh with details of his childish adventures, his flights of imagination, and the dragons he invented that kept the woods sister-free. It was a part of that magical spring, their laughter.

They grew closer. Sexual harmony was an ingredient of it. But there was far more. They walked for hours along secret trails in the forest, revealing hopes and aspirations to each other, and Sam began to realise that what he had thought was love – with Kimiko, or even Justine a year ago – was nothing. Love was now.

Claude knew. Angelique guessed. Justine's parents were uneasy and suspicious, but there were other events to distract them, for on the radio hidden in the house of the French Ambassador came tidings to gladden the hearts of many confined in Karuizawa.

Berlin was under siege.

In Asia, Iwojima was captured.

Okinawa, the last great island fortress only five hundred kilometres south of Japan, was invaded by a massive American army.

This rush of good news was disseminated with care, for the successes in the spring of 1945 made it a strange and dangerous time. Not everyone welcomed what they heard. The Nazi enclave in the town remained a dominant presence, swaggering in the streets, unable to believe defeat in their distant homeland was possible. They had lived with this arrogance for so long, their minds were closed to anything less than victory.

Throughout the winter, with so many nations compelled to coexist together, a bitter schism had developed between nationalist Germans and neutral foreigners. The Germans claimed a town full of aliens was a danger to security, a likely place to plot sabotage. These people, they insisted, had no allegiance; they fought on no side, they were concerned only for themselves. They were a motley collection of riffraff; Swedes, Swiss, South Americans, Spanish, Irish: some were even Jews, and should be removed from sight.

But they singled out the French as a main source of danger. After all, they had been allies of the British. The French needed watching. In fact, they no longer had a right to be considered neutral – or remain at liberty. They should all be interned. These were the undercurrents in the spring of 1945.

The Ambassador knew of this pressure. He reported it would be unwise to show satisfaction at Allied victories. Their status was being considered, but he was hopeful. Japan had a long history of trade with France. French people had spent their lives here; most Germans were transients, who would return to the Fatherland. Some were louts, parading the streets like storm troopers. Any move against the French, the government felt, was not an option to be taken lightly.

But Tokyo did send military police to check on possible espionage or insurgents. A Kempetai squad was dispatched to the mountains, and told to keep watch on *gaijin* who might be suspects. The man in charge of the detachment was Major Ito. The day after his arrival, he demonstrated he was now in a position to make Sam's life extremely unpleasant.

* * *

Major Ito came with a sergeant and corporal, announcing they were there to conduct a search of the house for incriminating documents. They arrived in two motorcycles, one with a sidecar for the Major. All wore uniforms as an act of calculated intimidation, for it was bound to spread word that the Delon house was being searched, therefore it was under suspicion, and it would be rash to associate with them.

They found nothing, for there was nothing to find, but it achieved its objective, provoking Sam and upsetting his mother, who had her own distressing memories of a previous police search and the ensuing gossip and embarrassment. It drew attention to the fact that Sam was a target for investigation, which was what Ito intended. After the search was over, he sent his men to wait by the transport. He bowed politely to Tamara Delon, explaining his duty sometimes caused distress, but there had been information laid before him, and as an officer he was obliged to act on it.

'What information?' she demanded, but the Major said it was classified, so he could not reveal that. Now he wished to speak to her son. However, he was sure they had no family secrets – he smiled as he said this – so what he had to say was not private. She could remain.

'I don't wish to remain,' Tamara said.

'I prefer you do,' the Major replied. 'I assume you do still regard him as your son, despite his birth in Australia?'

Tamara stared at him, thunderstruck. Sam knew Ito had done this deliberately. He wanted to lash out and hit the bland face, but that was the quickest way to a rope or a bullet.

'I know all about his mother, the late Miss Carter. And her sister, Florence Eisler. He's extremely fond of Aunt

Florence, but I expect you realise that – and I'm sure you're also aware that he foolishly writes to her.'

'Who told him this, Sam?' she asked, deliberately turning away to exclude the Major.

But Ito was anticipating it, and the first to answer.

'We have methods, Mrs Delon. I want you to prevail on him to cooperate with me. Then we'll leave you alone. You'll have no more trouble. And nor will I.'

They watched him walk away through the garden.

'What did he mean, cooperate with him?'

'Don't bother about it, Ma. Because I won't cooperate.'

'Is it true you're still writing to Florence?'

'No,' he said. 'I told her it was too dangerous.'

'You told her? When?'

'About two weeks ago.'

'How could you possibly do that?'

'I sent her a cable.'

'You're mad,' she said, her accent betraying her sudden agitation. 'Like your bluudy father was. Plain bluudy crazy. You'll end up like him if you're not careful.'

They stood in awkward silence, until the engines shattered the calm, and the motorcycles went away down the lanes.

Florence heard the news aboard the ferry, on her way to work. It began with a sudden clamour of ship's horns, freighters tooting, pilot boats too, and the clear sound of cheering across the water.

'Hitler's dead,' came the shout from a passing yacht, and everyone on board the Manly ferry began to cheer. Strangers shook hands, some hugged each other. At Circular Quay, the news vans were already delivering a special edition, and placards were in place.

HE'S DEAD, one said, and a well-dressed man walking up Castlereagh Street beside Florrie smiled at her and said it was the best news in years. He personally was going to the pub at lunchtime to celebrate the event, and intended to stay there until they turned the lights out. Would she, by the remotest chance, care to join him?

She laughed, but explained she had a full day ahead.

Me too, the man chuckled. Full as a boot, I hope, then he wished her well, crossing the street to greet another woman to whom he made the same offer.

Florence reached the office, and asked Dulcie if she had any influence at the local pub.

'Certainly have,' Dulcie said.

'I thought you might. When it opens, see if you can buy me a few bottles. Champagne if you can, beer or plonk if all else fails. Then tell all the staff we're having a drink at lunchtime. An office toast to celebrate that Hitler's dead.'

'Gotta be champagne,' Dulcie said. 'I'll get onto the guys at the PX.' She paused at the door. 'Will Carl be here?'

'I rather doubt it,' Florrie said.

'That's gotta mean he's somewhere far away.'

'Don't be nosey,' she laughed. 'But strictly between us, yes, he is away. Only don't ask me where.'

'Wherever he is, he'll sure as hell be celebrating this.' After she had gone, Florrie reflected there'd been so many Yankee boyfriends, even the accent was starting to rub off on her secretary – then told herself not to be such a prude.

Carl was in Munich, where the news had erupted hours previously. At first, it was a series of wild rumours, then facts emerged. Hitler had married Eva Braun in the last hour of his life, and in a bizarre pact they had suicided. According to reports, the Russians were at the doors of the Chancellery, while directly below them in his bunker the Fuhrer had put a pistol in his mouth and pulled the trigger.

'Some honeymoon for little Eva,' an American in their intelligence group said.

'Poor bitch,' Carl replied. 'What a pathetic life.'

'Window dressing,' another said. 'Adolf was asexual, but needed a woman around to create a semblance of virility.'

Everyone had their own theories. Carl wished he could join in the celebration that the beast of Berchtesgaden was dead, but was still in shock from his first sight of the concentration camps. He was assisting in compiling evidence at Dachau against the SS guards, both men and women. For hours he had interrogated the camp commandant, Josef Kramer, who was arrogant and unrepentant, claiming Dachau was no more than a political reformatory, where antisocial members of society were turned into useful citizens.

'Are *they* your useful citizens?' Carl indicated emaciated prisoners, so ill and demented by years of starvation and brutality that they were hardly recognisable as humans.

'Gypsies and Jews,' Kramer retorted, then aware of the anger he had aroused, hastily added, 'also communists, socialists, traitors opposed to the regime. I was only obeying orders.'

Carl and the intelligence team found a great many Nazis, who claimed to have only been obeying orders. He was appalled that young women were among the worst of the camp guards. Irma Greese aged twenty-two, a sadistic torturer at Belsen; Ilsa Koch – the commandant's wife at Buchenwald – who made lampshades from human skin of the prisoners; these were the darkest days and the lowest points of depravity to which humanity had yet descended.

Carl Eisler began to say so in public, loudly and often. He gave statements to German newspapers: editors, who wanted to suppress them, were ordered to publish by the Allied High Command. Headquarters encouraged his outrage; it was a useful weapon to berate the enemy into the act of final surrender. The Allies were also uneasily aware that their own leaders had known of these camps for a long time. Churchill and Roosevelt had kept silent; so too, it was now becoming apparent, had the Pope in the Vatican.

Carl was asked to speak on radio, and Germans listened to a German denouncing them, expressing his personal disgust at his own country. He told them it was not only the dreadful names in the headlines like Auschwitz, Dachau, Buchenwald and Belsen – there were over three hundred extermination centres. It was therefore impossible that the majority of the population had not known what was happening. Which made them all silent accessories to mass murder.

The war had only days to run, but in the eyes of a core of extreme Nazis, fanatics who called themselves the Werewolves, this German Jew was a traitor. He should be stopped, and the only way to show the world they were still willing to fight and were not yet beaten, was to illustrate this by killing him.

In Karuizawa, the Kempetai kept strict watch for signs of revelry as it looked certain the European war must end.

They were confused; the French seemed indifferent to the death of Hitler. The rest of the world might celebrate, but not here.

Here they played tennis or boule, met for drinks or cards, rode horses – did the same mundane things they had done for months past. It was a torment to Sam and his friends, who wanted to express their joy, to taunt the Nazis whose aggression they had endured. But the Germans had not yet surrendered. It was dangerous to show elation. The situation was fraught; the Kempetai roamed the streets, looking for signs of jubilation. Major Ito stayed in his office, but Sam was acutely aware of his presence.

In the intimate bedroom on the first floor of the building that housed the Red Cross office, Wilhelm Rambert passed passionate afternoons with Angelique Delon. He had never relished an encounter with any girl as much as this, for each time was not only a moment of sexual passion, but an act of revenge on her brother. A double enjoyment, he thought, as she cried out and he flooded her, feeling so aroused that he knew they would do it again before she went home that day. It still surprised him how eager she was, and how frequently he wanted her.

He had skilfully seduced her. On her first visit here, he had taken her on a brief tour. When she noticed the lack of staff, he said work was cyclical; he only needed staff when ships arrived with the letters and parcels to be sorted and delivered to those in prison camps. It was an economy, for the Red Cross believed every franc saved was money that could be used to help the unfortunate POWs.

'That's why Geneva is delaying their answer on whether I can employ you,' he had told her casually.

'My wages would hardly make a difference, Willy.'

He'd assured her he was working on it. He needed an assistant, and there was no-one he would rather have than her.

In showing her the premises, he had managed to include his own quarters. A comfortable room and an adjacent bathroom. Very different to the chateau where his parents lived, he remarked, which was the finest estate in the region, but this was a pleasant sanctuary of his own, a place to stay when he worked late.

'Sometimes I spend the night here by choice, instead of cycling home. Nice, isn't it?'

'Very nice,' she'd agreed, with a passing glance at the ample-sized bed.

He had been circumspect that first visit. Escorting her back to the office and making coffee for them both. Chatting on a variety of subjects, gaining her confidence, suggesting lunch the next day and in the meantime he would battle for her with the Swiss skinflints. Then at lunch, saying he'd attempted to contact Geneva but the lines were out of order, and he'd made a personal decision to request she act as his secretary one day a week. Very little money, he regretted, but would she please consider it? Having her company would make him very happy, and he'd keep trying to get her full-time work.

Angelique had said she was grateful, and a week later was in his bed proving it. After that, all pretence of secretarial work gave way to afternoons of sexual delight. He decided it was time for them to openly be seen together. It would swiftly be around town that they were having an affair. Gossip fed on innuendo in this place.

Time to let that bastard, Delon, know who was fucking his sister.

She knew that something was wrong the moment Frank Forbes came into her office. He was unshaven. He looked upset and exhausted, nor did he seem to hear Dulcie ask if he took milk and sugar with his coffee.

'No coffee,' he said when she repeated the question. Florence also shook her head. Dulcie went out and left them alone.

'What is it?'

'He's been shot. Some SS thugs...'

'Is he dead?'

'No, but...'

'But what, Frank. Please – for Christ's sake, don't try to spare me. But what?'

'He's in a coma. It's serious. They wanted to move him to St Bartholomew's in London, only it's too dangerous. Can you leave the office and fly to Berlin?'

'When?

'This afternoon. Some foreign office people are going to San Francisco, to discuss forming the United Nations. I can get you on that plane, then a flight to New York, and after that an American army transport to Berlin.'

'How long before I can get there?'

'God knows,' he said wearily, 'but I've been up all night putting this together. Trying to get more news. I know you'll wish neither of you ever met me, that Carl was still a lawyer here, I know all that – but I've done the best I can to get you a priority.'

'Why did they shoot him?'

'Because he was bloody marvellous.' The normally tough Forbes seemed close to tears. 'He gave interviews, went on radio and told the truth about the camps, how most people must have known. These fascist remnants, these guttersnipes, couldn't take it. They set up an ambush as he left his hotel, bashed him first and then shot him. Can you go? I'm afraid I need to know in five minutes, to confirm the seat.'

'Of course I'm going,' Florrie said. 'Just let me make one phone call.'

She dialled, holding her breath and hoping that James Lindsay was not on the beach fishing, or else on the golf links trying to hit a ball.

The engines vibrated. She felt exhausted and her head ached. It had been a hectic rush: finding James, being driven back to Collaroy to pack. After that, the hired car Frank Forbes had arranged, drove her to the RAAF field at Richmond.

As the land faded away and they were airborne, she felt thankful to James for his immediate agreement. Of course he would return and take over the office for a few weeks. For as long as it needed. The fish could wait; as far as his golf was concerned, he'd save a fortune in balls, the number of times he hooked them into the sea at the Palm Beach Club. She wanted to cry with gratitude, but there was no time. Just go, he'd said, keep them informed, please, because that godless bunch at the office would be praying for Carl and for her.

They went via Noumea and Samoa. Time became unreal as they crossed the international date line, and all of a sudden it was yesterday. She could only think about Carl lying in a coma, too ill to be moved, and recall the strange tremor of anxiety she had felt before he had left. It was too late for regrets; pointless to consider them, for he had wanted to do this. Denouncing his country and its people in the press and on the radio. As the plane droned towards the distant coast of America, she felt proud of him – and very afraid.

PART 5

CHAPTER 26

The news was flashed worldwide: the war in Europe was over. Admiral Donitz, who proclaimed himself Fuhrer after Hitler's death, had signed a document of surrender. In London and Paris, there were massive celebrations; in all the towns and cities of Western Europe and across America, people went wild with relief and joy.

In Sydney, James Lindsay looked down on the cheering crowds in the festive streets, and speculated on where Florence Eisler was, whether she had heard this news yet, and if Carl had any chance of survival. He had experienced injustices during the war; but to die in Germany in the final few days would the cruellest irony.

In Karuizawa, the French Ambassador heard the news on his illicit shortwave. The BBC Overseas Service had reporters in the crowd in front of Buckingham Palace, where the King and Queen appeared with Winston Churchill on the balcony. The Ambassador and his guests heard the cheering and singing, then switched to the Forces Network and heard how thousands were converging on Times Square in New York, and all over the world it was being called VE Day.

Florence was in New York, but not a part of the revelry. She had endured four exhausting days of travel, switching from one military aircraft to another, and was waiting at Rickett's Field for yet another plane. But the flights to Europe were delayed. Crews were the problem, a cheerful major told her. The guys were celebrating, and who could blame them? This was a day of a lifetime, and the streets were so crowded that even if the crew were stone-cold sober and trying to report for duty, the chances of them reaching the base before nightfall was remote.

Had she come far, he asked?

Australia, she said, unable to share in the euphoria around her, beset by a desperate feeling of dismay that she might not reach Berlin in time. This sudden outbreak of peace was one more hurdle, and she wasn't at all sure she could handle it.

Justine had spent part of the night with her parents, gathered around the embassy radio. She had stayed to listen while everyone gave opinions on the situation, then she rode into town. She knew Sam would be there waiting for her; he was sitting with Claude at the café by the tennis courts. She broke the news, and passed on a warning from her father and the Ambassador not to celebrate openly.

'But why the hell not?' asked Claude. 'It's great, the best thing that's happened in five years, and we ought to be cheering and dancing in the streets.'

'We ought to, but we can't,' Sam said. 'I'm with Justine. The most dangerous thing we could do is celebrate.'

'Thanks, Sam,' she said. 'I'll tell my father you agree.'

'That'll ruin his day,' Sam smiled.

She smiled in return, and rode off to call on other French nationals in the town.

'You agree with Justine,' Claude said, 'because you're head over heels.'

'Maybe. But we're on a knife edge. Any time, we could be classed as enemy aliens. Nobody knows what will happen then.'

'You mean we could end up in an internment camp?'

'Easily,' Sam replied. 'And if we start dancing in the streets, we'll be behind barbed wire the next day. It's bloody infuriating, but we have to hide the way we feel.'

He went home to tell his mother and sister. As he arrived, Wilhelm Rambert was leaving. Angelique was on the porch waving. Rambert looked so smug that Sam decided someone else could give him the news of VE Day. They barely nodded to each other, until the Swiss mounted his bicycle and spoke.

'Just bringing Angelique home.'

'Good.' He wondered why Rambert was lingering, with the trace of a grin on his face. 'Where from?'

'My place, of course. Where do you think we've been all night? Pretty hot stuff, your sister.'

Sam stood staring as the Swiss rode off. Then he heard Angelique's footsteps approach.

'What did he say?'

'That you stayed the night.'

'So? Why did he say that?'

'Obviously you did. And he couldn't wait to tell me.'

'I don't see why he'd bother. It's none of your business.'

'No, it isn't,' Sam said, 'but he wanted me to know.'

'I'm an adult,' Angelique said sharply, 'and if I want to fuck someone, then I can do it without your approval.'

'Of course you can, Angie. I just thought you'd have better taste.'

She slapped him as hard as she could across the face. As he held his cheek and she was about to slap him again, they heard the sound of a motorbike stopping at the gate. It was the Kempetai bike with the sidecar, and Major Ito was in uniform again, accompanied by the same sergeant.

'Have I interrupted a family quarrel?'

'What do you want this time, Major?'

'I want to make sure we missed nothing in our previous search. So we intend to search the house again.'

Sam saw his mother come out to the porch, agitated.

'We do nothing wrong,' she shouted, too upset to be cautious. 'This is bad – unfair!'

'I'm sorry, Madame,' Ito said politely, 'but my orders are to investigate all those considered enemies of the state. Your son has been asked to cooperate with me, but refuses. So I must conduct a campaign to convince him.'

'It's called harassment,' Sam told her.

'Assessment,' the Major corrected him, relishing it. 'An appraisal of suspects, to protect the homeland.' He stared at them all in turn, and his eyes locked on Sam. 'Don't deny you've heard the spineless Germans have capitulated. The news is known, and it could only be possible through an illegal radio. So we will search here for a short-wave set.'

'The Germans, they surrender?' Tamara asked, startled.

'Apparently, Mama. There are rumours in town.'

'And who spreads these rumours,' Ito demanded. 'You have names for me?'

'Sorry, Major, I heard the news but I have no names. You'd better waste your time and search the house.'

The two men went inside.

Angelique put out her hand and touched Sam's face where she had hit him. It was still flushed from the blow.

'I'm sorry, Sam.'

'Forget it,' he said.

'You know she sleeps with this Wilhelm, do you?' Tamara was badly rattled by this second police intrusion.

'She's grown up, Ma. She's entitled to do as she wants.'

'I thought you don't like him?'

'I'm not the one in bed with him, am I?'

Tamara frowned at this. Angelique smiled. There was a crash of glass from inside the house. As they turned to the front door, the beefy sergeant appeared. He had a shattered glass vase in one hand, something else in the other.

'Accident,' he said. 'The vase fell and broke this.'

He held out one of Paul Jacoulet's delicate wood carvings: it was his mother's favourite, Sam knew. It was smashed to pieces.

Berlin smelt of death and defeat. An army car met the aircraft at Tempelhof, and drove Florence through chaotic streets filled with rubble, past sad, begging children. A man in his *Wehrmacht* officer's uniform sat forlorn amid the debris of a shattered house, waiting for a family that might never return.

In the squalid side streets, young girls in shabby dresses bargained with American GIs, offering themselves for food or the higher prize of a packet of cigarettes. It was infinitely depressing, and she shut her eyes to close out the sight of so much misery. She must have slept, for the next thing she felt was the car stopping, and they were no longer in the ruined city, but at a small country house converted into an army hospital. A Union Jack flew from a flagpole. The driver took her suitcase inside, and told her someone would attend to her soon. No-one did, so she sat on a hard bench, leant her head against the wall and fell asleep again.

'You wouldn't happen to be Mrs Eisler, would you?' she heard a voice saying – a distinctive Australian voice, what's more – and saw a young officer with the unmistakable insignias of the AIF on his shirt. He wore hospital trousers with the khaki shirt. He was on crutches, and his left leg had been amputated at the knee.

'I certainly would be,' she said.

'Carl's wife? No-one looking after you?'

'Not so far, Captain.'

'What a dump,' he said. 'I'll take you to his room. The Colonel should be here to meet you, but he's a Pommy dingbat. The chief medical officer's a really good bloke, but he's flat out like a lizard drinking.' For a brief moment, the familiar expressions made her feel nostalgia for home.

'Is Carl . . . is he conscious? Has anything changed?'

'Not really,' he said. 'The doc'll tell you.' He called to an orderly hurrying past, and told him to look after Mrs Eisler's luggage. And why the hell hadn't anyone bothered to give her a cup of tea after about a week flying all the way from Australia?

'A dump,' he repeated, 'there's too many of us, and not anywhere near enough quacks or nurses. Carl's in here, it's a single room. I'm afraid he's still in a deep coma.'

He opened the door for her while telling her how they all liked Carl. He'd been really popular, cutting through the red tape at the POW camp when they were freed; some drongos thinking that as they'd been prisoners for four years, a few more days wouldn't hurt, but not Carl. He'd also spoken his mind about Dachau and the other cesspits, and it was a bloody shame some evil Nazi bastards had done this. The young Captain said his name was Jim Richardson, and he'd go and tell one of the docs she was here, or at worst it'd have to be Colonel Dingbat. And not to be too surprised if she found the Colonel a brick or two short of a full load.

There were tubes, some sort of monitor ticking with quiet regularity beside the bed. Carl was very pale, but he was breathing. For a moment, she felt terrified and uncertain what to do. There was no response when she spoke his name or gently touched his hand. She saw a wooden chair pushed against the wall; she moved it and sat beside his bed.

'Darling,' she said quietly, her eyes intent on his face, 'everyone at the office sends their love, especially Dulcie and the typing pool. And dear old James came back to take over for a few weeks, so I could be with you. Frank did his best to arrange all the flights. Not his fault, but it kept going wrong, and I got off-loaded several times for people described as VIPs, and I had to wait in huts at small island airfields for the next flight, and I feel as if I've been travelling forever. But I'm here and staying here until I take you home with me.'

She lost track of time, but sat at his bedside keeping up a steady flow of conversation. She lay the palm of her hand against his, so that if consciousness flickered, she would feel his response. She talked about what would happen now; with Germany beaten, the war could be directed against Japan. They couldn't fight the entire world; it must soon end. Then he could be a lawyer again. And Sam would be free to join them, and perhaps go to university in Sydney.

'Wouldn't that be wonderful,' she said, but there was no answer. Just the sound of a door flung open, and an irate voice that belonged on a parade ground, not in a hospital.

'What the devil do you think you're doing?' The words were snapped at her the moment he entered. 'Confound it, can't you speak English? Are you foreign? I asked what the devil you're doing in here?'

Florence thought Captain Richardson had been absolutely right about the Colonel. *A brick or two short of a full load.* He was in dress uniform, complete with Sam Browne and cap, and resembled a small strutting peacock puffed up with his own pomposity.

'Why are you sitting here? Why? Who gave you leave to stay in the room of an unconscious and critically ill patient?'

His voice was far too loud. Like a parade-ground bark.

'Please don't shout at me, Colonel,' she said.

'Shout at you? Shout at you?' He seemed to relish the repetition of a phrase. 'Who are you?'

'Florence Eisler. I'm Carl's wife.'

'Don't you know he's dying? He's dying,' he repeated.

'If he is,' she said, trying to ignore the insensitivity of the man and the remark, 'then I can't be doing any harm, can I?'

'That's as may be, Mrs Eisler, but I run this hospital and I want you out of this room.'

'You run this hospital, Colonel, but are you a doctor?'

'Of course not. I'm an administrator.' He said it as if doctors were from the lower ranks, not to be considered on his level.

'Then may I see a doctor? The chief medical officer,' she said, recalling Jim Richardson's comment. 'Because

I've come across the world, and I won't be turfed out of here unless he says my husband will suffer if I stay. Now would you kindly get him?'

The Colonel turned brick red; she thought he might have a stroke. She watched, mesmerised, as he strode to the door, opened it and bellowed at a passing nurse to get Major Darcy, the chief medical officer. Never mind if he was engaged in a vital life-saving operation, he barked – there was this awkward bloody woman from the Antipodes who demanded to see him.

Captain Richardson was too kind, she thought, listening to his bluster. One of her friends at home had an apt expression for an aberrant creature like this – *a man who wouldn't know if a train was up him until the whistle blew.*

She sat in the dim night light now, remembering. Major George Darcy, an English surgeon from Somerset, with a worn face and a soft burr to his West Country voice, had listened to her and given the opinion it could do no harm. For what Florrie proposed was that she stay there in the hospital and sleep on the floor if she had to; the rest of the time she would sit in the chair, and talk to Carl – keep on talking until he responded or he died.

'But it's against rules,' the Colonel had raged.

'Bugger the rules,' she said.

'It's insanitary,' he had insisted. 'No bed, no bathroom. Do you propose to use the patients' lavatory?'

'It's either that or Carl's potty,' she said, and saw from Major Darcy's responsive smile that she was winning.

'But what good can talking do?' the Colonel said. 'What possible good can it do?'

'I don't know,' she had answered. 'But nothing else

has worked. I know he's dying, you told me that. Twice. I happen to love him very much, and perhaps love can do what medicine can't.'

'Rubbish,' the Colonel had proclaimed, dismissively.

In reply, Florrie could only shrug at this discourtesy and look hopefully at Darcy.

'It's worth a try,' he had said. 'If you'd be kind enough to have someone bring her in a stretcher and a blanket, Colonel?'

'Good God! Do you suggest she sets up house here?'

'That's exactly what I suggest,' Darcy had replied. 'She can use the nurses' bathroom. I'll sort that out with Matron.'

She smiled at the memory of the doctor's quiet authority, and the administrator's indignation. He had stalked out after giving his opinion that this was a foolish waste of time and totally out of order.

'A very nasty species of dingbat,' she had told Carl when they were alone, after the arrangements had all been made at Major Darcy's insistence, 'definitely one snag short of a barbecue, that Colonel. I'm going to stay, my darling, and hold your hand and talk to you until that monitor says there's no longer any point. I'm not coming all this way to be told to go home by some jumped-up pompous jackass, because it's against his rules. I love you. And I'm going to keep telling you that until you hear it.'

Carl was mute and unresponsive. Deep in his prolonged coma, and beyond her reach. Towards the morning, fighting fatigue, and feeling desperate to stay awake, she found a photograph of Sam in her handbag, the last photo she'd received before the war when he was only nineteen.

'Help me,' she said to the smiling young face, but

no-one could help. She wanted to weep, but told herself it would achieve nothing. Nor would begging aid from Sam. Except perhaps to confirm Colonel Dingbat's opinion of her, if he happened to intrude.

'What do you hear, Sam?' the Count asked.

'Something different every day, M'sieu Le Comte. Not even our diplomats seem to know.'

'That doesn't surprise me!'

They sat on the terrace of his house, its extensive lawns in front of them. Moustique, slim, beautiful with her high cheekbones and almond eyes, joined them. She was wearing a silk blouse and skirt. As always she looked elegant. Sam admired and liked her. Whenever he had to come to the house for meetings with the Count, Moustique had always made him feel welcome.

'He worries too much,' she said to Sam.

'We all do, Madame.'

'Of course we do.' The Count was terse. 'Now the rest of the world can send troops it's a matter of time. But Japan won't give up like Germany did. They despise the Germans; to them it's inconceivable weakness. Look how they defend Okinawa, thousands dying each day rather than retreat – then think how they'd fight to save the mainland. They'll never accept unconditional surrender. That would entail turning their backs on the Emperor.'

'But meanwhile,' Sam said, 'the Emperor walks in his gardens and studies the flowers. Does he hear no air raids? See no destruction? Doesn't he realise women and children are dying?'

'It's the Japanese way. He's the Son of Heaven.'

'Protected from the hell outside his palace walls.'

'I've ordered coffee,' Moustique said. 'I don't think

either of you can solve the enigma of the Emperor or the devotion to him. I can't understand it, either. Not when it comes to a choice of people living or dying for a quiet man whom most have never seen.' She smiled. 'I suppose it's like the Christian martyrs who'd never seen Jesus, but were willing to die for him.'

They watched her walk into the house. She had deftly defused their argument, which was just as well. A servant brought a tray with coffee. Only diplomats and the wealthiest people now had staff. The farmers' sons were in the army, the daughters worked in munitions factories. *The Count is probably right*, Sam thought, *the war will go on. They'll defend Japan, until every son and daughter has given their lives for the quiet man.* And if the Emperor wished otherwise, intransigents would prevent it from being heard.

While they drank their coffee, the Count explained why he had sent for Sam. There was disturbing news, that must remain strictly confidential.

'A majority in the Japanese Cabinet wants to intern all French citizens. We've heard such rumours before, but this seems genuine. People have begun to resent Westerners living in what they think of as luxury, while they suffer hardship and food shortages. Rounding us up would be popular. There'd be stories in the papers, it'd be on the newsreels. You see what I'm getting at?'

'A morale booster. Take people's minds off the war. But if that happens . . .'

'If it should happen, God help us. We'd be out of touch with Zurich and Geneva. Any correspondence about the Swiss accounts would go straight to the Kempetai.'

'Major Ito would make certain of that,' Sam said.

'Our only hope is to use every scrap of influence to sway the Cabinet. I telephoned Prince Konoye's secretary this morning. To see if he would receive a message. The answer was yes, so I'm asking if you'll take it.'

'Me?' Sam was startled.

'He'd lose face if it were me, because it's public knowledge we've quarrelled. Also, your presence there would create less notice than mine would.'

'Am I taking him a written or verbal message?'

'A list of names. You know who they are. The Prince knows some: others may surprise him. I've pointed out the danger if this edict goes through. I want him to talk to those he can trust. In particular the War Minister, and two of the Cabinet. That's a useful trio, for a start. Plus the politicians and industrialists who might have influence.'

'When do you want me to leave?'

'I've taken you for granted. Refuse if you wish.'

I can't refuse and we both know it, Sam wanted to say. But he simply shook his head. 'When do I go?' he asked again.

'The Prince will be in his office tomorrow. You should leave on tonight's train.'

Tokyo was like an endless scrapheap of rubble and corrosion. From the train window he could see the devastation; it began in the outer suburbs and continued interminably. Vast patches of scorched land disfigured the view where tiny fragile houses had clustered in such close proximity that they had been simply and easily destroyed.

How many air raids had done this? Someone told him it was over a hundred, but at least half the damage had been inflicted in the two March raids. How many incendiaries had caused these miles of wasteland? Millions, people said. He knew from his own bitter experience that bombs had dropped continually out of a sky crowded with planes.

Tokyo had never been a beautiful city. It had none of the grace of Kyoto. Too damaged by the earthquake; then haphazardly rebuilt after that. But Sam had liked living there; in Nihon-bashi he had enjoyed the allure of the Ginza, and the maze of back alleys that had been his domain. Now, watching through the smeared window, the city seemed squalid: like a threadbare vagrant down on his luck, all vestige of pride stripped away.

There was nothing to delight the eye. The buildings that remained standing looked insecure, ready for their own demolition. Ueno Station, the terminus, had been severely damaged. Passengers had to use makeshift platforms. Sam had a wallet full of cash expenses; the Count had written down Konoye's office address, and advised him to take a taxi. Doubting this would be possible, he was surprised to see cabs with charcoal burners waiting outside the concourse. He hailed one, and asked to be taken to a street near the Diet Building.

Prince Konoye was an impeccably dressed man in his fifties. He did not appear to welcome the visit, nor invite Sam to sit down. His expression, while reading the list of names, was detached.

'De Boulanger seems to trust you. Surprising, in view of the trouble you caused. Do you know the contents of this?'

'Approximately, Your Highness.'

'Approximately?' Konoye studied him. 'You're strong on tact, even if your letter-writing was ill-advised and dangerous. Tell the Count I agree it would be stupid to intern the French community. But if the Prime Minister thinks it a popular move, no-one will prevent it. I'll use my best endeavours, but can promise nothing. Also kindly tell His Excellency it's safer if there is no further communication between us.'

With that Sam was dismissed, feeling it had been a long and rather futile journey. When he left, there was a sound he had not heard for months; the chilling wail of an air-raid siren. As no planes were visible, and people in the street ignored the alert, he assumed it was a reconnaissance survey. It was easy to become intuitive about such things; he recalled the pattern of the winter when he and most occupants of the city, bedevilled by alarms, had been aware when the sirens signalled genuine raids, and other times that posed no danger.

But whatever this warning presaged, it would delay trains until the all clear. He decided to visit the French Bank, and perhaps stay the night in the penthouse. Some of his clothes were still there, as well as some family photographs. He could pack them and tonight he'd hopefully find a restaurant. It would make a welcome break from the sparse food on which they existed.

He looked for a taxi. There were none cruising the street. He decided to walk, and crossed Hibiya Park, which should have been a mass of early summer colour, but the shrubs were stunted and scorched. Burnt trees leaned at grotesque angles. The flowerbeds were unkempt, as if the gardeners had fled to safer soil.

He detoured by the Imperial Palace walls, passing the Concourse, the huge space where crowds came to pay homage to their unseen Emperor. A national shrine; here, joyful parades had celebrated the victories, and soldiers had their photos taken against the famed Meiji bridges. People on passing trams – Sam had seen it – stood and bowed to the Emperor, while trying not to lose face by falling if the trams jolted.

There were no trams these days. Just a small crowd,

some kneeling, all showing reverence, a few watching him narrowly as he walked by without attempting to bow. He increased his stride; it was no place for a *gaijin*, not in these fretful times. He passed the Ote Gate and glimpsed the East Garden of the Palace. It looked tranquil and remote. No fires had blazed in this flawless place. He headed away from it towards Nihon-bashi with eager familiarity.

The sturdy buildings in the financial district were mostly intact. Built to withstand earthquakes, they were at worst scarred and windowless. But the bookshops were gutted. The tiny store that had specialised in English editions, where he had bought an encyclopaedia from elderly Mr Sato, was a burnt shell. Sam remembered the times he sat there and listened to Mr Sato – a former history teacher – talking of Edo Shigenaga, the original shogun who had ruled the city before the Meiji dynasty. He hoped Mr Sato had survived the ruin of his shop. But the desolate sight of incinerated books strewn there, made him doubt this.

He headed towards the canal and the Sumida River, and saw the huge Bank of Japan building unmarked, then the department store; its shattered windows boarded and other bomb damage repaired haphazardly like hastily bandaged war wounds.

He turned towards the French Bank, as if seeking an old friend. The ready smile froze on his face. The bank had gone, vanished, and where it had stood was only ashes and debris. No trace of anything else remained.

The English nurse was called Sybil – named after a famous actress by her stage-struck mum, she said, but confessed it had never rubbed off on her. Bedpans, not bright lights was her lot. She was friendly and cheerful; after her shift finished, she often came to chat, or just to listen as Florence talked softly to Carl as though he could hear her. It was Sybil who made her stop and rest late at nights, who insisted she relax each day in a hot bath, and who did her washing for her.

Jim Richardson limped in for a chat every morning. He was to be sent back to England soon, he told her, for an appointment with a new leg. Then repatriated home to Aussie. George Darcy would appear briefly, check Carl's pulse, smile encouragingly before being called to a new emergency. When she was alone, she often read aloud to Carl from books or newspapers; anything from the arraignment of Goering and other Nazis on war crimes, to the arrest of Lord Haw-Haw, or the scores in the special victory cricket match at Lords, where an unknown young Australian pilot named Keith Miller had made a dashing century.

But the days commenced to take their toll. Fatigue was inevitable; it was the stress that was undermining. She began to fear failure, sensed pity in the averted eyes of some of the nurses, heard murmurs of concern about brain damage after so long in a coma.

'Is that true?' she asked Darcy.

'Not necessarily correct at all,' he said, trying to be kind, but it left her unconvinced and fearful.

Was she doing something terrible here?

If he did awaken, would he be Carl Eisler or someone else – alive but lifeless – someone blank and incapable?

It was a long, tedious journey back to Karuizawa, for the line had again been bombed, and the engine had to crawl its careful way over repaired tracks. Often it stopped altogether, while there was a lively debate between the driver and his engineer about whether it was safe to proceed.

Sam kept thinking about the French Bank, and how it had become a piece of scarred ground, as though it had never existed. He had felt sick with the shock; in those first moments, bile had risen and remained a sour taste in his mouth for hours. He had thought of trying to search for Frankenstein and his wife and children, but knew they would certainly be dead. It was a direct hit by a fire bomb primed with high explosive, and no-one could have lived through it.

As the train began to move again, he tried to remember the children, particularly F Minor, the trusting child who had held his hand. But all Sam could recall was that the boy had been cold and frightened, and his name was Yoshi.

In the American forces newspaper, *Stars and Stripes*, there was an article about coachloads of Germans taken to see the camps, forced to witness the horror of what had happened there. The story said some left in tears, but others insisted it was just Allied propaganda.

'Those would be the bastards who shot you,' she told Carl, but there was no response, no flicker in the hand she held – just the same monitor at his bedside trying to insist he was alive.

'Do you think I'm crazy?' she asked Sybil. 'Come on, we're friends, you can tell me. It's an obsession, isn't it?'

'Nothing wrong with that. I'd be a bit barmy,' the nurse said quietly, 'if it was my fella. I really would, honest. I think it's quite natural to stay and hold his hand, and hang on to hope. You can't just walk away, Florrie.'

'I couldn't,' she agreed. 'But . . . to hold his hand, to sit waiting is one thing. But all the rest of it – reading to him from the newspapers, chattering about what we'll do when the pair of us get home. How Sam will survive in Japan and join us,' – Sybil knew all about Sam – 'and how Carl will come back to the law firm I run, and he'll be a partner.' She tried to smile at this. 'I'll tell you something. The bloody Colonel wonders how the hell I run a law firm. He can't believe it. He thinks I'm nuts.'

'The Colonel wouldn't know his arse from his elbow,' Sybil said firmly. 'You know his trouble?'

'I know he has lots of problems. And I'd hate to be his elbow – or especially the other bit. What is his trouble?'

'He sees the end of a really cosy life. Wearing a posh uniform, having a batman shine his shoes, dining in the officers' mess, people saluting him – all that's going to finish soon. It was a lovely war for him. He's going to hate being a civilian again. Because it's back to Barkers in Kensington High Street.'

'Barkers? What's that?'

'A big department store. Like Harrods, only nowhere near as grand.'

'And what is he when he goes back there?' Florrie asked. 'A manager?'

'A manager?' Sybil shrieked with contagious laughter. 'Oh, I love that! Love it, Florrie! Can you imagine old Dingbat managing anything?'

'Not really. Not even a hospital. So what was he?'

'He was behind the tie counter!'

'A tie salesman?'

'That's our poxy Colonel. And I bet he keeps his army rank, too, the silly old sod. He'll be the only colonel that's selling ties in Barkers.'

'Good God,' Florrie said, reacting.

'It's a laugh, ain't it?'

'No, I mean . . . Sybil, I felt something. I could almost swear I did. His hand moved.' She brushed her fingers across Carl's, while the nurse watched her intently. 'Sybil, it did, honestly. Oh, and it just did again,' she said with a sudden incredulous excitement, 'you feel for yourself. Feel his fingers.'

Before she could, Carl opened his eyes. He saw his wife and blinked with surprise and confusion. He spoke drowsily.

'What's funny? Did you laugh, Florrie?'

'No,' she said. 'Sybil was the one who laughed. She's the dearest girl, and a truly wonderful friend. She was telling me about Colonel Dingbat, who sells ties in a department store. And I think I'm going to cry.'

'Sounds like you've been both on the grog,' Carl said, and then her tears did come, as Sybil rushed out to summon a doctor.

'What is it, liebchen? What's the matter?'

'The matter is, I'm so happy I'm going to bawl my eyes out,' Florence said.

CHAPTER 27

The Count de Boulanger seemed unsurprised by the terse and rather negative message Sam had brought back from Tokyo. He merely observed they must continue being careful not to offend the Japanese, and to hope other ugly rumours that were prevalent would prove unfounded. As for the bank, he had been strangely philosophical about its destruction.

'We don't have to absorb the loss on our balance sheet. The premises were leased,' he said, which seemed to neatly circumvent the death of the caretaker and his family. But perhaps he had forgotten they lived in the building, Sam thought, for he had shown little interest in their welfare the day of the bank closure. He had left the decision of their future to Sam, who had felt it would be unfair to displace them from their basement. As a result of this compromise – what he'd hoped was a kindness – the Frankensteins were dead.

'What was the caretaker's real name?' he asked.

'I never knew. He was always Frankenstein to us.' The

Count expressed a remote regret. 'Poor devils, but I'm sure it would have been instantaneous.'

'I expect so,' Sam said, realising this rich aristocrat had few loyalties outside his own personal life. He left soon afterwards, riding back through the town on his way to meet Justine. Things had changed radically since the German surrender. The main square was no longer dominated by swastika armbands and fascist salutes. The strutting Nazi braggarts were not only humiliated by their country's defeat and their leader's suicide. They were also destitute.

Accustomed to being paid a salary by the embassy, they had lived high and handsomely. Many had been permanent residents at the Mampei Hotel, occupying the best suites and monopolising the bar. Now, the issue of funds had ceased. The German Ambassador had been forced to announce there would be no more payments; the edict to take place immediately. In response to complaints they would be penniless, he said he took instructions from Berlin, and the Allied Command there had given him orders to close the embassy and return home. His financial sources were frozen, so it was pointless anyone asking for a loan. In due course, they would all be repatriated.

Those locals who had suffered from the invective – and sometimes from physical violence – were moved to express delight. The Japanese, to whom defeat was dishonour, showed outright contempt for their former allies, and no longer cared if they were humiliated. Children in the streets gave cheeky Nazi salutes, brazenly mocking them. Claude taunted them with greetings of *Sieg Heil*, and always asked if there was any recent news of Adolf?

Aryan Herr Doktor Wirtz found he now had to care

for patients unable to pay. The Jewish doctors, Plessner and Wittenberg, were glad to treat those resident Germans whom they knew and had always attended, but declined goose-stepping party members on the grounds that examining these patients might contaminate them. Wirtz had the additional discomfort of calling at the Fournier house, to be told by Madame Fournier that Justine was not at home. At least not to him, she said apologetically. That was the message, and Justine had insisted she deliver it. Her daughter was proving to be rather a handful, no longer prepared to listen to her parents' advice, and spending far too much of her time with the young man she knew had never met with their approval.

Hans Wirtz clicked his heels and inclined his head in a stiff and formal bow. As he left, he was infuriated to see Justine riding off with Sam Delon. He felt affronted by his treatment. He had tried to be a gentleman and not rush things, even though there were times when he felt he could have taken advantage. He should have realised the French had absolutely no morality in such matters. He was so incensed, he almost returned to the Fournier house to tell her stupid mother that the daughter was deluding them, playing a game with the lot of them – but he decided they'd find out the truth for themselves before long.

Barely a week after his first hint of recovery, Carl was wheeled out into the hospital garden. He was an object of considerable interest; most patients convalescing there had heard of this German refugee who had told off his countrymen so thoroughly that a bunch of them had shot him. They'd also heard of his Australian wife, who had sat there and told him how she loved him until he recovered.

A bleeding miracle, it was. And according to one of the orderlies, she was Australia's top woman lawyer.

He was a big-time lawyer, too. When he wasn't tearing a strip off the Huns.

They had a grand mansion on some exclusive beach.

Nice chap, now he'd woken up and could talk.

Good-looking woman, even if she was nearly forty.

The power of love, eh?

Love, they all agreed, was a many splendoured thing.

Then, when they found out her name they couldn't help themselves, and started to call her Florence Nightingale.

'This is all getting a bit much,' Florrie said, hearing of her growing saga on the nurses' grapevine. She and Sybil digested these items in fits of laughter. But when she was brought a chair to sit in the garden beside Carl, all the convalescing patients put their hands together to quietly applaud her. She smiled and flushed with pleasure, for it was a rare tribute, a warm, spontaneous gesture.

After that, she accepted the situation: she was formally adopted by them all as Florrie N or Miss Nightingale. When she and Carl left the hospital, after he was declared well enough to complete his rehabilitation in England, most of the hospital patients and nearly all the staff turned out to farewell them.

'The Colonel regrets,' Sybil said as they hugged by the ambulance that would take them to the airport. 'He's rather busy drawing up tomorrow's standing orders.'

'Well, of course. How could you and the doctors hope to look after your patients without standing orders? Tell him I'll pop into Barkers and buy a tie.'

'And will he promise us a discount,' Carl added, 'if we salute and call him Colonel?'

'I don't know what I'll do without you two,' Sybil said, and stood smiling and waving until long after the ambulance was out of sight.

Sam tried to ignore the gossip about his sister and Wilhelm Rambert, but found it difficult. There were few secrets in Karuizawa. People had tired of the ordinary pursuits the town offered. Games of tennis or boule, horse riding, playing cards, these holiday pastimes had lost their appeal, and dispensing scandal was now the prime activity.

'Besides which,' Sam said bitterly to Claude, 'the bastard goes out of his way to make it obvious. Always got his arm around her. I can't protest or I'll be in the shit with Angie.'

'You need a drink,' Claude decided. 'And if you don't, I do.'

They went to the Mampei Hotel and had a beer in the bar. The place was empty. The barman, Joe Ishi, was bemoaning the lack of custom now the Germans could no longer afford to drink there.

'It's as dead as a whorehouse at breakfast time,' he grumbled while he poured their drinks.

'We always leave whorehouses before breakfast,' Claude said. 'The girls can't make a decent cup of coffee.'

'And they burn the toast,' Sam said.

'Comedians,' the barman muttered, and gave them their change. He asked quietly, 'Want any cigarettes?'

'Depends on the price, Joe.'

'Usual black market price. A fresh consignment. Top brands. Chesterfields, Luckies, Camels. All the cartons you want.'

'We'll think about it,' Sam said.

'Don't think too long. They'll all be sold by tonight.'
'How about a discount if I buy five boxes, Joe?'
'Yankee cigarettes, Sam. I don't need to give discounts.'

It was true, and they both realised it. The barman picked up a cloth and polished the counter, in no hurry for their decision. He knew what it would be.

They each took four cartons. Sam bought a box of Lucky Strikes for his mother to smoke, and three more she could use in exchange for food. It was an irony that his money could not buy fruit and vegetables from the farmers but that cigarettes were currency. They could readily be traded for provisions – which was fortunate – for they had bartered all the clothing they could spare, and Tamara had disposed of her last piece of jewellery. Sam was conscious of how she sometimes glanced at her left hand, and its missing wedding ring. Despite his protests, she had insisted on selling it, declaring that since the marriage was over long ago, a piece of beef would be more useful.

They sipped another beer while the barman went to collect the cartons. This abundant supply of cigarettes in a remote community like Karuizawa still posed a mystery. They were a scarce and precious commodity elsewhere. Local brands were rationed, foreign cigarettes illegal. Yet here people took it for granted that there was an unlimited supply. No permits, no coupons were necessary; all that was required was enough money to pay the inflated black market prices. It was a situation they often wondered about.

'Are they smuggled in, Joe?' Claude asked, as he brought them discreetly wrapped in newspaper.

'Now how the hell would I know a thing like that?' The barman waited for payment, then carefully counted it.

They finished their drinks, and went out to their bikes.

'He must know,' Claude said, 'he's the biggest dealer. He handles far more than anyone else.'

Sam shrugged; it was an enigma to them both. Neither felt the least compunction about buying on the black market; both families had experienced difficult times through a lack of rations, and every packet would be used in haggling for vegetables or rice. Or – with enough cigarettes – the rare luxury of fish or meat.

'I doubt if we'll ever know who's behind it,' Claude said, 'but someone's making a fortune. Are you coming to the dance?'

'What dance?' Sam asked.

'Your sister's dance, of course.'

'Whereabouts?'

'Where? At your house! On Friday afternoon, when your mother goes to play cards, Angie's giving a dance.'

'She didn't tell me. Is Swiss Willy invited?'

'I would imagine so,' Claude said, with a glance at him.

'That explains why I'm not. Anyway, I thought dances were prohibited? Banned as a decadent Western custom?'

'It's why we're all looking forward to it. Can't wait,' Claude said, and rode off clutching his illegal cartons.

The convalescent home was a graceful old house at Epsom in Surrey. It had a clear view of the grandstands and the racecourse where the English Derby was run. The previous week they had seen the huge crowds converge for this event, the first peacetime Derby for five years. Some had arrived in motor cars or charabancs; thousands came by train, others driving horse and carts because of the petrol rationing. There were gypsy caravans, tinkers, fortune-tellers; the Epsom Derby seemed to be a lively combination of the country's most prestigious race day and a fun fair.

Florence had found herself lodgings; a small boarding house within distance of the convalescent home. Sometimes in the early mornings, when the weather was fine, she walked the downs and watched the horses training, cantering against the dawn skyline. It was a majestic sight. She spent much of her time in the late evenings trying to make telephone calls to James Lindsay.

She felt guilty, for it was almost two months now since he had agreed to take over the office for a few weeks. But the phone delays were endless, and the line often so bad that most of their communication was by cable. James finally sent her a lengthy one, requesting she stop worrying, stop apologising, just make sure Carl was fully recovered – and when he was well enough, to try to get on a ship and come home. In the meantime, the same cable said, her secretary, Dulcie, had decided not to be a war bride after all, had waved goodbye to her last American fiancé, and wanted Florrie to know she'd met a nice young Aussie lieutenant.

Typical James, she thought. No fuss. *Typical Dulcie*, she smiled, thinking there would be another love in her life by the time they met, and how glad she would be to see her secretary. Glad to see them all, to resume her normal existence. It seemed an eternity since that long flight and the desperate weeks in the army hospital.

Today she really would call him, no matter how long the delay; she wanted to say, clean your golf clubs, get out your fishing gear, we're leaving. Frank Forbes had done it somehow; he had got them on a DC3 flight via the Middle East, for it was possible again to fly that route now the British had recaptured Rangoon.

Carl was well enough to travel: impatient and badgering the doctors for days. Frank had mentioned something absurd about him being recommended for a medal, but she paid no attention to it. She felt the zest of anticipation for her house, could almost hear the sound of the tide lapping on the beach, and see the familiar headland and the reef. Finally they were going home.

In Karuizawa, sexual heat rose like the midsummer temperature, impelled by a sense of fear festering in the town. Three hundred miles away, Okinawa fell; the Commander ceremonially committing harikari in front of his troops. The war had never been so close. No-one knew what might happen if invasion came. There was endless speculation on the fate of foreigners if Japan was attacked. Most believed they would be used as hostages to make the Allies hesitate, and that a first step on the country's sacred soil would result in the mass slaughter of civilians.

Feeling they could be living on borrowed time, people snatched at pleasure. The young were outdone by their elders in this lusty and libidinous pursuit. The Countess d'Almedia, widow of a Spanish diplomat, made it clear she was available to any man who asked her politely. Wealthy Madame Lelouche, who looked a chic sixty, but was reputed to be eighty, had been a great beauty in Paris and a siren of some renown. It was said she had bedded most of the crown princes of Europe in all the best hotels, and made love on the top of the Eiffel Tower to Monsieur Eiffel himself. It was known as the high moment in Parisian society.

She was rumoured to be having a torrid affair with the French Vice-Consul, but Sam and his friends were sceptical. For she was an aficionado of the physical; the Vice-Consul had only one leg, having lost the other in the first world war at Verdun. Their doubts were disproved at lunch one day at the Lelouche villa. Madame carefully placed her guests at the table. The Vice-Consul would sit beside her. During the meal Sam managed to drop his napkin, and bent to retrieve it. Beneath the table, he saw his hostess's still shapely legs tightly wrapped around the Vice-Consul's single limb. The male leg moved in lecherous rhythm, the female limbs ardently responding.

Other napkins were dropped, heads lowered, eyebrows raised, as they saw the proof for themselves. They were immensely impressed that throughout this, the elderly Frenchwoman kept up an animated conversation, as if nothing at all was happening beneath her dining table. Afterwards coffee and brandy was served on the terrace, and the guests dispersed outside. The house had a guest suite in the garden. The hostess and the Vice-Consul repaired there for an afternoon nap. The others played boule on the lawn, to the sound of bedsprings and ecstasy coming from there.

'It's indecent,' the Countess d'Almedia said, 'they're too old and decrepit to fuck like that.'

'You should know, sweetie,' Paul Jacoulet told her. 'You've been shafted more times than a milkman's horse.'

'Bloody poof,' she replied. 'Raving old queen.'

'Flatterer,' he said, and went in pursuit of a naval attaché from the Argentinian Embassy, for whom he had distinct hopes.

Their hostess finally emerged from her siesta, with the Vice-Consul gallantly escorting her.

'What a hero! What a shagger!' Claude was mightily impressed. He confided to his latest girlfriend, Lisette, 'She's used to the best, is Madame, so he must be an Olympian between the sheets.'

'Speaking of sheets,' Lisette murmured softly, 'my parents are visiting friends, and won't be back until late.'

'Anyone else at home?'

'No. Shall we go?'

'Yes, please,' Claude said.

Lisette observed it was strange about Justine and Sam.

'What do you mean?' he asked.

'I couldn't tell you, as you're his best friend. But there's talk about Justine . . .'

'There's too much talk in this place. Those two are in love,' Claude declared firmly. 'I happen to know they have this nest in the forest.'

'Then why are they going to the movies?' she asked.

The pilots seemed too young to die. They stood beside their aircraft – brave volunteers, the commentary said. The audience cheered as the young men waved, and although it was an image on the screen, many Japanese stood and waved back, shouting encouragement.

Justine shook her head in horror: Sam was mesmerised.

The planes were tiny craft, made to take only a crew of one. In the nose they carried a warhead containing 1200 kilograms of high explosive. Launched in mid-air from a larger plane, their range was fifty miles, before igniting the rocket engine and diving at the target. They had no defensive armour, for they needed none. These were guided human bombs, which would impact on the decks of enemy vessels and explode. Not one of these pilots would ever return from what was to be a glorious *kamikaze* mission.

The youngest spoke to the camera, and told the audience it was an honour to perform this duty. Already their comrades had scored great triumphs, sinking carriers and cruisers. These newer, better craft – eight hundred already built and more to come – would strike terror on the ocean. No enemy ship would be safe, and eventually the American fleet would have to surrender. He and his brother fliers pledged success. They were the Squadron of the *Divine Wind*, dedicated to give their lives for the Emperor.

Afterwards Justine said: 'Those boys . . . believing it's a privilege to die. War's disgusting. Don't you find that dreadful?'

'Yes. But what I heard is more dreadful. They're not really volunteers. The pilots are forced to fly those things, and their commanders get them drunk so they won't bail out.'

She shuddered, and took a sip of her drink. They had gone from the cinema directly to the hotel, and sat in the bar. The newsreel had made an indelible and disturbing impression on them. While the film had been a propaganda exercise, and they knew all about the *kamikaze* pilots – their acts of immolation had made international headlines – the extreme youth of the suicide fliers had shocked them.

Before they left, Sam asked Joe Ishi for cigarettes.

'We've run out,' the barman said. 'I'm expecting a new consignment later this week. I'll keep you some.'

'A consignment?' As they rode their bikes away, Justine

wondered how he could get such quantities of American cigarettes.

'One of life's small mysteries,' Sam said. 'Here's another. Why don't you like our forest any longer?'

'What do you mean?'

'We haven't been there for weeks. Or anywhere else.'

'Tree rats,' she shuddered. 'I've heard people say the place is full of them.'

'It's not true. I keep on telling you. But if it worries you, we'll take a room at the hotel. I'll organise it.'

'Let's not rush things, Sam.'

'To hell with your parents, or anyone else. Most of this town seems to be at it – except us.' He stopped and took her hands, and waited until her eyes rose to meet his. 'Is something the matter?'

'Of course not,' Justine said.

Florence and Carl left Croydon aboard a DC3. It was a sunny day in July, and their first refuelling stop was Malta, five hours away. She was nervously awake most of the flight, worried the vibration and turbulence would tire Carl. But he slept until an announcement told them they would shortly land at Valetta.

As they approached, the pilot spoke of the extraordinary courage of the Maltese through the early war years, when they had been battered day and night by German planes, had been besieged, almost starved into submission, their homes and historic buildings destroyed, and how, in 1942, the island had received the unique tribute of the George Cross awarded by the King.

The plane stayed several hours, and Florence and Carl took a local bus into town. In the shattered mediaeval streets they saw the extent of the destruction: not a hospital or monastery of the Knights of St John was left standing; the siege of Malta meant churches without steeples or roofs, most of the city in need of rebuilding, people living in the ruins of their homes, or in the rock caves which had served as air-raid shelters. The war was over, but bitter memories remained.

Down on Valetta harbour, some bars and cafés were back in business. A woman in traditional black came to take their order.

'Two beers,' Carl ordered. She nodded, then paused and stared at him. 'And some mixed sandwiches,' he added. She did not acknowledge this; instead, she went to the back of the premises, and conferred with a man behind the bar.

'Why do the women all wear black?' Florrie wondered, slightly uneasy at her attitude, and Carl was explaining that it was a Mediterranean custom when the man came to their table.

'You a German,' he said accusingly to Carl.

'Who said I am?'

'My wife . . . she say, he's a German. So I say get out of my bar. We don't serve bloody Huns.'

'Fair enough, sport,' Carl said. 'But don't call me a Hun. We're Australians. If you won't serve us, tough titty. It's your pub.'

'You Australian?' The bar owner frowned.

'My bloody oath, I am,' Carl said, and Florence who was about to support him, or suggest they went elsewhere, decided he was doing quite well without her help. 'And we'd like our beer real cold, mate,' Carl added. 'That's the way we drink it back home.'

The bar owner called to his wife. They had a conversation in Maltese. It sounded like an argument, but she returned calm and curious to their table. 'You call him ... *sport*?'

'That's right,' Carl answered. 'Why do you ask?'

She said something else in Maltese. The owner of the bar listened intently, then smiled and put out his hand. He shook Carl's with such force that the flimsy table rattled. Then he insisted on shaking hands with Florrie, fortunately for her with less vigour.

'*Sport*,' he said. 'Australians come with the ships to help break the siege. Very friendly, they call everyone *sport*. Good fighters, some of them die helping us. Some good blokes – that's what they call themselves.'

'Mixed sandwiches,' his wife went to the bar, 'and real cold beer. My bloody oath,' she said.

They almost missed the plane. They arrived at the airfield in a donkey cart, Florence feeling decidedly giggly, wishing they had been allowed to pay for at least one drink, but their new friends Louisa and Vittorio had insisted that this was their shout.

In Colombo, they were booked into the Galle Hotel, then spent a week in Kandy, after which Frank had arranged reservations for them on the Catalina flying boat to Perth. The big amphibian was a rare experience after the slow trip across Arabia and India in the cramped and noisy DC3. They had beds, space in which to move around, comfortable seats to relax in. One of the unknown success stories of the war, Qantas had been operating the Catalina service from Ceylon to Perth for the past two years. Despite having to fly past territory still occupied by the enemy, there had been no loss of an aircraft, or injury to any of the crew or their passengers.

From Perth they flew across the Nullabor, and finally

reached Mascot. It was early evening, and the airport seemed almost deserted and peaceful. Just one plane unloading near the small terminal building, and no sign of anyone to greet them.

'Let's go quietly home,' Carl said, but suddenly it was no longer peaceful.

Photographers appeared: flashlights began to pop. They had pictures taken of them together, then many of Carl alone. After that, there were reporters; a bedlam of questions, opinions about his former country, was he fully recovered, how did it feel to be a hero?

In the background she saw Frank Forbes, and realised James was with him, also some of the solicitors and the entire typing pool, of whom Dulcie was prominent with an enormous bunch of flowers. She waved excitedly, and Florrie waved back, then she saw beside Frank there was a formally dressed man.

'How does it feel?' The same reporter, getting no answer to his last question, repeated it.

'Me? A hero?' Carl said. 'It must be a mistake.'

'If it is, the government's made it. There's a bloke from the Governor-General's office here to present you with a citation.'

'But I did nothing.' Carl was bewildered.

'You got shot,' Florence said. 'Beaten up. You told the Germans what you thought of them. If you call that nothing.'

'What do you think of him, Mrs Eisler?'

'I think he's a hero. Now can we please go and say hello to our friends?'

It was a glistening morning, and she was awake, determined to be out on the beach in time to see the first trace of sunrise on the tranquil sea. She should have been exhausted, for it had been a long and late night; a wonderful reunion, hugs and joyful tears from the staff, the man from Canberra making an over-long speech about the value of immigrants like Carl, how he had enhanced the country with his conscience and courage, and how we should be proud of him.

All far too much, she had thought, aware Carl was uncomfortable with such excessive accolades. But the reporters had loved it, and the cameras had flashed as he accepted gracefully, and he had made a witty speech that seemed to be mainly about her, and how she had taken over the hospital to keep a vigil at his bedside. Then they had all gone back to the office where drinks waited, and many hours later James Lindsay had driven them both home.

The sun was up now, turning the water of the basin into a dazzling blue. Some of the fishing dinghies were coming home from a night's work, being winched onto the shore beneath the cliff. A neighbour called from his front garden to welcome her, saying there was a hell of a lot of news about them both on the radio, and in the *Herald*. Later, when Carl was awake and they had finished breakfast on the shaded verandah, Susan and John Dalby came by with copies of the morning papers.

'Good God,' Florrie said, looking at a big photo of them embracing on the front page of the *Telegraph*.

'Heroic Migrant,' Susan quoted.

Carl sighed. 'I suppose it's better than "Bludging Reffo".'

'A hell of a lot better,' John Dalby said, 'it'll stop a few people slinging off at migrants, even if it makes you squirm. By God, we've missed you two. Come and have dinner with us tonight.'

'You're on,' Florrie told them.

It was later, looking through the batch of newspapers, secretly quite proud of what they had written about Carl, that she saw the headline: ALLIED FLEET POUNDS JAPAN.

At first, people thought it was a distant storm. But the night was clear, the sky bright with stars, so they went to bed wondering if it had been a rock fall high up the mountain or a minor avalanche. But neither of these things seemed likely. The following day it was confirmed as the sound of gunfire. Japan itself had now become the last objective. Beleaguered, battered day and night by the air raids and now this, only the extremists remained adamant there could never be 'unconditional surrender'. Their despairing tactic was to dispatch more *kamikaze* planes to terrify the enemy, in the vain hope that a settlement rather than a surrender could be arranged.

In Karuizawa, so often hearing the faint thunder of the guns, people felt pity for those under fire. However, they also remembered the talk of being taken as hostages, which had never officially been denied. There were rumours the French had an undercover agent in the Foreign Affairs Ministry. He had reported that a fanatical element proposed all foreigners be shot if an invasion were attempted. It seemed to confirm the rumours circulating since the start of summer.

Tamara Delon believed the threat implicitly. Some of her friends and family had fled Russia; others were slaughtered by the Red Army. Mass killing did not seem implausible to her. Giving in to melancholy, she lost interest in card games, refused to be consoled by friends like Paul Jacoulet, and became convinced their continued presence in this isolated town was designed to make such a massacre possible.

Concerned about her, Sam sought an audience with the Ambassador, who brusquely said the matter was exaggerated. These were diplomatic issues best left to those like himself experienced in diplomacy; the spreading of alarming rumours was not in anyone's interests. Rebuffed, Sam went to the Fournier's adjacent villa in search of Justine. But she was not there.

Away. Visiting friends, her mother told him.

When will she be back, he asked?

Her mother said she had no idea. Justine was being stupid, and she did not wish to discuss her daughter's erratic behaviour – certainly not with him. Madame Fournier had rarely been more than distantly polite to him in the past, but never this hostile.

'May I leave her a note?'

Madame Fournier did not reply to this. She simply asked him to leave. The way she said it left him no option. Sam rode away, puzzled and concerned, thinking she had seemed almost deranged.

He called again the following day, and this time it was Justine's father who met him. There was absolutely no point, he was told, in pestering them like this. He thought his wife had made it clear. Their daughter was fed up with being confined to this village, and had gone to stay with friends in Shimoda. She missed the sea, and found daily life here tedious; the same small group of people, the lack of any excitement. She was in Shimoda for a prolonged stay, and he had no idea when she would be back.

'May I have her address?' Sam asked, and was told

they did not know it. This was clearly a lie, Sam knew. Diplomats were expert in the business of lying. But behind the bland facade, there seemed a sense of unease. It was a lie, but Pierre Fournier was not comfortable with the tale he was telling.

Sam rode into town. Her friends were surprisingly few, he realised, and all of them were vague. Nobody had an address, nor was quite sure why she had left so suddenly. She had not confided in anyone, or so it seemed. No doubt what her father had told him was true, they said; Justine was given to whims and had been restless.

'I know that,' he was able to assure them. He became angry with what seemed like deliberate obfuscation. The idea of trying to contact Paul Kranz in Shimoda occurred to him, but he had no address. He went seeking Claude to proffer a thought; that she might be pregnant, and had gone somewhere to seek an abortion.

'I doubt it,' Claude said.

'Why?'

Sam had the strange feeling his closest friend was uneasy.

'No particular reason,' Claude replied.

'Then what's happened? People as close as we were don't bugger off without a word, do they? No note, nothing. Her parents treating me like shit. I know they were never keen on me, but now they don't seem to like their daughter much, either. Which is why – lying wide awake for the past four nights – I got to thinking about an abortion. It seemed the only reason why she'd just vanish without a word.'

'I don't know why the hell I should have to tell you this, Sam. Why can't one of her bloody friends tell you?'

'Her friends seem thin on the ground. Tell me what?'

'Jacques Clermont was in town – about five days ago.'

'Clermont?'

'Full of the joys of spring. He was divorced – his father had died and he was going to inherit heaps of money and a chateau. Someone saw him leaving. There was a girl with him.'

'No, not Justine?' Sam was heated, angrily disbelieving. 'She hardly knows him.'

'She knows him well enough. Look, I don't want to tell you this. Other people make snide remarks. I try not to listen.'

'She told me he was here for New Year.'

'He was here before that. Often through the winter, when you were in Tokyo. He'd ski down from Nagano, stay overnight at the hotel. No girlfriend, people said; he must be reforming. But some gossiping bitch claimed Justine used to meet him there.'

'And did she?'

'I don't know. He came here a few days after Christmas. That's the only time I saw him with her. They were having drinks in the Mampei Bar. Jacques said he was celebrating the end of his marriage.'

'The end? A few days after Christmas?' Sam had a sick feeling, for it was the exact timing and the style of behaviour was pure Clermont. He knew it must be true. 'Why in Christ's name didn't you tell me?'

'Tell you what? That they had a drink together? Why would I tell you that?'

'Sorry,' Sam said, feeling numb and nauseated.

'I was more concerned about the bloody Nazi doctor who was making such a play for her, but she gave him the heave-ho when you came back to live, after we changed the nameplates around. And I thought things were fine and dandy between you two, until... well, until that crazy lunch party at old Madame Lelouche's.'

'Why then?'

'Because everyone seemed to be shagging or heading for the sack. But you two went to the movies.'

'And now she's gone off with Jacques Clermont.'

'I don't know,' Claude said. 'I can't say that.'

But they both knew she had.

CHAPTER 28

The neighbours in Collaroy were philosophical about fame intruding on their peaceful neighbourhood. Day after day, posses of reporters and press photographers came along the beach past their houses, trying to get interviews with Carl, or if that failed, then with Florence. To them, it seemed to be one of those heartwarming, good news stories; a refugee who endures hardship, makes good and then works for us. He upsets the Nazis, who bash him and shoot him, and his wife flies across the world to save him.

Put like that in the afternoon tabloids, Florrie thought it awful: simplistic and embarrassing. But journalists writing in the *Herald* and the Melbourne *Age*, some of them concerned with Australia's long and negative attitude towards displaced people, wrote more deeply about what had happened. In their stories, Carl Eisler became an immigrant symbol.

It had a strange effect. Refugees, some of whom had fled from various European tyrannies since the nineteen thirties, often at first rejected by their new country, wrote to express their admiration for what he had done. The letters came from all parts of the country, and from all nationalities including Hungarians, Czechs, Italians, even Germans, and to Florence's surprise, from a number of British migrants as well. Other letters arrived, saying their local communities – some until then prejudiced against foreigners, even racist – had done an about-turn after reading the newspaper stories and had begun to alter their opinions. It seemed Carl had done something in its way momentous; he had bridged a huge gap between the old entrenched inhabitants and the newcomers, and the new, in this challenging and often awkward society, were grateful.

It was unexpected, remarkable and rare. Florrie had loved him almost since the first day they met. Now she felt a sense of deep pride that she was going to share the rest of his life.

One night Angelique came home late. Sam was almost asleep when he heard the door of her room shut, heard her kick off her shoes and sit on her bed. The walls were thin and he could not avoid hearing her start to sob. He felt like an intruder on her grief as she sobbed as if her heart were broken. Eventually he tapped on her door.

'Angie . . .'

The door opened a fraction. Her face was tear-stained and angry. 'Go away,' she said. 'Go to hell. It's your fault.'

'What have I done?' He was bewildered. It was turning out to be a very traumatic week. Justine was gone, and clearly would not be back. 'What have I done?' he repeated.

'Ruined my life,' she said, shutting the door and locking it. She refused food the next day, and stayed in her room. Tamara knew the dark presage of Russian gloom, and did not try to speak to her. Sam did his best.

'Come on,' he pleaded, 'You're moping around like a tragic figure in a Chekhov play, blaming me for something, and you won't tell me what or why. Except I'd have to guess it has something to do with Swiss Willy.'

'He hates you,' Angelique said.

'I know. It's mutual – so what else is new?'

'He only fucked me as a sort of revenge.'

'I wish you'd quit using that word,' Sam said. 'Try saying he made love to you.'

'He never "made love" to me. Not once. He fucked me – that's all it ever was – to annoy you. Get his own back, he said, for when you knocked him down at school and everyone laughed.'

'You mean he told you this?'

'Yes.'

'When?'

'Last night.'

'But it happened years ago. Good God! Talk about elephants never forgetting. We were fifteen. He was bullying Bernhardt, and I stopped him.' He felt sudden anger. 'The bastard, getting his revenge like that. Did he just decide to humiliate you last night? Did you have a row, was that it?'

'Not exactly.'

'Angie, please. What happened . . . exactly?'

'It doesn't matter.'

'It does. Tell me.'

'Well,' she said, 'I spent the afternoon there with him. In the usual way.'

'You can skip that.'

'Then the truck arrived. The Red Cross truck, delivering letters and parcels. His regular workers would be turning up soon to unload all night. I said I'd stay to help. He told me to go home. When I said I was supposed to help, he said that was just a ploy to get me into bed, because all he wanted to do was fuck your sister.'

'He always was a charmer,' Sam said. 'But why didn't he want you to help?'

'He said he paid the others to work,' Angelique said. 'Except I got the peculiar feeling he was afraid.'

'Of what?'

'I don't know, Sam. It was strange, he couldn't wait to get me out of that building.'

'So am I to blame for that?'

'No,' she said, 'of course you aren't.' She kissed him and said contritely, 'I'm sorry. Forget the whole thing. It was a small incident in my life, and now it's over.'

It was later that same day that Sam found the sheet music. It was behind the piano, a single song sheet that must have slipped down and been forgotten. He was trying to decide whether to give it back, when he noticed the imprint of the music publisher and the date.

He sat staring at it for a long while, trying to work out what it meant. Later he took his bike and rode to Claude's house. He reminded him of a conversation they'd had nearly a year ago, and after Claude recalled it, Sam returned home with the song sheet.

'Angie, what's this?'

'Where did you get it?'

'Behind the piano. I think it was there since your dance.'

'We were wondering what had happened to it.'

'We? You and Rambert?'

'Well, yes. He played the piano while we all danced. I don't like to admit it, but he played quite well.'

'Bugger his talents. Where did he get that sheet music?'

'"In the Mood"? It's an old song by Joe Loss. He made a record of it before the war.'

'I know,' Sam said, 'but this is not the old sheet music of it. Look at the date. July 1944 – that was last year.'

'So?' She sound confused, uncertain what he meant.

'So how did it get here, in wartime? It's a new version, published in Chicago. It says so, there on the last page.'

'I don't know what all the fuss is about!'

'Angie, use your brains. How would he get hold of music published last year in America?'

'Perhaps he has connections?'

'How?'

'His job. After all, he runs the Red Cross.'

'Hardly. His father's influence got him a job, supervising delivery of mail to prisoners of war and internees, right?'

'You make it sound like he's a postman. That truck was full of sacks. Hundreds of letters and parcels. It's important work.'

'And he couldn't wait to get rid of you, you said.'

'Well . . . that's how it seemed.'

'A lot of the mail comes from America. Claude told me it arrives via neutral ships to neutral embassies, and is supposed to be distributed to all the prison camps and internees.'

'Supposed to be?'

'Last year, a journalist friend of his found out none of the parcels had been getting through. Letters, yes, not the parcels.'

'You mean the Japanese were stopping them?'

'His editor thought so. The journalist had another theory. That perhaps the parcels never left the Red Cross depot, which Rambert used to run in Yokohama, and now runs from here. You see, they have valuable stuff in them. Warm clothes, tins of food, cartons of cigarettes. And no doubt items like cards and books – and maybe for someone who plays the piano, even sheet music.'

'What the hell are you suggesting, Sam?'

'You know exactly what I'm suggesting.'

'Can you prove it?'

'No.'

'It's just guessing.'

'Perhaps it is.'

'Malicious guessing'

'If you think so. But I wonder what he'd say if I asked him how he obtained a song sheet printed in America last year?'

'You're stupid. Why would he steal Red Cross parcels?'

'For money.'

'Now you're really stupid. His father's rich.'

'Maybe his son wants to be richer. Greed is a disease, a craving. It's nothing to do with the state of your bank balance.'

'I'm sure there's a logical explanation for this.'

'There probably is.'

'You've jumped to conclusions, because you dislike him.'

'I'm inclined to. With good reason.'

'Even so, he couldn't do a thing like this.'

Sam shrugged and gave it to her. 'In that case, burn it. But please don't humiliate yourself by seeing him again.' He left her standing there, the music in her hand.

* * *

'So the bastard's going to get away with it,' Claude said.

'There's no proof. It's all supposition. As my sister says, a malicious guess.'

'Shit,' Claude's disappointment was palpable. 'We could find the journalist. He's still with the bureau here.'

'It was just his hunch. That's all. An idea that was never published. His editor overruled him, probably scared of a lawsuit.'

'You should've kept that piece of music.'

'What for, Claude? Nobody will ever believe the son of such a rich man did anything crazy like this.'

'But you believe it, don't you?'

'Yes,' Sam said, 'I believe it.'

'So do I.'

'Well, that makes two of us. A minority of two.'

'You feeling any better?' Claude asked, after a moment. 'I mean about Justine and . . . are you?'

'Not really,' Sam said. 'I'm trying to feel better. But I keep wondering where they are. Silly, isn't it?'

Sam was late for the meeting. The Count had sent word they had work to do, a transfer of a large sum of money to Geneva. It was a surprise; it had been weeks since any such arrangements had taken place, and he wished there was a way he could excuse himself from the proceedings.

As he cycled through the grounds of the estate, his mind was more on Justine than the transaction ahead. It had come as such a blow, but he began to realise he should not have been so shocked. After joyous months, it had become a changing relationship. In hindsight, it appeared apparent in minuscule ways: a lack of ardour; occasional excuses; it was difficult really to say exactly when he'd started to feel this, and perhaps he had been to blame in not confronting their loss of passion. Or would that have meant even earlier humiliation?

But Jacques Clermont!

That was what hurt. What an irony it had to be Clermont. She had been so convincingly loving with Sam until recently. The best time of his life. Yet the return of Jackie-boy was all it needed to shatter that. *Jackie-boy – the name Justine always called him should itself have been a warning*, he thought, as he arrived at the mansion.

The Count said the guests were waiting in the study. Herr Rambert and his son, Wilhelm. They had brought four million yen in cash, to be converted into dollars and placed in a Swiss account. As Sam tried to conceal his aversion and collect the paperwork, he heard Rambert say it was his son's money: while he would witness the transaction, only Wilhelm need be given the account number and the means to access the money.

Hans Rambert was in his late fifties. Although he owned a house on The Bluff in Yokohama, he rarely mixed with the foreign community. He had a circle of Swiss friends, a Japanese mistress, and with his Red Cross connections, was accorded a show of deference by politicians and bureaucrats. Rambert was a wealthy man, and although he and de Boulanger were acquainted, this request to transfer a large sum was a surprise. He would certainly have his own financial contacts, for much of his wealth would be regularly remitted to Swiss safety.

'It's entirely my son's money,' Hans Rambert repeated, as if wanting this acknowledged. He glanced cautiously at Sam, with a trace of recognition. 'I feel I know your clerk.'

'My assistant manager,' the Count corrected him. The

other shrugged, indifferent. A young man in a bank is a clerk, his attitude seemed to say, no matter what you may chose to call him.

'I was at St Joseph's school, Mr Rambert.'

'Then I expect you and my son know each other.'

'Yes. Hello, Wilhelm.' Sam knew his sudden appearance had disconcerted his former classmate. The father seemed surprised by this lack of response.

'Your friend said hello, Willie.'

'Father, I thought we arranged a private meeting?'

'Is there something wrong?' The elder Rambert seemed confused by the obvious tension that was now apparent between them.

'I'm afraid I'm not his friend, Mr Rambert,' Sam said. 'I never have been his friend, and I daresay he'd confirm that.'

Now the Count seemed equally perplexed at the curt reply. 'Sam, what the devil's all this about?'

'Your Excellency, if we're to transfer this money, I think we should be told more details. For instance, in this particular case, we're entitled to know its origin. And how it was earned.'

'I'm not staying to listen to this,' Wilhelm Rambert said.

'Be quiet a minute, Willie.' Now his father was uneasy, as he turned to the Count. 'I don't know what authority you allow your employee, but I will not have my son or myself disparaged. If we don't receive an apology, I think it best to cancel this appointment and make more suitable arrangements.'

'Sam,' de Boulanger's voice was frigid, 'are you going to explain those remarks and then apologise?'

'I'd like to explain, sir. When I do, an apology may not be necessary.'

'You listen to his stupid lies if you want,' Wilhelm's

burst of outrage startled them with its animosity, 'but I won't. I'm leaving.'

'One moment,' the Count said. 'If he intends to explain, surely it would be best to remain and hear what he has to say?'

'I think I know what he'll say,' Hans Rambert said. 'But whatever he says, it isn't true. And if he spreads any rumours, I'll call the police and have it stopped. Or sue him for defamation.'

'I doubt if you'll call the police...' Sam stopped abruptly as the Count moved to lock the door and pocket the key. For a stunned moment they were all silenced by his action.

'What the devil are you doing?' Hans Rambert demanded.

'It seems you all know something and, as you've involved me in a financial transaction, I must also know it.' As father and son remained mute, the Count looked at Sam. 'You wanted to explain. So explain, and be quick about it.'

'He works for the Red Cross, and he's been robbing prisoners of war. Stealing parcels from home that contain cartons of cigarettes, clothes, cans of food...'

'That's a filthy lie,' Wilhelm Rambert shouted.

'Is it?' The Count had become acutely aware that the father had said nothing. He stared at him and saw pain in the other man's eyes. 'Is it, Monsieur?' The silence seemed to go on and on, until the elder Rambert looked away. He seemed ashamed. His shoulders slumped, and he appeared incapable of a reply.

'If it's not a lie, then what else did he steal, Sam?'

'Whatever would sell on the black market. Most of all, American cigarettes. Things of no value in the parcels, photographs, letters – they'd be burnt.'

'You know nothing,' Wilhelm said. 'You bloody prick, you can prove nothing. He always hated me. This is nothing more than lies and spite. Because I fucked his sister.'

'Once in a while,' Sam continued calmly as if the other had not spoken, 'he might keep something, rather than sell it. My sister says he plays the piano. A song sheet published in America last year ... he kept that. I found it, after a dance she gave.'

'Where is it?' It was the older Rambert's voice, harsh with anguish. Despair was etched on his face.

'It's somewhere safe,' Sam said, hoping Angelique had not destroyed it.

'How much do you want for it?'

'For what? The sheet music?'

'How much?' Rambert insisted.

'Money? Does that buy everything, Mr Rambert?'

'For Christ's sake, boy, how much?'

'It's not for sale, sir. It's evidence.'

In Karuizawa, later that week, a police raid was carried out on all black market outlets. The barman of the Mampei Hotel was told he had a choice; he was either a loyal Japanese or a treacherous Hawaiian. The matter could easily be resolved; he could forfeit his citizenship and be moved to a prison camp in the far north, or reveal his source of supply and continue in his job as a barman. He decided his patriotic duty was to tell what he knew.

Shortly afterwards, the Rambert family left the village. Their chateau was locked. The departure activated rumours of scandalous conduct; Red Cross parcels and an illegal fortune made out of this plunder. There was talk that Herr Rambert had made an enormous donation to charity – as much as four million yen – and in return, his son might manage to escape prosecution.

A week later, the French Ambassador came riding his bicycle up the road to their house late one afternoon. He always looked as if he might fall off, and everyone felt sure it was a strain for him to spend months in Karuizawa, and not be able to enjoy the comfort of his car and chauffeur. But the sight of him riding all this way clearly meant something important, and Sam and Angelique hurried to the gate, while he straddled the bike and recovered his breath.

'There's a new sort of bomb,' he said.

'New?'

'Don't ask for details, Sam. I haven't time, and I don't know. It was dropped on a place called Hiroshima.'

'It's a seaport,' Angelique said, 'in the Inland Sea.'

'Not any more,' the Ambassador replied. 'There's nothing left. The place is destroyed.'

'Destroyed?'

'According to the reports. And most people are dead.'

'But wait on,' Sam was puzzled, 'how many bombs, Your Excellency?'

'One.'

'One? It can't be one.'

'I'm not deaf, Sam. The radio said it was one bomb. A small, special bomb.'

'Christ Almighty,' Angelique said, but the Ambassador was gone, pedalling away to the next house to spread his news.

* * *

An atomic bomb, the news on the ABC described it, and Carl and Florrie sat listening to the details. It had been delivered by one high solitary plane. The bomb, surprisingly small, had been dropped by parachute, and had exploded in the air above the centre of the city.

'A United States naval observer on board the aircraft, said that although they were ten miles away at the time the blast took place, the plane was badly buffeted by it. He described the explosion as being brighter than the sun, and the sky was filled with a giant mushroom-shaped cloud,' the announcer said. 'Reconnaissance planes over the target area, several hours afterwards, reported nothing could be seen of the city, but there was smoke and fires around the perimeter. Aerial photos indicate no buildings remain intact. There are no details of the casualties yet, but they are expected to be high.'

Florrie shivered. Carl sat listening intently.

'It has been revealed the bomb is the work of British and American scientists, developed in secret over the past several years in the New Mexico desert. A White House spokesman described it as the greatest scientific discovery in history.'

'No,' Florrie said, 'he must have been misquoted. What a mad thing to say.'

They switched off the radio. Dinner was ready. It was a silent, thoughtful meal. Later they went for a walk on the beach.

'Hitler could have had that bomb,' Carl said. 'He very nearly did. We were translating documents which showed how close he was, but I could never tell you about it at the time.'

'That's a terrible thought.'

'It is. He'd have used it until he obliterated Britain and Europe. Do you know the irony, my darling? Otto

Hahn, a German physicist worked on nuclear fission with a Jewish scientist. Then they were forbidden to collaborate because of the racial laws. If he hadn't killed so many Jews, the awful housepainter might've won.'

In Karuizawa, it seemed as if people held their breath. What would happen now? Either there must be surrender – for how could anyone oppose this kind of weapon – or else the round-up of people would begin, and the long-held threats to foreigners become reality.

How long became the question on everyone's lips, over the next few days. Whatever was happening in the rest of the world, life in Japan seemed unaltered. At least on the surface. Major Ito and the Kempetai were more prominent; Sam noticed this and it made him uneasy. The radio exhorted people to work hard in munitions factories, and prepare to resist the enemy. Should they dare attack Japanese soil, this would be repelled with catastrophic consequences. Patriotic music played interminably. Broadcasts constantly reminded listeners of the exploits by the *Divine Wind* pilots. The valour of these young men still terrified the Allied navies. Meanwhile, the BBC reported that Japan had no more pilots willing to fly suicide aircraft, even if ordered to do so. The days of the *kamikaze* were past.

'You could get very confused,' Claude said, 'between the radio broadcasts. There are two different wars going on.'

'And each side swears it's winning,' Sam said.

'So which side is winning?'

'Ours, of course. The Allies. It's obvious.'

'Not to the fanatical Japanese. They'll keep fighting,

building more planes and making ammunition until the sky falls in.'

'In Tokyo, the sky's been falling in for the past nine months. Can they still believe anything but defeat is possible?'

'They believe whatever their Emperor tells them.'

'But they've never heard their bloody Emperor's voice.'

'Makes no difference, Sam.'

'So what drives them? What makes them fight on?'

'Faith. Belief.'

'In the Son of Heaven, who they've never seen or heard?'

'How about God?' Claude asked. 'Has anyone seen him lately, or heard his voice?'

'What's that got to do with it?'

'The Americans always insist God is on their side.'

'It's a weird bloody world,' Sam said. 'And it's getting steadily weirder.'

The following day, the postman brought him a letter from Justine Fournier.

The handwriting was neat. Like Justine, he thought. Neat and alive, heartbreakingly alive. It was dated ten days earlier.

Dear Sam,

I don't know when you'll get this with the way everything is, but I want to say I'm truly sorry. I did love you, but there was never really a choice once Jackie said he wanted to marry me. Forgive me, darling Sam. I tried. I liked you so much, and there were some lovely tender moments, and some funny ones, too. Remember the golf course? We nearly fell off our bikes riding home. If we'd been two other people, we could have been so happy.

I've hurt you, and I'll always regret that. Until we can get a ship, we are going to spend time around the Inland Sea, and Jackie is going to give some tennis clinics while we wait for his lawyer in Geneva to send us money for the fare to Europe. We'll be in Iwakuni, and after that he's booked to play a week of exhibitions in Hiroshima . . .

He sat and watched her father read the letter. Fournier was silent for a long time.

'Perhaps they weren't there, after all, ' Sam said, but he knew it was a vain attempt to alleviate both their pain.

'She was always impulsive,' the diplomat said. 'Always unpredictable. When she was six years old in France, we had a country house. She used to sit on the steps, gazing out across the farm fields. Just sit there alone, for hours. I asked her once what she was thinking about each day. "Dreaming of leaving," she said. "Dreaming of leaving."' He sighed and shook his head. His eyes were red rimmed, as if he had slept badly. 'No, they were there. I had a telephone call last night. From the captain of a ferry that landed them at Hiroshima, the day before the bomb was dropped.'

He handed back the letter.

'Thank you for your courtesy, Sam. I'm sorry we never thought you were good enough for her. That was clearly a mistake.'

CHAPTER 29

Karuizawa, August 9th, 1945.
Dearest Florrie,
I don't know what'll happen now. After the horror of Hiroshima, tonight we heard the news about Nagasaki. Another bomb. Another aerial slaughter. Perhaps it will end the war, but we sat around in a state of bewilderment and shock. It seems unbelievable, knowing about the first bomb, the amount of death and destruction it caused within seconds – it seems insane and inhuman to use another. I feel sick and appalled.

You may disagree. Tamara disagreed. She argued that it was necessary. Or else Japan would never stop this war without there having to be an invasion, and that would destroy the entire country and cost far more lives – on both sides. My sister was quiet during this, then she voiced a question. She wondered what kind of a man this new American President Truman was, and if the thought of all those dead people from a single bomb would trouble him? Do you think, Angelique asked us, that he can sleep at nights? I also wonder what kind of man he is, and if the second bomb was necessary.

We heard on the short-wave radio that Truman has threatened even more – 'a rain of ruin from the air, the like of which has never been seen on this earth.' I think a man who can say that would probably sleep untroubled. But it troubles us – for this is a world we hoped to inherit, and with weapons like this, what does the future hold? Can there even be a future? We sat talking until late, unable to face being alone, wondering when this awful carnage would end.
With much love, and deep dismay,
Sam.

He knew there was no possible way to send this, but he wanted her to have it to read one day, so he sealed it in an envelope and left it in his desk. He had said nothing to her about Justine; the only time he had been unable to tell Florrie everything, but it was a grief too painful and too soon. It was bad enough to know she and everyone else incinerated in Hiroshima – yes, even Jacques Clermont – had been merely the first victims in the demonstration of this savage new weapon. Now another city lay black and dead, its inhabitants mutilated.

He wondered whether to write and tell Cecile but, unsure if he should send tidings that would only upset her, he put it off for another day. The news would soon spread. Perhaps the Count could decide what was best. For Sam it was difficult enough facing the well-meant sympathy of his mother and Angelique.

That morning, there had been an urgent summons to go to the French Embassy. News on Radio Australia had declared that after the Nagasaki bomb, the Japanese

Cabinet had met all night to consider if they could accept the terms of surrender. The announcer had said that, according to very reliable sources, the Emperor was no longer in control of his homeland. It was therefore distinctly possible that the war could be over within hours.

Claude and Sam were among others requested to help spread word of this. The Ambassador wanted people to stay home and remain calm. It might be a false alarm; nobody should celebrate prematurely. Claude went to the two doctors, who promised to inform as many of their patients as possible. Sam saw shopkeepers, asking them to advise their customers. Then he went to the Mampei Hotel. Avoiding the bar, he found Henri Barbusse, the Swiss manager, in his office. Barbusse agreed to circulate word to those guests he could trust. Sam said he was on his way to Count de Boulanger to pass on the news. Neither was aware that Joe Ishi had stood outside and overheard this.

Ishi returned to the bar. From a window he watched Sam ride away. Although it was de Boulanger who had reported young Rambert, the barman considered Sam even more responsible for the loss of his lucrative black market. Behind the counter was a telephone, for local calls. A local call was all he required. He rang a number and asked to speak to the officer in charge. Half an hour later, returning from visiting the Count and Moustique, Sam was arrested.

CHAPTER 30

He had no idea how many hours had passed. His watch had been smashed in the fall. He had been riding his bike home along an empty stretch when the Kempetai sergeant and two of his men had emerged from bushes at the side of the road. There had been no order to stop, so he was pedalling past trying not to show concern, when one thrust a baton between the spokes on the front wheel of his bike. He was flung forward over the handlebars, hitting the ground with a thud, landing on the side of his head.

Dizzy and feeling concussed, he heard the sergeant snap an order, and the military police handcuffed him. His bike, its front wheel mangled, was tossed into the bushes, while they pushed the hidden motorcycle and sidecar from the shrubbery. Sam was told that he was under arrest, charged with the crime of spreading lies about the Emperor and speaking against the war effort – then roughly bundled into the sidecar. He was forced down while the canopy was fastened tightly over him, obscuring him completely and making it difficult to breathe. After a short ride, still bleeding, and feeling sick and dizzy, he was pushed into a cell. It was dark and enclosed, somewhere in the basement of a building.

Dimly he was aware of Major Ito entering to state the charge equated to one of treason, for which death by hanging was the mandatory penalty. He was given no chance to reply. The door was slammed shut, and he was left alone.

The troopship was a British merchantman, crowded with Australian prisoners of war from the Crete and Greek campaigns, about to be welcomed home by the Governor-General, the Duke of Gloucester. Florence and Carl were among the special guests, because Captain Jim Richardson, complete with new leg, had cabled a request that the intelligence officer who had helped them so much, should be invited. After a hurried conference on whether a German being among the dignitaries would offend protocol, it was pointed out the English royal family tree had originally been called Saxe-Coburg-Gotha, before it was changed to the more English name of Windsor, and the invitation was issued.

The Duke was late. The ship was in dock, crowds were waiting. Reporters and photographers were there to record the occasion. Only His Royal Highness was missing. Prince Henry William Frederick Albert had been a far from unanimous selection as Australian head of state. A rather remote figure, known for some rather incoherent speeches and a liking for brandy, his first months in office had disappointed even the most loyal supporters.

An hour passed, then another. Families trying to push

forward for a glimpse of loved ones were being kept back by police. As time passed, their excitement turned to impatience and anger, and the police were obliged to use force to control them.

'This is a disgrace,' Carl murmured to Florrie.

When the Duke at last arrived, with an escort of Hussars, he was soundly booed by both the troops and their families.

'Couldn't get up early, you old bastard,' came the shouts.

'Curled up with the Duchess.'

'Curled up with a few grogs more likely.'

'Never mind us, mate. Only four years since I saw me wife and kids.'

'My family's being pushed around by coppers.'

'Look at him, staggering. Pissed already.'

'Had a few starters, eh, yer bloody old duck.'

The jeers and shouts reached a crescendo when His Royal Highness inspected the ship's company, followed by his plumed escort in tight maroon-coloured trousers. This provoked a storm of derision.

'Look at the buggers,' came a voice. 'Hardly got room in their trousers for their balls.'

'Who says they've got balls?' shouted another.

'Got feathers. Look like peacocks.'

'Who says they've got cocks?'

By now the packed vessel and crowded dock was in fits of laughter. On the platform, Florence wanted to join in the hilarity. She could see Carl having a struggle to contain himself.

The British crew members were grinning, the Hussars looked as if they would like to hurriedly disembark; the Duke alone seemed oblivious. It was either a splendid example of royal training, or else he had such a hangover that he was unconscious of the mockery. On the quayside, photographers took pictures, and reporters wrote of the incident in their notebooks; none of them knowing all this would later be suppressed from publication on the grounds that it would be unpatriotic to lampoon the brother of His Majesty the King.

Now there were footsteps, the sound of the key turning, the door being opened. A flashlight shone in his face; beyond the glare, he could faintly make out that there were two figures. One, in uniform, was the sergeant; the other remained indistinct until he spoke.

'Goddamn interfering cocksucking bastard,' he said, and Sam knew it was the barman. A moment later he felt a violent pain, as a boot lashed out and kicked him in the ribs. His involuntary cry of pain brought an angry shout from the sergeant, berating Joe Ishi.

'Stop that,' he shouted. He had a baton with him, and he lashed the barman with it. The torchlight made erratic patterns on the walls of the cell, as he held it in one hand and swung the stick with the other until Ishi cowed back in a corner. 'Do that again, and you'll be chained up. You weren't brought here to attack the prisoner. You're here to tell me exactly what was said, in front of him. Then we'll go to the office and write it down for the Major. Understand?'

'Understand,' the barman said, sounding surly and unsure of himself now. If he had hoped for a chance of physical vengeance, for which the Kempetai were renowned, he was disappointed.

'Well? We haven't got all night.'

So it's night, thought Sam. *Someone must be wondering where I am by now. Not that it can help.*

'He came to see the manager,' Ishi said. 'He told him he had access to a radio, and that the Emperor had been deposed . . .'

'That's a lie,' Sam said.

'You shut up,' the sergeant prodded him with the baton. He shone the beam of the flashlight into Sam's eyes, studying his reactions, while he told the barman to continue.

'He said the politicians had taken control, and wanted to get rid of Hirohito.'

'What do you mean by that? Assassinate?'

'That's what it sounded like. So they could make peace and surrender to the Americans. He was going round town to spread the news, so people would know it and be ready.'

'Ready for what?'

'To deal with the police. And military. Disarm them. Send word to the Americans. Find their prisoners of war and free them. They went on talking for a long time, but I couldn't hear the rest. I had to get back in the bar before they saw me.'

The light was still in Sam's eyes, blinding him. He could make out the Sergeant's face behind it. And then the figure of Major Ito, gazing down at him.

'I don't think your powerful friends can intervene on your behalf this time. You heard the evidence?'

'I heard a pack of lies,' Sam said.

'Then you didn't go to the hotel?'

'Yes, I went to the hotel.'

'You didn't see Barbusse-san, the manager?'

'I saw him.'

'You didn't talk about the end of the war?'

'It was mentioned.'

'How?'

'I said the foreign news thought it would be soon.'
'You listened to the foreign news?'
'I was told by someone who had.'
'Who?'
'I've forgotten.'
'You'll remember, when we finish with you.'
The Major snapped an order at the sergeant, then the flashlight was directed on the barman.
'You come with me,' the sergeant said to Ishi.
'Where?'
'We'll write down what you said, and you'll sign it.'
Sam caught a glimpse of Joe Ishi's face. He was sweating with fear. There was no chance he would dare change his story now. The lies would be written down and become evidence. If the barman admitted to any untruth, he'd be beaten and tortured until he signed the statement they wanted.

Most lights were out and all the adjacent houses were dark when the Kempetai sergeant arrived to search Sam's room, where he found the sealed letter addressed to Florence. Tamara Delon was in a state by now, demanding to know where her son was, and why this new search was being made. Angelique was equally agitated, but trying to calm her mother, who had made serious inroads on a bottle of vodka and was almost out of control. They were both ordered to sit down and shut up before they found themselves in serious trouble. The sergeant left with the letter moments before Claude arrived.

His news was not good. He had ridden out to see the Count de Boulanger and Moustique, who reported Sam had left their estate around midday, and as no-one had seen him since, there could only be one answer. If that were true, there was nothing they could do about it.

He tried to sleep, but the floor was hard, the concrete cell like an icebox, and he was hungry. Later he heard the tread of footsteps, and sat up with a feeling of hope. One of the uniformed Kempetai, who had arrested him, opened the cell door, and threw in a blanket. The other stood guardian in the stone passageway, holding a lantern and an unsheathed sword. Sam wondered why they felt it necessary to take such precautions, since he was still handcuffed.

'What about food?' he asked.
'No food.'
'My family. Have they been told where I am?'
'Nobody's family comes here.'
'It's my right to have them visit me.'
Both men laughed.
'No rights,' the man with the sword and the lantern said.
'No visits,' said the other. 'Not for you. Nothing for an enemy of the State. But we will tell Major Ito that you asked. It will amuse him.'
The door slammed shut, leaving him in the pitch dark.

It was long after midnight when Angelique and Claude saw the bright lights as they wheeled their bikes up the lane. They started to run, although both were very tired, having spent hours trying all the likely places Sam might be. After calling first on both the doctors, then the village hospital, they finally went to the police station.

They knew the constable on duty, but only by sight as

a local policeman. He had been polite, declaring there were no reports of accidents, and no arrests. It had been a most peaceful night. No drunks, no trouble anywhere. When Angelique asked if she could speak to Major Ito, in charge of the Kempetai, he regretted this was impossible.

Why, she asked.

He proceeded to explain that the village police were not a part of the same organisation. The Kempetai had their own rules and answered only to the chiefs of Intelligence and the Department of National Defence. He, the constable, had nothing to do with them, and preferred it that way. The Kempetai had their own building in town, but even if they knew its location, it would be most unwise for a young lady to call there at this time of night. He advised them to go home and rest, and felt sure their friend was somewhere safe. Probably out enjoying himself. After all, Westerners were well known for having parties, so perhaps that's where he was.

'I don't think we can do anything else,' Angelique said helplessly, when they were outside the police station.

'I'll ride home with you, in case he's there,' Claude said, but neither of them believed he would be.

They had ridden back to the house, which was when they saw all the lights blazing in defiance of the blackout regulations. For a brief hopeful moment, each thought it meant Sam had returned. But instead, Tamara was alone in the house. By now she was quite drunk.

'Ma, what on earth are you doing?'

'You can see what I'm doing. Breaking the stupid law, telling people he's missing and something's wrong. If I set the house on fire, they might take some notice! Bluudy bastards!' Her voice was slurred and angry.

'It won't help him if you're arrested,' Claude said, as he and Angelique drew the blackout curtains. They could see she was irrational; one empty bottle lay on the floor, while another was half finished. She stared at him without a sign of recognition.

'Any news from his friend Claude?' she asked. 'He hasn't bothered to come back. Probably in bed, canoodling with some girlfriend. It's all everyone does here; lots of funny business and rolling in the hay.'

'Ma!'

'Mrs Delon, I'm Claude.'

'You don't look like him,' she said, and collapsed as her legs folded beneath her and she landed on the floor.

'Oh God,' Angelique said.

'I'll help you put her to bed.'

'Let her lie there. I want her to wake up and realise she's a drunk, and she'll always be a drunk. She gave up for so long, but one crisis, one drink, that's all it takes. Leave her. In the morning she'll feel terrible, and the remorse might do her good.'

'I didn't know you could be so tough, Angie.'

'I'm not tough. I'm frightened.'

He heard distant voices, the clang of doors being slammed, and assumed it must be morning. He felt revolted by the smell of the slop bucket, but had to use it. No-one came near for what seemed like hours. The cellblock was quiet again, and the stillness seemed hostile and threatening. Finally a guard came for him, and he was hustled upstairs into a room, told to stand at attention and to wait.

For what, he asked.

The guard, not bothering to reply, sprawled in a chair, where he occupied himself with loading and reloading his revolver, like a child playing with a toy.

Sam felt weak, and the deliberate wait went on so long he began to feel dizzy. He had been given no food or water since his arrest and, as far as he could estimate, that was at least twenty-hours ago. Then, at last, there were sounds of voices approaching. The guard put his gun in its holster and jumped to attention as the sergeant entered followed by Major Ito. He carried a formal document, to which was attached several pages of Japanese writing.

'You'll sign this,' the Major said.

'What is it?'

'A confession.'

'I've done nothing wrong, so how can I confess?'

'We have witnesses and evidence. We even have a very treasonable letter you wrote to your aunt. Just sign your name at the bottom of each page.'

'I can't read Japanese, so I can't sign it.'

'Read it to him,' Ito directed.

The sergeant proceeded to read the transcript, which was an extreme version of what Joe Ishi had stated, as well as quotes from his letter to Florrie which sounded seditious the way they were read. During the recitation, his voice seemed to grow fainter, coming from a distance as Sam's dizziness returned. They saw him swaying.

'Stand up straight,' Major Ito snapped.

'I'm sick,' Sam said. 'I've had nothing to eat or drink since yesterday. No treatment for my head or face. And last night I was kicked in the ribs by the man who's told these lies. But then, you enjoy having your prisoners beaten up when they're defenceless.'

For a moment he thought Ito would strike him, but the Major merely smiled.

'Lies have certainly been told,' he said, 'vicious lies

against the Emperor. Even threats to his safety. A beating would never be adequate. On this charge, you can only be executed.'

The guard was instructed to bring a chair. Sam sat while the remainder of the confession was read. At the end of it, he was given a pen and told to sign the document.

'No,' he said.

'Sign, and you'll get food.'

'Major, I won't sign what isn't true.'

'You will eventually,' he was told. The Major smiled again, then, while still smiling, he slapped Sam viciously across the face. It was a blow so hard that it knocked Sam off the chair, and as the Major had chosen the side of his face, which had suffered in the fall from his bike, it was raw and bleeding again. He tasted a rush of bile and tried not to vomit. It would only bring another blow. On a signal, he was dragged to his feet by the guard. Major Ito surveyed him, the triumphant smile still in place.

'Take him back to his cell. No food at all. Just half a cup of water. He's to be kept handcuffed. In complete isolation. Regarded as extremely dangerous.'

The guard took him to the door.

'We'll see how you feel about confessing later today or perhaps tonight,' the Major said, 'when we get serious.'

The same tactics. Giving him time to contemplate what lay ahead. *You need a confession*, Sam thought, *because you are obliged to put me on trial, however brief and sham it is*. But to realise that was no comfort, because Major Ito had long wanted him dead. It had become acutely personal. So this time there would be torture until he signed the paper.

* * *

Florence installed a mantel radio in the office, so they could tune to the midday bulletin at lunchtime, or listen to any news flash. The whole city seemed on edge; the waiting felt endless. Two atom bombs, two cities demolished, yet the Emperor of Japan remained silent in his palace, and the fighting continued. Each day people woke in expectation, each night came disbelief that nothing had changed, and the growing anxiety that no news, in this case, was definitely not good news.

In Borneo, troops were regaining patches of ground, but on both sides soldiers were dying, and the delay of a surrender seemed unconscionable. With the liberation of prison camps came the first pictures of survivors, gaunt and weak from cruelty and cholera, worked and starved to the brink of death, bringing revulsion to a world that thought it was inured to sadistic and malignant behaviour.

On one of their night walks along the beach, Carl spoke of the department's fear for thousands in Changi. There had been civilian reports expressing alarm at treatment and conditions there.

'It must be over soon,' she said. 'Please God.'

'Once it's over, I'll be out of a job.'

She thought he was joking, but he seemed to be musing as they turned for home.

'No you won't. An office next to mine has your name on the door.'

'Frank keeps hinting he might stay in army intelligence. Make a career out of it. He asked me how I felt.'

Florrie had a dismayed feeling this might be the prelude to something unforeseen. Perhaps she had taken things too much for granted. 'What did you say?' she asked, as calmly as she could.

'I reminded him he was an engineer, and to go back and build something. Not to be a bloody idiot.'

She smiled. Things were coming good. With Sam's safe arrival, her life would be complete. *And about time, too*, she thought.

He survived the early torture, but much of it was concerned with the preliminaries, a calculated attempt to instil fear with Major Ito watching, commenting this could be avoided; all he need do was sign the confession, which must happen eventually, but this way he could save himself discomfort.

One of the interrogators chuckled when the Major used the word discomfort, and it was after that they drilled a hole into his thumbnail and he thought he heard himself screaming.

'God, that's nothing,' Ito said, 'just the *hors d'oeuvres*, isn't that your French expression? The appetiser before the main course.' The others chuckled. He nodded and they produced the electrodes and attached them to him.

'Quite sure you're not ready to sign?' one of them asked. Sam clenched his teeth and shook his head. A hand reached across the table where he was strapped, and turned a dial. The agony was instant; it seemed to spread like fire up through his body and into his mind, which was when he stopped remembering.

It was late afternoon when Claude rode back from yet another vain search. Though he kept looking, he knew there could be only one answer. For some reason, Sam was under arrest, but that could not be proved. Nobody would admit it, so it left them helpless.

The Kempetai was invested with unrestrained powers, and would never allow an interview with a prisoner in custody, nor give a reason for their actions. No matter how close the end of the war might be, their rigid code would not be moderated; Sam was in their hands and his best friend was truly fearful for his safety.

It was while reflecting on this, that he saw the sun's rays on a metallic object ahead. He realised there were slithers of metal spread on the road and, dismounting, saw they were fractured spokes from a wheel. He began to search, and within minutes found Sam's broken bike where it had been thrown deep into the roadside bushes.

The Inspector in charge of the local police force was a cautious man. He had served here for many years, first as a senior constable, then a sergeant and finally in command of the district as Inspector, and he knew most of the residents. He was aware of those who possessed authority, and those who didn't. He could dismiss Claude Briand, and this anxious young woman, the sister, as well as Madame Delon, but in view of the war situation, he was not at all sure about the French Ambassador.

Even as recently as a week ago, he could have been ordered out, told to go home and mind his own business, but the past few days had seen some radical changes, and the Ambassador might soon be a power to reckon with once again. Apart from which he had brought the Count de Boulanger with him, and the Count was said to be well connected in Tokyo. It was a time to be extremely cautious.

'So what are you saying, Your Excellency?' He realised both were Excellencies, but felt he should address the Ambassador as a matter of etiquette.

'I'm saying, Inspector, that we have sufficient evidence to accuse Kempetai Major Ito of a crime. We have proof he has harassed and intimidated Samuel Delon recently, and the Count de Boulanger will testify to his brutal treatment of Delon in Tokyo. I therefore officially inform you that a French citizen has been victimised, ill-treated, and wrongfully placed under arrest – with unnecessary violence.'

'But he is a young radical, I am told, charged with a most serious crime, advocating the assassination of the Emperor.'

'Rubbish,' the Ambassador said. 'Speak to the manager of the Mampei Hotel. You've known Monsieur Barbusse for years. He's a man of integrity. Then get the barman here, and question him. He's not only a notorious black marketeer, but a blatant liar.'

'But please understand, Your Excellency – I mean Your Excellencies,' he corrected himself, 'the matter is not within my power to investigate. I may be in charge of the region, but I have no authority in issues relating to the military police.'

'You have now, Inspector,' the Count spoke for the first time, 'I telephoned the War Minister. He's in full agreement, and you'll be granted your authority.'

'But when, Your Excellency?'

'It's being dispatched to you.'

'Until I receive it, I'm in a difficult situation.'

'Why?' De Boulanger was curt.

'I need this directive in writing, to be able to act.'

'We can't wait for that,' the Ambassador said.

'But I must wait for it,' argued the Inspector.

'Impossible. Urgency is imperative. Far too much time has already been lost by this police prevarication. We're not fools, Inspector. We realise you must have been well aware of this.'

'Aware of it, yes. But powerless to protest.'

'*Let's not even pretend that you'd have bothered to*

protest.' Claude and Angelique were stunned that the mild and elderly Ambassador could summon such outrage. 'The Count said you'll be given the power. The War Minister has guaranteed it. So stop this nonsense of trying to waste time. Kindly examine the witnesses, find out the truth.'

'But Excellency . . .'

'You listen to me, Inspector. Listen very carefully. What I will not tolerate for a moment longer is any more delay. You've wasted forty-eight hours since I asked for this meeting. Soon now, your government must agree to terms of surrender. If my French citizen is still in custody or harmed in any way – I do assure you the young man's father was a friend of General De Gaulle – this will go to the highest authority.

'And although you and I have known each other for some years, and I would be sorry to see you lose your post, nevertheless I can assure you the entire Kempetai corps will be interrogated and certain arrests will be made, while you personally will be held responsible for a dreadful diplomatic debacle. Which means your immediate dismissal without a pension, or else a new career in some distant province directing traffic.'

Bravo, thought Claude, standing with the others.

Amazing, thought Angelique, who had always considered him a charming old dolt.

There is no doubt about the French, thought Tamara Delon, *they do have great presence – even if they are full of shit.*

There had been two further sessions of torture, and after the second, Sam was ready to sign the confession, ready to sign anything to make them stop and put an end to the pain. But before he could manage to say this, he passed out again. The next thing he recalled was being woken on the floor of his cell, drenched by a bucket of icy water. There was no sign of Major Ito. The same sergeant was there. Instead of a whip or a gun, this time he carried a bar of soap and a towel. Accompanying him was a guard with a bowl of rice, who unlocked his handcuffs.

Sam ate the rice with his bare hands, scooping it from the bowl ravenously. The manacles were removed from his legs, and he was led to a room in which there was a steaming bath. It created a feeling of unreality; in the luxury of the hot water, he even wondered if he had signed the confession, and was now being prepared for his appearance in court.

'Where's Major Ito?' he asked the guard, who stared at him and did not bother to answer.

He dried himself, was given clean clothes to wear, and after putting them on, he was taken back to the cell. The sergeant was there, and with him was Major Ito in full ceremonial dress uniform. The sergeant snapped a dismissal at the guard, who bowed and scuttled hurriedly away.

Sam began to feel very nervous.

'I have been humiliated,' the Major said, 'I am to face charges of misuse of my rank, false arrest and excessive brutality, unless I make a formal apology to you. This I am not prepared to do, even though the instruction has come from my superiors in Tokyo. I am therefore left with only one honourable course of action. You cannot be allowed to go free, for you have committed crimes against the State, and my duty is to punish you for them. Afterwards, I will gladly die for my Emperor in the traditional way.'

He drew his sword so swiftly that Sam had no chance

to answer him. Only time to drop to the floor, as Ito swung the sword. It would have decapitated him, but he knew there was no possible chance to escape the next lethal thrust. He braced himself for death and heard the revolver shot as he saw the ceremonial sword tumble to the ground beside him.

'I apologise to you, Major,' the sergeant said as he shot him again, 'but I cannot allow you to do this. Even if it is just, if it is our duty, I cannot. For then, you will kill yourself and I'll be the only one left alive to take the blame.'

He shot him a third time, but by then Major Ito was dead.

CHAPTER 31

It was a strange sensation. The news spread slowly, with shocked disbelief. Japan had surrendered. Not everyone yet knew this, or was prepared to accept it. Even after Sam was at last released, after hours of formality and a full investigation into Ito's death, there were people still ridiculing the idea, dismissing it as a trick by the enemy. These sceptics had not read the *Nippon Times* that morning, in which the Imperial Rescript had been published in full. It was the Emperor's own signed and official statement, dated the previous day when terms of surrender had been finally accepted.

No-one had been told the time of Sam's release, so there was nobody to greet him. He expected they'd all be gathered at the café by the tennis courts, and set off in that direction. Halfway through the town, he realised there was an unusual silence. People, a great many more Japanese than were usually seen in this part of Karuizawa, farmers and their families from outside the town, were standing in the streets, all waiting. There was a particularly large crowd gathered around an electrical shop, which sold and serviced wireless sets, and one of the new models had been placed on a table in the doorway. A longer cord was being fitted, so it could be moved further out onto the pavement.

Sam began to realise what was happening. He could see no other foreigners as he stopped at the back of the crowd, almost unnoticed. Everyone's gaze was fixed on the shop, mesmerised by the sight of the set. The proprietor checked his watch and switched it on. For a few moments, until the valves had heated, there was no sound. Then the radio began to broadcast a recording of the national anthem.

The atmosphere became quite eerie. Men took off their hats. Most of the crowd bowed their heads. The anthem ended and an unfamiliar voice began to speak:

'*To Our good and loyal subjects*:

A whisper, a murmur of comprehension and recognition went through the crowd. Although they had never heard him speak publicly in their lives, they instinctively knew the rather hesitant and apologetic voice, unschooled and unfamiliar in public speaking was that of the Emperor, their 'living God'.

'*After pondering deeply the general conditions of the world, We have decided to effect a settlement of the present situation by resorting to an extraordinary measure.*

We declared war on America and Britain out of Our sincere desire to assure Japan's self-preservation . . .'

Like hell you did, thought Sam, glancing at the crowd, but the faces were frozen in deep concern and concentration. Some were staring at the set from where the voice was emerging. Others had their heads still bowed in deference. They were all, in their own different ways, trying to grapple with a situation they had never imagined they would experience.

Down the street, Sam could see several other groups of people – once again almost all of them were Japanese – gathered around doorways, where another wireless set was broadcasting the only voice that the entire country was listening to:

'But now the war has lasted nearly four years. Despite the best that has been done – the gallant fighting of military and naval forces, and the devoted service of Our one hundred million people, the war has developed not necessarily to Japan's advantage.'

Sam could hardly believe the phrase. Nobody laughed; they would hardly dare; no-one smiled, they just listened mutely to what was one of the great political understatements of all time.

'Moreover, the enemy has begun to employ a new and most cruel bomb, the power of which to do damage is indeed incalculable, taking toll of many innocent lives. Should we continue to fight, it would not only result in the collapse and obliteration of the Japanese nation, but also it could lead to the total extinction of human civilisation . . .'

A rather dignified and elderly woman was quietly, almost soundlessly, crying, the tears streaming down her cheeks. Sam glanced around at others near him. Children were wiping at their eyes. Their mothers were starting to sob. More astonishing for this country, there were a great many men – some of them police and soldiers in uniform – beginning to cry openly and despairingly, as the voice continued his halting speech:

'Such being the case, how are We to save the millions of Our subjects, or to atone before the hallowed spirits of Our Imperial Ancestors? This is the reason why We

have ordered the acceptance of Our people to lay down arms...'

Most of the crowd were now sobbing loudly. From further down the street, where a speaker was broadcasting the speech, there was almost mass hysteria. Sam had never seen – nor could he have imagined – such an exhibition of national anguish. If this was the grief in Karuizawa, where no bombs had fallen, he felt that Tokyo and all the other cities in ruins must be awash with tears.

'According to the dictate of time and fate, We have resolved to pave the way for a peace for all generations to come – by enduring the unendurable and suffering what is the insufferable...'

If there were other words, Sam could no longer hear them. The mass of people mourning and weeping for their lost cause drowned anything else that their Emperor might have said.

CHAPTER 32

He was on deck before sunrise, too excited to sleep, and as the day began, he could see the hazy shape of the distant coastline. There were headlands and beaches, but the ship was too far out to distinguish any of them, until the giant bulk of the North and South Heads became visible, like sentinels at the harbour gates.

The SS *Kanimbla* was due to transport occupation troops to Japan, and on its southward journey was bringing home the last of the internees to Australia. Sam, having no priority of this kind, had been on the waiting list for two months, and had eventually secured the final berth available, on one of the lower decks. It was a cabin for six, and the other five occupants had spent the war in a camp in the far north, enduring harsh treatment, boredom and near starvation. They were older men, tourists and businessmen inadvertently caught by the outbreak of the war, and from the start they were resentful his nationality had spared him their years of suffering.

In the heat of the tropics he sometimes wished he had waited for a more congenial passage, for they became progressively bitter that he had managed to evade imprisonment and live in apparent comfort. It was pointless to try explaining to them his three and a half years of evading Major Ito, or the trauma of the carnage in Tokyo, and his escape in the March air raids. Even the anxious months of wondering if neutral aliens would be used as hostages.

Or Justine. Especially Justine.

It was a relief the voyage was almost over.

The ship made its slow way through the Heads. In the distance far to his right he could see the shape of the Manly ferry terminal and, beside it, the netted swimming enclosure, where he and Florrie had made their turreted castles in the sand when he was ten years old. And rising above this, the same familiar outline of the Hotel Manly. It felt like yesterday, but it was thirteen years ago. Just seeing it brought a sudden excitement, and a rush of memory.

A ferry passed across their stern, crowded with people on their way to work. Soon – in a little over a month – it would be the Christmas school holidays, and the same ferries would be packed with families of day trippers. *Seven miles from Sydney, and a thousand miles from care.* He had never forgotten the famous slogan, nor the musical trio on board who played for passengers during the half-hour trip.

'I'll be back,' he had told Tamara and Angelique, but they all realised this was unlikely. Certainly he would return some day, when it became possible, but only for a visit. Claude he would miss greatly, for childhood friends are rare and often remain for life. Claude had asked him to check if there were film units in Sydney, and might some day join him.

There was really no-one else. The Count de Boulanger had insisted that after he attended Sydney University and obtained his degree, there would always be a job for him – in the French Bank or whatever other financial institution he controlled at the time. Sam had thanked him, but they both knew this would not happen.

The ship was close to the Woolloomooloo wharves now, and his eyes searched the crowd for her. They had spoken by phone a month ago; Carl, who seemed to have a lot of influence, had somehow arranged it, and he had taken the call at the Swiss Embassy, courtesy of the Vice-Consul, his school friend, Bernhardt.

It was a crackling line, a terrible connection with their words echoing, so that everything was said at least twice and there were long pauses while they had to wait for the resonation to end, but he had been able to ask if Sydney University was possible, and when she had said it was, he had told her in that case Harvard was off the agenda. And he'd heard her say, that was just wonderful, that things were really looking up, and she felt as if all her Christmases had come at once. At least, that's what he thought she had said, but perhaps it was the echo and the bad line.

'Sam!'

A hand was waving from high up, well above most of the people gathered there and, as the pilot boat eased them in, he realised it was Florrie, sitting perched on the shoulders of a tall man in his early fifties, who clearly must be Carl. She waved both hands as he started to wave in reply, laughing, delighted that she hadn't changed and never would, happy that at last he was home.

AUTHOR'S NOTE

This book could not have been written without the unique assistance provided by Alex Faure, who was at school in Japan when the war began. I thank him for his patience, and the wealth of background detail which he provided. My sincere gratitude to John Croyston, who carefully analysed the first draft at my request, and supplied a solution which had eluded me, important enough to make me tear up four hundred pages and start again! In saying this, I want to express my appreciation to Cate Paterson, who was supportive enough to read both versions. To have such a publisher is not only fortunate, but a real stimulus to any writer.

It was a pleasure to work with Sarina Rowell as my editor, and Carolyn Beaumont. As in previous novels, my thanks to Brian and Mary Wright for the use of their precious reference books. Also to the Japan Cultural Centre in Sydney, where I was able to find letters and oral histories which revealed an insight into the lives of

Japanese civilians, particularly during the air raids which destroyed Tokyo.

As an eighteen year old with the BCOF occupation force, I saw these ruins for myself, and also the rubble of what had been Hiroshima. Both made an impact that remains to this day. Both were horrific. But one was the result of hundreds of massed raids. The other was a city devastated beyond recognition by one small bomb.

Peter Yeldham
Yarramalong Valley,
2001

MORE BESTSELLING FICTION AVAILABLE FROM PAN MACMILLAN

Peter Yeldham
Against the Tide

Helen and Michael Francis are Hungarian refugees with no country to call home, Sarah Weismann is a survivor of a death camp piecing together the shattered remains of her life, and Neil Latham is an ex-commando unable to return to his peaceful village in rural Kent. All four leave war-ravaged Europe for Australia's golden shores.

It may be a new beginning, but for these refugees the work camps of Cooma and the inhospitable landscape are a far cry from the idyllic existence they have been promised. Alienated by the communities around them, they each struggle to forge a new life. But Helen and Michael's past in Europe contains a secret that has the power to destroy all their futures. It seems only a matter of time before the truth will be revealed.

From the best-selling author of *The Currency Lads* and *A Bitter Harvest* comes a startingly frank account of post-war migration and a compelling saga of friendship, love and survival.

'an epic read and totally absorbing'
SUN-HERALD

Peter Yeldham
The Currency Lads

Sydney, 1883
Daniel Johnson and Matthew Conway are currency lads –
born and bred in the new land now being called Australia.

Daniel, ambitious and determined, escapes a brutal
childhood to find wealth and success in the bustling
maritime world and happiness in an unconventional love
affair with an older woman.

Matthew, well educated and fired by a passion for the
truth, becomes a journalist on his father's news sheet.
But will his desire to fight injustice jeopardise his family's
precarious position in society?

These two friends also share a secret that binds them
together, their destinies intertwined as their lives and
loves span two decades. But when they find themselves
on opposite sides of a fierce conflict, their friendship is
pushed to the very edge . . .

'The master of the Australian historical blockbuster'
DAILY TELEGRAPH